NETWALK

THE NETWALK SEQUENCE BOOK TWO

JOYCE REYNOLDS-WARD

Cover art by GrinPhoto, purchased from Depositphotos

Design by Joyce Reynolds-Ward

Created with Vellum

CHAPTER 1

CALL. CALL. CALL.

The overlay blinked steadily in red-edged black text at the lower left corner of Melanie Landreth's vision, starkly superimposed over the snow and the lift shack. Black and red, the text identifier for a call from her estranged grandmother Sarah, president of the North American Confederation, such as it was in 2075.

Tyrant. Bitch.

Melanie scowled and shook her head, dismissing the text and disconnecting the call.

She didn't need to think about Sarah now. Not on a day like this, with the early morning sun glittering down on the crystalline, flaky powder snow so rare for December in the Cascades. Not with only a single precious hour to ski. A single precious hour that was almost over. No need for distractions, especially from the Bitch Queen.

Too little of her time was her own; had been that way for the past seven years. This hour belonged to her. Not to her grandmother, not to Do It Right. To her.

"Problem?" asked Angela Garcia, the head of Security for Melanie's company, Do It Right.

"Sarah starting something," Melanie said. "I'll deal with it when we get back to the office."

CALL. CALL. CALL.

This time Melanie's dismissal headshake rocked the chair slightly.

"Still got your com on?" Nik Morley, Angela's companion and Melanie's Security Number Two, frowned. "Turn it off or deal with it, *now*. Especially since it's Sarah. Conditions are too good and too fast. You don't want that distraction."

"I know." A third headshake shut the com off completely while leaving Melanie's other Dialogue implant functions operating. "Turned it off."

"Good," Nik said.

Their chair entered the tunnel for the upper end of the High Reaches ski lift. Melanie slid off of the chair as it spun around the bull-wheel. She glided through the narrow tunnel to the edge of the run.

Sarah could wait. As far as Melanie knew, there wasn't anything that urgent. Especially with this sweet, sweet snow on the Reaches today. Fluffy, wonderful snow.

Best December snow in fifteen years. Maybe even in thirty years.

Melanie threw her arms wide and sucked in a deep breath of cold, clean air. Low clouds shrouded the desert lands to the southeast of Hood, threatening to pour waterfall-like over the ridges containing them in the lowlands. Soon enough, the clouds would build up high enough to break over—not that she would be here to watch the phenomenon happen, though it was one of her favorite things to see when on the slopes. It would take at least an hour for the clouds to overpower the ridges—and by then she would be hard at work.

The toothy ridges of Mt. Jefferson to the south glistened dark blue through the fresh covering of snow starkly outlining the rocky points and edges. A single lenticular cloud clung like a tattered banner to the top point while pale skiffs of clouds wrapped around Jefferson's lower slopes. Far below them, a wisp of fog drifted over the classic lines of the Reaches Lodge and briefly hid the lift shacks.

She blinked twice to check her time display. Just enough for this last run and no more. Melanie glanced at Nik on her left, Angela on her right. Nik gave her a thumbs up.

"Yeehaw!" Melanie pushed off. She caught the rhythm of the slope, picking up speed as she pointed her tips more directly down the fall line.

Nik passed her halfway down. Melanie pushed to catch up, glorying in the hypnotic rhythm of turn, straighten, turn, feeling the pull of gravity throughout her body. She didn't expect Angela to keep pace with them, not after Angela's bad crash two years ago. Plus, once Ange had become the head of Do It Right corporate security, she'd developed a strong sense of caution.

Got to teach that girl that leadership doesn't mean you have to give up playing!

Melanie certainly hadn't stopped playing.

Wonder what Sarah wants?

The thought intruded unexpectedly. Nothing good, that was for certain. Hadn't been that way for seven years.

Not now!

Melanie dismissed the thought. Still off the clock, still on the snow. It would be time soon enough to worry about what Sarah wanted. For now, it was swoop, straighten, *feel the soft powder crystals push away underfoot, balance, rasp of ski edge on snow.*

All too soon it ended. Nik waited near the long lift line forming at the Low Reach lift entrance. Melanie sent snow spraying over Nik as she cut a fast, fancy racing stop.

"Hey! Take it easy, Mel! I don't want to argue with Ski Patrol!"

"C'mon. You have to *hustle* if you're going to keep up with me!"

"Yeah? Who beat you down the hill?" Nik threw a handful of snow at her. Melanie threw snow back.

"Can't I ever take you two out in public?" Angela laughed. She scooped up snow in both hands and nailed both Melanie and Nik. For a couple of minutes, they chucked snow at each other, laughing and yelling as if they were kids again.

Then the alarm pulsed in the right-hand corner of Melanie's vision. She dropped her handful of snow, as did Nik and Angela, all business again. They glided over to the old day lodge to change.

Melanie cast one longing glance back at the slope as she stepped out of her ski bindings, then continued inside to the private locker room that Do It Right maintained in the day lodge. She quickly changed out of ski gear into work sweater and slacks. Nik locked the gear up.

"Ready?" he asked.

She nodded and gave her jacket collar a final tweak, pulling on a hat and sunglasses before leaving the locker room. Nik and Angela took up their positions, Nik on Melanie's left, Angela on her right. The three of them walked to the tram. After the noisy crowd swarmed out of the tram, they entered, the only skiers going back to the parking lot this early in the day.

Melanie leaned against the glass and looked back up at the bright shining promise of the Mountain, eyes fixed on the stretch of the High Reach that seemed to go to the top, turning her eyes away at last when the trees blocked her view.

At the bottom, another loud, raucous crowd waited. Nik pushed through the crowd, Angela behind Melanie, tense, waiting for something to happen.

Uneventful. No one recognized Melanie, no one challenged her.

Not my day to get harassed. Good.

Rarely, they encountered a Sarah partisan who remembered that Melanie and her renegade mother Diana had openly opposed Sarah—that is, until Sarah had forced Diana Landreth to leave the country, relocating Do It Right International's headquarters to Nagano, Japan. Those situations could be touchy.

Worse, there was always the possibility of a Corporate Assassination Contract that the Corporate Courts hadn't announced yet. That was one reason why Nik and Angela pressed close to Melanie as they walked through the parking lot to her secured skimmer in the VIP lot. Melanie shivered as a group of snowboarders burst from between skimmers, Nik and Angela wheeling in close just in case—

The boarders ignored them, running for the next tram.

Melanie tightened her lips, once again annoyed by thoughts of her grandmother. She *should* have more Security with her, all things considered. But the damn Courts restricted her to only two Security in public, unless she had an active Contract sworn on her.

That's why we have the Contracts, Grandmother Sarah had said in that snarky-sweet tone of hers when Melanie dared to complain about the restriction after the Courts handed down *that* decree five years ago.

So we don't have excessive Security staff waving weaponry around in public. It's a public safety matter.

The lack of an Assassination Contract hadn't stopped Nikos Antonelli from getting shot down on the steps of his California headquarters five months ago.

I need weapons, Melanie, Nikos had pleaded with her just two days before he was killed. *There's been threats.*

I can't do weaponry, she had been forced to say, by all the damn agreements restricting her. *You have to talk to my father.*

And when Antonelli—good friend, bioremediation equipment supplier—was killed, neither the Confederation nor the Corporate Courts did a damn thing about it. Antonelli Farms had been subjected to a Notice of Takeover, and was now part of Stephens Reclamation, headed by Melanie's brother Andrew.

Worthless fucking Courts.

She had no use for the shadowy international organization. Or for the constant political juggling that seemed to be leading to a new name and flag for the Confederation of North American States every few months. For her own safety, Melanie did her best to stay out of politics—in part to avoid stepping on someone's toes and provoking the creation of a Corporate Contract on her, or those close to her.

Do It Right North America is just a bioremediation and tech company. All of our security products come from the Nagano division, where my mother and father are located. I don't have time for politics. I develop biobots for environmental remediation. Nothing more than that. You want security work, talk to Do It Right International in Nagano.

Or at least that was Melanie's standard statement whenever anyone—including her grandmother, her dangerous uncle Peter, or Peter's protégé Andrew, Melanie's older brother—pressed her about political involvement. She knew too much about Sarah's role in the events that made her Confederation President. And her uncle Peter was toxic and twisted.

Too bad Drew got sucked into Sarah and Peter's circle.

But that had happened years before, when the two of them were teens. Not something Melanie understood—or why her parents hadn't objected to their grandmother Sarah enticing Drew into her entangled web of toxic politics.

And then there was the Gizmo, ostensibly the rationale for the creation and continued existence of the Corporate Courts. Originally, from what Melanie had learned after taking her mother Diana's place as President of Do It Right North America, the Courts upheld the protection of a device called Gizmo.

Melanie had never seen Gizmo itself because for whatever reason, she hadn't been cleared to come into its presence. It was some sort of war machine, or at least that was what she had been able to puzzle out from rumors and limited access to data. Responsible for the destruction of twenty cities worldwide when she and Drew were little, with no logical reason behind the cities that were destroyed. Then it had been known as the Disruption Machine. But it took digging to tie the Gizmo protected by the Corporate Courts—in some remote, undisclosed location—to the Disruption Machine.

Oblique suggestions in family history hinted that Sarah's former lover Francis Stewart was somehow tied to the Gizmo, and that its capture brought about the final split between Sarah and her daughter Diana. No one that Melanie knew regularly referred to it as "the Gizmo"—just "the gadget," "the device," and other workarounds.

Melanie sighed as they approached her small skimmer in the VIP lot.

She was *tired* of playing this role, of acting like the airhead ski bum heiress. Sarah showed no signs of weakening, even though she was in her nineties. Didn't display any apparent interest in handing over political and corporate power to a subordinate, either to Melanie's uncle Peter or to her brother Andrew—both likely successors. When her mother had fled North America, both Melanie and Diana had thought the situation with Sarah would resolve soon.

It hadn't—seven years later.

As they reached her skimmer, Melanie waited for Nik and Angela to lower its shields and clear it before entering. She punched in her autopilot routing code for Do It Right North America's corporate headquarters in Hoodland.

As the skimmer glided down the Mountain, Melanie tapped her

fingers on the console between her and Angela. Lousy connectivity and the shortness of the trip meant too little time to pull up any work. But the drive was just long enough for her to brood about the day ahead.

Especially with Sarah so impatient. That never boded well. Her grandmother was fully aware of the time differences between D.C. and the Mountain, hell, her spies knew Melanie's daily routine better than Melanie herself. The fact that Sarah was pushing this call this hard, this early, was not good at all.

Damn it, what is she slamming us with next?

Melanie sighed and leaned her head back against the seat, cataloging the tasks ahead of her today to distract from her worry. Nothing special, nothing exciting. Except for what might result from Sarah's call, just another day of bureaucratic B.S., shot through with occasional interesting nanobot bioremediation research pieces.

How much longer will it be like this? I want some action!

Especially as friends and colleagues like Antonelli were cut down or driven away from Melanie and Do It Right. She had been stuck on hold in Hoodland for seven years. Too long. Her fingers tapped harder, until Angela gently rested her hand on top of Melanie's fingers.

<Patience,> scrolled across Melanie's Dialogue overlays, with the pink-lined aqua tint that meant it came from Angela. <One day at a time.>

<How much longer?> Melanie subvocaled her text back. She caught the quick flash of her black-lined teal text across Angela's eyes. Her fingers stirred impatiently under Angela's light pressure. <How much longer do we put up with this?>

<Things change,> Angela sent. <Run your company. Wait. It has to break soon.>

<*Tired* of waiting,> Melanie answered. <We have to do something. Soon.>

<Wait,> Angela repeated, as the skimmer settled within the main Do It Right compound. <Wait for Ness and Marty to come back.>

<It's been seven years. They aren't coming back.>

Melanie's control slipped for a moment, her words threatening to slip from subvocal to vocal. Ness Ryan and Marty Fielding had been two of Do It Right's top researchers, Marty acting as Head of Research for DIR North America. But when Sarah conscripted them for the National Security Research labs, well, Melanie had no means with which to object. Sarah Stephens hadn't clawed her way into the presidency of what remained of the United States by allowing people to say no to her.

Especially not family.

Melanie heaved a sigh as the door opened. "Back to work."

"Have a good day," Angela murmured before she followed Nik to the Security wing. "Don't get too frustrated."

"I'll try," Melanie said. She took a second deep breath, her eyes tracking wistfully to the snow-dusted ridges around her.

Work. Now.

She trudged to her office.

Janine, Melanie's assistant, multi-tasked between her computer projection screen and the hologlobe simulator while talking to Anna, one of the data clerks in Mapping.

One of Liam's—no, Sarah's spies.

Melanie tensed. Along with Sarah's persistent calling, Anna's appearance in the office didn't bode well. Anna was an agent for Sarah's spymaster Liam Jeffreys, Melanie's ex-fiancé. The woman made no secret of her role, and much as Melanie wanted to—*do something*—about Anna, she didn't dare. Not unless she wanted to consign Do It Right to Andrew's control.

And Melanie wasn't ready to burn those bridges just yet. The best she could do was stick Anna in a position where she could cause as little disruption to Do It Right as possible—and still appear important.

"Sarah's been calling repeatedly," Janine said to Melanie. "In a mood because you were out skiing."

"I know," Melanie said. "Got the text at the top of the High Reach."

Anna stiffened, using her height to loom over Melanie. "Your grandmother *is* the President of the Confederation of the United States," she said. "Don't you think you should talk to her right away?"

"My grandmother doesn't have anything to do with this business," Melanie said. "My mother founded it. Grandmother's the one who insisted Mom choose between exile or Do It Right North America facing Takeover. Grandmother chose politics. Mom chose business and family. Mom's the one I answer to. You don't like it; you leave the company."

I wish. Bitch. She's probably here to report to Liam every word I say about not calling Sarah right away.

Bugging Janine by hanging out in her office until Melanie returned from skiing *was* the sort of petty thing that Anna did—or was it Liam who directed Anna? Whoever's idea it was, the behavior was annoying. Obnoxious. Anna flaunted her not-so-secret ties to Liam and National Security in everyone's face at the slightest opportunity, gleeful that she was untouchable because of it.

"Well! *Some* of us have to work, instead of living the ski bum life!" Anna sniffed disapprovingly and turned to leave.

"*Anna.*" Melanie's voice was low, quiet, and menacing.

Anna stopped at the door, visibly tightening her shoulders, still keeping her back to Melanie.

"I meant what I said," Melanie continued after a pause, keeping her voice quiet. "You have a problem with how I manage things, you get the *hell* out of this company. Understand?"

Anna nodded. She continued to face away from Melanie.

"*Look* at me. *Do you understand?*"

Anna turned reluctantly, her shoulders slumping, looking down at the ground.

Melanie drew a deep breath. "I should fire you right now."

That brought Anna's head up. "You wouldn't dare."

Unfortunately, she's right. My hands are tied, unless I want to directly challenge Sarah. And I'm not—Do It Right's not—in the position to do that yet. Damn her.

"Don't expect your ties to Liam to protect you forever," Melanie said in a voice just barely above a whisper. "Especially from *me*."

"There's nothing there now," Anna said, focusing on her feet instead of Melanie.

Melanie laughed, one short sharp burst. "Unless he snaps his fingers and calls you back? It may be eight years since he and I broke up, but I still remember his blarney." She allowed herself another single, soft breath. "You came close to crossing the line, Anna. There's a point at which I'll say to *hell* with your connections to Liam and National Security." She snapped her fingers. "Then you're gone. Remember that. Liam may snap his fingers to bring down wrath on people, but I can do it too."

"You know what will happen."

Melanie inhaled.

I so did not need this crap today.

"You go running to Liam or my grandmother to blab about what a meanie I am, just keep one thing in mind. I may be a bitch and you their visible spy, but Sarah's worse than I am about trivialities. Go do your job and stop bugging Janine. There's nothing for you to report on here. Understand?"

Anna nodded, and fled.

Melanie sighed and raised a brow, looking after Anna.

Shouldn't let her get to me like that. But damn it, Janine has enough to do without handling the taletelling from Sarah's spy.

"What the hell was she pestering you about now? Damn it, despite the consequences, I'd fire her in a minute, if she doesn't leave you alone."

Janine shrugged. "Drama. Nothing you need to deal with directly. Minor stuff."

Melanie frowned. "*Should* I know about this?"

Janine shook her head. "I put a note into your daily briefing. It's personalities, and I've assigned Kelly to deal with it. Should have stayed at that level."

"Thank you, dear." Melanie snapped open her viewer and slipped on her fingertip stylus, pulling up her daily files. "Any priorities in today's docs?"

"The usual," Janine said.

Melanie Landreth, President, DIR NA, Melanie scribbled at the bottom of the first document, approving the hiring of two new staffers to monitor bioremediation bot performance on the Gulf oil spills, dismissing it to Janine's queue.

"Thanks for not routing the call to the skimmer. What's Grandmother mad about now?"

"Not a clue. She was unhappy that she couldn't raise you directly."

Melanie chuckled softly. "Well, I'm grateful for that." Uncertain wireless connectivity was another plus of working on the Mountain. Sometimes. There were moments when she cursed the connectivity issues, and others, like now, when she praised them.

"How was the snow this morning?" Janine asked.

Melanie scribbled her signature at the bottom of the second document before answering, authorizing the sale of bioremediation bots to a company near the Florida War Zone.

"Marvelous." She sent that one to Janine and opened the next one. "You going skiing after work?"

Janine made a face. "Not tonight. Takeover Day. That's not the crowd to ski with."

"Oh. Yeah. Right." Melanie frowned. She had forgotten about Takeover Day celebrations.

Takeover Day and DIR's lack of appropriate response to it was probably why Grandmother Sarah was burning up the lines today. That is, if Melanie was lucky.

Melanie frowned at her next document. A budget report for Dialogue chip upgrade research. She needed to look at this one in depth. Melanie flicked it to her files.

"Make sure you book yourself time to ski tomorrow morning, okay? Come up with us."

"I will."

Melanie finished signing the other documents, then went into her office, opened up her hologlobe, and activated her protective datasuit for deep immersion into the upgrade budget reports. She was inside the first sub report when Janine's blue and red text popped up.

<*She's* on the line. Worse than she was before.>

<Thanks,> Melanie texted back.

She closed out the Dialogue budget and shut down the hologlobe. No sense leaving anything open, just in case Grandmother Sarah had a snooper program running. Dialogue *was* still a DIR secret project. Sarah would snatch anything she could, and Dialogue wasn't something Melanie wanted to gift her by accident.

You want it, you develop it, was Melanie's philosophy with regard to competition, and Sarah's National Security labs were definitely competition.

Melanie counted to five before she brought up Sarah's image on her computer viewscreen.

"Ness Ryan's dead," was the first thing that Sarah Stephens said, her short, stiffly styled white-blond hair looking more like a wig than usual. "She crossed the line. Treason. You and your mother are behind it. Either give me the data to support the charge in Corporate Court to justify her execution, or I'll throw you into jail, have your mother extradited from Japan, pronounce your company under Interdiction, and take what I want. Or have Andrew file a Notice of Takeover from Stephens Reclamation in Corporate Court and get what I want that way. What's it going to be?"

Ness is dead? Crap! What about Marty?

Brief panic surged through Melanie.

Sarah charged Ness with treason. Crap, crap, crap. Ness is dead. What happened? How did Ness get caught? Oh shit. We're dead.

She forced her hands to unclamp themselves from her chair's armrests, all too aware of Sarah staring at her fixedly, noting her every reaction.

Never show weakness to Sarah, she reminded herself. *Not even in a situation like this.*

"So, Grandmother. How are you today?" Melanie kept her tone light though she wanted to scream. "Snow was pretty good this morning. Best it's been in ages."

Don't react don't react don't react. Ness. Oh God, Ness. And Marty. Where's Marty?

Her gut tightened.

Don't think about this now. Can't think about this now. Focus on Sarah. Think about skiing this morning.

Sarah snorted at her. "If you have time to waste on skiing, then perhaps you ought to shut your company down for Takeover Day like most everyone else."

"I've bots to ship and research projects to monitor."

"Yet you have time to ski."

"Before work!" Melanie snapped. "Keeps me centered. At least I have a life. Maybe it would be better if you did." She gulped and stopped herself as a faint smile twitched the corner of Sarah's right lip.

Damn it, I reacted to her, just like she calculated. Oh Ness....

"Girl, I have more important things to do. I want the data from you."

"If you have enough proof to kill Ness Ryan, then you have enough proof to support your charges." Melanie dropped her hands out of sight of the screen, digging her nails into her palms.

"What the hell makes you think I had anything to do with her death?"

"You think I'm an idiot who can't connect the dots? Come *on*, Grandmother!"

Sarah waved one hand dismissively. "If you know what's going on, then it shouldn't be a problem. I want the data she's given you. Willingly or by force. It's up to you."

"You think I'm going to answer right here, right now, without proof that she's dead?"

"Of course not. There's evidence. Your brother will courier it. I'll expect a response promptly. Remember, your choice is simple. Cooperate, or I take Do It Right. I want a response by four o'clock this afternoon, Pacific time." Sarah's face flickered off the screen.

Melanie slumped back in her chair. Damn. Damn. Damn. She stared at the screen. She *could* try to contact Marty. Sarah hadn't said anything about Marty. Maybe he was okay.

No. That could expose him.

And handing Ness's data over to Sarah came dangerously close to revealing the existence of Dialogue, because Ness was tracking the parts of National Security's research that paralleled DIR's. That risked the Dialogue implant's computer command and communication secrets.

Damn it. Dialogue. How much information about Dialogue development had Sarah gotten out of Ness before her death?

Melanie sighed. She needed to report this to her mother. She blinked twice to activate her Dialogue, then called through her secured, highly illegal hologlobe.

Her priority code got her through immediately. Not a relief this time.

"Hi, Mel." Diana Landreth's smile faded as she studied Melanie. "What's wrong?"

"Mom," Melanie said slowly, "we have a situation."

HER BROTHER ANDREW SHOWED UP ABOUT NOON. HE DROPPED A DATASIM on her desk.

Melanie picked it up slowly. The movement triggered a slow, jerky video of Ness Ryan's body, followed by document views. Melanie examined the documents carefully, surreptitiously running an authenticity check through Dialogue. More overtly, she ran a check through her hologlobe and conventional methods.

Both matched. Real pictures and real data, not fake, as far as she could tell.

Damn.

Hope faded that this was just a bluff. National Security had the ability to fake out her conventional software. But Dialogue, with all of the safeguards that her father Will and his researchers had stuck into it? Not yet.

Her blood chilled as she looked at a still. Their uncle Peter stood over Ness, gun in hand. Peter, who like his nephew Andrew, jumped to Sarah's tiniest command. Peter the killer. She stifled a shiver.

"You could have simply emailed these over," she said to Andrew as he paced back and forth, watching her every move, snapping his fingers absent-mindedly. "And why you don't *sit down,* damn it!"

"What's the matter, making you nervous?"

She didn't answer, already regretting her reaction.

Up to his old tricks.

Andrew had never been diagnosed with ADHD like her, but he had some of the behaviors, especially when he thought he could annoy Melanie.

She tabbed through the pictures and documents, stalling for time. She blinked at one picture. Was that Marty Fielding cleaning up the mess that was left of Ness? His dust-brown skin pale, thin instead of the chunky, bear-like man he had been when working at Do It Right?

Oh God. It is Marty.

Of all people, damn it.

For his sake, she hoped Marty and Ness hadn't revived their relationship while they were at National Security.

Melanie forced herself to relax.

I hope he's safe.

Keeping all emotion off of her face, she looked up at her brother.

Andrew craned his neck to see which pic it was, grinning at Melanie, waiting to see if she would react.

When she didn't, he shrugged, answering her earlier question. "Grandma wants the personal touch. You know how she is. By the way, Liam says hi."

Melanie kept her face blank. Five years as Peter's personal assistant hadn't improved Andrew's manners any.

"So what does she want?" Melanie steepled her fingers and turned her chair away from him so that she could stare outside instead of at Andrew. Give her a chance to think about that morning's glorious skiing.

"What she's always wanted. The company. You. Mom."

"She won't get it from me."

"You need to give her what she wants. She's not joking about Interdiction or the Notice of Takeover."

Melanie spun her chair to face him. "She can't do it to an offshore company."

"DIR's not an offshore company."

"Do It Right, International, is based in Nagano with sub-headquarters in Rio de Janeiro. Do It Right North America is a wholly-owned subsidiary of the Rio operation. As it's always been. We've downplayed the Japanese and Brazilian connections to get our American contracts."

The smirk left Andrew's face. Then he laughed, one short sharp bark. "You sneaky little bitch. You and Mom have been planning this all along, haven't you?"

"You wearing a wire?"

"No. Grandmother gave you until four this afternoon. Let me talk to her. Give me something to play with. I can talk her into twenty-four hours if you give me a token. But that's all I can do. Twenty-four hours, and then you'd better have something for her, or, offshore or not, DIR is dead on the North American continent."

Melanie stood. "Don't waste your energy."

Andrew towered over Melanie. "Let me give you a word of advice, little sister. I'm the good guy here. If you give me *anything* about what Ness Ryan was leaking out of National Security, I can save your smart little ass. Then you can caper off to Mom in Nagano or Rio, and live whatever ski bum life suits your fancy."

Melanie clenched her fists. "Knock it off, Andrew!"

"Don't count on Mom to save your butt, Mel. I won't be the one who comes next. It'll be Peter, and you don't want that. You really don't." His voice softened. "Trust me, Mel, our uncle has gone crazy these days. The man loves killing. I don't know what Grandma's had her pet scientists do to him."

"You're the one who's trusted him. Never me. And I think even he would find that we're not as helpless as he thinks."

"What? Your little bioremediation company has some teeth?"

"Bioremediation is only one of our specialties. You must not be up on your research if you aren't aware of our other subsidiaries."

"Space stations," Andrew scoffed. "Computer chips. Nanobots. Whatever happened to that neural interface research?"

Too damned close to Dialogue!

Melanie shrugged, trying to relax. "That's our Japanese branch. Not my responsibility."

"Huh. Then why was Ness Ryan working in North America? Why didn't you claim Japanese employment for her when we conscripted her?"

"Because," Melanie said slowly and carefully, "we were using her neural research to interface with bioremediation nanobots. Come on, Drew! You know I'm not going to give you what *she* wants just like this!"

Andrew sighed, dropping his flippant mode. "It was worth the try. Look, Mel. Our grandmother is seriously pissed off, and she's as bad as Peter when it comes to being bloody-minded. Heading up the Confederation really has done a number on her head. Peter's not the only one who's gone off the deep end."

If Melanie didn't know better, she would think he was sincere.

She snorted. "Since when did you get so concerned about me?"

"You *are* my sister." He continued, more quietly. "Mel, she'll kill you if you don't give her what she wants. I don't know what those nanos are doing to her or to Peter, but they're both pretty crazy these days."

"Drew, I don't know why in hell you're so concerned about my welfare now, but let me tell you this. When this stuff blows, you'd better get away from the two of them."

Andrew stared back at her. "She's made me her heir to Stephens Reclamation after Peter. I can't leave."

"There it is, then," she said. "You're in with her. And I won't leave Mom's side."

"Damn it, then it's another generation," Andrew said. "I'd half-hoped you and I wouldn't be like Mom and Peter."

"It's not too late for you to jump ship."

"It is." His voice was dead now, drained of all emotion. "They've made sure of it. I have no choice. Do you?"

"You know Mom would take you back. Maybe not top level in the business, but there'd be something."

"It's too late. They put an implant—" His voice cut out as his face paled and he winced. He pressed his lips together tightly and half-closed his eyes, then opened them again. "You have twenty-four hours. After that, you'll answer to Peter. God help you then." He turned and left, quieter than when he'd come in.

Melanie collapsed into her chair. She blinked to her Dialogue, then subvocaled a text command.

<Condition Yellow Alert. All Do It Right Dialogues. Two-minute countdown.>

Maybe it would be enough. She wasn't ready for Condition Red, much less Condition Orange. She fumbled in her desk drawer and pulled out the small box that held the Burnout amphetamine tabs, staring at the red and black dragon hologram on the front of the lacquered box. Then she tossed it back into her desk drawer.

Not time for that—yet.

Dialogue links started shutting down without warning. After several hours of escalating reports with no results, Melanie snapped up a globe to trace the problem. Working inside hologlobes was tricky and tiring, but they gave the best three-dimensional visual images of Dialogue network schematics.

<Melanie.> Janine texted.

<Yes.> Melanie texted back.

<Ness Ryan's death is confirmed. Marty's on his way.>

<Thanks.> She considered quitting and pulling together support for Marty. No. Neither Ness nor Marty would want her to stop work for this reason. <Confirm his arrival and condition. Streamline arrival process.>

<Will do.>

Less than a half hour later, the globe went black around her.

What the—?

Not a power outage. That was what generators were for. A denial-of-service attack? Possible, except that the servers at Do It Right HQ were sufficiently robust to handle such attacks.

The globe flickered back to life.

A good third of her Dialogue links were gone. Blank. Like they'd never existed.

<Melanie. MELANIE!> Janine texted. <GET OUT! NOW!>

She quickly shut everything down. No sooner had the globe retreated into a swirling ball next to Melanie's computer screen than Janine burst into Melanie's office.

"*She's* dead." Janine's face was fishbelly-pale. "And there's a world-wide systems crash. Systems coming back online slowly."

Chills ran up and down Melanie's skin as she stared at Janine.

"Are you sure?" Her numb lips suddenly refused to work as well as she wanted.

"Same time as servers went down worldwide."

"We have a cause?" Sarah's death wouldn't be enough to cause this level of disruption. Unless National Security had planted some sort of cyberbomb triggered by her grandmother's death.

"Look for yourself. I sent you a link."

Melanie commanded Dialogue to bring up that link. It popped open to footage of snowy, rugged canyons. She didn't need the subtitles to identify it as the Blue Bucket Canyon area along what had been the Oregon-Idaho border. Melanie swallowed hard as she recognized the location. Grouse Creek. She studied the still photographs of the wreckage of the helicopter, taken by older technology that hadn't been disrupted by the weapon that had killed Sarah. Stared at the close-ups of Sarah's dead body.

Authentic, or a creation by Peter, to justify coming after Do It Right? For there was a Do It Right connection. No coincidence, not in that location. Not from the reports of that brief but worldwide crash. The weapon had succeeded, much more spectacularly than she had ever expected it to perform.

Dad will be thrilled to know it works.

Will Landreth was probably dancing with glee in his Nagano labs.

Janine gasped as the picture of the suspected killer flashed up. Melanie stared at the face of her old mentor, Kathy Miller. Ness Ryan's aunt. Ness's only surviving kin.

She knew about Ness's death. I don't know who told her because we couldn't reach her, but she knew.

Confirmed Do It Right setup. Real or not, Peter would now pin it on them.

Her father and Kathy Miller were the developers of Joseph's Ghost, the electromagnetic pulse disruptor (and more) that had brought about Sarah's death. Do It Right had quietly sold it to the native peoples now controlling Blue Bucket and Skene County, to protect their reservation during the chaos that had preceded Sarah's coup. They had devised milder versions for other Indigenous Nations. Joseph's Ghost and its cousins had kept the reservations free from the Confederation's influence.

This changed *everything.*

Melanie turned to Janine. "Go to Condition Orange, pre-Diaspora. Get everything and everyone moving. Clear HQ of nonessential personnel, put essential personnel on Diaspora alert. But before you do that—Anna's fired."

"*Good,*" Janine said. "Shall I do the honors?"

"No. I'm sending Nik and Angela." Melanie clucked up her link.

<It's time. Get Anna the hell out of here,> she texted Angela.

<About fucking time,> Angela answered. <Easy or rough?>

<Fast,> Melanie sent back. <Cut her links, *now*. We're going to Orange but I won't do it until she's gone.>

<I'll let you know when it's clear.>

<Thanks, girlfriend.>

<De nada.>

"That's done," Melanie said aloud. "When I hear back from Angela, kick in Orange level. Got it?"

"Got it." Janine left the office.

Melanie scowled at her hologlobe.

I need to figure out what's killing those links.

Flight would do them little good if National Security had hacked into the secure Do It Right networks. They'd have motivation to act on whatever secret capability they'd acquired now.

Meanwhile, she had one more duty to do. Slowly, she commanded her Dialogue to bring up her mother's most secure address.

Diana's face flashed on her screen. "I'm clearing my schedule. I'll be there day after tomorrow."

"Mom, it's not safe. We're losing links. I've fired Sarah's spy Anna. As soon as she's gone, we go to Orange."

"Good."

"It's not safe for you to be here."

"I'm doing what I can to clean up this mess. To save you. What I should have done instead of running away." Diana's tone hardened. "Melanie, you let me deal with Peter. Keep yourself safe until I get there. You figure out what's wrong with those links, and be ready to run."

"Mom, it's not safe," Melanie repeated.

"Life's never been safe in *this* family. Let me be the one to pick up the pieces. You're the future. You know too much. Wait until I get there, and then you go. Got it?"

Melanie sighed. "Got it."

She frowned at the screen. Then, slowly, she reached into the desk and pulled out the lacquered box of Burnout tabs, putting one under her tongue. This would require an all-nighter.

<Done,> Angela texted. <She was already packing up. Maria checked her bags. Nik and Sergio are taking her to the bus off the Mountain. She's clear.>

<Good. Institute Condition Orange.>

<Condition Orange activated,> Angela texted.

It was done. For better or worse, she was committed to the whirlwind. Melanie heaved a deep sigh.

Long night's work ahead.

CHAPTER 2

MELANIE BIT BACK A SURPRISING DESIRE TO HUG MARTY FIELDING AS HE shambled into her office the next morning.

She *wasn't* going to think about their past, when they'd almost been a couple. Before Liam.

Maybe that impulse was triggered by Marty's appearance. He looked like hell. Gray streaked his long, black hair bound back in a ragged ponytail, and deep lines marked his haggard, dust-brown face, making him look twenty years older than when National Security had conscripted him seven years ago. Skin sagged on his jaw and neck, pulling tight over his cheekbones. He had lost a lot of weight.

God. He looks awful.

At least Marty had passed his preliminary clearance, including scans to reveal whether he was under any compulsion to deny he was under the influence of either National Security, Liam or Sarah.

Melanie took a deep breath, and plunged right into her questions. One way to keep those *feelings* at bay.

"You're entirely positive that Ness's dead?" she asked. Doubts about the provenance of those pictures had roused her in the middle of the night. Her uncle was capable of deepfakes to promote his goals.

"Yes. I was assigned to close out her lab and clean things up."

"There's been some anomalies." *Yeah, that's one way to put it!* "I'm sorry, Marty. We should have fought my grandmother, kept you two here."

"Sarah was convinced she needed us." Marty sighed. "But at least we learned a lot. I hope what information we passed on was useful."

"It was. But you look like hell."

"That place *is* hell." He stared at her with dull eyes. "You can't imagine it. Not without being there."

"Are you *sure* they haven't figured out a Dialogue equivalent?"

"They have an implant. It's inferior to Dialogue, doesn't have even half of Dialogue's capacity. Their focus has primarily been on nanos. But—" He raised his right index finger to emphasize his point, bringing back fond memories of past days. "The interface between their nanos and the implants could be a Dialogue equivalent. I wish I knew more, but *that* research was limited to Ness only. I wasn't allowed anywhere near it."

Melanie flopped back in her chair. Damn. If only there was a better way to put the pieces together. She stared at the hologlobe spinning over her desk. More Dialogue links gone.

"We'll have to figure that out at some point, but right now we have other issues," she said.

"Such as?" Marty leaned forward, brows furrowing with sudden interest. "I've noticed the activity and wondered what was going on. Asked questions; was told you would brief me."

"We're in Condition Orange, about to go Red," she said. "We're losing Dialogues and non-Dialogues links to National Security sweep squads, although no one's hit here in Oregon. Yet. I think they're saving the Mountain for last."

Marty frowned. "Ness's death did that? What's going on?"

"You haven't heard?"

"Heard what?" he asked. "I'm sorry, but I was in a total com blackout. Any kind of connectivity was too dangerous for the folks who got me out of D.C. I had to shut everything down, and they talked to me as little as possible."

Melanie tightened her lips. "Some big changes have happened. *She's* dead. Grandmother's helicopter was shot down yesterday afternoon. Grouse Creek, near Blue Bucket Canyon." She pulled up the pictures on her viewscreen to show Marty.

Understanding followed by shock flitted across Marty's face as he clicked through the pictures. "Kathy did it. Kathy Miller, right? Has to be since it happened there. Too close to her cabin."

Melanie nodded.

"Damn." He dropped his head in his hands, shaking it back and forth, then rubbing his face and eyes. "Damn. Melanie, I'm sorry. I didn't think she'd do anything like this. I told Kathy about Ness as soon as I could, before I left D.C."

"So she knew."

And we couldn't raise Kathy. She must have shut down her com once Marty told her.

"Yeah. I told her. She took it hard. Mel, I'm sorry. I didn't think she'd do this."

"It's not your fault, Marty. From what I've been able to figure out, Sarah went after Kathy. She didn't go looking for trouble, it came to her."

"She would have been looking for trouble hard enough," Marty said. "That's Kathy. She hates Sarah enough to kill her, and Ness's death—" He shuddered. "Sarah just gave Kathy the chance to do it in her own backyard."

"Well, while it's causing us a lot of pain, Kathy also helped us."

"What do you mean?"

"Where the hell do you think Sarah would have come next, after chasing down Kathy?"

His brows raised. "Oh. Yeah."

"Kathy's still alive," Melanie said. "She got in touch with our Security once she reached safety. But she took out Sarah by triggering Joseph's Ghost. The electromagnetic pulse from that baby did what it was supposed to do. Did it ever. That's part of the problem I'm figuring out right now. The rest is the politics. Peter's in charge, and he's headed this way. I have no idea how much time we actually have. The Warm Springs Nation has offered us asylum if we need it. Warm Springs is where we'll bug out to, from here."

"What do we do about your uncle? Isn't he in line to be Confederation President?"

Melanie pushed herself up and began to pace. That latest tab of Burnout was fading. If she didn't move or take another tab soon, she'd crash. No sleep last night, little likely tonight.

"We still have a few friends. That's what's keeping him from going to full Interdiction. He doesn't have Grandmother's power, not yet. That's why Mom's coming back, to stop him." Melanie drew a deep breath. "I guess. Something to do with the Corporate Courts. Joseph's Ghost apparently triggered enough of a crisis to activate emergency provisions involving the Courts."

"Is it safe for your mother to come back to the States?"

"Of course not! That hasn't changed at all. Marty, I'm sorry. I wish I could give you time to recover. I know you two went through hell. But I'm losing those Dialogue links. I have to get everything ready for when Mom gets here."

"Ness and I knew we were going into hell when Sarah grabbed us. We knew that passing on what information we could to you was likely to lead to our deaths." He spread his hands. "Frankly, I'm surprised that my escape plan worked. The whole time I half-expected those smugglers getting me out of D.C. to shoot me or take me for ransom. Even though they claimed ties to your father—on the other hand, I thought it was better than waiting for Peter to come after me."

She dropped back into her chair. "It's just—Damn, Marty, I wish I could make it better."

He gazed at her with dull eyes. "You can make it better by giving me a job to do."

Melanie reached back into the desk. Feeling Marty's eyes analyzing her every move, she popped a tab of Burnout, steeling herself against Marty's inevitable criticism.

"We're losing too many Dialogues, and I can't explain it. Our security shouldn't be that significantly breached. I need you to find out what's going on." She took a deep breath. "Will you be my Head of Research? Things are happening fast, and I need someone *here*. Not in Nagano."

"You certain you want to trust me after seven years in National Security?"

"Who better to trace what they may be doing to us?" she countered.

A faint smile quirked his lips. "I'll try." He got up slowly, then turned back to face her. "You know what you're doing with that?" He gestured toward the Burnout box.

"I'm *okay*, Marty!" She knew what he worried about. Redline. The dragon's tail turning on her. Forced crash, collapse, possible death.

But she was an experienced Burnout user. Burnout had gotten her through more than one all-nighter. This was nothing more than what she'd done before.

Granted, Marty's right to be concerned. He's not seen me for seven years.

Marty *had* bailed her out of that nasty crash when they were younger. But she was no longer a rank beginner when it came to using Burnout. She knew when she was edging close to Redline and trouble.

"You've said you were in control before. Mel, you trust that stuff too much."

"Too much to do, too little time to do it in. Dad still uses Burnout. Not as much as he used to, but all the same, he's using it. Even in spite of cancer."

Marty opened his mouth, as if to say something more. A moment passed. Then he sighed, a deep sadness sagging his face.

"If you say so, Melanie." He shambled out of her office.

His old line, when she refused to stop taking Burnout.

She sighed. Maybe she wasn't the only one fighting with old feelings.

No. Focus on what they were dealing with.

Maybe Marty could find their problem. If anyone could, it would be him.

I'm glad he's back. I just wish—

Right now, she wasn't exactly sure what she wished for.

BY AFTERNOON, MELANIE WAS READY TO COLLAPSE. THE DIALOGUE LINKS still kept going down without warning or pattern.

If it's a virus, it's a weird one.

"Melanie." Janine's voice sounded tired through the com.

"Yes." Given the situation, they were using voice-only communication. No text. No Dialogue.

"It's Andrew."

"Got it." Melanie clicked up the link in her globe.

A small taste of satisfaction flooded through her when she saw how haggard Andrew looked.

I'm not the only one pulling late hours!

"You have twelve hours to cooperate," Andrew growled.

"Say what?"

"Twelve hours. Hand over Ness Ryan's data, and you might get out alive."

"Excuse me?" She wasn't sure what he had said.

"Twelve hours. Tomorrow morning. Nine o'clock. That's all the time I can get out of Uncle Peter. If he has to come to the Mountain, Mel, he's going to kill you."

"He'll have to come through my Security."

"You're damned lucky he hasn't nuked you."

"That's not luck. He knows better."

Chills pulsed through Melanie. Sarah had known about the networked explosives that stalemated the family upon her ascent to power, seven years ago. Two people held that dead man's switch, Melanie and Diana. It was enough to keep Sarah at bay, at least as long as she wanted DIR and the Confederation intact instead of destroyed. Any takeover on her part had to be negotiated, or face major impacts upon the Confederation's organization.

Peter must know about it too. A saving grace.

Andrew shrugged. "I don't know why. He was set to do it, and then he stopped the countdown."

Melanie fought to keep herself calm.

He didn't know. Somebody told him.

"It's because he found out about our explosives network," she said, barely able to speak through the tightness in her throat. "If you're in Grandmother's old offices, you'd be dead, too."

Andrew laughed one short, sharp bark. "That explains it. Damn, he was pissed about that."

Peter was set to nuke us.

Melanie dug her nails into her palms. Not even Sarah would go that far. But Peter?

"Mom and I hold the dead man's switch," she said. "And Mom already told Grandmother, years ago, *if something happens to me, she won't override.*" Melanie swallowed hard. "The same holds true for me, if something happens to Mom."

"That changes in twelve hours," Andrew said. "Grandmother didn't figure out the way around your cute little dead man's switch. Peter has. Twelve hours, Melanie. Then we'll be there. The only thing saving you will be the data on Ness Ryan."

"He'll have to pick up that data himself, then," Melanie said. "In person."

"That'll spare your business, then. Probably not you."

"We'll see in twelve hours," Melanie said.

"Twelve hours, more or less, Mel. Twelve hours."

"I hear you," she whispered. Andrew switched off. Melanie buried her head in her hands. When it came to a showdown between National Security and Mountain Security, she had no doubt who would win that round.

The fucking crisis she had been trying to avoid for seven years. Well, it was here.

I'd better tell Angela.

She called Security.

"We're on it," Angela responded tersely after Melanie finished explaining. "Have been. Ness and Marty weren't our only sources, Mel. We already knew what Peter was planning to do."

"And you didn't tell me?"

"Did you need to know? Peter would never have gotten those nukes off."

"You're sure of that?"

"We've got people on the ground there, Mel. Little brown people that Peter doesn't even notice. We don't exist to him, or to his Freedom Army buddies." Angela tiredly flicked back a strand of hair. "Be grateful for your uncle's racism, Mel. Our invisible people pulled the teeth on that threat. For now. The cousins are watching over us."

"Gracias, Ange."

"De nada. Get some rest, because it's going to be ugly tomorrow. I want you fresh and ready to go."

"I will," Melanie promised. She pushed back from her desk. Enough was enough for today. Time to check in with Marty.

As Melanie walked down the hallway to Marty's office, something *slammed* inside her head. She dropped to her knees, clutching at the area behind her right ear, the site of her Dialogue implant.

What was that?

<Dialogue!> No response. She blinked three times for a reboot cue.

Nothing.

She tried again. This time, the reboot overlay stuttered across her visual field, went down, then came back, stronger.

What kicked off the reboot? Something Marty did?

She staggered upright and ran for Marty's office. Knocked. No response. Slammed the door open, and froze.

Marty curled in a fetal position inside a hologlobe. *Damn!* She activated her datasuit, then slipped into the hologlobe, wincing as she passed through the enclosure. It shocked her because she wasn't the person attuned to this globe—but not bad, nothing she hadn't encountered before.

Melanie rolled Marty over, mentally reviewing Dialogue crash recovery procedures. He moaned before she could do anything.

"I lost them," he groaned, throwing one arm over his eyes. "I lost them. A whole line of linkages."

"Shh. It's okay. We'll get them back." Melanie rocked back on her heels. This wasn't the standard Dialogue crash.

He dropped the arm and his eyes popped open. The agony and pain that looked back at her made her stomach clench and go cold, his face gray under brown.

"You don't understand. I *lost* them. We *can't* get those lines back,

Melanie. They went Suicide Red. Most of them went Suicide Red. I couldn't help them. I couldn't stop it. I was *there*, Melanie. I *felt* it!"

She froze, staring at him.

A whole lineage of Dialogues went Suicide Red and he felt it? God.

Pushing away all caution, she took Marty into her arms and held him tight.

God. What he just went through.

Marty buried his head deep into her shoulder, shaking all over, quivering as if he wanted to cry but didn't quite dare let it go.

"Shh. Shh," she murmured, stroking the faint wetness away from his eyes. "You did what you could, Marty. If you couldn't have saved them, no one could."

This and Ness too.

For a moment, she thought about sending him on Diaspora with the others, getting him away from the nightmares clustering around them. For a moment. Then she dismissed the thought. She needed him here. God, did she ever need him here.

"You can't send me away," Marty said.

"Did I say it out loud? I didn't think I did."

"I didn't hear that through my ears, Melanie. I heard the voice in my head. It was different from your spoken voice." His voice trailed off and he swallowed hard. "It's the same voice I hear when I call up Dialogue. When I'm getting a response back from Dialogue. But this time I knew it was your thought, your subvocal voice."

"There's no such thing as telepathy."

"No. No. And we've not built a mind-to-mind speech capacity into Dialogue." He kept staring at her. <But all the same, here I am, talking to you via Dialogue.>

<How the hell?> She moved away, dropping all physical contact, and a connection she hadn't noticed before went dead. Marty picked up her hand. Once again, she felt that rush of warmth, a sensation of *contact*.

<You hear it now?> he asked.

<Yeah.>

<Physical contact in a hologlobe. Have we tried this with the latest generation of Dialogue?>

<No.> She slipped her hand from his and leaned back. "And, fascinating as this is, we still have a problem. Hold it. I have an idea." She picked up his hand again. Could this be a solution to their Dialogue problem? <Show me where we lost the links.>

His pain and fear radiated into her, but he slowly rose, using her shoulder as a brace, then helped her up. They twined their hands together. Marty led Melanie into the virtual world, through the colored schematic of links to where they were broken. Blood-red shadows roiled from that schematic, oozing down the lines.

They stopped. Melanie and Marty coalesced into one unit. The shadows formed into a red blob, projecting a malevolence that made her shiver. Melanie used their joined hands to trace out a blocking link, while tapping code with her other hand. She was peripherally aware of Marty typing a similar code. A thin purple line slowly circled the red blob. The blob fell apart, returning to shards of churning shadows, contained by that purple line.

Brightness flashed. The shape of a copper-colored spiky ball about as big as she was momentarily strobed in Melanie's vision.

What the hell?

The ball faded.

<Do It Right Dialogues,> she subvocaled, using an All-Call universal text command. <Disconnect all Linkages and Lineages. Now. Establish independent contacts. No new links. No following links. Use independent nodes.> She and Marty added their authentication codes to the message.

They released their hands. Then studied the roiling shadows that strained against the thin purple line.

"We better shut this process down," Melanie said.

Marty nodded. "That line won't contain those shadows for long. We'll have to figure out something else soon."

"We'll deal with it. For now, we've got them contained." She hesitated. "Did you see—*that*? There at the last?"

"Sh. Not here," he said. The urgent tone in his voice silenced her.

They backtracked carefully out of the virtual world. Then Marty tapped the code to close the globe. They watched as the hologlobe tightened around the shadows, until the globe was no more than a swirling baseball-sized sphere.

Marty fell to his knees. Melanie grabbed his shoulders, holding him upright as his upper body sprawled against her. He took a deep breath, shook his head, pulled himself up and away from her, and took her hand. The contact rocked through them. She wanted. He wanted. *They* wanted.

They stared at each other for a moment, eyes wide, sharing the shock at that reaction.

Marty gently pulled his hand away from hers.

"S'okay. Damn it, Melanie, I'm going to be no good to you without some more rest. Not going to do Burnout. And with that deadline coming…."

"It's okay. It's been put off until tomorrow."

"Huh. Wonder if it had anything to do with *that* thing."

"The shadows or the other thing?" Melanie asked. "Just what the hell was that?"

"Something you really don't want to know more about."

Melanie stared at Marty, wanting to slap him in sudden sheer frustration. "Now's one hell of a time to start fussing about secrecy and confidentiality."

Marty sighed and looked away. "Tired. Sorry. Conditioning. Mel, I hope that's not what I think I'm seeing. Because if that is, we have a bigger problem than those shadows."

"A bigger problem?" Melanie repeated, a chill running over her as she suddenly suspected what Marty alluded to. "The gadget?"

Mom never calls the Gizmo by its name.

Marty nodded. "Mel, we don't want to mess with—it. We really don't."

"I have no intention of tangling with it, if I can avoid doing so," Melanie said. "Look. Mom's getting in later tonight. We can take this issue up with her then. Why don't you rest?"

"Only if you do, too." He looked steadily at her. "I promised Ness that I'd keep you safe."

"Before all this happened?"

A confused look crossed his face. "No. Something happened. I'm supposed to protect you. It's what Ness wants."

She decided not to push him further. "I'll rest, if you do too."

Marty nodded. He shambled down the hallway toward his quarters while she wandered back to hers.

Just what the hell was that moment all about?

Melanie thought about it while doing her evening workout, but no answers came to her, other than the obvious. She and Marty had been lovers once, before she became involved with Liam after Marty became entranced with Ness. And now, with Ness dead and Liam revealed as the slimy betrayer he was....

She wasn't the only one struggling with old feelings.

That night she dreamed about the skimmer crash with Liam and woke up screaming. It took more exercise and a stiff drink to clear the images from her brain.

No more time. Melanie woke to a gentle shake from her mother Diana, one of the few beyond her personal Security who had the access code to her quarters.

"Take Marty and the rest of the essential personnel, get the hell out of here," Diana said. "Angela's connections saved your butt earlier, but no guarantees that will continue."

"What about you?"

"Your dad gave me some tricks to deal with Peter."

Melanie frowned at her mother. "You got the all call about no Dialogue links?"

Diana nodded. "We set up floating addresses while you were sleeping. No statics."

"There's some new stuff." Quickly, she told Diana about the shadows, and the contact technique she and Marty had discovered yesterday. "And—" she hesitated. "There's more. The gadget may be interested in us. Marty and I saw it."

Diana flipped her left hand dismissively. "Not for you two to worry about. I'll deal with the gadget for now. Marty sent me a short description of what happened, so I knew about the shadows. That shadow worries me more, since your father thinks it's what has been killing our Dialogue links and lineages. However, I'm intrigued by this contact conversation technique Marty described. That's not anything we've known about before now, is it?"

Melanie shook her head. "Maybe it's a hologlobe thing. That's the first time I've had my thoughts picked up when touching another person with a Dialogue."

"Try it with me." Diana took her hand.

<I'm worried about you,> Melanie thought, careful not to use subvocals, which would trigger the Dialogue text function.

Diana shook her head, then slipped her hand free.

"Nothing," she said. "You and Marty should look into this more deeply when you reach a safe place. At least we've found something that works against the shadows. Here." She held out a small vial.

"What is it?" Melanie studied the vial.

"Silicone-based bioinoculate. Modified enough to be digestible."

"What does it do?"

Diana paused. "Your father discovered part of how those shadows operate. They're similar to a virus, and access Dialogue through internal links—that's the part we don't know yet. The shadows jump into the chip and activate the Suicide Red trigger that blows the chip up. If a shadow gets into your Dialogue, this treatment shuts it down without compromising you. The Dialogue's unusable and will have to be replaced, but at least we'll stop people dying."

"That Suicide Red trigger had at least three redundancies."

"I know. Someone's damned good at this stuff, Melanie, and we're just lucky that we're better so far. I wish we still had Ness in those National Security labs. Marty doesn't know who developed this shadow stuff." Diana rested a hand on her shoulder. "Let's get you out of here."

Melanie gulped down the vial's contents, frowning at the taste. "Mom, I don't want you meeting with Peter alone. Send the others away, fine. But you need someone by your side to face Peter. Let it be me and Marty, with my Security. We can move pretty damned fast."

"You'll lose the chance to take skimmers."

"There's stealthsuits for us and some horses, right? Won't be that hard to ride over to the Warm Springs Reserve—they're expecting us. Ride up to snow level, turn the horses loose if it's too deep, snowshoe and hike the rest of the way if we have to. It's not like there are clear-cuts all the way between Hoodland and the Reserve. And we have scatter generators. The blacksuits of National Security don't. Kathy created those for us while she was at Grouse Creek. Ness never knew about them."

"If anyone could do that, you and your Mountain Security could," Diana murmured.

"We've done a lot of winter training for bugging out into the mountains ever since you left for Nagano seven years ago. Horses, no horses, snowshoes, cross-country skis. All options."

"Okay," Diana conceded. "You, Marty, and your Security stay. I want the rest out of here now, especially your Janine. She knows too damn much, and you'll need her in Nagano."

"Nagano, not Rio?"

Diana gave her a withering look. "Your dad's in Nagano. Research facilities are better there. Besides, the snow's good in Nagano this year. I *assume* you'd rather have snow than beaches, right?" A faint grin twitched her lips.

"Mom, you know me too well."

"Good. I'll get Diaspora going. You brief Marty. Meet me in your office. Half an hour."

"Okay."

Melanie gathered up her clothes, showered, and went to find Marty. He was in the cafeteria, morosely chewing on a muffin while staring into his coffee cup.

"Hey."

He faintly smiled as she sat down, his face coming alive as he looked at her. "Hey."

"You doing better this morning?" she asked.

He shrugged. "I guess I'm doing as well as could be expected." He took her hand. <I'm curious to see if this works without a globe.>

She half-jumped, as much from the wash of feelings that spilled over her as from the mental voice. <It didn't work with me and Mom!>

He pulled his hand back. "That's something we'll have to figure out after we get out of this situation. So what is our plan?"

She quickly told him. "Oh yeah. Did you get the bioinoculate?" she asked.

"Two hours ago." He got up. "Ten minutes before we meet up with Diana. Sounds like I'd better pack a light bag if we're cutting out of here by horseback. You sure there's a beast big enough to carry me?"

"Several," she told him. "And they've been getting regular workouts. I've been keeping ready for something just like this."

He nodded. "Should be interesting. I haven't ridden since I left."

"It'll come back to you."

She hurried to her own quarters. What to take? Her data was portable; a must over the past few years. Most of the personal items that meant anything to her had been shipped out seven years ago to Nagano, in case she ever needed to flee the Mountain.

Seven years. Seven tough years in hell.

For better or worse, it had ended.

She packed a very small bag, and slung it on her back.

Marty was already with her mother when Melanie reached her office.

"This is what's I'm planning," Diana said, tossing Melanie a stealthsuit. "I'm going to take Peter down. Sedate him if I can. He's already pretty damn upset, and when he gets upset, he gets unbalanced, thanks to those damn nanos in his system, just like my mother insisted on using. Damn unstable tech, and *neither* of them would listen to me."

Melanie snorted. "As if we could tell the difference between regular Peter and unbalanced Peter." She pulled on the stealthsuit.

Diana frowned at her. "Maybe you can't. I can." She sighed. "I'm pretty dang sure that your grandmother's death triggered a king-hell of a reaction in him. Add to that the effect of that systems crash on his nanos. I doubt he's rational now. Takes after my uncle Brent in the face of a crisis. Hell, most of the Stephens men are certifiable. I'm sorry Andrew seems to have taken after them."

"I'm sorry, Mom."

"I wouldn't be surprised if one of the first things Peter does is to try to kill me," she said.

"Mom—"

"It's not the first time. He tried it before I left seven years ago."

"Why didn't you do something about it then? Why wouldn't Grandmother listen?"

"Her nanos." Diana frowned. "I warned them. Unstable, especially in the amounts they were using for anti-aging processes. They augment any mental instability. And Peter has many more problems than she did." Her mother shivered. "I wasn't ready to go all the way. Then. I am now."

Melanie bit her lip. "What's our strategy?"

"I'm armed and ready. While the plan is to sedate Peter and defang his support staff, I'll kill him if I have to. Your dad prepped me with a bunch of built-in hidies that Peter and his National Security aren't about to find."

"Why wait around here for him and his goons? Why not blow the place and leave?"

"Politics. We've been in a state of war for seven years. It's just out in the open now." Diana fixed Melanie with a stern gaze. "Before I left Nagano, the New Federated United States Government in Exile appointed me as Interim President. No money for support, of course. But the Do It Right cells that you created around the country will be more effective than cash right now. Getting our government back will take stealth and underground work. Direct confrontation won't be. At first. Except for Peter. I have to take care of this. And Andrew, too, if it comes to that." She shook her head. "Your worst enemies are from your own family. Thank God I at least have you on my side."

"Are you sure you want those of us who are left to go?"

"You're Research, not politics, hon. If something happens to me, the company's yours to run. Political side as well as research side. But you're right about one thing. You need to be here, to witness what happens. This is family business. I need you here for that."

"I've never thought of you as a killer."

"I hope it doesn't come to that." Diana rubbed her eyes. "If I can sedate Peter, we can ship him to Tokyo and try him for war crimes. The

New Feds are ready. That's what they really want." She cocked her head. "They're here."

Marty handed Melanie her riding coat, a long, black oilcloth duster. She slipped it on, then pulled her bag on over it. He shrugged into his own coat and they followed Diana out, along with twenty armed Do It Right Security troops. The implications of her mother's words struck Melanie as they walked toward the door.

The New Federated United States Government in Exile appointed me as Interim President.

Her mother had never talked much about political involvement in the past, except for the sparring between Do It Right and Stephens Reclamation, which had been going on as long as Melanie could remember. This was serious.

She shivered. Marty's hand brushed hers.

<It'll be okay.> His voice sounded clear in her head.

She glanced up at him, startled. <I'm just a techie. I don't do political stuff. I facilitate the research. That's what I do best.> She didn't text, but subvocaled words back without the text prompt. The new skill came to her surprisingly quickly.

<Right. And I just hack the small shit. You've been doing this political stuff with the Do It Right underground, Mel. You just don't think of it in those terms. You'll pull this off.>

<I'm scared.>

His hand tightened on hers, then dropped. She triggered the shielding on her stealthsuit as they went outside. It wouldn't be a complete protection against any gunfire, but it wouldn't hurt.

Melanie glanced up to the high ridges that, with any luck, they'd be headed for shortly. Wisps of fog wrapped around the tops, hiding them.

Perfect weather, and stealthsuits plus scatter generators give us even more of an edge. If we can get enough of a start ahead of the National Security blacksuits, we just might make it to Warm Springs.

Melanie stood at her mother's right side as Peter's skimmer slid to a halt, followed by a National Security contingent. Standing like this, she was aware of the difference in their height. Diana towered over her, always had. Melanie was the short one of the family, shorter than her father, shorter even than her grandmother.

Peter stepped out of his lead skimmer, gaunt and dissipated-looking, gray-blond hair disheveled. Andrew followed their uncle, looking like he had aged twenty years in the past two days.

I wish you'd chosen differently, brother.

Melanie's ex-fiancé Liam climbed out after Andrew, looking not one day older than he had when Nik had booted him out of Nagano, eight years ago. Still slender and slightly stooped, limping from the skimmer accident. A sneer twisted his lips as his eyes met Melanie's.

She looked at him, and for the first time in eight years, felt nothing.

Tension radiated from her mother as Peter and Andrew marched toward them, Liam behind Andrew.

Of course, the slimy little jerk hides behind Drew.

She swallowed hard, trembling slightly. Marty's hand brushed against hers, a quick wordless sending of comfort and support. It eased her trembling.

Peter and Andrew stopped about twenty feet from them. The end blacksuits came face to face with the end DIR Security, no more than two feet between them. Both groups of Security simultaneously shifted to battle-ready positions.

We'll be lucky to get out of this alive.

"So. You're back, *sister,*" Peter said. He took three steps forward. Diana matched him. "I hear that you've been appointed Interim President. Congratulations, for all the good it'll do you. It'll make it easier for me to take control of your company."

"Interdiction and Notice of Takeover cannot be applied to an overseas company," Diana said.

Peter laughed, a forced laugh that went high and screechy. "Come *on,* Diana! Now that you're back, DIR is no longer an overseas company. Your mistake! You know Confederation law on the subject!"

Diana shook her head. "Will's the current head. I resigned when I was appointed the New Fed Interim President."

"Sneaky. Sneaky. So. Are you going to try to drag me to Tokyo? You can't. You'll lose in court."

"*You'll* lose in court if you try to take my company."

"Not with the Corporate Courts under my control." Peter's eyes darted toward Melanie and Marty. "For the good of your daughter, I'd suggest you surrender now."

"For the sake of my son, I'd suggest that *you* surrender peacefully."

Peter laughed again. "Looks to me like we're at a stalemate." His right hand twitched, and a gun appeared in it. "Want to play chicken?"

Marty moved closer to Melanie, his arm brushing against hers. She blinked as he sent her the sequence of the moves they should make when the shooting started.

"I don't play those games," Diana said forcefully. With a fingersnap, a similar gun appeared in her right hand. "You've forgotten too damn much about me and my husband, *brother.*"

Peter bared his teeth, shaking his head. "Oh no, little sister. I've not forgotten a damn thing about you or your Will. Not a damn thing at all." He circled to her right, toward Melanie, his eyes darting again toward Melanie and Marty. Marty shouldered Melanie away from Peter. "Oho. Who's this? Haven't I seen you before?"

Marty remained silent, but slid slightly in front of Melanie, still keeping a light contact. <Watch out for Peter's left hand. He's sneaky with it.>

<Understood.>

"Marty Fielding, head of DIR North American Research," Diana snapped, turning to face Peter, holding her ground.

"That's not where I saw him. Ah. You were with Ness Ryan, weren't you?" The grin split his face. "Little sister, here's my proof of treason right here. Your Head of Research's been sitting in my National Security Research labs for seven years. Try and tell me that he hasn't been feeding you information."

"My entire company was sworn into service by the Government in Exile seven years ago. No treason at all. We're enemy combatants."

Peter laughed at her. Suddenly, his left hand flicked, and a knife darted toward Diana. She feinted, ducked, and shot. Marty's hand closed around Melanie's wrist. His other hand on her shoulder turned her sharply, pushing her through the line of DIR security, but not before she saw Peter Stephens fall as the two lines of Security converged. Then she was running hard, struggling to keep up with Marty's long strides.

More Security met them with the horses. She grabbed the reins of a small brown mare, her favorite, the granddaughter of her mother's famous cutting horse mare.

"Good girl, Mocha," she murmured. Then, to Angela, who'd followed her from the melee, "My mother—is she—do we know—"

"No idea!" Angela yelled back. "We've got to ride!"

<DIASPORA NOW!> Melanie texted. Then she urged Mocha into a gallop, along with the other riders.

CHAPTER 3

DARKNESS FOUND THEM HIGH IN THE MOUNTAINS. AFTER THE INITIAL WILD stampede, Angela herded them across the Salmon River and along the slope of Huckleberry Mountain, heading deep into the heart of the old Salmon-Huckleberry Wilderness. They bushwhacked part of the trail when National Security skimmers roared overhead, but the surveillance wasn't as bad as it could have been.

It was a tough, torturous route, however, hacking their way along a thin trail through heavy underbrush and around downed logs. Even at that, they made better time than Melanie had expected.

Angela dropped back to her. "Sergio's found a good spot for the evening, down in the canyon. I'd hoped to be closer to some of those grown-over logging roads in the Roaring River area but those damned blacksuits worry me. Someone in their crowd might be competent enough to find an old Forest Service map. Even if they're too damned citified to follow us across the terrain, they could be waiting for us on the other side."

"Maybe. And maybe they think we're on the other side of Hunchback. They don't know the country very well. Straight line extrapolation."

"We can hope. Sergio's site has water and a reasonable flat space, though it's snow-covered. Not too exposed, perfect setup for the scatter generators to hide our heat signatures, even allow us a small campfire."

"Good," Melanie said. "Any news?"

Angela shook her head before riding on ahead. "I'll brief you once we're settled. Nothing that can't wait. Our people got away with no significant casualties, that's the short version."

Melanie rubbed Mocha's neck, gently breaking up the dried sweat that had formed there. At least there had been a chance to cool out the horses from that first frantic run.

It wasn't long before they skidded down the side of the canyon to the creek. They splashed across the belly-deep water to a small flatland sheltered by trees, where the snow settled to a six-inch depth.

After setting up the scatter generators, Angela directed them to specific duties. Melanie helped Sergio and Nik tend the horses. Once the horses were cool and dry, Melanie staggered toward the main encampment set up around a tiny campfire. She warmed herself by the fire, along with Nik and Sergio.

Angela handed her a mug of something steaming. Melanie sipped gratefully at it, pleased to find the mug contained a salty broth which warmed both her gloved hands and her insides.

"Thanks," she said to Angela.

"That's the only hot stuff we can do right now," Angela said. "Just a little something to warm you up."

"Can't be *that* warm, there's no booze in it!" A grin snuck up on Melanie as she remembered past riding campouts, acting as guides on tourist trips as a cover for Security survival training.

Angela guffawed. "What do you want, Mel? A luxury outing?"

"Damn, Ange, I just thought this was some sort of fancy extreme ski trip that involved horses. Ain't seen no skis yet, though!" Melanie said, trying to keep a straight face. It worked until their eyes met and they burst out in giggles, remembering *that* client.

"Jesus, Mary and Joseph, girl! You're going to have me thinking this is a luxury trip yet!" Angela quoted the client.

They collapsed against each other, giggling.

Angela was the first to sober up. She passed Melanie a flask. "Here's the booze. You might want to check in with Marty," she whispered in Melanie's ear. "He's been quiet. I can't tell if he's having physical problems or if everything's getting to him. You know him better than I do."

Melanie took a swig. "He's been running pretty hard," she whispered back. "We all have been."

"Yeah, but we're used to it. He's not. He's been a city boy for the past seven years." Angela reclaimed the flask and took a drink.

"True."

"I've also put you two in the same tent. I want you to keep an eye on Marty."

Melanie stiffened. "Angela—"

Angela shoved the flask back into Melanie's hand. "You two are our Primaries. I want you in one place if we have to run. Besides, you've trained for this, and he hasn't. If you're watching him, it makes my life simpler."

"Ange, that's not fair. I can't do this."

Angela frowned at her. "Mel, come on. What the hell is going to happen? Or are you still carrying a torch for Liam? I thought you were over him long ago."

"I am over Liam. Been over Liam for a long time. But still, Ange, this is really awkward."

"Why? You two are just sharing a tent."

"But does it look professional? Considering who we are?"

Angela shrugged. "Who the hell cares? Mel, we're on the run. I could be shaking you two out of bed in the middle of the night because we've got an alert. I don't want to futz around finding my Primaries." She peered closely at Melanie. "Girl, you sound like an anxious virgin on her wedding night. This is a Security run, not a lifetime commitment."

Melanie's fingers tightened on the flask.

I don't know if I can handle it if something does happen.

"I'm just concerned," she said.

I don't know if I can handle a relationship.

Angela gave her a playful shove. "Look, you need to loosen up. Relax a little. Who the hell keeps lecturing me about the need to play more? Seems to me you need to be taking your own advice." Her face straightened into a sober line. "Trust me, it's not my intention to play the matchmaker, especially given these circumstances. But as your friend, not your Security head, I'd like to see you break out of that freeze that Liam shoved you into."

"Thanks. But I'll work it out. In my own time."

Angela sighed, exasperated. "Look. We're all exhausted. You're the only trained spare I have. That means you're the one to monitor him. That's me speaking as Head of Security to trained Primary. Period. Chill out and take another drink. You need it. You're jangled."

Melanie didn't argue further. She took a deep drink and handed the flask back to Angela.

I have my assignment. Better do it.

She wandered over to Marty, sitting on a stool by the fire, and squatted next to him, flinching at her aching thigh and calf muscles.

Damn. That hurts. I'm not in as good a shape as I thought.

That raised another worry. If she was feeling this sore and tired, then how was Marty doing? Yeah, Ange was right, damn it. Marty needed one-on-one attention to make sure he could keep up. He was their weakest link.

"You holding on okay?" she asked.

He nodded. "I'm going to hurt bad in the morning. Am hurting now. Every muscle I've got is yelling at me. You?"

"I've been riding and skiing as much as I can to keep in shape. But I don't think it's enough. This hurts."

"Good. I don't feel so bad, then." He shifted his weight on the stool. "You can sit here. That's got to be more comfortable than what you're doing now."

"You sure? Doesn't look like enough space."

"I'll hold you." He flashed her a grin. "I don't bite, and I won't let you fall."

"I'm depending on you." Melanie settled cautiously on the edge of the stool, making sure there was the slightest space between them. He firmly pulled her closer. She stiffened, then relaxed. It made sense to sit like this. Together, they were warmer. Still, she could feel that quivering sensation inside of her.

I can't afford to have this happen.

At least the contact didn't trigger their Dialogues.

We have to figure this out.

But not while they were on the run.

Sergio passed out dried food bars along with water. Melanie and Marty kept up the contact, strangely reluctant to pull away from the warmth and comfort of each other. She noticed that most of the Security crew stayed alert.

"Ange," she said. "What's the latest news? If any."

Angela shook her head. "Not heard anything. I know some of our folks survived, and your brother made it out of HQ with some of his blacksuits. Peter was hit, but I don't know if it was a killing shot or not. I got this info before we got too deep into the canyon. Now?" She shrugged. "Not only are we too far in to get a good connection, I'd just as soon not attract attention."

"And Mom?"

"She went into full safe mode shortly after we left. No more news. Sorry, Melanie. I know she's alive. But whether the blacksuits got her, whether Peter's alive or dead, whether she's on the run with him in tow, I don't know."

"It's okay."

Angela hesitated, then continued. "I have most of my folks on watch. We're going to keep it that way, with two-hour rotations. I want you two in this tent—" She gestured to a centrally located tent close to the fire. "—the sooner, the better. Then we can kill the fire."

"Okay."

"Ladies first," Marty said.

Melanie grimaced, but headed for the tent. Two mummy bags were already laid out for them. She pulled off her coat and laid it on top of the bag she chose for herself. Then she eased off the stealthsuit. Sleeping in stealthsuits was uncomfortable, and even on full equipment training runs, the rule was to shed them at night, with scatter generators running, to diffuse heat signatures. She slid into her bag, slipping off her pants and outer sweater and kicking them down to the bottom of the bag to stay dry and warm for the morning. She ran the zipper up high and nestled in, shivering as she waited for her body heat to warm the bag.

Marty grunted as he ducked into the tent. She watched in case she had to give advice, but he quickly shed his stealthsuit and crawled into his bag. From the thrashing, she could tell he was doing the same thing with his clothing as she had.

"Night, Mel," he murmured.

"Night."

Despite her worries, Melanie fell asleep quickly once the bag warmed.

THRASHING AND MOANING, FOLLOWED BY AN INARTICULATE CRY, WOKE her. She quickly blinked up her time display. Two o'clock. She lightly shook Marty's shoulder.

"Marty. Marty," she hissed.

He woke with a start, gasping and shuddering. "Ness—oh god, Melanie. Ness. Oh God. *I saw it all over again!*"

Half-asleep, she freed her arms from her warm and toasty bag and pulled him to her. He nuzzled his head into her chest while deep, shuddering sobs shook his body. She stroked the back of his head, murmuring softly while he cried.

<Take care of him for me, Mel.>

"What the *hell?*" she whispered. That was *not* Marty's subvocal voice. It almost sounded like Ness.

<Take care of him, Mel. He's a good guy, but he doesn't do well alone. Take care of him.>

<Who are you?> she thought hard.

No answer.

Marty's tears slowed and he raised his head. He squeezed her tighter. <You heard it, didn't you? That other voice.>

<Who is it?> she asked.

<I don't know.> She felt his bewilderment and worry. <It sounds like Ness. But she's *dead*!>

This time his agony and emptiness spilled over. Melanie tried to push it away. She could barely make out his mournful face in the shadows. Another wave of sadness and pain radiated from Marty as she held herself apart from him.

Something broke deep inside of her as Marty sagged his head resignedly against her chest again, accepting her rejection; bewilderment and pain radiating from his deepest self.

No. I can't do this to him.

She pulled him tightly to her, trying to project comfort. His head lifted. His lips brushed hers, softly, gently. She resisted, but only for the briefest of moments. Then they were kissing furiously, a fire lighting up deep inside of her.

This isn't smart. This isn't wise.

Melanie shuddered. Too much had been going on over the past two days. The past seven years. Hell, the past eight years. *She* wanted the comfort as much as *he* did. Ange was right. She had been frozen for too damn long. Marty wasn't Liam, would never be like Liam. It was time to break free from her past.

Still she eased back, briefly. <You sure about this?>

His answer was to pull her closer. <Yeah. Yeah.>

Then she felt the touch of the *other*. <Take care of him, Mel. Take care of him.>

The unknown person faded away. All she was aware of now was Marty. They fumbled with sleeping bag zippers and what little clothing they had been wearing, until they were flesh against flesh. As Melanie's body pressed hard against Marty's, and he slipped inside her, something expanded inside her head.

She wasn't alone. He was there. They were there. *Together.* She was part of his arousal, his surprise as that *something more* opened up. She viewed Marty as he saw himself, a smaller, stooped, older version of the real man. Melanie sent back images of how she perceived him. The Marty she knew, the man that she was glad had made it back from National Security.

In turn, he showed Melanie the image he had of her, a more elegant, polished and skilled person than she recognized.

Brightness. Words and images faded away, massive warmth sweeping over them in waves as Marty pressed deeply into Melanie and she rocked her pelvis against him, their hearts pounding in sync, their breaths matching, a bright glow rising higher, higher, higher.

Marty. Melanie. Them. The blazing intense spark that was the deepest part of who and what he was, what they were, what they could be, together.

Union. Two together. One. She couldn't tell where Marty began and she ended. She'd never been this close to anyone else before, not even Liam. Not even Marty the first time they had been lovers.

They quivered together, and were finished. Marty collapsed onto Melanie, resting his head on her chest. She held him tight as she shuddered a bit longer than he did, still one, still not sure what was him and what was her.

Marty raised his head and slid both of his hands on each side of Melanie's face, running his fingers through her hair, covering her lips, her nose, her cheeks with small soft kisses as her breathing slowed. She blinked, finally aware of herself alone.

No. Not alone. Not completely. She could feel him not just physically but mentally, brighter and more confident than he'd been.

Marty rolled onto his side and pulled her close to him. She leaned against him, resting her head against his chest. His lips played over her forehead, over her hair. She raised her head and nuzzled him back.

"You okay with this?" he asked. "I might have been a bit abrupt."

"No problem. Entirely understandable."

His arms tightened around her. "You okay staying like this the rest of the night?"

"If you are. But we'd better fix the bags. My butt's starting to get cold."

"Agreed. You take your side, I'll do mine."

They rearranged the bags, zipping them together before they snuggled, Marty's arms wrapped around her. She remembered what he had said to her earlier that evening.

I won't let you fall.

Years ago, when Sarah came to power, Melanie had put away all thoughts of relationships.

Did this change things, or were they just comforting each other?

She decided to worry about it in the morning.

Melanie and Liam fought in their skimmer, something that became more and more common once he found out she was pregnant and planning to keep their child. It was late at night, and they were on their way back to the Nagano Do It Right compound after watching the ski races. She couldn't remember what the fight was about, only that Liam slapped her. She raised her arm to counter his blow, and in the kicking, slapping battle that followed, her right leg knocked the autopilot loose. They went spinning, spinning, crazily flipping end over end, crashing at high speed. It seemed like it would never stop and she was screaming, screaming—

Someone shook her. "Mel. Melanie. Stop. It's safe. It's okay. You're okay. It's a dream. *It's just a dream.*"

Marty's voice. Marty's hands. His naked body against hers. She stiffened.

What the hell?

"It's a dream," Marty repeated. "Easy. It's okay. A bad dream. That's all it is."

She shuddered. He kept talking softly and soothingly to her, stroking her forehead.

"Come on," he said, coaxing now. "Cry if you need to. It's okay."

She shuddered again, afraid of what would come out.

"It's *the* crash, isn't it?"

She nodded, wetness starting to spill out of her eyes. "It was my fault. We were arguing. He hit me, and I knocked off the autopilot while blocking him from hitting me. My fault."

"He shouldn't have hit you. There's no call for that. You were just protecting yourself. Simple bad luck that the autopilot blew. Not your fault. Not at all."

She kept shaking.

This is a really bad one. It's usually not this graphic. I felt it all, just like the time it happened.

"I did it, though."

Marty gently took her head in his hands, and kissed her forehead, then each eye. "He shouldn't have hit you. It's not your fault. Listen to me. *It's not your fault.*"

She gulped, still shaking, tears breaking loose. He pulled her close, crooning softly as she sobbed quietly into his chest. At last, her tears eased off.

"Does this happen often?" he asked.

"Two or three times a week."

"You've not gotten any help?"

She shook her head. "No time for help. Besides, where would *I* find help? Secure help that I could trust, in today's political environment?"

He was silent for a few minutes. "Melanie," he said finally. "Has there been anyone else since Liam?"

She shook her head. "No," she whispered, feeling very small and shamed.

"I'm the first lover you've had since Liam?"

She nodded.

"Jesus. What a fine pair we are." He rubbed her back in a soothing rhythm. "A pair of walking wounded, that's us. I've not had anyone since Ness and I split."

She gulped. "It's just—I can't afford to mess up bad, there's too much at stake, I messed up so bad and made such a bad choice with Liam, and I'm so *damned* lousy at this relationship stuff, I work too hard and get too damned intense and active, you know that about me, and because of who I am and the way I am there's just been no one I can trust or who really can handle who I am and who I'm related to—"

"Breathe, Melanie. Breathe," he whispered. "That little son of a bitch did a real number on your head, didn't he? I didn't help when we were together the first time, did I? Damn. I'm so damned sorry. I was young and stupid and arrogant then."

"You didn't have anything to do with it," she whispered. "I was young and awkward and didn't know what to do."

"I was afraid of you then," he said. "You were the princess. Smart. Self-assured. Bashing your way through the World Cup circuit while going like hell in the labs. No fear at all. I didn't think I had a chance with you. That one day someone else would slide along and scoop you up because, after all, I was just the hired help. When Ness came along, and then Liam, it was just like I'd foreseen."

"You were never *just* the hired help. But Ness was so right for you, so much into the same things. I was just a spoiled brat, rich ski bum."

"No," he said softly. "Never that. And Ness wasn't right for me in the long run. She knew it and I knew it. God, Melanie, how could we have been so stupid?"

Melanie shivered again, this time from a very different, intense sensation of oneness with Marty. He held her until she fell back into a dreamless sleep.

No longer alone.

A SCRATCH AT THE TENT DOOR WOKE HER.

"Let's get moving," Angela said. "Looks to be another wet day but not bad. Drizzle. Let's make time while the weather works for us. I think we can make it without ditching the horses if we hurry."

"Gotcha," she answered.

Marty stirred. She turned within his arms. He smiled at her, kissed her forehead, her eyes, her lips.

"You okay?" he asked.

"Yeah. You?"

"Mmhm. I meant what I said last night. I won't let you fall, Melanie. Everyone needs to watch out for each other. I don't like being alone, and you shouldn't be either. If something more than that happens from this, then great."

"I'll still worry about the timing," she whispered.

"Don't," he said quietly. "I'm forty years old. I've learned by now that the best things don't always happen at the right time."

"I'm still learning that."

"Doesn't mean we won't have more nightmares like last night, or that we're magically healed. We both have some pretty deep hurts."

She pressed her head against his chest, briefly, then dug around with a foot to bring up her pants. "Right now, we need to get moving."

"Yeah." He grinned at her. "Ladies first."

"Figures," she grumbled back at him as she climbed out of the bag to wrestle into her pants and the bottom half of her stealthsuit. When she sat down to pull on her overshirt, he slid out and pulled his pants on. They shared one quick kiss before climbing out.

Angela smirked at her knowingly, but said nothing.

This day's ride was as hard and as fast as the previous one. But it brought them to the edge of the Reserve by nightfall. This time Angela directed Nik to supervise camp setup while she headed east to find connectivity.

She came back with a grin. "Got our No-Fence codes. We'll be hooking up with Warm Springs Security about ten tomorrow morning." Angela glanced at Melanie. "There's news. Peter Stephens is dead. Your brother's announced Succession to the Presidency, although it's unlikely he can hold onto it."

"And Mom?"

"One quick transmission, announcing her appointment as Interim President. We don't know where she is. The Warm Springs Security know something, but they ain't talking."

"Good."

Angela paused. "We're close but we're not in the clear yet. I'd like you to eat and hit the sack fast. I don't trust these scatter generators to cover a fire's heat trace in this location. More open than last night. Harder to hide."

"Okay."

Angela jerked her head toward the edge of camp. "Mel. I want you to look at some horses."

Melanie raised one brow, but followed Angela to the highline where the horses were tethered. They started fiddling with Mocha's feet.

"Okay," Angela said. "Are you still on the same tack you were on last night about sharing the same tent with Marty? Because tonight I can give you the space if you need it."

Melanie shook her head. "No. No problems at all."

Angela grinned at her. "Thought so. You look five years younger, and he looks one hell of a lot better. So am I a matchmaker or what?"

"I should kick you in the ass for this bullshit," Melanie said.

Angela snorted. "You haven't the training or the conditioning to kick my ass." Her voice softened. "Ride with it, Mel. I really didn't think anything was going to happen. You've been pretty defensive and self-protective since Liam, and I didn't think either one of you were in the mental space to crack it open. Boy, was I wrong."

"Nightmares," Melanie said.

"Shit," Angela said. "The big one for you?"

Melanie nodded. "Worse than I've had for years. And he had one about Ness."

Angela rested her hand on Melanie's. "Just keep me posted on the sleeping arrangements. Or any other changes I have to make."

Melanie grinned at her. "Thanks, Ange. Thanks."

"De nada, girlfriend." They headed back to camp.

After a quick dinner, Angela herded them into night formation. Marty and Melanie crawled into the tent together instead of separately. Marty snorted at their already-zipped together sleeping bags.

"No secrets from any Security," he said.

Melanie shrugged. "That's my Security. They grew up with me. Know me well. Almost too well. That's the level of detail we pay them for."

"Yeah." He caressed her, and they made love again, this time less frantic than before.

That night they both slept well.

CHAPTER 4

"It's taking us too damn long to get out of here," Melanie growled to Angela, the morning of their second day in Free Victoria. The stillness after the frantic horseback ride, moving from vehicle to vehicle for three days before getting smuggled across the border, then that nerve-wracking ferry ride—

Yes, she was tired. But Melanie was at that stage of exhaustion where she operated on sheer nerves. And someone had identified her on the ferry, damn it, which meant the media was hovering outside—how soon before someone stormed the house to either kill or kidnap her? Sure, there were a handful of police around the Do It Right safe house, but not enough to stop a determined assassin.

At least they had reached the house before the media descended.

Melanie paced around the small living room. It seemed smaller than it was because they didn't dare open the miniblinds and risk sniper exposure. The walls closed in on her, and she desperately wanted the blinds open. Otherwise, it felt like everything was pushing in on her.

Two days of stillness. Two days of waiting. Two days with no further news from her mother. Two days of waiting under observation.

And there was only so much work she could do off-site without access to internal networks. She needed access to her mother's files, to figure out what had been compromised—and until she had internal network access, she couldn't do any of that.

"It'll happen, Mel," Angela said. "Patience."

"What good is a place with a view if we can't open the damned blinds?"

I'd feel one hell of a lot better if Marty and Nik were back!

"They'll be back soon, Mel. We'll get out of here today."

"We should have gone with them."

"Mel. Marty and Nik are less recognizable by themselves than they would be if we were with them." Angela's tone sharpened. "They're okay. They'll be back soon."

Melanie clenched her hands into fists and continued to pace.

I need to stop taking out my nerves on Ange.

No chance to ski, which meant she was more jangled. She wasn't sleeping well and that caused more issues. Last night was rocky for Marty. *Her* nightmares seemed to have calmed, but Marty's yells jerked her out of sleep and, as she woke, she saw an image of a grotesque figure cloaked in the shadows they had blocked at the Mountain lab. No nightmares after their first night on the trail, no nightmares at Warm Springs, none at the Makah Reservation, but then, *here,* there were nightmares again. Both last night and the night before.

Last night was the first night that form bent over *her,* not *him,* before it snapped out of sight. She had the distinct impression, from what Marty had *not* said, that the figure was threatening her in his dreams.

At least the gadget seemed to be leaving them alone.

God. I just want to clear this up.

Which meant they needed to get to Nagano.

She lifted one slat of the miniblinds to peek out at the overcast, drizzly day. Not enough to expose herself; barely enough to see something besides walls and blinds. The media flocked just beyond the fence and the police cordon, complete with bug cams, robotic reporters, and emaciated low-level, live reporters huddled under umbrellas and clutching warm drinks from a portable espresso cart that had set up shop across the street. The motion of the blind was enough to stir the mob into a feeding frenzy concentrating on the one raised blind, voices raised in excitement.

Melanie dropped the slat and grimaced. Marty and Nik had slipped out through a side door and cut through a friendly neighbor's side yard to an alley to avoid the paparazzi and bug cams.

"They're not going to go away, Mel," Angela said. "You're hot news."

"Ange, I know that!" Melanie snapped. "But is this the way things are going to be from now on?" She resumed her pacing.

"It'll be better in Japan. Then we don't need to worry about someone shipping you back over *there* as easily." Angela jerked a thumb in the direction of the Olympic Peninsula. "Come on. Let's do some moves."

"This is my last clean jumpsuit. I don't want to sweat it up."

"You've got others in the wash. They'll be done soon."

"Yeah, but if we go today, I may not have time to change."

"Mel, *damn it*!" Angela took a deep breath. "We'll have time. That shuttle doesn't board until eight tonight. Let's blow off some of your energy, before I clobber you with a clue-by-four!"

"Sorry. I'm being that much of a pain?"

"And more. Look, I know you're worried about the boys getting the paperwork from the New Feds in exile. But damn it, if I could get my hands on some Ritalin, I'd stuff it down your throat right now."

"Like hell you would," Melanie muttered. "My Ritalin days are long over!"

Angela gave her a sidelong, calculating glance. "Don't think I wouldn't or couldn't do it. Look. Help me move some furniture. Put that energy to good use."

They slid the furniture back against the walls and rolled out a practice mat. Angela stepped onto the mat and took up her position. Melanie bowed to her, then stepped onto the mat. She followed as Angela led her through a warm-up, then worked the kata that she'd most recently been learning. Angela pressed Melanie hard, not giving her time to think. Her anxieties and worries flowed away and she was absorbed in nothing more than the motion, anticipation of Angela's next move, and her own response.

Suddenly, Angela signaled a stop.

"About time you guys got here," she said.

Melanie whirled. Marty and Nik stood behind her. "Did you get the paperwork straightened out?"

"All done," Nik said. "Marty here was the biggest hang-up. Thought we were going to have to leave him behind or else stay for another month. Had to promise his first-born son in order to leave Free Victoria. And a few pints of blood."

Melanie glanced quickly at Marty, worried. He grinned and shook his head.

"Nik exaggerates," he said.

Melanie called up the time. Eleven o'clock. "How much longer before we leave?" she asked Angela.

Angela rolled her eyes. "Six hours. At least. That's more than long enough to pull a clean jumpsuit out of the wash."

"Yeah. You're right," Melanie said.

Wish I had something better to wear.

Even her best jumpsuit was faded and worn enough to make her self-conscious.

I'll get something more stylish in Tokyo.

THEIR COMMERCIAL SHUTTLE TOUCHED DOWN AT NARITA IN DRIZZLY DUSK. Clouds obscured any view they might have of Mt. Fuji.

The noise and lights of Narita were a contrast to North America.

Bright. Loud. Overwhelming. People, *so many people.* The building didn't stink of unwashed bodies and sickness. People actually walked around with their heads up, wearing brightly colored clothing, not looking around cautiously and huddled into themselves. Or blustering around bullying others they perceived to be weaker, with alcohol on their breath.

Normal. This is normal. You haven't been living in normal for over seven years, she reminded herself.

Marty wrapped an arm around her waist and she gladly pressed close against him.

<It's a lot,> he said.

<Yeah,> she agreed, glad she wasn't the only one suffering from sensory overload. Grateful that Angela and Nik escorted them through Customs, that Steve and Paul handled luggage.

"We shook the media?" she asked Angela.

"I booked us under pseudonyms, and got alternate bookings under our own names for Rio," Angela told her. "It won't last long."

As Security rushed them through the main terminal, Melanie heard excited voices. They picked up a bug cam, followed by a couple of paparazzi.

"Told you it wouldn't last long," Angela muttered as one camera flashed. "They know we're here now. Damn. Let's move it."

Before the crowd got too large, they popped outside. A long black skimmer waited for them. Angela and Nik bustled Marty and Melanie inside and closed the doors quickly.

"Melanie." Her father stiffly rose from his seat.

She crossed the skimmer cabin to hug him, careful not to press too hard on his frail bones. Never a big man, Will Landreth's translucent skin now clung tightly to his slight frame, and his clothing hung loosely from his body. It was a striking contrast from the stylish, elegant and athletic father she remembered. At least his hands were as steady as ever, not palsied and shaking as she had feared when she heard how far he had declined in the seven years it had been since she last saw him.

Mom said his health was problematic. But I didn't think it was this bad!

"Dad. It's been ages."

"That it has been, baby girl." Will patted her on the back, then turned his attention to Marty. "Marty. I'm sorry about the way things blew up at National Security."

"So am I, sir," Marty said, shaking Will's hand.

"We're leaving," Angela's voice echoed through the front speaker.

Marty guided Melanie to the seat across from her father. He rested his arm across the back of the seat behind her. Her father raised one brow.

"So," he said. "One room or two for you two?"

"One," Melanie said quietly, leaning into Marty. "Security didn't tell you?"

Will waved his hands. "No, no. It's pretty easy to put two and two together when you two are together in every mediacam shot. So. The state of affairs at National Security?" he asked Marty.

"It's worse than you could imagine," Marty told him. "Ness got sucked into trying to save everyone we saw. That's what killed her. She tried to save the wrong person. She got reckless."

"That's too bad. I've never thought of Ness Ryan as reckless."

"I hadn't either. I'll always wonder if I did something wrong, or not enough." His arm tightened on Melanie's shoulder. "You know how she could be."

"Uh-huh," Will said. "We shouldn't have left you and Ness in there that long. How bad are the aftereffects?"

Marty hesitated.

Melanie jumped in. "He's had nightmares the last two nights," she said. "Something funny has been happening with our Dialogues. And —the gadget."

Will's brows shot up. "Tell me."

"We can *talk* with our Dialogues. Full speech, no text. Words. Phrases. The voice we hear is very close to the real-life voice."

"I sure as hell didn't design *that* into Dialogue."

"There's more," Melanie continued. "We can transmit emotions, pictures, schematics."

"When did this happen?"

She described the hologlobe incident. Will leaned back, steepleing his fingers and tapping his lips with his index fingers.

"Does this work with anyone else?" he asked when she was done.

"No," Marty said. "Just the two of us."

"Did you try it with your mother?" Will asked Melanie. "Her chip's the same generation as yours."

"Yes. Nothing."

"There's another thing," Marty said. "I hear another voice. It's Ness."

Will's eyebrows shot up higher than ever. "Now this *is* fascinating. Tell me more."

"We hear her on the nightmare nights," Melanie said. "It's not just Marty. We don't have to be touching, either. I hear her when we're not touching. That's the one exception to the touch rule that we've found."

"Do you two absolutely have to be touching to make this new ability function between you?"

Marty nodded. "We've tried it."

"Hmm. Sounds like we have some interesting work to do. What about the gadget?" her father asked.

"We've seen it once. Mom told us she was handling it—"

"Then she is. No need for you to follow it further." Her father's voice suddenly sharpened. "The gadget is strictly need-to-know, and so far, you're not in that loop."

"Okay," Melanie said. "Have you heard anything from Mom?"

A shadow crossed Will's face. "Nothing new for the past twenty-four hours, probably nothing that you don't already know. But I haven't expected anything."

"Dad, I'm sorry."

"Melanie. Honey. Your mother and I have been through this type of situation before. Usually, I'm the wanderer. This time it's her turn. She'll do fine. She's a tough girl. She has more friends than any of us over there, and she'll be the one to pull this off for the New Feds. If anyone can. We know it. They know it. I was glad to hear she had hooked up with Kathy Miller. Kathy's kept Diana safe and alive before; she'll do it again."

"I didn't know that. Warm Springs Security were keeping things pretty quiet."

The skimmer glided to a stop. "Well, now you know as much as I do." Will reached for his cane and started to rock to his feet. Melanie offered her arm so he could pull himself up, then steadied him as they left the skimmer. He leaned on her as they walked into the tiny walled yard that was part of the Do It Right Tokyo Shinjuku compound. He felt light enough to blow away in a stiff wind.

What's wrong with him? I thought the nanos got all the cancer.

"Let's put some tracker leads on you," Will said. "See what feedback we get if this midnight visitor appears tonight. Or any nightmares. Tomorrow we'll head to Nagano, start trying to figure out what's going on with your Dialogues, and devising a strategy for the shadows. The bioinoculate is not going to be a perfect solution. It's too transient. We have to figure out what's going on."

THAT NIGHT WAS QUIET, WITH NO NIGHTMARES, VOICES, OR VISITATIONS. Melanie woke and found herself alone. Marty had been stirring before her, ever since they had spent the one quick night at Warm Springs. Usually, he foraged some food for them to share, got a morning briefing from Nik or Angela, and gathered household information for the day, wherever they were staying, then briefed her on what he'd learned.

Part of my role as Head of Research, Marty had said in Free Victoria. *More expansive because we're lovers. Make it easier on you.*

Melanie smiled to herself and lay back. She could get used to this life. Their private breakfasts ensured that she was eating better than she had in years, and their morning discussions helped her prepare for the day. She was starting to gain a greater appreciation for the team her parents had formed as President and Head of Research for Do It Right. She'd never considered that possibility for herself—until now, with Marty.

Her thoughts turned to the daily schedule. Traveling to Nagano today. No internal networks here, not yet. She'd tried last night. The Diaspora order had frozen her links, and Marty needed final clearance before he had full access. Unfreezing links would happen in the Nagano labs. Not here. Necessary security, but still frustrating.

So maybe there would be time to slip in a ski session tonight. She sighed wistfully, missing her snow. Then she dismissed the notion. Will was determined to figure out this Dialogue anomaly. He would want to hit research hard once they got to Nagano.

In-person shopping in Tokyo before they left was a necessity. Melanie didn't want to wait for autotailors or bespoke outfits to replace her faded jumpsuits, and she had lost enough weight to trust past sizing. Security *should* work—the *only two Security with you at a time* rule no longer applied. Perhaps a cautious, careful expedition with lots of Security around them could happen. Nik would tell her if it were possible.

The shoji door slid open. Marty delicately maneuvered the lacquered tray with teapot, cups, pickled vegetables, rice and two bowls of steaming miso soup through the doorway. He slid the door shut, then placed the tray by her side of the bed. He shrugged out of his robe before sitting, cross-legged, on the mat beside the bed. She sat up, running her hands through her hair, rubbing around the wireless leads still in place from last night.

"Figured we could do breakfast in bed," Marty said. He poured her some tea and handed it to her. "Angela's given me a heads up that your dad's not moving too fast this morning. He worked late last night."

"What's up?"

"Andrew. Pestering. Our arrival made the news, and he wants us back in North America. Your dad videoconferenced with some Interim Government representatives, as well as the Japanese Government to fight his attempts." He poured a cup of tea for himself. "Your dad's failing pretty damn fast, too. Those meetings were rough on him."

"I know he's fading. Mom didn't tell me everything."

Marty shrugged. "What could she do? What could you do? Up until the last few days, you didn't dare leave the West Coast, much less the country."

"I should have known," Melanie fretted.

"And done what?" Marty frowned into his cup.

"I don't know." She took a deep breath. Time to stop fussing. "We need to get up to speed on DIR International corporate operations, Marty. I want you to shadow Dad in Research, with the idea that you'll become International Head of Research, not just North America." She sipped her tea. "If we can figure out our mental speech capacity, and work out a means to connect without touching, it would be even more convenient. Especially if others can do this as well."

"Yeah. You're right about that. But this touch stuff can be nice sometimes." He took her free hand and squeezed it. She smiled at him, enjoying the simple warmth. The fact that a lover was so happy to be around her—did it say something that this felt entirely new to her?

After they finished eating, they quietly made love.

<Wonder how that showed up on the sensors?> Marty thought at her as they lay curled together.

She slapped him playfully. <Always the research!> But she added a laugh to ease any sting the thought might carry.

He rolled onto his back, staring up at the ceiling thoughtfully, flopping one leg over hers to keep the physical contact. <If we can mask the leads so they're not visible, I'd like to keep them in place all day. It could be useful. I know your dad kept copies of our brain scans from the Dialogue initialization process. I'd like to compare them.>

She nodded. <You've a train of thought going.> She tossed in a picture of an old-fashioned steam train chugging down a track.

Marty chuckled and sent back an image of a Shinkansen. <I'm wondering if Ness didn't tinker with something.>

<What could she have done? Could it have been tied to—the gadget?> She found herself very seriously *not wanting* to think about Gizmo by name.

He was slow to respond, and she sensed reluctance, dread, and worry cluttering his thoughts as he frowned up at the ceiling.

"I don't think—*the thing*—has much to do with what's happening with us. Nanos," he said out loud. "It could be nanos. Ness might have slipped me some nanos. The National Security labs under Sarah used them in conjunction with implant chips. How I could have passed them to you before we became lovers, I don't know. But that's one thing we need to look into when we're safe in a lab."

"Yeah." They drowsed for a few minutes.

Finally, he stirred. "Let's get going."

"I'd like to find out how slowly Dad is moving today. If we've got time, I'd like to do some clothes shopping, get something more up-to-date to wear than faded jumpsuits."

"Never knew you were such a style girl."

"Glam sells. I don't have squat to wear that's current, and what works for the Mountain won't work if I'm going to be the public face of DIR International. Mom and Dad have set a high standard. Learned that trick from Sarah as well."

Marty sighed. "Your princess role. Guess I'd better join in."

She tickled him playfully. "Remember, Dad has always dressed the part. He's set the standard. As my Head of Research, you need to look good."

"Geez, you're demanding." He playfully grabbed her hands, wrestling her underneath him for a kiss.

"Get used to it." She twisted from under Marty, kissed him, laughing, then sprang out of bed, heading for the shower.

Both Angela and her local counterpart Hideo, head of Will's Security, vetoed the notion of shopping in the well-known districts.

"Too much exposure," was Hideo's verdict. "But, here in Shinjuku, yes, we could handle a quick expedition. I know just the store. Safe, plenty of options. Specializes in Corporate items, clothing, electronics, that sort of thing."

"Then let's make it happen."

Clothing needs had been one thing at Do It Right North America. She needed to fit in. Not standing out, even when she left Hoodland. Jumpsuits in drab colors. Perhaps some slacks and shapeless blouses.

But Do It Right International required a more sophisticated look. Part of establishing credibility.

When they walked into the department store that Hideo deemed safe, Melanie was grateful that they were *just* going to this store. So many *things* to choose from! So many *new* things! Sanctions had restricted options even for Melanie.

The electronics department drew both of them like a magnet. Where to start? There were items that had been in prototype seven years ago.

Marty lingered over a few items, then put them down with a wistful look.

"Why don't you get those?" she asked, checking out the full-body immersion games he was handling. *Hmm. Interesting.* Far more sophisticated than anything she had access to for some time—and these were the simple games.

He smiled ruefully. "My bank account, for one. You're right about my needing to upgrade the wardrobe. That'll suck up most of what credits I have left. The amount of time I'll have to use the fun stuff, for another. I don't see myself having a lot of free time to do pleasure reading or gaming."

"Marty. The clothes go on Corporate. So does this other stuff." She picked up the things he'd put down, adding duplicates for the things she wanted. He wrapped one hand around her wrist to stop her.

<Mel. I'm not a kept man.>

<No. You're not,> she agreed. <You're my Head of Research. As such, you need to dress appropriately. That's why the clothes go on Corporate Account.>

<And this stuff?> He nodded toward the electronics in her hands.

Melanie shrugged. "I had to dump a lot of clothes and electronics seven years ago. I might have to do it again. It's just *stuff*. C'mon, Marty, it's not only you. I'm getting it too."

He shook his head, but smiled. "I'm not going to win this one, am I?"

"No," she said firmly. "The prince needs stuff as well as the princess."

They finally tore themselves away from the electronics to pick out clothing. Current styling for both men and women trended toward minimalist, understated cuts and narrow collars in bright colors with white contrasts. So different from the beige, gray and black shades and the over-ruffled Edwardian designs currently common in the Confederation. Melanie preferred her dingy jumpsuits to *that* stuff.

And the Shinjuku store had a broad selection of high-end clothing with built-in body armor. Perfect.

"How much more time do we have?" she finally asked Angela, once she and Marty finished selecting clothing.

"We've reserved a private Shinkansen for fourteen-thirty."

"I suppose lunch at a restaurant is out of the question."

Angela rolled her eyes. "Things aren't *that* better over here, Mel."

"Worth a try."

"We can order in. Plenty of time for poison checks and all without having to rush."

"Then let's head back." Melanie took Marty's arm, and fell behind

Hideo and Angela as they headed for the skimmer. Nik and Steve followed with Paul pacing to her left, Hideo's partner Mizuko on Marty's right. She noticed that both Hideo and Angela carried weapons palmed in their right hands.

Is it really that bad?

<Your mother is the Interim President,> Marty thought at her.

<I sure hope this eases off.>

Something exploded to her right. Security clustered around them, urging them into a jog trot through the corridors and down a freight elevator to an underground garage. They broke into a run before skidding to a stop in front of their skimmer. Angela and Hideo unceremoniously shoved Marty and Melanie inside, forcing both of them down on the floor, lying on top of them with weapons drawn.

The skimmer took off quickly. Melanie realized she was breathing fast and hard, almost gasping for breath. Her eyes met Marty's, and he reached out and took her hand, sending reassuring feelings.

Angela's hand on her back eased. "Okay to sit up now."

"What was that?" she asked as she slid onto a seat.

Hideo held up one finger, blinking rapidly as he processed bright flashes of Dialogue text. "Nothing to do with us," he said finally. "Yakuza infighting. Better to react and be safe than be sorry."

"Hideo, how much of this Security is defense against stray Yakuza attacks and how much of it has to do with actual threats against us?"

Hideo hesitated. "I'll need to speak to your father."

"No. You tell me what's going on. Now." She hated to push, but it was time. Before, she was simply the daughter of the family to be protected. Now she was in a leadership position. "What exactly is the political and the corporate threat level?"

She could see the loyalties warring within him. He frowned, glanced over at Angela, looked back at her.

"I don't want to find out about it all at once when something happens to Dad and it gets dumped on me," she continued. "I need to know. *What is the threat level?*"

Hideo heaved a sigh. "We just got notice, five minutes ago. Stephens Reclamation has registered a Contract with the Foreign Office."

"Personal, Political or Corporate?"

"Corporate."

"And the level?"

Hideo hesitated again. He shared another quick glance with Angela. "Highest level," he said finally. "Death. For both of you."

"And the principal filer?" She hated to ask, suspecting the answer already, but needing the confirmation.

"Andrew Landreth-Stephens, for Stephens Reclamation," Hideo said.

CHAPTER 5

THEY ARRIVED AT THE SHINKANSEN STATION UNDER TIGHT SECURITY. WILL traveled in a floater chair, for speed and safety, with four of his Security surrounding him. Melanie wore one of her new outfits, a black miniskirt with a red sleeveless turtleneck, both with built-in body armor. The matching black suit jacket held hidies in the sleeves, and her knee-high black boots concealed a throwing knife in the loose-fitting top of the right boot and a derringer in the top of the left. Marty carried a walking swordstick, wore an armored polo, and had a couple of knives stashed in the lining of his jacket as well as hidies in his jacket sleeves.

Getting hidie weapons around Dad isn't hard—and how many weapons does he have stashed in that floater?

As far back as Melanie could remember, her father carried lots of weapons, even before she and Drew had been kidnapped as teens. He had been a weapons designer for his father's company, Landreth Technologies, before dissolving it once his father Parker Landreth died. Even now, security was one of his corporate design priorities, along with other tech work related to communications and wireless chip implants. Nanos and bioremediation devices were Diana's focus.

Melanie learned weaponry from her father almost as soon as she could walk.

"You think we have enough armament?" Marty whispered into her ear.

"Probably not, by Dad's standards," she whispered back, and rested her hand casually on his. <But then I think he'd be happiest if we were packing visible heat and he had a pocket nuke stashed somewhere.>

<I wouldn't be surprised if he didn't have something like that in his chair,> Marty retorted.

<Exactly.>

And then the media was upon them. Melanie flinched at light flashes from the bug cams. Security clustered close as they hustled Melanie, Marty, and Will through the train station. Media, both live and robotic, shouted questions. The blare was so loud she couldn't make out individual voices—*aggressive* media here. And she had thought that Free Victoria was bad!

<What do they want?> she texted Angela.

<Andrew's Contract on you is news. Big news. Plus you're a high-profile refugee from the North American war zone.>

<We'll give them something?>

<Not here. Not now.>

<Janine here?> After the whirlwind of the last few days Melanie barely knew where *she* was, much less her staff.

<At Nagano,> Angela answered.

They trotted up the stairs to the main Shinkansen platform. Security escorted them to the sleek white train with its single car. The window shades were already closed. Security encouraged them to sit in the middle of the car, moving the seats to accommodate Will's floater. Melanie remembered this level of Security from right after she and Andrew had been kidnapped. Only then she had been a kid, scared to death by what had happened to her, terrified that she could be snatched again.

She wanted to be back on the Mountain, free to ride horses and go skiing with minimal Security.

Those days are gone for good, now.

She settled in next to Marty, tossing her jacket onto another row of seats.

"So," Will said. "It seems your brother's decided you two are best off dead. Makes life interesting to be under Contract, doesn't it?"

Melanie shivered. "I guess you could call it that."

"Girl, your mother and I deal with such things all the time." Will shrugged. "A Contract's a game, as much as anything else. Even at the highest level. One day you have one on you, the next it's gone." He grinned suddenly, a big death's-head grin that dropped years off of his face and jolted Melanie. She glanced down to hide the sudden wetness that came to her eyes.

This was a fleeting glimpse of the father she had grown up with, not the sick skeleton of a man he now was.

As Marty talked to her father, Melanie clicked up a hologlobe and contacted Janine, relaying some short details and directions about a public statement.

<I'll have it to you before you reach Nagano,> Janine texted.

<Thanks,> Melanie sent back. She shrank the hologlobe back to a palm-sized ball, slid it into her travel case, and closed her eyes, taking Marty's hand as he and Will continued their discussion.

<I could get used to this,> she thought.

<Me too,> he thought back. She drowsed off, comforted by Marty's bass rumble, saving her energy for Nagano. Let Will and Marty have bonding time.

"Melanie." Her father's voice changed in tone. "Hideo said you wanted to make a statement in Nagano."

"We need to say something since we're high-profile refugees. Maybe that will get some of these folks off of our backs." Melanie straightened up. "Janine will have something ready for me by the time we arrive. Nothing elaborate."

Will snorted. "I say, let them wait."

She shook her head. "I want to give Mom a statement of support."

"Politics." Will frowned.

"I don't have anything complicated in mind. A brief castigation of Andrew's unprofessional behavior. Denial of any validity to the Notice of Takeover from Stephens Reclamation. Express my support for Mom and the New Feds, then emphasize how Do It Right is just trying to serve the best interests of all the citizens of the former United States while maintaining a responsible international relationship. Unlike Stephens Reclamation, which can't seem to separate personal vendettas from Corporate."

"They'll want to know why Marty's with you."

"He's my Head of Research." She met her father's eyes. "Just because we've changed locations, I don't expect that role to change. I won't say anything more than that—gets into those National Security issues."

"Ah. Now we're getting into these concerns," her father said.

"Meaning?"

"What role do you expect to be playing in DIR International?"

She took a deep breath. "How committed are you to continuing as Mom's substitute? If you really want it, then I'll be happy and proud to be second to you. But I'm in limbo right now. Am I a figurehead with DIR International, or am I in charge for real?"

"You look at me and see how frail I am compared to what I used to be," Will sighed.

"I'm sorry. But I'm worried about your health. I fear being in charge will draw down your strength. And I," her voice faltered. "I don't like seeing it. I'm worried. I won't forgive myself if you run yourself into the ground. I want you to be safe and strong for when Mom comes back."

Will raised a hand. "Girl, I understand. You've been running the show in North America for seven years, and doing a pretty decent job of it. Your mother and I talked about this possibility before she left. I *had* thought I could maintain this position. But."

"But?"

Will shook his head. "Then I had to face certain realities. First, I don't have the stamina or the patience to run Corporate, Political, and Research all at once. Second. Even Research is becoming difficult. I talked with Marty and got his results back from my Security investigations. His vision for Do It Right Research works for me. I'm more than happy to have him be in charge of Research for International as well as North America. With me as an advisor, of course."

"Thank you," Marty said.

Will sighed, and his face softened, making him look even older.

"Third. I tried to talk Andrew out of filing Contract last night. I thought he listened. I was wrong. Arguing with him most of the night wiped me out. I can't handle situations like that anymore. So, my dear, I am very happy to hand DIR International over to you, while maintaining an advisory role."

"I appreciate that vote of confidence."

"Will you take some advice about how to handle this statement, from someone who's done his share of dancing around Corporate Contracts?"

"Advice is always welcome, Dad."

Will leaned forward. "I'll introduce you as your mother's replacement for Corporate and Political for Do It Right International, and Marty as my replacement for Head of Research. That changes the level and focus of Andrew's Contract. He'll have to refile. Corporate Assassination Contracts are no longer viable when titles and responsibilities change. I'll set the official record to go up when I announce the change."

"Sounds good to me."

Will grinned at her. "Then you drop your rant about Andrew's bad behavior, and how he can't keep Corporate and Political separate from personal."

"After that, Dad, we leave. Let's keep the exposure down. Make it short, because Security will have a major fit."

"Girl, you *definitely* take after me. Your mother would have wanted to take questions."

"Mom's more political than I am. I just want Corporate to go smoothly."

"You're more political than you give yourself credit for."

"Not really. I'm not as interested in those political power games as Mom, or Grandmother. Research is my game."

Marty stirred. "Speaking of Research, sir, what areas do you want to keep to yourself?"

Will chuckled. "Security, of course. You need me to figure out what's happening with your Dialogues." He sobered. "It's going to take all three of us plus my top folks to figure out these shadows. I want you two to replay what you did to stop them when you were still at Hoodland. Your fix been working, but small leakages are stirring again."

"We probably need to redo the barrier," Marty said.

"I want to check the nature of that barrier." Will smiled, fatigue easing off of his face. "It's not something I've seen before."

"Me neither. Melanie did it by instinct."

Melanie pulled out her hologlobe and checked with Janine while Marty and her father talked. She scanned her updates and did what she could—nothing major yet, not until her father made the transfer official. More limbo.

But at least I see an end to it.

She reviewed the statement Janine had written for her and uploaded it to her Dialogue for easy reading. Then she unwrapped her personal electronics, pulling up a ski simulation game.

Reading required too much thinking, and she needed a break.

As the train slowed for Nagano, Melanie put away her things and reviewed the statement Janine sent, checking her Dialogue to ensure the whole thing was downloaded for easy reading.

She handed her bag to Angela, then slipped to the restroom to check that she looked every bit the corporate professional. Melanie stared at the woman in the mirror, quickly brushing her hair over the exposed sensors, studying her reflection critically, with the perspective gained from both Free Victoria and now Japan.

Need to get that hairstyle fixed. And God, I look emaciated in comparison to everyone else.

Certainly not the same as she had appeared seven years ago. Stress, and restricted diet.

Well, maybe that was one way to raise awareness of the current state of affairs in North America. Someone would dial up her pictures from seven years ago, and run a comparison.

She gave herself one last lookover. Marty rose as she rejoined them; his expression solemn. She slipped her hand into his, quickly, and he squeezed it.

He dropped her hand, but placed his hand on her back, keeping up the contact as they walked behind Will's floater. They left the train and went down to street level, where Janine, surrounded by even more Security, waited with the media.

This is it. She swallowed hard. *Showtime.*

Will settled his floater. She moved to his right side, with Marty next to her. Security reluctantly parted, to let the media see them.

"Howdy, folks." Will exaggerated his slight drawl. "Good to see you here. We won't be long. My last Corporate announcement was that my wife Diana Landreth, the head of Do It Right International, had resigned her position with our Company to accept the position of Interim President of whatever they're now calling what used to be the United States back when I was young, and that I was taking her place." He paused, waiting for reactions.

"I'm announcing another change, effective immediately," he continued. "Our daughter, Melanie Landreth, head of Do It Right North America, has joined me here in Nagano along with her Head of Research, Martin Fielding. Melanie Landreth is now officially replacing me as President of Do It Right International as well as retaining her position as head of Do It Right North America."

Not quite what I expected. I thought they'd stick the North American title on Mom. Maybe that's to keep Andrew confused. But doesn't that interfere with the goal of breaking Andrew's Contract?

"I also yield the International Head of Research position to Martin Fielding. These two have shown their mettle in managing a difficult situation in North America. Diana and I have no doubts about their ability to continue their fine work at this high level. Melanie—" He gestured to her. "Your turn to speak."

Melanie blinked to her Dialogue to bring up the statement.

"First, I want to let everyone know around the world that I support Diana Landreth as the Interim President. Not just because she's my mother." She paused to allow an appreciative chuckle to circulate around the crowd, drawing energy from their attention. "But because it's the right thing to do."

She drew a deep breath. "We need to save a detailed discussion for another time. Let's just say that things are very tough in North

America right now. Very restrictive diets. Movement restrictions. Assorted atrocities—I could be here all day giving you details about why my mother is a much better choice for leading the country than my brother Andrew. However, Mr. Fielding and I are under Corporate Contract at this time, with a rather high bounty. We need to minimize our exposure."

"Does it make you nervous?" an anonymous voice called from the crowd.

"Right now, *everything* makes me nervous. That said, Do It Right, International, wants to be viewed as a good international corporate citizen. The typical reaction on the part of a corporate head like myself would be to file Corporate Contract in retaliation against those who filed on me and my Head of Research. I choose not to do that."

Indrawn breath around the crowd. She grinned at them, well aware of how unusual that choice was. Another jolt of energy pulsed through her. This was *fun,* playing the reporters like this. She hadn't expected to feel anything other than nervous when making this speech.

"Part of being a good international corporate citizen is discerning between Personal and Corporate actions, or Personal and Political actions," she continued. "This choice by Stephens Reclamation to file Corporate Contract on me is a failure to discern between the areas of Personal, Political and Corporate. It serves nothing more than a futile hunger for personal vengeance."

"But he's your *brother!*" another anonymous voice shouted.

"He *is* my brother," she responded. "Let's not forget that. I believe he's unduly influenced by recent tragic events. Do It Right International, *and* myself, choose not to get sucked up in feuds more appropriate to medieval Italian city-states than to the corporate world of the late twenty-first century. There is no legitimate, corporate reason for this filing. This is a personal attempt to play political games. We regret that our close corporate relative cannot seem to separate the Personal and Political from Corporate motivations. That's all I have to say."

Take that, Andrew! Dare to file Corporate Contract on me, your own sister —I'll show you.

"What about Melanie Landreth?" a voice screamed.

"At this time, Melanie Landreth's interests must be aligned with Corporate interests," she said. "I refuse to make the mistaken choices that others of my family have made. I support Diana Landreth fully in her goal to reinstate the Interim Government of the New Federated United States of America, in the form and function designed by that Government's original founders nearly three hundred years ago. I do this both as head of Do It Right, International, and personally as Melanie Landreth, Diana's daughter." She paused, surveying the crowd.

Yes. Give them more.

"Things have been done in the name of my family for which atonement must be made. I commit myself to what it will take to make those things right. Do It Right was founded on the principle of making things right, and I swear to uphold that basic principle." She stopped, reluctant to do so, but it *was* a good ending. "That's all."

Pew! Unmistakably gunfire.

Something grazed her forehead. Melanie staggered, groaning as pain lanced through her face. Marty's hands guided her as liquid spilled into her eyes, blocking her Dialogue overlays.

<I can't see! Marty, I can't see!>

<Don't panic. Here.> Vision opened up from his perspective. At least she had some notion of where they were going as they ran yet again, heading for another Do It Right skimmer. Marty flung her into the skimmer and fell on top of her, holding her tightly. The vision clicked off and she realized he was shutting himself away, hiding his feelings from her.

How the hell did someone get past Security? I want a report, and soon!

"Marty," she gasped. Was he all right or had he been hit, too? There had only been the one shot, hadn't there?

"Steady," he murmured. "Close your eyes. You have a forehead wound that's bleeding badly. Looks superficial, thank God. We'll clean you up."

His hands remained steady on her upper arms as someone—*Ange,* she realized—gently sponged her face, then applied a liquid bandage. It stung as the goop oozed onto her forehead. Her father spoke urgently in the background, too softly for her to hear. Angela answered, interrupted by Nik. Marty's hands left her shoulder. A soft, wet cloth repeatedly wiped her eyes. Then Marty gently grasped her chin.

"Open your eyes," he commanded. She obeyed, blinking carefully so she wouldn't call up her Dialogue. He daubed expertly at her eyes, gently clearing them.

"Now boot Dialogue."

She obediently did so. The remaining text from her speech hovered in her overlay.

"I just see my speech."

"Reboot." His tone wasn't that of her lover, but of her Head of Research investigating an issue. She took comfort in that, unsure if she could deal with a panicky lover right now.

She blinked carefully and the reboot screens came up.

<All clear?>

<Yes.>

<Show me what you see,> he demanded.

She hesitated, unsure. <How?>

<Think of me behind your eyes. That's what I did for you.>

Reluctantly, she tried it. <That feels weird!>

He withdrew. <You look okay.> "She checks out," he continued, aloud.

"Are you sure?" her father asked.

"I looked for myself. Through her eyes."

"You can *do* that?"

"Just figured out how. These new skills appear to manifest when we're under stress."

Will shook his head. "We need to figure out what this is all about. Melanie, my dear, that was a bit too exciting. But it should make excellent press. You handled that very well."

"Yeah, well, getting shot at once is enough," she grumbled, settling back against Marty. "I want to know just how the hell someone got through the Security cordon with a weapon."

"My people are on it," Will said. "I'll let you know what I find out."

"As for the presentation—should we follow up from a secure location?"

"Might be worth it," Will said. "Give the clips a couple of hours to get to Andrew first, see what his private reaction is. Could be enough to stir things up in your mother's favor. I just hope she's reasonable about her security."

Melanie nodded. She sat up slightly, still maintaining contact with Marty, and commanded Dialogue to show her the replay from news recordings.

It was bizarre watching the blood spray from her face. A faint smile twitched her lips. She had *enjoyed* making that speech, more than she had expected. It showed in that smirk on her face, and *damn,* she looked good. Especially when bantering with the media.

Was this what hooked Sarah on politics?

She remembered the rush of power she'd felt when talking to the press. It stirred a wish to do this again.

I could start to like this.

She shivered.

God help them all if she fell prey to the same urges that her grandmother had.

IT TOOK UNTIL MIDNIGHT BEFORE MELANIE COULD FINALLY CALL IT A night. "So where are we quartered?" she asked Angela as they left Diana's offices, now Melanie's.

"Your old quarters. Same for Nik and me." Angela said. "Don't worry, there's nothing of Liam's left in your place."

"He was cleared out of that space eight years ago. I'm not worried."

"Good. I'll walk with you."

They walked to the personnel compound adjoining the DIR offices. Years ago, Will and Diana had planned for housing on or near the sites of the major DIR offices. Some of the rationale had been land costs, but the heavier weight was proximity to Security and Research while raising Melanie and Andrew. Their version of integrating personal and work life.

Nagano had been the second residential facility, after Hoodland. Melanie had lived in corporate housing adjoining DIR offices for all of her life, with the exception of a short time rooming with Angela, Nik and Liam on the Mountain.

Moonlight spilled through the reinforced glass of the walkway to the personal quarters. Melanie shivered. Liam. Too much about Nagano reminded her of Liam. Much of their relationship and the drama around it had taken place here.

She stopped to look at the moonlight playing on the snow-covered mountains.

"We'll make it up there, Mel. Don't worry," Angela said.

"I don't know, Ange. This International responsibility's awfully damn heavy."

"You can do it. You handled North America."

"Ange, it's getting so big. So fast. So much. And then there's Marty."

"What about Marty?"

"Am I making the same mistake I did with Liam? Too soon, too fast, too deeply involved?"

Angela gently shook her shoulder. "Melanie. Honey. Marty is as opposite from Liam as it's possible to get. This relationship didn't happen as fast as you think it is. You and Marty have been carrying a torch for each other for years. *Years.* Even when you were with Liam and he was with Ness."

"Come on, Ange. No way. I was *obsessed* with that sick little shit."

"Yeah. But you were always different around Marty. Lighting up around him." Angela paused. "It was the same for him, too. Yeah, he and Ness were intense. But Marty was always softer around you. Looking at you in a certain way. Nik and I had solid bets that the two of you would finally hook up. And then National Security snatched him. Geez, you were droopy after that."

"Yeah." Melanie wrapped her arms around herself. "I looked at you and Nik, so smooth, so comfortable together. Then I'd think about what it was like with Liam, and figure that something was screwy with me, that I would never find someone who fit me like Nik does you."

"Mel, that son-of-a-bitch had your brain twisted in so many different ways, it's no surprise you blamed yourself."

Melanie shook her head. "Then he ran off and spilled every nasty little thing he could about me to Andrew and Peter. Ange, I worry if I can put a decent, lasting, relationship together. I fell for his lines."

"Mel. Honey. This is Marty. He's a nice guy. He's not a sack of shit like Liam was. Marty adores you. Has for years. Look. Nik and I have had our tough times. It's *hard* being both a couple *and* Security partners. Sometimes it's crazy-making. But I wouldn't trade it for anything else." Angela paused. "Remember when I got pregnant?"

Melanie nodded.

"Nik and I fought hard over it. I was ready to quit Security, ready to settle down and be Mama. Nik talked me out of that option, but we argued about it. He was right, and I was wrong. And now Sophie's with Mama Brenda," she sighed. "Hard. But she's safe. That's what counts. And I realize I'm happier doing this than being Mama, and worrying about Nik's safety with another Security partner."

"I'll always wonder what would have happened if I made it through my pregnancy."

"A kid? You and Liam? Consider yourself lucky you have no ties to that asshat. Remember when Marty brought you flowers, when you were in the hospital after the skimmer crash?"

"Yeah." Melanie smiled. "He said they were from him and Ness. But I always wondered why Ness never came, and why she was so funny about it afterwards."

"Honey. Ness had *nothing* to do with those flowers." Angela smirked at her. "I heard all about that one from Steve. Marty and Ness had a nasty fight about those flowers. He did it without telling her, and when she found out, oh, mama, was he ever in for it. Mel, girl, I tell you this. Everyone around knew the two of you would be an item someday. Ness knew it. Liam knew it."

Melanie shivered again. "Then why am I worrying? Wondering what the hell I did and how this happened so fast?"

"Look. You're tired. It's late. It's been a crazy day, and the last time you were here, you and Liam were on the rocks. Memories carrying over. Even though Liam's in the past and you're with a sane new guy, that past is still going to grab you in the ass now and then. You know that. But what you really need is some rest, and some time on the slopes. You need ski time."

"Too much to do. Too little time."

"Yes, you *can*, and yes, you *will*. Trust me, as your friend and Head of Security. I'll drag you out at six. You and Janine both. I'll set it up so it's secure. We'll sneak out without the boys. Nik just texted me that they're going to be working a while yet, so they'll want to sleep in. We'll blow it out on the slopes to start the day. You'll feel better. I'll feel better. Janine will feel better. We'll all be fresh and ready to tackle monsters. Sound good?"

"Yeah."

"The boys will give us hell for sneaking off to ski without them, but neither of them will be in shape to go with us."

"Thanks, Ange. Thanks for everything," Melanie said.

"It's my job, isn't it?"

"But you go beyond it. In a good way."

They stopped at the door of her quarters. "You make it easy, most of the time," Angela said. "Ever since I decided to follow my mama's footsteps by going into Security, I knew I wanted to work with you. It's easier doing Security for a friend."

"Thank you."

"You're welcome. See you in the morning."

Melanie entered her quarters and headed straight for the bedroom, not stopping to check on any changes to the suite. She could do that in the morning.

After she got back from skiing.

CHAPTER 6

A crisp, snowy morning on the slopes. Melanie blew hard to catch her breath as she clambered into the gondola. Tired, yes. But glad that Angela had pulled her out here. Another run would clear the remaining tatters of fog from her brain.

They had the entire slope to themselves, except for a gaggle of media that more Security kept at bay. Even the bug cams appeared to be interdicted. Only a few interviewers tried to ski with them, and aggressive Security (including the periodic skimmer overhead) ran interference. The one reporter who tried to catch up with them was left behind when Melanie opted for a double black diamond route.

Ski Patrol hauled him out on a stretcher.

Don't mess with someone who grew up on the slopes.

Harsh, but they had been warned. Private ski day, no interviews. No followers allowed.

"So?" Angela demanded as the gondola headed uphill. "Didn't I say you needed this, Mel?"

"You're right, Ange. You're *so* absolutely right," Melanie admitted. "Any flak from Nik?"

"I left him a text. What about Marty?"

"Same. I don't think they got in until three o'clock."

"Men." Angela shook her head. "Nik said that they were deciphering shadow code. When your dad and Marty get together, they don't like to stop."

"That's for sure." They reached the top and unloaded. Melanie pushed off first.

This run, she skied her hardest and fastest. By now she had the feel once again of her old equipment, the boots that canted her slightly further back, the skis a hands-width longer and fingertip wider than what she had been riding on the Mountain for the past seven years. She needed to spread her toes and flatten the ball of her foot differently because these boots were larger than the tight-fitting custom ones she had left behind. But boots and skis felt like extensions of her feet now.

The fine-grained powder snow pushed away easily as she rode the contours of the slope, chasing the seductive pull of gravity both side-to-side and down the hill. Angela yelped a few times behind her. Janine, of course, was far behind them. The Nagano Security, while good on their skis, weren't as aggressive as either Melanie or Angela.

I suppose I should be nervous about running ahead of Security.

But she trusted their ground crew to keep things clear. Besides, Melanie didn't feel like being careful. She *wanted* to ski hard. The harder she pushed, the better she felt.

Blow out the stress.

An urgent Dialogue text signal flashed yellow. She blinked at it to hold and wait. It persisted. Melanie chose a less risky line so that she could find a good stopping place. Nik would have nagged her about still having her Dialogue running. But she wasn't comfortable skiing on a new slope without Dialogue being active. Especially given the current situation.

Probably Marty or Nik being cranky at us for sneaking out without them. Damn it, when will I learn not to ski with the com on?

The text was from Will.

<View this. Now. Media wants response.>

Now what?

Angela pulled up next to her.

"What's up?"

"Didn't Nik send you an urgent text?"

"Yeah, but he always does that when I ski without him. I ignored it.

You get one from Marty? Girl, you've got to learn to manage these men."

"Not from Marty. From Dad. With a link." Melanie blinked up the attached link in her father's text as Janine and the rest of Security joined them.

Copy of a message addressed to the Corporate Courts.

Cancel Contract on Melanie Landreth and Martin Fielding. No further Contract at this time. AL-S.

"Andrew cancelled the Contract," Melanie marveled. "He actually did it. I thought he would fight canceling it."

"He probably did," Angela muttered. "Most likely took his Security this long to beat some sense into his head. But what the hell else does he have up his sleeve?"

"Let me check the news feeds," Janine said, sidestepping closer to Melanie. Angela and the Nagano Security closed ranks around them. "You'll want to give a response at the bottom of the run."

"Checking my mail," Melanie said.

As she expected, there was a message from Andrew.

Okay, little sister. You won this round. But you better watch out.

She showed it to Angela. Angela pursed her lips, nodding. "He has a plan," she said. "But you did a good job making him look like an idiot in the world media. Stupid place to try an assassination."

"Did they ever catch the guy?"

"Yeah. He 'fessed up right away. Small freelance indie journalist, tied to the Freedom Army."

"What the hell is a Freedom Army connection doing in Japan? I thought they were only in North America. Working for Andrew? They're fucking *anarchists*, for God's sake."

Angela frowned. "Hard to say. I downgraded the Freedom Army to a lower priority screen once we left North America, because we didn't have evidence that they had much of an international presence. That has changed."

"Good, and thank you." At one time, her uncle Peter had developed connections with the Freedom Army, an anarchist group that wavered between support and opposition to Sarah's rule. Melanie hadn't thought that Peter passed the connections to Andrew, but it seemed safest not to assume anything now.

She turned to Janine. "What do you suggest for a statement?"

"Go with your instinct. You did good impromptu when you went off-script yesterday."

"If I tell them I'm glad my brother came to his senses, wish my mother well in deposing him, using this as an example for the need of older but wiser heads to run the company, I wouldn't be going too far?"

"You mean older but wiser head to run the *country*," Janine corrected.

Melanie shook her head to clear it. "Yeah. Right. Sorry. I'm thinking in corporate mode, not political. But I'm not going too far?"

"Start with coming to his senses. Don't talk about your mom until they ask. Appear gracious and relaxed. Give them your flashiest, fastest stop like you're still a hot high school race kid who does ski jumps for fun, and for God's sake, don't fall down! Look like you're just another ski bum goofing off. That there's nothing urgent waiting for you back at the office. *They* don't know you ski like a bat out of hell when you're freaking out and need to blow off some energy."

"Let's allow the media to come in closer," Angela said. "I'll call the others."

"Let me work on your face." Janine produced a tube of concealer from one of her pockets. "Pop off that helmet and goggles for a moment. We want you looking glam when you push those goggles up, not tired and hard-working."

"Good grief, what *else* do you have hidden in your pockets?"

"Honey, if you need it, I probably have it. Always do when we're skiing together." Janine frowned, then applied concealer to another spot. "There. You're good to go. Remember, fast, furious, but relaxed and casual. Strike a pretty pose. Do the glam thing. Ski bum forever. Andrew can't touch you for glam, and glam is what makes you look good. Especially in ski gear."

"Got it." Melanie readjusted herself. "Ange. Security clued in?"

"Yep. Think you can pick up the pace again?"

"You bet." Melanie pushed off, skiing hard and fast. Out of the corner of one eye, she saw a drifting bug cam move uphill, focusing on her.

Security's set them free.

Time to showboat for the cameras, focus on slowing down her perception of time, just like she used to do when she was racing.

Big, dramatic swoops at speed, making her moves flashy while staying within her limits. Pop over a mogul, catch air, and whoop. Overbalance on one turn but recover, remembering to make it look easy. Carve the turns, skating on the edges of her skis. Pick a spectacular jump that looked harder than it was, do a cross and grab. Almost wiped out at the bottom of that one, but the adrenaline kicked in to save her.

Bet Angela's cussing me now and wishing Nik were here.

The end of the run. Melanie carved a flashy turn as the media surged forward, held back by Nagano Security, and executed a sharp stop that sent snow spraying, taking a deep breath before pushing up her goggles and kicking out of her skis. Someone from Security gathered her skis and poles, while the rest clustered protectively around her as she strode toward the media mob.

"Ms. Landreth! Ms. Landreth! Have you heard the news?" several voices shouted at her.

"I think it's wonderful that my brother came to his senses," Melanie said. "Personal affairs should not be brought into the Corporate world."

"Your mother has made no comment on this matter. What do you think that means?"

"She's probably too busy organizing to set herself up as a target. I don't expect her to draw attention before she's ready. Just another example of why we need older and wiser thinkers to be in charge of the country."

Angela and Janine shouldered in beside her.

"Let's wrap this up," Angela muttered. "Might not be a Contract out there, but that doesn't mean there's not some freelance idiot from the Freedom Army who hasn't gotten the stop order."

"No more questions," she told the crowd. "My Security's still worried." She flashed them a smile. "They would just as soon not have any more incidents like yesterday's, thank you very much." She forced herself to look calm and relaxed as Security muscled her to the waiting skimmer. Once inside, Melanie wrenched out of her boots, swapping them out for lighter slippers, and leaned her head against the seat.

"Whew. Think I gave them enough visuals?"

"I thought you were going to wipe out on that jump," Angela said. "I just about peed my pants when I saw you take it."

Melanie chuckled. "So did I. But it felt *good*. Damn. I didn't realize I could still huck it like that!"

"That'll be plenty to give them enough to talk about for a while," Janine said.

"Feel better?" Angela asked Melanie, half-smiling.

"Yeah." Melanie grinned back at her. "Yeah. Now I can do fifty impossible things before lunch."

Angela's grin grew wider. "It was worth it to see you stick that jump. Nik will give me shit for not getting after you to play it safe, but —worth it."

"I bet Marty's not going to be too happy with me, either. But absolutely worth it."

At this moment, with the adrenaline still pulsing through her veins, Melanie didn't care what Marty might think. Nailing that landing felt good.

MELANIE BARELY GOT INTO THE SUITE BEFORE MARTY SCOOPED HER UP IN A big hug, spinning her around. "Good Lord, girl, it scared the crap out of me when you took that jump!" He kissed her hard.

"So it played well?"

"Holy crap, did it ever. I didn't realize I was hanging with such a hot skier chick. I know you used to be a racer girl, but now? Damn. It scared me to watch it. You almost lost it at the bottom, didn't you?"

"Almost," she admitted. "It wasn't as bad as it looked. It's just been a while since I did anything like that."

"Makes me wish I'd been riding with you girls." He tapped her nose with his index finger. "No more sneaking off, even if you have to rent me a board, 'kay? Someone has to keep up with you."

"Got it."

"Yeah." He looked closely at her. "Makeup while skiing? That's new."

"We got the message about the Contract cancellation mid-slope. Janine dolled me up before I did that last run for the cameras."

"C'mon, I'll show you the footage." He paused. "I think you'd be more comfortable without those cold clothes on. Let me help you." His help consisted of kissing her while deftly stripping off her clothes. Before he was finished, she was fumbling with his clothes as well, kissing him back passionately. They barely made it to the couch before they coupled, fast and hard.

When they were finished, Marty slipped off of her, sliding her gently against the back of the couch, arms wrapped around her, nuzzling her neck and shoulders. "Mmm. You looked pretty intense during that last run."

"If I can't do my morning ski to blow off stress, I usually ride horses," she told him. "Puts me in a better frame of mind to deal with the workday."

"Hate to see what your horseback riding usually looks like, then. Judging by the way you rode through the mountains, anyway. Poor horses."

"Oh, I have to be nice to the horse. Warm-ups and cooldowns. Nik doesn't do the riding stuff. Angela does it, and she's *tough.* She's demanding when it comes to jump schooling."

"What did you have for breakfast?"

"An energy bar. I don't usually eat before skiing."

He scowled at her. "I'll get you something."

While Marty prepared breakfast, Melanie huddled into a blanket and turned on the newsfeed. There were more cameras out there than she'd suspected, including one that shot her jump from below.

Unfortunately, the audio commentary wasn't as good as the video. She flicked over to the headlines and crawls. Most commented on her calm attitude.

She piled into the food Marty brought back. "I'm going to get fat if I stick with your cooking," she said as she came up for air.

Marty snorted. "You? Fat? With *your* metabolism? Mel, you're still way underweight. I'm where I should be, but you're too damn skinny."

"You? Where you should be? *You're* way underweight."

"I was overweight to start with, Mel. You're too damn skinny."

"I looked at myself in the mirror yesterday. It's scary." She changed the subject. "What's on tap for you today?"

Marty frowned. "We're hot on the trail of dealing with the shadows. Your dad left a process going. I'll check on it—" He blinked up his Dialogue. "About an hour left to go. And you?"

"Corporate paperwork, mostly. Shipments I need to follow up on. Track the political stuff Andrew's stirring up."

"Think we might snatch lunch together?"

"Let's *plan* to do that," she said. "That way we'll both take the time to eat."

He grinned ruefully. "Watching out for each other, right?"

"Who else will do it?"

He chuckled, and kissed her forehead. "I'd stay a bit longer, but I need to get going."

"So do I." She headed to the shower.

It was a good thing they made that commitment to having meals together. Melanie broke off work to grab Marty for lunch; Marty did the same for her at dinner. She suspected that they both might have skipped meals without the other reminding them it was time to eat.

It was almost midnight when Melanie made her way back to their quarters. This time, as she went in, she spent a couple of minutes looking around, letting herself think about the changes she had noticed but not considered before.

Nothing was left of Liam. A few of her favorite ski and ballet sculptures were placed strategically around the room. Some abstract paintings from Marty's old quarters on the Mountain, before he and Ness had been grabbed by National Security. Old photographs of Diana riding Mocha's granddam in reined cowhorse competitions—*hope Mocha's doing all right on Warm Springs Rez.*

New furniture, of course. The walls were a different color as well, a light, spring green instead of the bright yellow Liam favored.

Good. The whole place seemed lighter, and it didn't stir memories.

Melanie changed into a casual robe and poured herself a single malt scotch. She curled up on the couch, sipping the liquor while watching a kabuki performance. Drowsiness soon followed, her eyelids drooping hard. The glass nearly slipped out of her fingers and she set it on a side table. The liquor was hitting her hard. Well, she hadn't been drinking much the past few years. To be expected.

It was too far to walk to the bedroom. She snuggled around a pillow and fell asleep.

She woke to Marty's soft kiss on her forehead.

"Come to bed," he whispered.

She groaned softly, stiff from the hard skiing that morning. Marty carried her to bed. She nestled into his chest. <Tired,> she complained, unwilling even to speak.

<Me too.>

They settled into bed. Melanie dropped back into another dreamless sleep.

Then Marty jerked convulsively. She rolled over as his body writhed and contorted.

<Marty! MARTY!> She couldn't sense him, even when she shook Marty as hard as she could.

Then what was happening to him crashed over her.

Quivering. Twitching. Electric pulses lashing them. Hot rivers of pain cascading up and down her body. Memories. His and hers, all mixed together. Something beating at her brain, pounding, pounding, POUNDING. Agony knifing behind her eyes and around her Dialogue. Desolation. Rage. Anger. Sorrow. Dizzying array of zigzag multi-colored lines flashing in her vision so that she didn't know which way was up.

Someone raging at her.

why did this happen to me why can't i feel anything where am i who am i whywhyWHY?!

Fleeting image of Ness Ryan.

Visuals abruptly fading. Her head throbbed *hard,* centered behind her right ear where her Dialogue implant was located.

Darkness.

MELANIE WOKE IN A HOSPITAL BED, ALONE. <MARTY?>

Nothing.

She sat up quickly, her head aching, the world around her spinning.

"Don't do that!" Marty grabbed at her shoulders. "Don't blink for Dialogue," he added. "We're both shut down."

She closed her eyes and breathed slowly, trying to keep from hyperventilating. "What the hell happened?"

"Our little visitor," Marty said, a grim tone in his voice. "It hit you worse than it did me, this time. Induced a seizure in me, then jumped from me to you."

"Do we know what's behind it? Is it tied to the gadget?"

"It's complicated," he said. "Not the gadget. But based on the brain scans, we have a pretty good idea."

"It's Ness, isn't it?"

He nodded.

Desolation surged through Melanie. How could she fight someone who managed to come back from the grave?

"How?" she asked.

"We're not entirely sure. It's an electronic personality, with Ness's brainwaves. Ness, but not-Ness, too. Almost like a digital thought clone, but not that, either. A full personality upload. I didn't think such things were possible."

"Do you regret us?" God, but it hurt to say those words.

His head shot up. "Melanie, get that thought out of your brain, damn it!" His hand clasped hers firmly. "I. Have. No. Regrets," he said firmly, squeezing to emphasize each word. "No. No regrets."

"I had to ask," she said.

"It's not her," he said. "It's after power, and revenge, and a warm human body, *any* human body. It's not human, Mel. Not anymore."

"Then how do you know it's her personality?"

"I talked to it," he said. "Your dad and I managed to herd it into a chip. His latest Dialogue upgrade. We've been tweaking Dialogue further, based on brain scan data of how you and I talk without words. We call this chip version Netwalk."

"Netwalk? How does it all fit together?"

His eyes lit up. "My God, Melanie. It's a combination of nanos and neurals. We can do telepresence with Netwalk. You aren't just looking, you're *there*. Any place there's an access node, or a Dialogue, or any sort of electronic chip, you can be there. But the drawback is that you end up creating digital personality uploads. I *knew* about the technology, but I *didn't know* it, either. Ness planted the data in my memories, without my knowing, before she was killed. I've been accessing those techniques unconsciously."

"How did she do it? How did she keep National Security from figuring it out?"

Marty shook his head. "I don't know. I don't know how the uploads work. I don't know the rules of the upload. Your father is ripping out what's left of his hair because he can't figure it out either. We're hoping that Ness can eventually tell us more. The telepresence factor is why we dubbed it Netwalk. Apparently, I left something open to it in my Dialogue, and that's how we got nailed."

"But if it's Ness, *how?*"

"You can upload your memories electronically with an enhanced Dialogue chip, park them in a data node, and they'll exist after you die. That's the concept behind digital thought clones. I had thought you needed to create an algorithm to develop a digital thought clone—but there's no algorithm in this manifestation. The personality is the same, and it throws off measurable brain waves that match the living person."

"You sure it's not a digital thought clone?"

"Positive. The brain waves don't exist with thought clones, and Netwalk is more independent of data nodes than the digital clones are. It's Ness's memories, and knowledge, and to some extent her reasoning skills. She was constantly uploading, until she was killed." He scowled. "Problem is, apparently these uploads go insane without continuous live human contact. Electronic personalities need a committed, stable host that they are permanently connected to so they can prune themselves to just one version, instead of multiple variants. That's a huge difference from digital thought clones."

Melanie shivered. "What does that mean?"

"This being needs a human host to be sane. Or we have to kill it. Again."

She shivered. "And the possible host?" she whispered.

"Me. Or you. We can't trust her to a lower level of Dialogue. She knew too damned much, and her first host has to be very strong."

"My God. What does that do to you and me?"

"I told you just a few days ago that I wouldn't let you fall. I meant it then and I mean it now. I won't sacrifice you for her. She damned near killed you."

Melanie stared at him, speechless.

"You've been out for nearly a day and a half," he said grimly. "We almost lost you." He shook his head. "No. I won't let her, let *it* do that to you. It's not her. Ness wasn't that way. I won't let a warped electronic shadow of her continue to exist."

"Shit." Melanie fell back against the bed and closed her eyes. She already had a lot to do. She didn't *need* wandering electronic personalities wanting to possess her body. Much less someone who had been intimate with her lover.

"On the positive side, this does give us a clue about what the shadow is," Marty said.

Shadow, singular.

She dreaded the implication. Melanie opened her eyes. "Was it Ness?"

He shook his head. "No. Worse, much, much worse."

Dread tightened her gut, and she *knew*. "Sarah?"

He nodded, slowly. "Your father and I think it's after your mother."

"So what do we do now?" Her voice cracked slightly, despite her best efforts to control it. Out for a day and a half. Ness back. And Sarah.

Damn it, Sarah, how on earth did you manage to resurrect yourself?

"First, let's run checks to make sure you're all right."

Melanie frowned. "What's been going on while I was out? Any further reaction from Andrew? What's the word on Mom's progress with the New Feds?"

"Your dad will brief you on the Corporate matters. We've let it be known that there was another assassination attempt. That's won you some sympathy. Even better, it's influenced a group of governments to support your mother over Andrew."

"Good. But Mom? What's happening back home?"

"Everything's erupted. Civil unrest, riots, different groups vying for power. National Security doesn't have the lock on things it used to have. Doesn't mean that Diana's in charge yet. A lot of local feuds are breaking out now that Sarah's gone. Eventually things will settle, but what that looks like is going to be anyone's guess." He stroked her forehead.

She closed her eyes, relaxing under his touch. "I guess things haven't gone to hell as badly as I feared."

"And I've worried about you. You scared me."

She opened her eyes. "It—Ness—looked like it was killing you. I just can't believe you aren't in as bad a shape as I am."

"Your reaction is what caused your problems, Mel. You tried to chase it down. Acted as if you had hologlobe protections when you went after it, and when you did engage it, well, it took your dad and me ten minutes to disengage you two. We went through a whole sequence of Dialogue disconnection strategies before we hit on the sequence to get you free."

She shivered. "Marty, I don't remember one bit of those details."

"You wouldn't. Not from the meds we gave you. But it's taught us a lot about Netwalk. Hologlobes are crucial, and we've upgraded our datasuits. When we bring the Netwalker electronic personalities out, at least at the beginning, we do it with the new suits and in a hologlobe." He squeezed her hand. "Your abilities are interesting. I burned out my Dialogue in the process, but there's something about the way you do things in Netwalk that not everyone can do. You're very intimidating and dominant. It could have interesting implications."

"Such as?"

"Well, once we figure out how to protect you, it's very possible that you might be able to control Netwalkers. I don't know how far this possibility extends, and I'd much rather learn these things less dramatically."

"So would I."

A light tap sounded on the door. Marty turned his head. "Yes?"

A Chinese woman in a white coat bustled in. Melanie faintly remembered her as one of her doctors from eight years ago.

"Doctor Liang?" she asked, as the doctor bent over her wrist to check her pulses.

That won her a quick smile, confirming she had the name right, before Dr. Liang refocused on her examination.

"I am pleased to see that you are alert and have long-term facial memory retrieval. That bodes well. Let me look at your eyes."

Melanie followed Dr. Liang's directions as the doctor peered into her eyes, checked her reflexes and vitals, and ran through the other, more esoteric blinking and visual checks familiar to her from standard Dialogue maintenance.

"Your Dialogue's still viable," Dr. Liang said, finally. "There appears to be no residual damage. Neural repair systems are doing what they're supposed to. You appear to have a nice set of repair nanos doing their job in you."

Melanie arched a brow at Marty questioningly but didn't say anything. *Later*, he mouthed.

"So I'm free to get back to work?" she asked.

Dr. Liang produced a vial. "Drink this, please. More of the bioinoculate."

Melanie wrinkled her nose at the bioinoculate but drank it anyway, frowning. "How often do we need to take this?"

"I'd recommend a maintenance dose every forty-eight hours," Dr. Liang said brusquely. "That provides optimal protection. Not what we first knew. I do not recommend much activity today. You need more time to rest and recover. No online activities yet. Wait for twelve hours before reactivating your Dialogue. Rest one hour for every half hour you're on your feet."

Melanie started to grumble, but Marty scowled at her. "I'll make sure she does that."

"Good. We don't want you overdoing today. You may go ahead and overdo tomorrow since that seems to be your pattern." Dr. Liang unbent enough to wink at Melanie knowingly. "Please keep from doing that today. Give yourself some recovery time."

"Skiing?" Melanie asked, suddenly hopeful.

Dr. Liang shook her head. "Snow's not that good today. Should be better tomorrow. Forecast is for fresh snow tonight." She bowed slightly. "Good day. Remember, no overdoing, at least today!"

"Can't even *ski*," Melanie muttered. "Do you have any clothes for me?" she asked Marty.

"Yes."

Melanie scowled at the workout suit he handed her. But as she slid out of the hospital gown with his help, she realized how achy and sore she was. Bruises covered her arms and legs.

"What the hell happened?" she asked. "I'm sore, but I thought it was just from not moving around after skiing."

"*It* was whacking you electronically," Marty said. "Pretty damn ugly. I couldn't see what was raising marks on you until I pulled on a datasuit. I was in pretty poor shape myself, from what *it* did to my Dialogue getting to you. But *it* was slugging and kicking you. Without a datasuit and a globe, you couldn't see it."

"You could just see bruises popping out on me?" Melanie had a hard time visualizing how that could happen.

Marty nodded. "Marks. Welts. Not bruises, then."

Melanie shivered. "Do you know why?"

"*It* hasn't told us yet. And I don't trust myself to ask why. Not yet." His voice turned sharp again. "Until I knew what was happening with you, I didn't trust myself alone with *it*."

"Should I detach these?" Melanie pointed to the wireless leads on her head and body.

Marty shook his head. "Not until after we activate your Dialogue. We need to keep monitoring you. We don't know what will happen. There could be aftereffects."

Melanie decided not to say more.

"Want a floater?" he asked when she was ready to go.

Melanie shook her head. "I'm okay. I'm still able to walk, damn it!" She gritted her teeth. She should be able to overcome this. After all, she recovered quickly from skiing and riding injuries. This recovery shouldn't be that different from those times. Nothing was broken.

It didn't take her long to change her mind. She needed to stop and catch her breath after three or four steps.

This is crazy, she thought after the second stop. *It's as if I'm completely out of shape. What the hell is going on? What isn't Marty telling me about this?*

She tried again. But after four more steps, the world spun around her and Melanie grabbed tight to Marty's arm, feeling sick to her stomach.

"Mel. This is ridiculous. I'm getting you a floater."

Melanie nodded, unable to say anything. Marty guided her to a bench. A few minutes later, Security showed up with a floater. Marty took over the controls with a quiet thank you, and stepped up on the jumpseat. Melanie sagged into the floater seat.

"Don't think I could overdo now even if I wanted to!" she grumbled.

"Easy. You'll do better once you eat and relax. You've not gone through a cybercrash before, have you?"

"Cybercrash?"

"Dialogue crash gone really bad. Not something you would experience normally. Something we see a lot more of in the labs."

"No. I've not gone through it. But how am I going to work without my Dialogue?"

"How did you do it during upgrades?"

She made a face. "Physical contact with keyboards. So damn *slow.*"

"Yes," he agreed. "It is. But just listen to me for a while, okay? This is my area of expertise. Trust me. Your recovery will happen faster if you don't fight it."

She was quiet for a few minutes. He *was* her Head of Research, after all. While he had seen situations like hers before, there was something about his reaction which bothered her. Was it personal or professional?

How bad had this crash been?

"How many Dialogues have you had to nurse through something like this?" she asked.

Marty frowned. "During the course of chip version developments and fine-tuning, I've seen too damn many cybercrashes." He shook his head, tightening his lips. "I've lost a couple."

The grim look on his face sent chills down her spine. "Lost as in lost their minds, or lost as in dead?"

"Dead," he said sharply. "Mel, I take recovery pretty seriously. It's very easy to underestimate the degree to which you've been injured in the cyberworld. I've seen hologlobe burn, and neural mismatch, as well as electronic malfunctions and partial Suicide Red triggers." His voice trailed off.

"And?"

He paused, then sighed. "Melanie, I've not had anyone else survive something as bad as this." His hand tightened on her shoulder. "Without the trace of bioinoculate in your system, you'd be dead."

"I didn't realize the situation was that bad," she whispered.

"I was afraid I was going to lose you."

"Do you think Ness was aware of us, and jealous?"

Marty shook her head. "Not from what we've picked up from interrogation so far."

Melanie shuddered. "So how do we stop personality takeovers from happening now? We implant another chip into someone's head, right?"

"No. The host process is a wireless transfer to an existing Dialogue chip."

"Then how do we control her—*it*?" She didn't know why Marty was calling Ness *it*, but if that was going to be ongoing Netwalk protocol, then she needed to cooperate.

"Your Dad thinks contact with a living mind is crucial. We've been feeding *it* contact on a very limited basis. The more living human contact *it* gets, the saner *it* becomes. At least *it* can carry out a reasonable Dialogue discussion now."

"If your Dialogue's burned out," Melanie said, slowly, "then who's been talking to *it*—her?"

What the hell *could* she call this thing that apparently was Ness

Ryan returned from the dead? Melanie didn't like the idea of calling that entity *it*.

"Your dad."

Melanie tensed. "Is *it* safe? I thought you said only you or I could safely handle *it*."

"For brief contacts to bring *it* back to sanity and see what we have to work with, he's fine. As are other people. Mel, we can't keep him away from this. Too much to figure out with Netwalk. He's fascinated by this new research. Keeping him away from *it* would break his heart."

"I worry about him."

"He's in good hands. His Research crew takes care of him. They're having fun, they're making progress, and, to all reports, *it's* enjoying the contact now. I hope we can get to the point where we can start pumping *it* for research information. I'd like to think *it* will become Ness again, and help us."

So Marty doesn't think it is Ness—yet. Telling. Now I understand.

"I wonder if there haven't been other Netwalkers before, but they either faded out or fried the brain of their host."

"Or triggered Suicide Red," Marty said. Again, his hand tightened on Melanie's shoulder. She recognized the reaction by now.

"How many triggers did I go through?"

He looked sideways at Melanie. "You don't need our silent Dialogue speech to read me, do you?"

"How many?" His evasiveness worried her.

"Two and a half."

Two and a half. Of the three safeguards.

Melanie shivered.

"Am I still at the half safeguard?"

"Resetting is standard. You're protected again."

"I'm sorry. I really did put you through hell, didn't I?"

"And if you hadn't been my tough Melanie, I'd have lost you. Even with the bioinoculate. Please take it easy, okay? I don't want you to relapse. What I need you to do later on will be tough enough."

"What's that?"

Marty took a deep breath. "I want to put one of the new datasuits on you, with exterior links, and see if this Netwalker reacts to you negatively. I don't think *it* will. But I want to be positive. I want to be sure what happened was a seeking of energy rather than an attempt to destroy a rival. I *meant* what I said when I said I'd kill *it* again rather than let *it* destroy you."

"Let's hope we don't have to do that. But what happens if *it* becomes Ness again, and one of us hosts her? Can she peek in on us?"

"Different levels of security are possible. That's why we're running all these practice simulation sessions. *It's* too dangerous otherwise."

"Okay. So how soon are we doing this?"

"Later." He steered the floater to a stop, stepped down, and opened the door to their quarters. "I want you to rest. You'll have laptop and pad access. Nothing more until I say so. No excess walking around without my permission."

Melanie scowled at him.

Nonetheless, it felt good to be settled in their own quarters, on the couch in front of a simulated fire, a highly sweetened fruit drink along with high protein snacks on a table next to her, and a handy laptop. Melanie worked on the important things she'd missed while Marty shambled in and out of their quarters on his tasks.

At some point, she slept. When she woke, fresh food and drink waited for her.

Now who's being kept?

Melanie remembered their conversation in the Shinjuku store a few days earlier.

She wasn't about to object. How long had it been since someone had taken care of her like this?

Too long. If ever.

CHAPTER 7

HER STOMACH CLENCHED AS THEY PREPARED TO MEET HER FATHER AFTER Marty and Dr. Liang pronounced her clear twelve hours later.

"No floater," she said as Marty started to call one for her.

"Are you *sure*?" Marty asked. "Your vertigo's gone?"

"Pretty much."

"I don't want you walking if you have *any* vertigo," he said. "That's a sure sign you're headed for problems."

She shook her head, slowly. "No. I get occasional wobbly legs but that's all about strength, not vertigo."

"The minute you turn green on me or start to faint, I'm calling a floater. No arguments," he said firmly. "Mel, don't try to tough this out. We can't take the risk."

"I'm just weak. I know this feeling. It's not like the vertigo I had earlier. Plus I don't know if I'm ready for this. It's not a physical issue. It's a mental issue. I feel like the Other Woman."

"It won't be as bad as you think."

"I hope you're right."

Will wandered from monitor to monitor when they walked into the lab, stopping to tap on keyboards or study the monitors, frowning at what he saw, going back to change little things before moving on. Melanie recognized her father's nervous mechanisms.

He's worried, too.

"Good to see you on your feet, girl," was all he said. "Looked bad there for a while."

"That's what Marty said."

Will nodded. He peered at a monitor. "She's stabilized quite a bit more in the past hour, Marty. Almost like chatting to her in the flesh. It's a good time to run this test." He pointed to a door. "Melanie, dear, you'll find one of the upgraded datasuits in there. Dispose of your old ones and add the upgrades to your daily wardrobe. Necessary for Netwalk."

She glanced at Marty. He nodded in confirmation. "I have a new version on," he said, tugging at his collar to pull out the tell-tale tabs tucked underneath. "Our old versions just aren't going to work."

"Eventually I want to develop clothing that transforms into datasuits easily," Will eyed another monitor. "That will fit Netwalk parameters much better than one you change daily. But for now—" He jerked his head toward the door, his voice changing to the fatherly firm, no-argument-now tone she remembered from her earliest childhood. "Put the new one on. If the sizing works, then I'll print you some more. You need the heightened protection at all times."

When she came back out, Marty attached a remote Dialogue lead to her temple. Then he stood behind Melanie.

"Let me tell you what to expect." Will's brow furrowed as he spoke. "Don't be surprised at what you see. She has some challenges connected to appearing with her head half blown off, and she's sensitive about it."

Melanie nodded. "Understood."

Will's voice sharpened. "I don't want deep thoughts. I want small talk. We'll eventually get around to picking her brain for the information we want. She's still disoriented, and has no idea that she nearly killed you. She's working through death trauma. Right now, we're just making connections."

"What if she asks about my relationship with Marty?"

"Be honest with her. Marty's worried she may try to attack you. I don't think that will be a problem. But we'll see. I'm controlling the connection. Anything gets out of line, I'll pull your connection and shut her down."

"You will see oscillations in her—*it's*—form every time she remembers something. That's when things get touchy and *it* might lash out unpredictably. Be prepared, all right?" Worry shaded Marty's voice.

"I'll be ready. Let me know if I don't see problems in time."

"Here we go." Will nodded toward one corner. A hologlobe expanded. "She'll appear there."

The hologlobe enlarged to a size big enough to hold a person. A shadow formed inside of it, developing a shape, then solidifying. One side of the face twisted into a wavy shape which barely resembled Ness, clothed in a standard National Security jumpsuit. There didn't appear to be any open wounds or blood.

"Hello, Ness," Melanie said.

The apparition faced her. The misshapen part of her face was fuzzy and unclear, only the right eye, part of the right side of her nose, the right cheek and all but a corner of her lips and chin clear. It stared at her.

"It's Melanie, Ness." Her stomach tightened.

Don't react.

Finally, slowly, a faint response. "Mel-anie?"

"Yes."

The image grew firmer. "I'm—sorry. I just—barely—remember—you."

"It will improve with practice." Melanie projected a reassuring tone.

"Yes. Yes."

"Do you remember anything about Do It Right?"

Her gaze moved past Melanie, focusing on Marty. "Mar-ty?"

"We've spoken before, Ness. Do you remember?" His hands tightened on Melanie's shoulders.

She frowned, and started to fade a little bit. "No. May-be. Yes. You—were—"

Marty's hands clamped down hard on Melanie's shoulders and she bit her lip to keep from crying out. She slipped her hands up and slid them under his, trying to pry them loose. He caught the hint and moved his hands, wrapping them around hers. The motion caught the Ness thing's attention.

"You—two." Agitation crossed her face. Her image fuzzed, then strengthened. It pulsed, growing in intensity.

Melanie tried to ease her hands away, but Marty tightened his grip.

"No," he said softly. "No. Example of one of those processing moments. They are really, really unpredictable."

"Yeah," Melanie whispered, her mouth suddenly dry. "I see."

The pulsing stabilized. The image reestablished itself stronger than ever, except that this time the fuzzy left side of Ness's face looked like a melted ruin. Melanie saw traces of the damage she had seen in the pictures taken after Ness's death.

"Marty." The voice was stronger, more certain now. "You and I—we were—were—"

"Yes," Marty said. "Before you died, at one time, we were lovers. Although that ended seven and a half years before your death."

"Why?"

"You were so deep into doing both research and sabotage that there was just no time for a relationship."

"Sorry. I just—I just can't remember. Can't remember the relationship!" The image pulsed again. "I-I-I-I CAN'T HOLD THIS INFORMATION! WHY CAN'T I REMEMBER?" The image collapsed into a red cloud.

Melanie hesitated, waiting to see if her father or Marty would react.

Up to me. Of course. She needs soothing. Why can't they see that? Men!

"Ness. Easy." Melanie projected her broadest reassuring tone. "Easy. This isn't just an aftereffect of what's happened. Steady." She shrugged off Marty's hands. "You probably don't remember this. But before you left for the National Security labs, you and I worked together quite a bit. You were often absent-minded, especially when it came to everyday things. Don't beat yourself up over this. Please. Don't blame all this on your current condition. It was easy for you to get overloaded. Give yourself space. Give yourself time." She walked closer to the image, doing her best to project a safe, comforting profile. "If you were still breathing, I'd say take a deep breath. But you're not. So settle. It will to take time to get your memories back."

She stood a mere foot away from the agitated, cloudy swarm that was Ness. Following an instinct, she held up one hand toward it, pushing her hand through the hologlobe boundary, wincing at the sting. Apparently even the new datasuits wouldn't modulate the bite of someone else's globe.

A hand formed from the cloud, reached out, brushed against hers. The image began to form once more, oscillating yet again between intensity of bright and dark.

"You trust," it said—*no. Ness. It's Ness. You have to think of her as Ness. Not it.*

"Yes," Melanie whispered.

"You trust," Ness repeated. "But you lack—ahHHH!"

Sharp shocks shot through Melanie's hand, but she held steady, looking deep into the dark swirl of Ness's remaining eye, until someone wrenched her away from the globe.

"What are you *thinking?*" Marty growled.

"What are you *doing?* Putting yourself at risk!" Will snarled.

Don't they see it? Don't they understand? Marty's the one who says she needs living contact to remain sane, but neither he nor Dad get it!

Rather than snap back, Melanie took a deep breath. "She needs the contact in order to ground herself and become sane. Can't you see that?"

"She damned near killed you before!" Marty shouted, his eyes wide, brows furrowed, glaring at Melanie.

At least he's not calling her "it" anymore.

"Listen. We're not the only ones learning right now. She has to learn how to do this."

Melanie turned to face the rapidly pulsing cloud. "Ness. Ness. *Stop.*" She projected the same vocal tone that she would use with Mocha when the chestnut mare decided to act up, *feeling* it through her entire body. Steady. But not a yell, never a yell. Just a firmness that conveyed that the next action would—not be something the object of Melanie's attention would want to experience.

It worked. The pulsing gradually slowed. As Ness started to reform her shape, Melanie turned her attention back to her father and her lover, both of whom glowered at her.

"Now. You two. If you're going to use the relationship that Ness and I had to get her back in one piece, then, damn it, you have to trust me." She used a milder tone than she had with Ness.

"Melanie, she's dangerous," Will said.

"Give me some space. Let me try some things. If it looks like I'm getting hurt, *ask me, damn it!* The problems happened previously because we were asleep. I'm sure of it. She's *not going to hurt me.* In fact," she drew a deep breath. "Restore my Dialogue. Now."

"Mel," Marty groaned.

"We have to take this step sometime. One of us has to be her host. We can't tippy-toe around her any more. I need my Dialogue. You need your Dialogue. Let's go into a globe with her and talk this out. Now."

"No," Will said. "No Dialogue. Yet. You need a longer recovery before that level of interaction, both of you. You risk your neural circuits."

Melanie expelled a deep, exasperated breath. "Dad, is this for real? Or are you trying to protect me? You're being a dear, but you're smothering me." She turned to the now stabilized Ness. "Ness, are you following this discussion?"

"I don't understand it all."

"Did our touching help you?"

"Yes. Oh yes. Yes."

"Tell me what you remember."

"I remember Marty. And you. I remember that I could always trust you. I remember worrying about what would happen. And in that last second—oh God." She started to fade away again.

"Ness. Don't push it. Don't rush it. You're still learning. So are we."

"I remember regrets. Hoping that you could take care of Marty before it all, before it all ended."

Melanie held up a hand. "Don't go there yet. Don't."

"I'm so lonely, Melanie. It's so cold." Ness started to oscillate again, but kept speaking. "I remember agony. Pain. A shadow trying to grab me. Trying to touch Marty. Him screaming. God, I—tried—you're such a temptation. Both of you. Breathing and alive. With those chips—if only I could find a way inside—" She shuddered from a body shape into the cloud form again, keening. "I'm so *aloooone.*"

"No. You're not. You have us. You'll always have us, or someone like us."

"I—too much information. Data overload."

"Go process for a while. Meat and electronic, we still have to rest and put things back together. But when we're ready, we'll return with our Dialogues active. Both of us will spend time with you. You're not alone."

"I did that to you, didn't I?"

"Did what?"

"Your Dialogue. Why it's not active. I did that."

"Yes."

"Sorry. Just—so—*alone*."

"We'll make it better. You aren't alone. Go process."

"Okay." The cloud winked out.

Will jerked his head toward the door. Melanie's knees buckled and the room swayed around her. Marty steadied her.

"Sorry," Melanie murmured. "That took more out of me than I expected."

"The vertigo's back?" Marty asked.

"Yes."

"Too much, damn it! You're going right back to our quarters and resting rather than debriefing further," Marty said, his face grim. "Vertigo's not good. That's a relapse. Damn it, Melanie, I told you not to push it!"

She gently pressed a finger against his lips to shush him and nodded, recognizing his concern.

"You're right. I feel sucked dry. I pushed it too far. I do that. It's what I'm good at doing. It's getting better. But."

Melanie squirmed out of his arms, grabbing him to keep herself steady against the swaying that started again.

"Both of you," she continued. "If we're going to get Ness back and keep her sane, we have to risk contact. She doesn't want to hurt us. She's not malignant. She's just trying to figure out how to communicate. She needs practice before she gets better at it."

"The problem is that if she misjudges her touch, she can kill," Will said.

"Yes. But keep in mind that besides the shock of her death, she's still recovering from a long time of being very alone except for Marty, at National Security." She leaned hard into Marty, fighting to keep upright, half-closing her eyes to stop the room from swaying around her. The vertigo was rising again, but she needed to say this last bit. "I don't think we should judge her for what happened. I think she was so desperate for contact, so inexperienced with Netwalking, and so alone that she tried possession."

"You could be wrong," Will said. "She might be tricking us."

"Maybe. But I don't think she is." Melanie shifted her weight even more onto Marty.

"That's enough for now," Marty rumbled. "Mel, *that's enough*. Vertigo's back?"

She nodded. "It was okay before I stood up."

"That's typical. We can discuss this further in our quarters. Will, Mel needs more food and rest. We've done enough."

Will nodded. "I'll run more diagnostics. Collect some more data, then I'll drop by to talk to you."

"Give us a couple of hours at least," Marty said.

It was oh-so-easy to let Marty hold her up as they waited for another floater, sagging into his chest, letting her eyes close to stop the room from swaying around her, allow her muscles to relax and know that she was safe.

Know that he wouldn't let her fall.

Most of all, be aware that she still lived, still breathed, still moved in a world that was only partially electronic, where she could still walk in the snow, go skiing, ride horses.

Still *feel* sensations. Taste things. Smell things. Touch Marty.

One thought kept circling around as she thought of the electronic hell she had just glimpsed.

Poor Ness.

THE ROOM WAS DARK WHEN MELANIE WOKE, NO SUNLIGHT COMING through the high skylight over the bed. Male voices rumbled somewhere nearby—kitchen area. She started to blink up the time, then remembered. No Dialogue yet.

Melanie got up and pulled on a robe and slippers, then ran her fingers through her hair to straighten it. She wandered out to see who was talking in the kitchen, the world still fuzzy and blurry around her. *Something* smelled really good. Her stomach rumbled—*food. NOW.*

She followed the delicious scent to the kitchen/dining area. Her father and Marty ate donburi while sitting at the breakfast bar. Rather, Marty methodically shoveled bites of chicken and rice into his mouth while Will talked, waving his hands, his fingers and chopsticks outlining a schematic.

Marty grinned at Melanie. She sat on the stool next to him, leaning against him.

"You look better."

"I *feel* better," she said. "What time is it?"

"Four-thirty am local time," Marty said.

"We need a clock to supplement our Dialogues." Melanie snitched a chunk of chicken from his bowl. *Mmm. Real meat, not fake.* She grabbed another piece. "I couldn't figure out what time it was."

"Hey!" Marty playfully batted her fingers away. "Hold on. I ordered one for you. Leave mine alone!"

"Mmm," she growled at him. "*Starving.*"

"Good. Means you're almost through recovery."

Marty went around the breakfast bar to retrieve a fresh bowl of oyakodon from the preserver. He set it and a pair of chopsticks gingerly in front of Melanie, as if she might sample his hands instead. She grinned at him before diving into the egg and chicken combination.

Delicious. Extremely delicious.

Marty grabbed his bowl and resumed shoveling his food down—eating almost as fast as Melanie.

At last, she finished eating and slid the bowl away. Marty deftly gathered their empty bowls, leaving Will his barely-touched bowl, and put them in the recycler.

Will studied her critically. "Marty's right. You look better. I'd say you're nearly ready to reactivate your Dialogue."

"How's Ness?"

Will frowned. "Her signal's stronger than it was before you met with her. I'm a bit nervous about trying this again so soon. The two of you dived right into deeper contact than I think you should have."

"Dad, there's a connection between the way Marty and I originally developed our ability to communicate and what's happening with Ness." She smiled at Marty as he came back with bowls of miso for them. She rested her hands around the warm bowl, waiting for it to cool. "Of all the senses we have available to us, touch, smell and taste are the ones least likely to carry over to netspace. Seeing and hearing travel well across the electronic barrier."

"Tell me more." Will leaned back, fiddling with his chopsticks, picking idly at a sliver of chicken, then dropping it and picking up a slice of carrot instead.

"Integrating an electronic personality with living human personalities may depend on the degree to which they can compensate and adjust to the loss of those three senses in particular." She took a big gulp of miso, savoring the broth. Almost too hot to drink this fast, but it tasted *so good*. Just the right mix of salty flavor.

"That's an interesting thought," Marty said.

"Remember what Ness said? Last physical memories of agony and pain. She used physical imagery to describe how we were a temptation to her. That imagery wasn't by accident, although I doubt she's that self-aware yet. Touch is the sense she longs for."

"That can lead to dangerous behavior on her part, if she's obsessing about touch," Will said.

Melanie nodded. "We need to orient her electronic version in small doses, with multiple people. Also, she reaches overload very quickly. That's a good reason to keep her sessions short. Monitor her closely, and see what it looks like when she hits that overload point."

"The spike shows up well on the monitors," Will said. "I tracked it in real time. When she started falling apart, she spiked high on all levels."

"A direct touch may not be the best thing for either side," Marty said, rubbing his chin thoughtfully. "We might have more productive sessions if we can develop further protections for her as well as us. Buffers or barriers."

"What do you mean? More than the cage we've got her in?" Will asked.

"We may be able to have longer, less intense sessions for both sides if we rig up an electronic version of a datasuit for Ness to use. Maybe just a dataglove, one for her, one for us to provide additional protection as well as the new datasuits. It's going to be a long, slow, process otherwise. We went for ten seconds in this first session. She was in overload and Mel was wiped out when that was done. Yeah, Mel was in recovery mode, but I just don't see it happening any faster if we don't find a buffer." Marty frowned. "I'm worried about Ness's reference to that shadow. I think the process of orienting her may teach us a way to control it. But to do that, we need to find a way to make those sessions workable for both flesh and electronics for longer."

"Sounds like you've bought into Melanie's hypothesis about touch being the key."

"It makes sense to me, the more I think about it."

"Hmm. Well. Let me go back to the lab and have a chat with my people. You two need to take it easy until the regeneration process is finished." Will pushed away his bowl of barely-touched soup, and reached for his cane. Melanie started to get up, but he waved her away. "Girl, I'm fine. You're the one who still needs to be resting." He hobbled toward his floater.

"Any news from Mom?"

Her father stopped, one hand clenching quickly into a fist, then releasing. Then he sighed, turning away from his floater, frowning at Melanie.

"Nothing. Very little reliable news is coming out of North America. Our best sources are the Indigenous reserves, with their independent communications, and they're choosing to lie low. All I know is that she's still alive. I'd know if she were dead. Trust me."

"Tracking device?"

Will made a face. "You know me too well, girl. Yes. Among other things. I know she's alive. But where, I don't know. Andrew—Andrew's not talking to me. I don't know what that boy's thinking. I can't predict him. I don't advise you talk to him until your Dialogue's up, running, and fully tweaked."

"I wasn't intending to do so." Lie. She *had* considered the possibility.

Damn. He still knows me pretty well.

Will glared at her. "You're just impulsive enough to try it. I'm not about to mess with him after our last go-round. He's suddenly turned into a younger version of Peter. Don't mess with him until your Dialogue is powered up. You need its protection."

A sudden thought came to her. "Dad. He told me he didn't have a choice. That they put an implant in him. Is this tied to Netwalk—or the gadget?"

"It's not the gadget. When did he tell you that?" Will stepped closer to her, eyes fixed intently on her face.

"Just before everything went to hell. Sarah sent him with pictures of Ness's body and an ultimatum. He tried to talk me into cooperating, said some weird things about those anti-aging nanos. Added something about Liam saying 'hi' as well. I don't think that was an accident."

"Liam. That little bastard," Will muttered. "It figures. Did Liam know anything about Dialogue?"

Melanie shook her head. "Liam never got close to that research. His only exposure would have been information from here. Eight years ago. That's an eternity in Dialogue development time."

"And you were doing a good job of keeping things under tight wraps." Will's frown deepened. "I still wonder."

"Liam was no scientist. He's always been more Political than Corporate or Research," she said.

"Yeah. He's a little shit but he's not stupid," Will grumbled. "I wonder how much influence he has over Andrew these days? Peter and Liam both. Damn." Will waved a hand in dismissal. "Enough about Liam. What did Andrew say to you about the implant?"

Melanie stared thoughtfully into her miso cup. "I tried to talk him into leaving Sarah and Peter. That's when he told me he had no choice, that they put an implant into him, and then he broke off from that comment pretty damn fast, like he was being monitored."

"Some of his mannerisms the other night were a lot like Peter's." Her father scowled thoughtfully.

"Do you think they found a Dialogue analogue that would let them control Netwalkers?" Melanie asked.

"*I* don't know," Marty said. "If they did, Ness would know. They didn't let me work on anything like that. At the end she was working on a special project for Sarah that she wouldn't or couldn't talk about. Makes things more urgent for figuring out what she knows." He frowned, tapping his fingertips together as he stared at the wall. "Any Dialogue copy they might have come up with would focus on nano/implant interfaces. Nanos over implants is their preference. What I don't have figured out yet is the actual upload itself. They wouldn't just upload personalities without setting boundaries, tying them to a single host. They couldn't. They wouldn't be that stupid."

"You sure about that?" Will asked.

Marty sighed. "You're right. They would, and they could. No wonder Ness is in bad shape. We have to figure out their process, because my guess is that it's traumatic, and is likely to fry Netwalker cognition. Which would be a method of control."

"You're saying that Andrew might currently be subjected to possession by Peter?" Will frowned. "With none of those safeguards you've been devising for us?"

"Knowing what I do about their systems, and judging from Ness's reactions and responses to me and Melanie, yes, I think he is under Peter's control," Marty said, scratching his chin.

"That would explain going to Contract like he did," Melanie murmured. "Grandmother or Uncle Peter. They're both dead, and potentially controlling Andrew." She felt sick. *Damn them.* "What do we do about Drew?"

"Pull his Netwalker link," Marty said. "Get Peter or Sarah out of him. I think they've been doing this half-assed Netwalk method for a while. I'd like to know why you haven't seen this before."

"Maybe it's because the Netwalkers they create go crazy or glitchy, and become that weird Dialogue stuff we run across at times. Those anomalous Suicide Reds we get," Melanie offered.

Will straightened up. "You two may be right. But that means we don't have a lot of time. Let me get our crew working on a dataglove for Ness. You two rest." He hobbled over to his floater. Melanie got up and, over his protests, helped him settle in, then kissed him gently on the forehead, something she hadn't done since her teen years.

He glanced up sharply, then smiled. "I'm okay, girl. I've been fighting Sarah for ages. Just looks like there's another form to deal with. If only Andrew had made better choices." His voice softened. "I'm glad to see you're better. You take care of yourself." He turned the floater away and headed out the door. Melanie crossed her arms across her chest and watched him go.

As the door closed after him, Marty came up behind her and rubbed her shoulders, then slid his arms around Melanie and pulled her close to him.

"He's not eating much, is he?" she said.

"No. Not at any one sitting. But he does seem to munch constantly. Maybe that makes up for it. No one seems to be concerned about it. They just have food handy to put in front of him at all times."

Melanie sighed. Another old pattern, only more so.

We have to solve this situation and get Mom back here. That's the only thing to keep him from undereating and overworking.

She wrapped her hands around Marty's.

I'm not ready to lose Dad.

Even though their Dialogue links weren't working, Marty seemed to sense her thoughts.

"I'm here," he whispered into her ear. "I'm doing what I can to watch out for him."

"Thank you," she whispered back. "Thank you."

CHAPTER 8

"I *HATE* THIS STUFF," MELANIE MUTTERED DURING A BREAK IN THE Dialogue reprogramming process. She flexed against the chair restraints. Necessary, because they held her steady once she reached the stage where she would be inverted and rolled through various positions to check for vertigo. But tight and uncomfortable all the same.

Marty grunted sympathetically from his automated lab chair. "You think this is bad, you should be on the other side." She was still upright, but he was tilted back with his feet in the air while his chair began the vertigo check. His tweaking was going faster than hers. "But at least we're on the home stretch."

"That's good."

Soon enough, the program finished checking her overlays and diagnostics. Now came the worst part—the vertigo check.

Melanie clenched her teeth as the chair started the rolls and inversions slowly, then sped up. Test overlays flashed across her eyes. At least she didn't experience any dizziness or disorientation.

A good reprogramming.

"Boot up," Julia Hawkins, the head Dialogue maintenance engineer, finally said.

Melanie blinked through the initiating boot sequence. Her Dialogue overlays popped up faster than ever, scrolling through the initial startup routine in a less harsh blue and green than before.

Finally, the startup ended and she parked her standard faint blue Dialogue icon in the lower right corner of her visual field. Good. The Netwalk upgrades appeared to have enhanced and sped up her Dialogue performance.

Back in the world of Dialogue. She blinked, subvocaled, and set up her visual displays so that she could reference local and Northwest time simultaneously. A faint green icon indicated that she had text messages waiting, probably Dialogue-specific and not accessible by computer.

Melanie pulled up the list and started reading while the techs bustled around her, finishing their work.

One message pulsed an urgent red.

<Once you two are cleared, come see me in my office. Dad.>

Wonder if the touch-talk with Marty is still there?

She couldn't try it just yet; their chairs were too far apart for touch.

<Don't need touch anymore.> The voice in her head was faint, but it was still Marty.

Her head jerked sharply toward Marty. He grinned at her. <It works for me. You?>

<Yes. Oh yes. Any idea how far our range is?>

<We do have limits. Just not sure how far, yet. Probably pretty short-range.>

<But we have this.>

<Yes.>

She slid out of her chair and walked over to him, picking up his hand. <I still prefer this.>

<It's different when we're touching and not-touching, isn't it?>

<Yes. Not only is your voice stronger when we're touching, but,> she stopped to consider the feel of the link. <Emotions come across better. More vivid backgrounds when we touch. Tonal variants. Colors. Warmth. It would be interesting to play with nonverbal sendings to see the degree of difference.>

"I think it definitely bears out your touch hypothesis," Marty said, climbing out of his chair.

"Speaking of that, do we know how far along the dataglove research is? Julia?"

"I believe your father has something ready."

"That must be why he wanted us to come to his office. Thanks, Julia."

"Thank *you*," Julia said. "These Netwalk updates are interesting. Now that we're done with you two, we're adding them to every Dialogue here. Upgrading." She grinned and tapped her temple. "Already have my upgrade. It does nice things for Dialogue!"

"Processing seems to be faster."

"It should be," Marty said. "We added some resets that have the effect of speeding up Dialogue processes. It's a major Dialogue upgrade as well as a Netwalk launch."

"It's all good," Julia said. "Anything that speeds up the processing is good."

"I just hope this Netwalk stuff continues to be good for us in the long run," Melanie said.

"Take it one step at a time." Marty placed his hand on her back, gently but firmly guiding her to the door. "Let's find out what your dad wants."

He kept the hand resting on her back until they walked out of Julia's lab and turned the corner toward Will's office. As his hand slid off of her back, she caught his fingers in hers and squeezed them. He smiled at her, and they walked down the hall, holding hands.

Will's office was just around another corner. The unstaffed reception desk was now being used as a workspace for two lab techs working at fingertip level in a small hologlobe. Melanie stopped to observe, noticing that they both wore datagloves.

<Looks like he's made some progress,> Marty commented.

<That's good.>

They continued to Will's main office. Melanie knocked. Her father grunted, and they walked in. Will slumped in his chair, staring at a hologlobe, twirling an elaborately lacquered hairstick that belonged to her mother. She sat down quietly, waiting for him to come out of his reverie and acknowledge her, blinking to set her Dialogue's timer running so she could tell him how long they had been there. Marty sat next to her.

They waited. At last, Will jerked slightly, then looked over at them. He set the hairstick down carefully.

"How long have you two been here?" he asked.

Melanie blinked the timer to a stop. "Five minutes," she said.

Typical Dad.

Will nodded. "Did it work? You two still need to touch to talk?" he demanded.

"It works," Marty said. "We don't know range yet, but we have noticed a distinct signal drop off between touch and no-touch."

"Good information to have." Will picked up the hairstick again. "I've been looking at our data. Ness's strength keeps building with every auditory and visual session she has. I've had unfamiliar lab techs work with her. No touch, just auditory and visual. She's not real comfortable with me or with strangers yet, but when I talk to her, she's definitely fluctuating less. All the same, you two are the only ones she trusts right now."

"That fits her pattern," Marty said. "Ness never trusted anyone until she got to know them really well."

"Kathy's like that too. And Kathy raised her," Melanie said.

"I keep forgetting about that connection," Will said. "So. Girl. You ready for another session?" He looked hard at Melanie.

She nodded.

"I've designed a slightly more stylish next-gen datasuit that looks more like clothing," Will continued. "It's still rough and fit isn't the best, but it's better than nothing. Definitely make sure you're wearing this latest upgrade when you talk to Andrew. I'm hearing weird news about him. I'm certain now that either Peter or Sarah have a grip on him."

"Unless it's Liam pulling the strings," Melanie said.

Will shook his head. "No. This has the feel of Sarah or Peter. Liam has a certain style. There's a bit of flair around what he does. What's coming from Andrew is blunt stuff." He hesitated. "There could be further influences. But I do not have the authority to talk to you about that. Your mother does."

"The gadget?"

Will nodded sharply. "I can't talk about it, Mel." He jerked his head toward the wall. "There's that datasuit. Tell me what you think."

Melanie rose and examined the thin fibers of the datasuit hanging on the wall. While still clearly a datasuit, it had small designs on the arms and legs to create a decorative touch if worn under a sleeveless dress or tunic. She picked it up, noticing that it moved freely in her hands, almost as if it were crocheted from cotton or other fiber, with only a faint resistance from the thin metallic protective threads.

A good start toward integrating datasuits with clothing.

"Wonder if this is something we could develop for the Corporate market? Once we go public with Dialogue, it'd be nice to have some stylish datasuit designs to market as well. Maybe talk to designers about integrating datasuits into clothing."

Will rolled his eyes, but nodded in agreement. "Trust you to figure out these things, girl. Sounds like a good marketing device."

Melanie examined the suit further. "Once we get out from under this mess, I'll think about it more."

"*This mess* is likely to last longer than you think," Will said. "Get one of your marketing people to do it."

Melanie nodded. "I'll tell Janine to call Rio. It's the best place to develop something like this for the fashion market, and Janine will know who to call." Melanie took a deep breath before changing subjects. "About this session with Ness. Marty, I'm wondering what would happen if you and I both tried integration with her."

Marty shook his head. "Let's see how this session goes with the datagloves."

"I still might want to link with you for part of the briefing. We need to explain our theories to her. Get her engaged. Ask her advice. She's isolated from outside contact so she can't leak information, right?"

"As far as I know she is," Will said. "Can't guarantee it one hundred percent, but I've not seen anything to suggest otherwise."

"Okay." Melanie looked at Marty. "I'll explain why we want her to try a dataglove, then move into contact."

"Agreed. No more than thirty seconds for contact, though. And I want to track your brain waves."

Melanie nodded. "Okay. I'll change, and then let's get started."

"Wait until I put these monitors on you."

She stood while he carefully placed the wireless leads.

"I'm done," he said finally. "Want me to wait for you?"

"I'll meet you in the lab."

She slipped into the small restroom off of Will's office, frowning as she spotted the box of Burnout tabs sitting on the counter.

Wonder how hard he's riding the dragon?

She pushed back the temptation to check up on her father's Burnout use and changed. She had to admit, looking at the datasuit once it was on, that it resembled a lacy catsuit with gloves more than it did a datasuit.

Combine the datasuit with the right skirts and tops and it would be a cutting-edge style to appeal to fashionistas in Tokyo and Paris. At least she didn't need to wear a hood with these newer versions of both Dialogue and datasuit. The Dialogue itself created a protection for her head, in combination with the datasuit. The hood might be a detriment to style.

Then again, given the right designer, it could be really glam. And I am so ready to get back into glam, after seven tedious and boring years being plain.

She tapped the linking patches on her temples twice to extend the datasuit protection to her head. Then she blinked to make sure all was clear with her Dialogue linkages.

Everything worked. Melanie pulled on the rest of her clothing and joined the others.

Marty and Will chatted with Ness, both within the hologlobe. Melanie joined them, getting a faint zap from the edges as she walked into the globe. Ness's form was more solid, except for the left side of her head. It blurred and fuzzed, tiny spots of bright neon colors erratically firing and fading.

Wonder if she'll ever be able to fix that?

Ness brightened as she spotted Melanie.

"Melanie! I'm glad to see you."

"I'm glad to see you, too. Have these two briefed you on what's up yet?"

"Not a word."

"You're talking better."

"It seems easier now, since we touched."

"We think that touch is going to be a factor in helping you remember and to help you hold data. It's based on something that happened when you first tried to touch Marty."

Ness looked perplexed, at least as much as her remaining face could show an emotion. "But I thought I was hurting you." She faded a little.

"You were. I'm not talking about when you crashed our Dialogues. I'm talking about the very first time, when Marty found the shadow. You were there, weren't you?"

Ness pulsed slightly, fading in and out. "I-I c-can't completely re-mem-ber that."

She stutters when she's stressed. It might be a trait which continues.

Ness when alive had not been a stutterer. Did that hint at data corruption?

"Then let's not worry about it. Let me tell you what happened." Melanie briefly described how she and Marty were suddenly able to speak to each other while touching.

"You speak with your Dialogues?" Ness sounded even more perplexed. "No texting? Voice? In your heads? Like telepathy?"

"Yes, very much like the notion of telepathy. It comes in words, tones, sounds very similar to our own voices when we subvocal, only I'm hearing Marty's subvocal and he's hearing mine. No texting. More than that. Emotions. Schematics. Visuals. I got a scalp wound that bled into my eyes so I couldn't see, and Marty sent me a visual of where we were going, so we could run. But we had to be touching each other."

"That's interesting." Ness pulsed again.

"Is there a possibility that you may have given me some nanos that facilitated this happening?" Marty asked. "Melanie and I are the only ones who can do this so far. We have nanos in our bodies that we can't account for. They appear to be easily transmitted, at least between the two of us."

Ness pulsed, frowning as each pulse hit the solid phase. "I can't remember giving you anything, Marty. But if you're right about me being able to remember more later, maybe I will. I don't know. There's *something* interfering with what I recall. Some sort of spiky sphere."

Her father briefly tightened.

Spiky sphere? Is she talking about the gadget? Dad can't or won't talk about it. Can Ness? Get her stable, and maybe we can learn more without waiting for Mom.

"We think that with each touch you'll remember more."

"Wish I had more memories *now*. There's just enough that makes me think it makes sense, but I can't grab it."

Was that a grumbling tone in Ness's voice? If so, it showed improvement in her orientation.

"That will come. Let's do it. Dad will explain the process."

Will handed a dataglove to Melanie. "Melanie, put this one on. Ness, materialize a hand inside this other dataglove." He placed the second one within range of Ness.

"What's the theory of the dataglove?" Ness asked.

"You and Melanie hit overload in ten seconds last time. We're hoping to buy thirty seconds in this next session, maybe even longer, without frying either of you."

Ness nodded. She dissolved into a red and black cloud. It swirled around the dataglove, then moved inside of it, filling the glove. Ness took her shape again and lifted the glove.

"Interesting sensation." She flexed the glove, then touched a table-top. "I *feel* things with this. I couldn't do that before."

"Good," Marty said. "Let's get started. I want you two to start slowly. *Slowly*. Fingertips first. I'll give five second countdowns. Progress to full hand contact at your own rate. Let Melanie govern the process. No more than thirty seconds this time. Period. If either of you senses a problem, I want you to break it off. I'm trusting you two. Okay?"

"Okay."

"Okay."

"If this session goes well, I'll try a second thirty second interval. No more than that. We need to assess the impact on both of you. Got it?"

"Yeah," they said, together.

Melanie faced Ness. This time, the thought of deliberately touching

Ness seemed more frightening. Slowly, Melanie raised her hand. Ness's dataglove rose to match hers. Their fingertips touched. At first, Melanie felt nothing. Then a slight tingle.

"Five," Marty said.

Melanie pressed the joints of her fingers delicately against the joints of Ness's glove. The tingling followed, but at the same intensity. Ness's form solidified as Melanie felt something *pulling* at her. At first she wanted to break away, but schooled herself to stick with it. It wasn't too much, not yet.

"Ten," Marty said.

She pressed her upper palm against Ness's. Tiny darting lights danced in her vision.

What is that?

The same lights flashed across Ness's remaining eye, forming into a schematic.

"Fifteen," Marty said.

On a sudden hunch, Melanie pressed her entire hand against Ness's. She and Ness stared at each other. Ness yanked at Melanie. Suddenly Melanie was following Ness through that brightly colored schematic that had been in Ness's eye. Needles prickled against her hand as they passed through a doorway and Melanie separated from Ness.

She chased after Ness through a long passageway of brightly colored lights. She'd glimpsed this before when working with links via Dialogue in a dataglobe. Only then, the passage had always been behind that door. Transparent, yet closed. Now she had actually gone through that door, and she didn't know which way she wanted to go first. So many different paths called to her. So many possibilities.

The copper-colored spiky sphere Melanie glimpsed previously suddenly strobed in front of her.

<No!> Ness yelled, and pulled Melanie away.

The flashing bright lines around Melanie faded and she was back in the lab, still tightly clinging to Ness's hand.

"Thirty!" Marty said. "Melanie. *THIRTY!*" He tugged her hand free from Ness's unresisting grip.

Melanie stared at Ness. "That's what you see, isn't it? Brightly colored schematics? And that copper-colored spiky shape?"

"I-I-I-yes." Ness pulsed anxiously.

"Mel. Look at me." Urgency tinged Marty's voice. She looked at him, wondering why he was so upset. "Didn't you hear me?"

"Pretty," she told him. "It was so pretty, with all those schematics. Except for that spiky sphere at the end. It's scary."

<Melanie!>

His mental roar snapped her free. She shook her head, dropped her eyes to combat the sudden wave of vertigo that swept over her. The world steadied. She looked back up at him.

"I think I started Netwalking," she said. "It's not like Dialogue at all. Nothing like Dialogue."

"I-I-n-no more ri-ri-right now," Ness said. Melanie turned to face her. Ness pulsed rapidly. "P-p-process! Needed. Now. C-c-come back. Later."

"Sounds like a plan to me," Will muttered.

Ness winked out slowly. Marty firmly took Melanie by the elbow. "Let's go."

The world sparkled around Melanie as they walked back to Will's office, brightly at first, then gently winking out. The pressure from Marty's fingers grew stronger. She realized he lurked quietly in her mind.

What the hell?

<Don't go there, Mel. Don't.> Tension filled his mental voice. She stopped dead, staring at him.

<What happened? Why are you reacting like this?>

<It's easier to show you on the monitors,> he answered. <Meanwhile, Mel, just trust me, okay?>

She nodded, and let him guide her the rest of the way to Will's office. Bewildered, she dropped into a chair.

Her father stared at her grimly. "You can't keep this up," he said finally. "You bond with her far too well. And you attract—the attention of things that shouldn't notice you."

"What do you mean?"

"This." Marty clicked up a hologlobe and started running two tracks through it. "These are your brain waves. These are her pulses." He started a third process, a video of the contact. "Watch the two monitors along with the process."

She watched, listening to Marty's count, observing as sparks shimmered around their gloves when her hand pressed hard against Ness's.

Bright light flashed from the contact. The spiky sphere flashed copper, then disappeared.

So it does exist. Is that the Gizmo?

"Look at your waves!" Marty hissed. "I'm going to slow-mo it."

She looked, and gulped. The two waves matched. Pace for pace, until the very end.

"Now look at the video," Marty said.

At his fifteen-count, after the light flashed, she looked upward, a beatific expression on her face. Then she faded slightly, as the copper-colored spiky sphere appeared, then winked out.

"What the—" She leaned forward and clicked it to a stop, then clicked it back. "Now just how did *that* happen?"

"Here's your other vitals," Marty said grimly. "I'm syncing it with her strength."

She watched as her heart rate and respiration dropped, matched by a corresponding weakness in Ness's signal.

"What's going on?" she asked.

Marty shook his head. "I don't know. What did you mean when you said you went Netwalking?"

She described running down the schematic, passing through the door with Ness.

Will and Marty looked at each other. Marty turned away and stared into the hologlobe, face tightly set.

"You started an uploading process," he said. He pointed to a small, nebulous gray blob that she suddenly recognized as a shadow of herself. "Damn it. I wish I knew how you were doing it! Things were going fine until that fifteen second count."

"Fifteen seconds may be all they can do until we understand this mechanism," Will said. "I don't like the appearance of the—gadget, yes, Melanie, that's the gadget. And I can't talk about it. But this adds a worrisome dimension to this whole process. There's risk to you if it becomes too aware of your presence."

"I don't know," Marty said, shaking his head. "I just don't know."

"Well," Will said, leaning back in his chair, "Let's see what happens after Ness has had time to process, then we'll see what she remembers. The gadget's appearance may not be a problem. All the same, Melanie, I want Julia to check your Dialogue before you do anything else with Ness."

She nodded, overwhelmed. "Does this mean I've uploaded a piece of me?"

Marty nodded.

"We can't let it sit there without contact, can we?"

"As long as you're alive, it's okay," Marty said quietly. "It doesn't appear to be moving around. There must be some sort of trigger process which activates it."

"Should we kill it?"

"I'm—I'm not ready for that. Yet," Marty said. He winced. "Silly and superstitious of me, but it reeks of killing you."

"I'm not comfortable with that upload's existence," she said.

"I'll monitor your upload while we figure out what to do about it," Will said. "I want to study it further. Meanwhile, Julia has to check you out, Melanie," he repeated. *"Now."*

"Okay. But you'll keep an eye on that part of me, right?"

A thin smile touched Will's lips. "I'm researching it. You bet I'll be watching."

"Come on, Mel. Let's have Julia run the check. I'll go with you," Marty said.

They walked down the corridors quietly. At least this time she didn't feel fatigued or dizzy, except for that first quick wave of vertigo.

Progress, of a sort.

CHAPTER 9

"BACK SO SOON? WHAT'S UP?" JULIA'S LEAD TECH REIKO ASKED AS THEY entered Julia's lab.

"Mel had an *incident* while working with Ness," Marty said.

"Ah. Okay. Let me get the boss." Reiko bustled into the main lab. She talked to Julia, gesturing toward the window. Two DIR staffers Melanie didn't recognize were strapped into the chairs.

Julia meant it when she said she wasn't wasting any time upgrading other Dialogues with the new tweaks. Good.

Julia nodded, pointed to each chair as she spoke to Reiko, then showed her some screen results.

"All right, Mel," she said as she came through the door. "Have you *already* been wrecking my handiwork? Tell me what happened."

"We tried the touch test with Ness," Marty said. "It went well, for the first fifteen seconds. Then Melanie started to upload."

Julia raised one eyebrow and ran her hands through her short, brownish blond hair. "Huh? Mel, how did you do *that*?"

"Darned if I know. I just followed Ness."

"Just followed—Mel!" Julia shook her head.

"*Well,* it *was* cool-looking! And I've always wondered about it. I've seen the passageways and the schematics, but they've been locked behind a transparent door. This time I followed Ness through the door." Given Will's reaction about her seeing the spiky sphere, Melanie decided not to mention it.

"Through the door," Julia mused. "I've seen that. And—more. Did you see something else, that you can't talk about?" She side-eyed Melanie.

Melanie squirmed. "Yeah," she said. "Dad keeps sending me mixed messages about whether it's a problem or not, but he's pretty adamant that I really don't want to be the focus of its attention."

"He's right," Julia said, her brusque tone akin to Will's. "If you're lucky, this won't continue to catch the whatchamacallit's attention. You need to talk to your mother or Kathy Miller for more information." Her shoulders sagged. "You said you followed Ness through the door? Mel, I swear you can be the queen of impulsivity sometimes!" She shook her head. "Okay. Come with me. We'll use the auxiliary lab."

At least I don't get the chair.

Julia linked in to her Dialogue and quickly ran through the diagnostics.

"Okay." Julia unhooked the link. "Nothing wrong, Mel. This time. But will you be more careful in the future?"

"I'll try."

"You always say that." Julia's smile took the sting out of her words. "I want to talk to you later about what you saw. Not everyone sees the schematics or the door. Or the other. That's definitely what you think it is. Again, talk to your mother or Kathy. They have the clearance to talk. As for the schematics and the door, I got a brief glimpse, but I'd like to see it first-hand. I want you to take me into the globe and show it to me. Soon. It could be useful with Netwalk management, especially with adept risk-takers like yourself. Did you see what she's talking about, Marty?"

Marty shook his head. "I don't see schematics in the same detail Mel does. My operations are more intuitive, more text-based. I've never seen that transparent door."

"I'd like more time to look into this," Julia said. "I can't do it now. I have to monitor uploading this Netwalk protocol for local staff. But after that, I want to check this phenomenon. We may have different categories of people accessing Netwalk and interacting with Netwalkers, and Mel might just be one of the rarities. I'll know more once I have a bigger Netwalk database and see the variations. This matches what we've talked about with Dialogue performance variants."

"Sounds good," Marty said. "Keep me posted."

"Okay. I need to get back to my current process. Check in with me later, Marty. Let's talk about it."

"I'm going to my office," Melanie told Marty as they left the lab. "While I'd like to ski, I have work to do."

"Maybe we could do something later. Want me to have Nik check the possibility of private night skiing? He said something about that earlier. If you think you'd be up to it."

"Me not up to skiing? I have to be as out of it as I was yesterday to keep me down."

"I'll let you know. Maybe just a short two-hour break."

"Sounds good to me."

They kissed outside her office suite. She smiled at him, then went in.

"How's it going?" Janine asked.

"Dialogue's up and running. I've been checking my messages."

"Good. Then you're up-to-date. Andrew keeps on calling. Not emails. Calls."

"That's—*interesting*."

"He's had Liam call a couple of times for him. Sounds like Liam's his number two. May be Andrew's spymaster, like he was for Sarah."

"Lovely." Melanie rolled her eyes. "I'll call him. Marty's trying to set us up with some night skiing. Up for it?"

"Yes," Janine grinned at her. "Here's the number Andrew's been leaving." She flicked it to Melanie's messages.

Melanie went into her office.

Call first, or wait for Andrew to call back?

Call, she decided. She coded the number into her Dialogue's contacts before calling, noting that it was a new one.

"Hello. It's about time, Melanie." Liam's face appeared on her screen.

Deep breath, Melanie. Don't react.

"Hello, Liam." She kept her voice quiet and neutral, professional in tone. "I'm returning Andrew's call."

"What's up on the slopes, girl?" He grinned at her, rocking back in his chair. She looked at his sharp, angular features. What the hell had she ever seen in this man?

"I'd like to speak to Andrew, please." She kept her voice in professional, detached mode.

Liam raised one eyebrow. "Come on, Mel. Getting too big for some friendly conversation?"

"I'd like to speak to Andrew, please," she repeated, clenching one fist out of Liam's line of sight. "If he's not available, then he needs to call me back. I don't have the time to play these games. Is he available?"

"Can't you joke around with an old friend, at least?"

She schooled herself to keep relaxed. Liam knew too many of her nervous mechanisms. "If he's not available, then he needs to call me back. I've a corporation to run." She let her voice sharpen.

"My, my, my. Melanie the busy corporate lady. You weren't that way before. What happened to my fun girl? C'mon, Mel. Let's drop the seriousness here."

"A lot happens," she said. "I've grown up. Liam, are you telling me that Andrew's not available? If not, please put me through."

"Aw, honey—"

She switched him off. "I'm *not* your honey," she said aloud to the empty office. "And you're wasting my time." Then she messaged Janine.

<Liam calls, message only. No talk. Talk only if it's Andrew.>

<Liam just called. Huffy. He says no call from Andrew. Not soon.>

<Thanks.>

She turned to the ever-present datafiles and began the reviews. The first one she started to sign *Melanie Landreth, President, DIR NA* before catching herself and substituting *International* for *NA*.

It took several hours, but she got through the files. Melanie sighed, wondering how soon it would be until Marty let her know about skiing.

Why wait? After all, they didn't need to touch to mindspeech anymore.

<Hon?> she sent.

<Just a sec. In a process.>

Melanie half-frowned, shaking her head ruefully. The odds were good that he had been locked into doing the process ever since he went in the lab and hadn't come up for air. Had Marty even talked to Nik?

Typical scientist.

<Mel?>

<You had a chance to check out the ski possibilities?>

<Ski? Oh. Yeah. Nik's got us set up for six tonight. Sorry I didn't pass the word on sooner. That time work for you?>

<Sure. Add Janine to the group. How's the process going?>

<Okay. Following some tags from Julia. Have to talk to you about that. And you?>

<Andrew was trying to call me. But I got his pet butthead instead.>

Marty was quiet for a moment. <Liam?>

<None other. In his finest, most flowery, glorious buttheadesque mode. I think it's safe to assume he's now Andrew's spymaster. Or something.>

<You okay?>

<Makes me wonder what I ever saw in him.>

She sensed a chuckle. <Makes me feel good. Got to go. Love.>

<Love,> she sent.

That left one more major problem. Her mother.

Where the hell *was* Diana?

Melanie decided to try the direct approach. She cued her Dialogue for Diana's private address, half-expecting a NOT IN SERVICE icon to pop up on her viewscreen.

Instead, she got a connection. A static image of Diana appeared. Text slowly scrolled across the bottom.

Melanie. If you've gotten this message, I'm still on the run but alive, well, and uncaptured. I can't tell you much more than that. I will be updating. You can input text to me, but I won't promise I can answer any questions.

A blinking icon indicating more updates appeared at the end of that text.

Melanie chewed her lower lip, noticing that the date was a week old. She toggled the blinking icon.

Update number one. I see you've not accessed this message yet. Your father tells me you're alive and well, and on your way to Nagano. That's good. He also tells me that you and Marty are together. I'm glad to see it. He's good for you. You've needed someone in your life, and I wish you both the best.

She didn't wait before toggling the next icon.

Update number two. I see you've not accessed this message yet. I don't know what's going on with Andrew. His actions have drawn several Contracts on him from companies allied with us. I've contacted them and asked them to lift their Contracts. You don't need the interference.

I caught video of your press conference. Good job. I've always told you that you have excellent PR instincts. But Mel, your father—

This update broke off suddenly. She looked for an update icon and was comforted to see another.

Update number three. What the hell is going on? Something cut into me and knocked my Dialogue out of commission for half a day so that I couldn't finish that update. Then your father tells me about that latest attack and your contacts with Ness. And the other. Melanie, be careful with the online world. It comes too easily to you. Depend on Marty to keep you safe. Don't engage—the other without talking to me, Kathy, or Zoë Wright. Furthermore, don't be Ness's host. Marty won't betray you, neither would Ness, but you'd push her to do unsafe things. You're always pushing the boundaries. You can't push him.

Melanie snorted at that comment. If there was anything she had figured out about Marty by now, it was that.

She returned to reading the rest of Diana's text.

Something is not right with Andrew, and I'm thinking it's Netwalk. And other things. I don't know how much longer I can keep posting these updates. They make me too vulnerable. I'll check when it's safe. Post me something so I know you're all right. Keep posting even when you don't get responses. It's easier for me to read than to text.

No more update icons flashed after this message.

Melanie chewed nervously on her lower lip, thinking about what to say. Finally, she composed a response.

Got your updates. I'm worried about you. We're tracking a theory with

Ness right now. She's getting stronger, and that may give us more useful information. You're right in your hypothesis about Andrew. I'm trying to talk to him but no luck yet. Just getting Liam. He may be Andrew's spymaster, or—

Another thought came to her.

Perhaps his controller, she added.

She paused, thinking hard about what she wanted to say next.

Dad's hitting the Burnout, she finally wrote. *Not eating well. Marty says he sees everyone offering him food, but he's—I'm worried, Mom. I can't call you back from your Interim President work, nor do I want to, but what can I do to help things along for you? What about Dad?*

She frowned at her text, debated about editing out the last part, then decided to keep it. Before second-guessing herself further, she sent the message.

It had been a while since Melanie skied with Marty. Ness had not been into either skiing or snowboarding, so Marty's occasions out with Melanie's group of skiers had been rare. While his first runs with the snowboard were tentative, by their fourth run, he was easily keeping up with Melanie at her relaxed, non-racing pace.

"I'd forgotten how good you were," she said as they rode the gondola up to the top of the slope.

He grinned and squeezed her hand. "I didn't grow up doing it like you guys. But riding's always come easily to me. Not so with the skis."

"I want to push Nik this next time down," she said. "It's the last run. I've still some stuff to blow off, and I want a hard, fast line. You have a problem if I race?"

He shook his head. "I'd like to see it, actually. I've just heard about Crazy Mel on skis. And seen the vids from the other day. You've not done that around me."

She grinned and looked down at her boots. "I guess I've saved that for more private times than the previous occasions you've come skiing."

Marty lifted her chin with a finger. "So? This is one of those more private times. Show me your stuff!"

She winked at him. "I will."

Nik picked up on her cues as she paused at the top, adjusting her gloves and goggles, checking her bindings and boots with more detail than usual for a casual run.

"You up for a race?" he asked.

"Yeah."

"You're not concerned about Marty?" He looked back. "I normally wouldn't ask."

She grinned at Nik. "Marty said he's never seen Crazy Mel on skis. I figure he's okay with Ange and the rest of our team. He's not half-bad on the board."

"Yeah. No need to push him past his comfort level. But—Crazy Mel, huh? That mean you're going to do the cliff again?"

She snorted. "Not tonight, not after this kind of day. But fast and sharp, yeah."

"Five second start?"

"Sure. Why not?"

"You'd better ski your skinny ass off, then. I'll make you work for it."

"I wouldn't have it any other way."

Melanie took a deep breath, dug in with her poles, then pushed off, tucking low and hard to pick up speed, seeking the fastest line down the slope.

Slick, fast stuff tonight.

She carved a good, tight turn, then caught some air, landing it hard and good and pushing herself down the straightest, fastest line she could spot. Her world became a blur of reflexes, following the line down, following her balance. She might have been a mediocre World Cup skier, but dear God, she loved the speed, the feel of her boards on the snow under her, the trees whipping by her, the way it became a flowing gestalt of white and forwardness at one with the mountain under her.

Nothing else was like it.

Snow. Speed on snow. The fluid grace of moving down the slope in rhythm with her speed, hearing the rasp of the dry, crusty snow on her skis. It was the closest she could come to flying.

She heard rather than saw Nik catching up to her, and tucked harder. Out of the corner of her eye, she saw him paralleling her for a short distance, then outpacing her as his greater size and strength allowed him to take a straighter, faster line than she could.

The end of the run came too quickly. She slowed easily, not bothering with the flashy turns, and skied up next to Nik.

"That was good. How much did you beat me by?"

"Not much," he said. "You were sizzling tonight."

"Snow's different from home."

"It's not Cascade concrete."

"Yeah."

"Thanks for setting up the private run."

Nik chuckled. "It's easy when you've the power of DIR behind you."

"They want an endorsement, I suppose."

"It'd be a good thing."

"Send me the info when we get back. There are a few things I need to wrap up before I quit for the night. That can be one of them."

"Will do."

They watched as the rest of their group made their way down the slope at a slower pace.

"That was *interesting*," Marty said as they headed back.

"Glad you liked it."

"Yeah. Hey, when we get back, I'd like to spend a couple of hours in the lab. Okay with you?"

"I have more stuff I need to do. But I'd like to show you something before we call it a night. Not urgent."

"I'll come by when I'm done with my processes."

"I'll drag you out if you take too long," she threatened.

He laughed. "There's a time limit on this current process I'm developing."

SHE ENDED UP BEING THE ONE WORKING LATER AND LONGER. SHE WAS analyzing bioremediation progress reports from Rio when Marty walked into her office.

<Mel. Time to call it a night.>

She blinked up the time and realized that she'd been working for three hours.

"This is what I want you to see," she said, calling up the texts from Diana.

Marty read through them, frowning.

"I wondered how she was keeping in touch with your father," he said. "That's a lot of risk to her, though. Puts her easily on someone's radar, even with the floating addresses."

"How easy?" she asked.

"Too damned easy for my liking. Your father's dropped hints of stuff he did to make your mother more secure before she left, but this is still information being transmitted online, with the potential that it'll catch someone's attention. Those floating links aren't perfect." Marty brought up the message that had been abruptly cut off and pointed to the date and time stamp. "Timing on that one's significant."

"How so?"

"Matches when Ness attacked you."

"That couldn't have been Ness too, could it?"

Marty shook his head. "No. The shadow was getting restless as well. I would have to scan Diana's Dialogue, but my guess is that something happened online to rile up more than one Netwalker. Maybe it's tied to—what you've been seeing. That's one of the processes I've been tracking today." He stared at the message, tracing a circle on her shoulder. "I wonder."

"Wonder what?"

"You ever hear back from Andrew?"

"No."

"He dropped out of sight publicly about the same time you did, after Ness's incident. Just how many Netwalkers got lively, willing or unwilling, at that time?" He sighed. "Another issue to consider, when I'm so damned tired I just want to eat, curl up with you, and sleep."

"Should we follow up on it?"

He shook his head. "No. I've been wrestling with aspects of this all day. This just gives me more data to think about. Right now, I'm so tired I can't see straight. Anything more would be useless."

"Sounds like I'd better take you home."

He squeezed her shoulder. "Damn right."

She shut her work off. He slipped one arm around her as they left her office and they walked down the hallways like that, arms around each other like they were teens in love instead of adults.

"At least we've got an excuse to break it off and crash," she told him. "Otherwise, I'd keep on going."

"Me too," he said.

She leaned her head into his chest. At least she wasn't facing these crazy times alone.

CHAPTER 10

"ANDREW'S CALLING REPEATEDLY," JANINE SAID THE NEXT MORNING WHEN Melanie entered the office. "Himself. Not Liam. Five-minute intervals. Rude. Pushy. Demanding I put him through."

Melanie raised a brow. "Did you notice any changes in his behavior or speech patterns?"

Janine twisted her lips and tapped one finger on her desk. "It's very subtle," she said, finally. "But yes, there is a difference. While he's always been pushy in the past, he's never been directly rude. This was more like the way Peter used to talk to me."

"Did you notice any resemblance to Peter in his actions?" A chill ran down Melanie's spine.

"Sorry. I wasn't looking for that. Do you want me to?"

"Yes. Put him through next time he calls."

"You won't call him?"

"He's the one making urgent noises. Let him make the contact." She went into her office and sat down. <Marty.>

<What's up, darlin'?>

She hated to wreck the good mood he had been in this morning. <Andrew's been calling. Janine says he's pushy.>

<And?>

<She noticed a change in behavior. She didn't notice any particular physical mannerisms, but he acts like Peter.>

<Damn. Are you calling back?>

<No. I'm going to let him call me.>

<Good. I want to be there. Wait, no, I can't. Not physically. Can't leave this process, it's tricky and I'm doing it with Ness active to advise me. Netwalk stuff. But link into me before you open the line. Let me see through your eyes. You're wearing the latest datasuit upgrade, right?>

<What are you worried about?>

<If Peter's in Andrew, the odds are good that Peter's a predatory Netwalker. He may try something. We have to assume that the Dialogue secret is compromised, Mel. I'm starting to suspect it has been known to our foes for a long time.>

She frowned at that thought, tapping her upper lip with her finger. <Perhaps it's time to prepare for the public Dialogue launch?>

<Looks like it. Remember, link to me before you open the line. Love you.>

<I will. Love you.> She signed off and started work on her dailies.

Andrew's call came just as she finished reading messages.

Trust him to always be timely.

She sent Marty an alert. He was suddenly *there,* almost as if he were standing next to her. A reassuring presence.

Melanie opened the projection.

"Andrew," she said.

"Where the hell have you *been?*" he snapped.

"And how are you today?" she retorted. "What's on fire?"

Instead of the rolling eyes she expected, he growled in exasperation. Her right hand clenched, out of sight under the desk.

Not a typical Andrew behavior.

Even when he had been pushy in the past, she had been able to get a smartass response to a smartass comment. One of the few sibling behaviors they shared, cultivated by their father.

This had to be a Peter reaction. Her uncle hadn't possessed even a shred of humor.

"Damn it, I expected you to call back," he snarled.

"I'm on Japanese time. I just got up a little bit ago. I've been working and recovering from assassination attempts."

"And playing the hot-shot ski heiress," Andrew grumped.

"So? I have a life. Besides, I called you and got Liam. I don't appreciate that."

"He *is* my assistant."

"Assistant what? Butthead?"

Hm. Demoted from spymaster to assistant—or is he controlling Andrew for someone else?

"That's not exactly a professional attitude."

"Well, *excuse* me, but Liam was hardly professional himself. *My* assistant doesn't treat you or anyone else the way Liam did me. Now. What do you want?"

"Get Mom out of here."

"Why?"

"You know why. She's interfering with my government."

Melanie quickly called up a status report on Andrew's confirmation. "Right now, Andrew, you don't have the authority to govern. If anyone does, it's her."

Andrew's lips tightened. "That's what I'm talking about! Do It Right International is interfering with the internal affairs of the North American Confederation!"

"*I'm* not the one interfering." She blinked to check on Diana's status. A new icon flared at her. *She's still going. Good.* "Besides, she's officially the Interim President for the New Federation. Take it up with the New Fed Congress if you have a problem."

"Yeah, yeah, we know who's really driving this cart. You tell her to knock it off." A sneering tone came into his voice. "This is her warning. I've had just enough of her meddling in my internal affairs." Lights started pulsing at her from the screen, the same flickering lights she remembered from the last session with Ness. The spiky sphere glowed in the background.

<*Melanie!* Break off the connection *now*!> Marty bellowed.

A sudden flood of memories cascaded through her brain, a recap of the last few days.

Then Ness was in her brain along with Marty, flashing out through her own eyes, forcing Andrew—*dear God, he looks like Peter*—back. The sphere disappeared. Everything went black and the memories shut off.

She blinked. <Marty? Ness?>

No response, as the world slowly returned into focus around her. Cold sweat trickled down the base of her neck and her hands clamped tightly on the arms of her chair.

Just what the hell was that?

<Mel.> Marty's voice. <You okay?>

<I think so.>

<I'm on my way. If he calls back, don't take it. Don't use Dialogue at all. Not until I've checked you. I'm talking to your dad, *now!*>

She sensed him breaking into a run.

"Janine?" she said through the speaker.

"Yes, Melanie?" Janine sounded surprised at the audio call. "You're not messaging?"

"No. No Dialogue until Marty approves. Listen. If Andrew calls back, I'm in a meeting. Okay?"

"Got it."

She fell back in her chair, trembling as she finally was able to unclamp her hands.

What the hell is going on?

Marty burst through her door. He skidded to a stop next to her chair and dropped to his knees.

"Look here," he demanded, holding up a scanner while he leaned over to peer in her eyes. "Blink. Up. Down. Left. Right."

Dialogue failure diagnostic.

That set off another attack of trembling.

He rested one hand on hers. "It's okay. It's going to be okay. You check out fine. Easy now." The fear and tension in his voice belied the soothing words.

"What happened?"

"Peter has him. No question about it. Peter tried to get *you*. And your dad thinks Andrew's tied into the gadget somehow, not directly or it would have come after you."

"But how?"

"The light flashes are the key. A hypnotic signal to trigger a reaction sequence in a Dialogue, and probably whatever analogue they have. Thank God I put those fail-safes in before we regenerated our chips.

The memory cascade was the first phase of the attack. Thank God I was talking to Ness when it happened. *She* recognized it and responded."

"How did Ness get into the connection? Is she working with him?"

Marty shook his head. "I don't have a clue. She was just *there*, Mel. She shut Peter down, and I'm hoping she nailed him hard."

"You mean she confronted him?"

"Yeah. Barged through my link to you, shut down his signal and I think did more damage than that. Then she returned."

"I thought you had her isolated."

"So did I. At least she came back."

"We *have* to talk to Ness. We need to know more about what's going on," Melanie said grimly.

Marty helped her up, pulling her close for a tight hug. She leaned hard into him, reassured by his presence.

"NESS HAS BEEN DEMANDING TO TALK TO YOU EVER SINCE MARTY BLEW out of here," Will said as they came into his office. "Fortunately, it looks like the gadget's not directly a factor. Melanie, you wouldn't be on your feet if the gadget were after you."

"She's clear," Marty said. "No damage."

"Good. Let's talk to Ness."

Melanie twined her fingers with Marty's as they walked into the lab. Ness paced back and forth, brighter than ever. Her ruined face was distinct in every feature now, sparing them only the blood.

"What the hell's going on, Ness?" Marty demanded.

"They're moving. They're going to attack Diana," Ness said out loud, her voice clearer than before. "It's harder because she's staying offline, but they're trying to locate her."

"How do you know this? For that matter, *how did you attack Peter?"* Melanie asked.

Ness shook her head. "Memories are coming back, Melanie. There's a tiny trace of me in that upload that links you and me. Kill it. Now. It leaves you wide open to attacks like Peter's. Or me, if I were a predatory sort." Her pacing sped up. "So much to share. So much to tell you. Peter has Andrew. Or had him. Thank God you linked with Marty; I was able to piggyback through him to nail Peter. Andrew's not his primary host, and neither of them are directly tied into the gadget. They're pulling on it in some way I don't see clearly. Have you been briefed on it yet?

"No," Melanie said. "I have to talk to Mom or Kathy Miller—and they're in North America. We're in Japan."

"Okay. Somehow, Peter and Sarah are doing a dual host thing. I don't recognize that aspect of their technology. But." A fiendish grin twisted her lips. "I was able to get *some* payback for what Peter did to me. That set their plans back, and they don't know how good I am. Still. And with you two, I'm even better."

"Thank you for stopping Peter. But how did you know he was doing that? How do you know their plans?" Melanie repeated.

"That light flash is a common cue they use for their implants, followed by the gadget image. And unfortunately, it also transfers directly across to Dialogue. Similar programming. Marty and I were talking about that when Andrew called. As for the plans, I stole them. When I blasted Peter apart. He's not very sophisticated at hiding his information. Andrew's not in very good shape, either. Their implants aren't as good as our Dialogues, and he's hurting. I hit them hard, as hard as I could without a full host link." She paced faster than ever, her image blurring. "We can't waste any time. They're planning to launch a full online war on us, as soon as they upload more personalities. They'll kill people to get their shock troops. They have at least twenty uploads in readiness."

Marty held up a hand. "Ness. Slow down. We need as much data as you can give, but it has to be in a form that we can process."

"We *have* to stop that shadow. It's Sarah. So far, every one of their uploads are linked to her. What you've done has split me off from her and Peter so that I'm my own person now. Peter belongs to the gadget but Sarah doesn't. There's some sort of war going on there."

"That's interesting," Melanie said.

"It gives us leverage," Ness said. "Thank you. I'm sorry I've done so much damage to you. I know how we can set up a cleaner Netwalk transfer process." She quivered, pulsing brighter. "That attack brought me fully back, but damn it, we have so little time! I wish I could have gotten away alive! I can think faster, move faster, like this, but *we've lost so damn much time getting me back again!"*

<This is what she was like before the end. Manic. Spilling info constantly to me,> Marty told Melanie.

She nodded. "Ness, we need to be cautious about this. They may have their twenty uploads, but how many of them will be sane and functioning?"

"They won't *need* sane and functioning," Ness said. "Sarah draws on the captive uploads for energy so she stays free from a host. Peter goes back and forth between drawing on Sarah for power and charging in Andrew. And he has another living host. Andrew's his primary living host, but Peter's upload isn't that strong. Not like hers. When I hit him and Andrew, Peter had to run back to Sarah to recharge. Or to his other living host. I can't tell."

"*Another* living host?" Marty scowled. "How does that work?"

"I wish I knew more. There are at least three models of Netwalk. Do It Right, National Security, and this mysterious third version. Peter can't feed off of the other uploads independently of Sarah because she's locked them all to her. That's why you need to kill your upload, Mel. I don't want you accidentally harnessing it to me, and that will happen if you don't kill it. It's just too easy to do."

"How?" Melanie asked.

"Both the National Security model and this unknown version of Netwalk are based on a structure of a primary, controlling Netwalker who dominates their living host and weaker uploads. Andrew is one of their harnessed hosts. Other victims are the weaker uploads—and I left you open to that process, damn it. Unavoidable because I'm created on the National Security template."

Melanie shuddered. "Does our version have that structure?"

"No. I *like* the Netwalk process that you've been developing."

Will frowned. "Just how aware are you of what's been going on?"

"I've been picking up bits and pieces of data leakages. Another reason to stick me in a host. That contains a Netwalker more than if they're free."

"How can I trust what you say?" Will asked.

"You can't. Not really, not like this. I can download what I know, but you need to check it. It's urgent. I'm worried that they'll go after Diana. She can't do any more online communication. It's not safe for her. *You have to tell her that!*"

"I'll message her. Is there any way you can download the plans and other information we need to know? We can split it up, put different groups to work on parts of it, get things assimilated faster," Melanie said.

Ness nodded. "Doing that now. But get me into a host and kill that upload."

"You are aware that your host will be one of us, right?" Marty asked.

"It should be you, Marty," Ness said. "You'll be more useful to Melanie when you host me, and it's unexpected. They'd expect her to be my host. Not you."

"But our past relationship might be a clue."

"It's not something *they* would do."

"Ness, you won't be getting *me* back. You know that. Melanie has a right to be worried if you go into me."

"Marty. Hon. I can't have that kind of relationship anymore, not with anyone who's flesh and blood. I'm *glad* you have Melanie. I'm not interested in human relationships. I just need a host to be effective. I want to make Peter and Sarah pay for what they've done to me. To you. To a lot of other people."

"I—have to do some things before I can go through the host process. Download what you can, all right?"

Ness nodded. "Give me an address, and I'll start downloading."

"Here it is." Marty tapped out a code. "I'll text Julia and let her know it's coming in. You'll organize it?"

"Yes. I'll start with the Stephens plan, then the data on their version of Netwalk. Hurry, Marty. Sarah's in full hunt mode. And Melanie, *kill that upload before much longer!*"

"Do you have any recommendations?" Melanie asked her.

"You and Marty do it together. Don't download it back into yourself."

"How the hell would I do that, even if I wanted to? I can't even tell you how I uploaded it, much less how I'd download it into myself."

"Herd it into a storage chip. It'll listen to simple, basic commands. Then short out the chip. Incinerate the chip after you short it out. You should know if it worked because killing your own upload will make you feel like you've been run over by a freight train and had your brain sucked out." Ness made a sour face. "Sarah made me do it to at least five of my uploads. You won't be good for anything much else today. Sorry. It's the safest way I know of to kill an upload."

"We'll do our best," Melanie promised.

"Good. Get this solved. I'm free from Sarah and Peter now. I don't want to be harnessed to them for the rest of whatever electronic time I have left!"

Ness's shape drifted into a red cloud, and hovered over the hologlobe next to her cage. Then the cloud formed a slender gray thread, tying into the globe.

"Data's feeding to Julia," Marty said. "Let's go."

Once again, they filed into Will's office.

"Do you think she's reliable?" Will asked. "I have to depend on your judgment. Both of you also know her better than I do. Did."

"I think she's straightforward," Melanie said. "If she hadn't been, I don't think she'd have stopped the link during our last contact, or returned after hammering Peter. Marty?"

"Her behavior patterns fit the way she was at the end. Loaded with information, and too little time to pass it all on."

"What do you think about her plan to kill my upload?" Melanie asked.

Marty shrugged. "It makes sense. It does worry me that killing the upload should have that great an impact on you. But if that upload leaves you as vulnerable as she says, it's not safe for you to use Dialogue until you kill it. Especially after that encounter with Peter."

Melanie took a deep breath. "Then let's get going. You and Dad check the data. Tomorrow morning, let's make the decision about the Netwalk hosting issue."

"So fast?" Will asked.

Marty stirred, sighing. "I don't see a lot of options."

"Okay," she said to Marty. "Let's kill an upload."

THE UPLOAD DIDN'T WANT TO BE KILLED.

Even with all the precautions, including isolating the upload into a secured hologlobe, *it* resisted their efforts to drive *it* into a sacrificial chip.

<We need to create a chip that sucks the damn uploads in,> Marty said at one point while they took a break, the upload bouncing against the far side of the globe from Melanie and Marty. <An attractant. A trap door chip. Something that can catch rogue Netwalkers as well as uploads we want to kill.>

<Sounds like a good idea. Not that it helps us right now. I wish Ness had gone into more detail about this process!> Melanie dove for the upload as *it* slowed, *finally* getting her hands on *it.*

The upload stung her repeatedly as she dragged *it* over to the chip. She and Marty needed to shove *it* into the chip together.

"Considering what Ness said about how this is going to make you feel, you'd better sit down," Marty said as they emerged from the hologlobe. He held the chip gingerly between thumb and forefinger.

Melanie laughed wryly, shaking her head. "Not gonna fight the suggestion. I already feel wiped out." She dropped into one of the computer chairs, pulling down the arms.

Marty delicately initiated the shorting-out process. Melanie gulped as *something* slugged her in the gut. She bent over, clutching the chair arms as *heaviness* dropped over her.

"Are you all right?" Marty's voice seemed to come from far away.

Melanie waved her fingers—lifting her hand felt too hard. "Don't—stop." She panted as the *heaviness* increased.

Then it lifted. She straightened up, gasping.

"God. You're all right? That's just the short—what's the destruction gonna do?"

Melanie nodded. "Ness survived the process. I can too. Just get it done!"

Marty tightened his lips. He switched on the lab's small incinerator, letting it heat up. Then he fitted the chip into a pair of tongs, and put the chip inside.

Heat. Heat. Burn. Burn. Melanie shrieked as agony flashed through her.

And then it lifted, leaving her sweaty, wrung out, and barely able to lift her fingers.

"Shit. This is—we have to find a better means of handling uploads," Marty muttered. He went outside the lab and brought the waiting floater inside—they had both decided it was safer to have it outside of the lab, not inside. Just in case something happened to screw up its programming. "Now I know why I found Ness crashed in the labs. Five times."

Every part of her body ached as Marty helped her onto the floater. Melanie closed her eyes as he guided it to their quarters. When they got there, Marty tucked her into bed, plying her with fruit drink and protein snacks after she settled in. This time he added a painkiller.

"Your Dialogue's still functioning, so I don't need to worry about the painkiller interfering with the integration process." he said. "Going back to the labs now. Call me if there's an issue."

"Thanks."

Had Ness had underestimated the effect of killing the upload? She hurt all over; her stomach queasy, head throbbing, and joints aching. Melanie lay in bed, waiting for the painkiller to take effect so she could fall sleep.

But sleep evaded her. The painkiller kicked in. The easing of pain had the paradoxical effect of spinning her brain into action instead of easing her into sleep. She kept visualizing potential scenarios. At last, Melanie got up, staggered into the living area, and turned on the video. If she couldn't sleep, maybe she could keep her brain distracted.

She was deep into the plot twists and turns of an anime classic when the first jolt hit her brain. It was a sharp, hard thud, like the one she felt when Joseph's Ghost spun into action. She sat upright.

What was happening now?

A second jolt.

<MELANIE!> Will's panicked, subvocal voice hit her Dialogue, and jerked her into sudden, frantic motion. She threw on shirt and pants.

Then she ran from her quarters, all fatigue gone, driven by the urgency in that one call.

Melanie gasped for breath as she skidded to a stop at the door of Will's lab. Marty was already there, wrestling with the door handle, futilely flinging himself against the door.

"I can't get it open! Autolock has kicked in!" He groaned. "Security's on their way; whatever happened didn't trigger their alerts."

"Let me try my access." Melanie kept her voice quiet—no need for *both* of them to panic, and if Marty's accesses as Head of Research didn't work—surely *her* access as International DIR President would work, wouldn't it?

If not, then they were *really* in trouble.

Thankfully, the door yielded to her universal code, and they burst into the lab.

Ness raged in a small hologlobe, pacing back and forth, oscillating between a red cloud and her human shape, her thin screech whining from the globe. A black cloud swarmed over Will's limp body. Blood spurted from his torn throat and smashed head.

Melanie darted forward, but Marty held her back.

"Mel. *Don't.*"

"That's Sarah!" she yelled.

Marty gestured to Ness while grabbing a dataglove and tapping up a hologlobe that swelled to take in the room.

"Set Ness loose. She's the only decent tool we have! Link up with me in Netwalk after. It may take all of us. Call Julia and get the crew down here, NOW!"

With fumbling fingers Melanie tapped Ness's hologlobe to free her. Ness transformed into the red cloud as Marty faced her, dataglove raised high. The red cloud shaped itself around the glove.

Melanie frantically messaged Julia for help.

Once she got a response, she turned back to her father.

<Netwalk access!> she subvocaled to her Dialogue.

Immediately she was flung back into that brightly colored schematic world. Lights flashed, but she disregarded them, searching frantically for Ness and Marty.

There they were!

Ness was still a red cloud, while Marty took the avatar of a big, shambling bear that roared and swatted at the black cloud that sat on Will's chest. The black cloud devoured memories—pictures, music, voices, more—that swirled out of the exposed sections of his brain.

Melanie threw herself next to Marty, not sure what her shape was, or even if she had a separate form. She tried to touch Marty, hoping to link up and help him through her touch but he moved too fast.

What the hell can I do?

Help Dad.

She turned to Will.

Memory cascade is a part of the attack. What can I do to stop it?

She knelt beside his head, trying to keep the memories from the black cloud. To her surprise, she could seize them in her hands. Melanie caught one and slapped it back into his brain. Then another, and another. At last, she was able to block the escape route off and keep the rest inside. The others were gone, but at least she had saved this much. She moved her hands over his head, a blue glow forming which seemed to stop the escaping remembrances, though they roiled underneath the glow.

Shadow roared at her. She startled, staring deep into the heart of it, rocking back on her heels but still keeping her hands in position. The spiky sphere flashed at her but it felt toothless, like the other appearances.

You have no power over me!

The sphere winked out. The black cloud took a shape. Sarah in human form looked back at her. Her face twisted into a gargoyle-like rictus as she raked out at Melanie with glowing neon-red fingernails. Shards of the stealthsuit she had been wearing when she died hung from her skeletal body.

Melanie held strong, keeping her hands tight on her father's head, staring Sarah down as she ducked the fingernails.

I will not yield. I will not let you do this to him.

She dared not move her hands from Will's head. The blue glow was so fragile. She didn't dare let it slip. One of Sarah's fingernails whacked her face, and she flinched but did not move, trusting that Ness and Marty would find a means to protect her.

I will not let you bully me. I will not yield to you.

She stared at Sarah, holding firm.

Ness took the shape of a screaming falcon that dived hard on Sarah, hitting her with talons and beak. Marty knelt beside Melanie. He leaned forward, growling and *pushing* on Sarah.

Sarah's form started to shrink.

Melanie followed Marty's lead, *pushing* with one hand while protecting her father with the other. She was faintly aware of the distant presence of Julia and her team, touching her, lending her power and strength. She used their freely given power to throw at Sarah.

Sarah's shape collapsed into the black cloud. Then the cloud receded, retreating down a tunnel until it faded. The falcon followed it for a short distance, screaming, until Marty—once again human—whistled it back. It landed on his shoulder, preened, then slid off and became the red cloud around Marty's datagloved hand. Then the red cloud retreated to a corner, becoming Ness again.

<Netwalk off,> Melanie whispered to her Dialogue.

Slowly, the lab shimmered back into place around her. She and Marty knelt by Will's still body, her hands on his broken head as Julia and the other techs worked on him. Marty pulled Melanie away from her father. Julia took her place.

<Nothing more we can do. Let's get out of their way.>

<Is he?> She couldn't say anything more, either silently or verbally.

Marty shook his head. <It's bad, hon. It's bad. That head injury—> He wrapped his arms around Melanie and held her close as she collapsed against him. He rocked her gently back and forth as her shivering increased, stroking her back.

<If only we'd gone for Netwalk sooner. If only I'd tried to stop the memory cascade sooner. If only—>

"Shh. Shh." Marty said aloud. "We could have done all that and it wouldn't have made a difference."

She turned her head slightly to watch Julia and her team work. <Did he upload?>

<I think so. We'll ask Ness to look for him.>

<Would there have been enough time for him to find a safe place, or did Sarah get him?>

<I don't think she got him. Hey! Something's happening.>

Julia suddenly stiffened, her eyes going wide. She pressed both hands to Will's temples as he convulsed.

"Ness," Melanie croaked. "Help. What's happening?"

"Oh my God," Marty whispered. "It's a direct Netwalk transfer. They've figured something out! But how?"

Will's body sagged. Julia toppled to one side, staring up, her eyes blinking rapidly. Marty let go of Melanie and crossed over to Julia. The rest of Julia's team tried to resuscitate Will, while Marty worked on Julia.

"Ness," Melanie whispered.

"Can't do much," a whispery electronic voice came from beside her. "T-tired. P-process."

"What's happening?"

"D-dead. They t-tried transfer. S-sneaky bu-bastard! Will. Pumped me. Got info. Told Julia earlier today. Can't tell. If it worked. Yet. Might be. Better. For Marty. For Dialogues. S-sorry. Process." The cloud winked out.

Reiko finally looked over at Melanie. "I'm sorry. I think we can keep on doing this from now until forever with the same result. He's gone. I'm sorry."

Melanie shook her head. She crawled over, shut her father's staring eyes, stroked what remained of his forehead, gently picked up his lifeless hand. A hand she'd clung to as a child. A hand that had wiped away tears, had guided her first steps, held up her up on her first skis. Once strong and powerful, it was so frail and fragile now.

I failed you, Mom. I couldn't keep him safe until you were back!

Now the tears came. She dropped her head on her father's chest and sobbed.

Marty lifted her from her father's body when she was cried out.

"It worked." His face was pale and drawn, but his lips were set firmly. "Your dad's traumatized, but Julia got him and he's orienting fast. Nothing like Ness. We have the trick of it now. I plan to review the process, with Ness's help, and then we're going to train every damned Dialogue on how to perform a Netwalk transfer, whether as host or Netwalker." He raised his voice as he held Melanie tight. "All of you. Listen." He paused. "Will is dead. But not completely. He's a Netwalker now, with Julia."

Murmurs arose.

"I speak as your Head of Research. This is war. We were attacked in our own labs. From now on, this is what we do. Datasuits on at all times for everyone, not just crucial personnel. Monitor each other. We don't dare be alone in case of an attack."

"His throat, how can a virtual being rip someone's throat?" Reiko looked up from working on Julia. "And smash his head? How can we stop that?"

"We don't have an answer to that yet," Marty said. "But we will learn." He inhaled deeply. "We didn't lose Will. He's dead but we have him as a Netwalker. I swear to you, *we will not lose anyone.* We will all learn how to run Netwalk as hosts or as Netwalkers. We will destroy Sarah and her pack of Netwalkers. *We will win this war.*"

"What do we do?" Reiko asked.

Marty glanced at Melanie. She nodded. "It's your lab. You're in charge." She swallowed hard, tears forming in her eyes once again.

Dad's gone.

She fought back the howling cry that wanted to break free from her lips.

"Reiko. Take care of Julia. Standard Dialogue regeneration treatment. David. Contact Janine and have her prepare a statement about Will's death, but not release it until Melanie's had time to review it. Ken. Can you help Melanie by getting funeral preparations started?"

Melanie tuned out the rest of Marty's directions.

Dad's dead. Her gaze kept straying toward Will's body. *He's dead.*

Marty kissed her forehead. "We're almost done. Can you hold up for one more thing?"

"What?" She raised her head, tears blurring her eyes.

"I need you to monitor the Netwalk transfer for me and Ness. We should have done it earlier. Maybe things would have turned out differently if we had already been Netwalker and host—maybe I could have gotten into the lab sooner, stopped Sarah."

"It's not your fault," she whispered. "Don't blame yourself."

"Maybe. But I don't want to risk it any longer. We need Ness's data and input. *I* need her input as a Netwalker."

"She's pretty wiped out, went to process. Will that be a problem?"

Marty shook his head.

"What do I need to do?"

"I'll send you a checklist."

The icon was blue. Melanie blinked it open, the instructions overlaying her vision as she helped him settle on the floor. She brought Ness's hologlobe over and sat down next to Marty.

"You ready?" she asked.

He nodded, clenching his teeth slightly. "As ready as I'll ever be. Better get me a mouth guard before we start. I'm afraid of biting my cheek or tongue during the process. Julia did."

"Do you know where they are?"

"Top drawer, over there." He pointed toward a storage cabinet. Melanie got a guard and handed it to Marty. He inserted the mouth guard, settled it in, then nodded.

She sat down again and took his hand. "Ready?" she asked again.

Marty nodded.

Melanie snapped the globe open. Ness-as-red-cloud stirred as the globe enveloped the three of them.

<Ness, it's time. Go into Marty's chip,> she ordered.

The red cloud responded by pulsing at her.

<Ness, let's do it>

<She may not be able to move very quickly,> Marty said.

<What should I do?>

<Try touching her.> He grimaced. <Not perfect. Keep it to a minimum. She'll drain you in this mode.>

<How about the dataglove we used before?>

<If you can find it.> He lifted one hand. <I'll try to lure her over. I'm surprised. You'd think she'd be eager to join up.>

<Maybe because she's drained.> Melanie got up. <Be right back.>

<Hurry.>

<I will.>

Luckily, she remembered where Will put the dataglove. Melanie slipped it on and hurried back inside the globe.

It didn't take much to get the red cloud moving. A light touch, and Ness stirred forward a couple of feet. A second touch, and she moved closer to Marty. By the third touch, Ness formed a tiny, vaguely humanoid shape, still bright red, and crawled toward Marty. Melanie scooped her up in the datagloved hand and held her next to Marty's chip site. Ness pressed miniature red hands against his head, nodded to herself as they disappeared, then lowered her head and pushed on in. Melanie shivered as Ness's feet finally disappeared from sight.

Marty stiffened, jerking. Melanie took his hand. Wordless experiences flooded over her.

Memory cascade!

Something was wrong—Melanie grabbed at one fleeting thought.

<No.> Marty stopped her. <Part of process. I'm in control.>

She instinctively slipped into Netwalk to monitor the rest of their integration. Soon she spotted the patterns as Ness carefully overlaid her memories and self into Marty's chip. Before long, she helped Ness tuck strands and pieces of herself into the chip's circuitry.

At last, they were done. Ness settled into a tiny piece of the chip schematic and slowly turned into a faint, blinking red light.

Melanie exited Netwalk and helped Marty to his feet. Summoned a floater for him. Guided him to their quarters. Got him settled in bed, after pouring fruit drink down his throat and urging him to eat protein snacks. Melanie sighed and unsnapped her shirt, fatigue from this hell of a day finally, *finally* exhausting her.

"I'm beat but I can't sleep," he said.

She curled up against him. "That's okay. Just hold me. Please."

This time she was able to drop off into sleep.

CHAPTER 11

MELANIE SLUMPED IN HER DESK CHAIR, STARING AT HER MOTHER'S LATEST text.

Mel, I hear your worries about your father. He made me swear not to tell you, but the cancer's back. He's in a race against time. He won't give me the details either, if that's any help. Do what you can. Find a way to help Andrew and shut down that shadow. I feel it coming after me in the dark. Make further contact through Kathy. Good luck.

She sighed.

Damn it, Dad!

But now she had to break *this* news to her mother. How? The news of her father's death had hit the media by now. Diana would expect it to be the cancer progressing more quickly than expected. Telling her that it was murder, that Sarah had struck from beyond the grave, was going to be *hard*.

Especially after reading the condolences pouring in from around the world.

Will Landreth had been admired and respected.

Melanie had never considered her father to be as prominent as her mother. He was always in the shadows while Diana was the public face of the company. To her, his focus had been fiddling with security devices as well as other tech. Nothing that particularly attracted attention. Not as spectacular as Do It Right's bioremediation bots.

But he was just as well-regarded in his circles as her mother was in hers. Circles that valued his covert knowledge.

Bigger issues. How was Diana going to react to the reality that Will was now a Netwalker residing in Julia's chip?

Melanie's feelings about Ness tucked inside of Marty's chip were confusing enough. After last night, and this morning, she was certain that the boundaries between Ness the Netwalker and Marty would hold, but it was an intellectual certainty, not an emotional one.

Can I entirely trust her? Trust them?

Her mother also needed to know about the urgency of training North American Dialogues in Netwalk procedures.

And I damned well need to know about that damned gadget. I don't like the way it keeps popping up.

At last, she called up the address for Kathy Miller. She typed into a keypad instead of subvocaling, giving herself time to think about her words as she wrote.

Mom. You've heard about Dad by now. Here's what happened.

She paused, thinking hard about what to say. Then she remembered Marty's words.

He went down fighting. It wasn't the cancer. He was attacked, by the shadow. It's Sarah. I saw her myself.

Now here came the hard part.

Dad got enough information from Ness before the attack to devise and implement a Netwalk upload, different from what National Security and Ness created, in a way we had not thought possible. His current host is Julia Hawkins.

She chewed her lip, considering her next words.

We are training every Dialogue in the Netwalk transfer procedures he discovered. I will contact you about training North American Dialogues, when we know more.

She pushed send.

The funeral was the next thing on her to-do list. Preparations were based on a detailed plan Will prepared six months ago. Online feedback criticizing the speed with which she arranged the ceremony, and the smallness of it had already come her way. Melanie reviewed the public statement she had written earlier in the day, a revision of Janine's draft.

The Landreth family, and myself in particular, do not have the emotional energy for a long, protracted public ceremony to commemorate Will Landreth's death. I understand many of you loved and respected my father. Please feel free to memorialize his death in any manner that fits that love and respect. This service was requested by my father, and designed by him. For better or worse, I am complying with his wishes. Melanie Landreth.

His planning had foregone the traditional wake. She was grateful, because a wake was more than she could handle. Melanie reread her statement, and nodded, changing "do not have" to "lack". Then she pushed "send," with universal distribution. Maybe that would keep the complaints at a lower volume.

Next came dealing with Netwalk. Setting the training protocols for Netwalk took more time than they had anticipated. She skimmed the latest update describing current training status, frowning.

So many issues.

But the biggest one was that Dialogue upgrades were taking longer than originally planned. Participants needed down time for regeneration after upgrades before they could begin the training, more than anyone realized. How on earth had so many Dialogue users, especially in lab settings, avoided necessary upgrades?

Why? Complications? How do we make the need for consistent, regular upgrades attractive?

If implementing full Netwalk procedures provided this many challenges in Nagano and Rio, where Do It Right had full labs, then just how tough was it going to be in North America, where they would have to do it in the field, without lab facilities? Almost impossible to hope that upgrade discipline had been better in the field.

And yet it was entirely possible, after all, that the Dialogues in the field had kept up with maintenance. After all, *she* routinely kept updated, out of security concerns. Entirely likely that their field workers felt the same way. This might be one case where the field was in better shape than the labs—but there was no way to know for certain, until they were out there.

One issue that Marty was wrestling with.

And he's not going to North America alone. I'm going with him.

Supporting Marty was one reason for her decision. Confronting her mother and Kathy about that damned gadget was another.

<Melanie?> Janine texted. <Andrew. For you. Old-style behavior.>

<I'll take. Wait.> Just to be cautious, she signaled Marty, and waited until she felt his presence before opening the connection.

<Ness is on alert,> he told her.

<Thanks>.

She snapped the link open, in a protective globe to minimize any Netwalker tricks.

"Andrew." Melanie choked back her shock at his appearance.

He stared at her instead of responding right away. Dirty, oily blond hair coiling every which way instead of clean and neatly corralled into place. Stained, wrinkled shirt.

Andrew never appeared like that. *Never.* He would change shirts three times a day rather than look disarrayed. Under normal circumstances he would *never* appear with his hair dirty and oily. Even as a teen, Andrew had been meticulous about his grooming.

"You should have let Sarah take him!" he snapped. "Then we'd still have access to what he knew!"

"Just how the hell do you know the way he died?" A disappointed chill ran down her spine. It was one thing to know what Andrew was, and what he knew, but another to hear him confirm it like this.

He's not mourning Dad, but the loss of a Netwalker. Drew, couldn't you be human for once?

Andrew ignored her. "He's gone. All that knowledge and skill is gone. And him. Who and what he was. Gone. He's *gone.*" He shook his head.

"Andrew. Listen to me. *How do you think he died?*"

Is he really mourning Dad or does he just want what Dad knew?

Andrew stared at her for a moment. "Why—um—cancer, right?"

"You're a shitty liar. Why would you want her to have taken him? What else did Sarah tell you?"

They stared at each other. Then Andrew slumped back in his chair, looking down and leaning his forehead on his right hand as he shook his head.

He rubbed his eyes, sighed, and raised his head, his lips tightening as he met her gaze again. "How long have you known about Netwalk?" he asked.

Melanie raised a brow. "At least you're using the same terms we are. Two weeks. Maybe longer."

A wry smile twisted his lips. "About the same here for your Dialogue. We've suspected for longer, but Sarah confirmed it."

"You know she killed Dad. Did she tell you that?"

Andrew shivered. "I try to talk to *her* as little as possible. I'm not her host. Thank God she's not interested in me that way. She has no living host. She doesn't want a living host. She wants mindless energy slaves." He shuddered again. "Seriously. But she, God, she was in a mood after losing Dad. Bad enough with Peter. Your blowing him out of me was the confirmation of your Dialogue. That was the only thing my people could think of that could have had that level of impact on him."

"She's predatory, Andrew. So is Peter." *Andrew isn't even hinting at the gadget. I guess that's a good thing.* "And he has other help."

"I know. God, do I ever know that. But if you had let her take him, we would still have something of him in a safe repository, out of Peter's reach and the—" Andrew stopped.

"What do you know about the gadget?" Melanie asked.

Andrew paled and his eyes widened. He looked around. "Mel, if it comes down to Peter versus Sarah when it comes to the gadget, you want to bet on Sarah."

"What do you know about it?"

"Not enough and too much." Andrew licked his lips nervously. "No more than it's tied into the Corporate Courts. Mel, it's not involved except with Peter!" He flinched. "That's all I can say. Meanwhile, we've not just lost Dad's skills, we've lost *him.*"

"I wouldn't let Dad within a mile of *her*, especially the way she is now," Melanie said.

Andrew looked confused. "What do you mean?"

"*We* have him. The transfer was successful. It was one hell of a fight against *her*, though."

"You *have* him?" A faint smile touched Andrew's lips.

"Successful Netwalk transfer."

"But how?"

She smiled at him, baring her teeth. "We also have Ness Ryan. Surprised?"

Andrew shook his head. But the faint smile was still there.

"Drew. Make a run for it while you can, before Peter gets back to you. We'll help you get rid of him. We'll figure out a way. I know more about your situation than you realize."

Listen, big brother. Please. Listen to me.

"I'm in too deep," he said. "Too much at stake in Stephens Reclamation and in the Confederation. They would kill me before I could reach you." He hesitated. "Liam, well, he's my minder. You probably suspect that already."

"Who is he working for?"

Andrew winced. "I've told you too much already. But not—*our*—dead."

Our dead? Peter and Sarah. But if Liam wasn't working for Peter and Sarah, then who pulled his strings? There was one other option.

No. He couldn't be. Melanie shook her head even as Andrew's stricken look answered her question.

"Let me guess. Liam's part of the Freedom Army," she said. "That assassination attempt on me. Yeah. Liam's doing in your name, right?"

"I've told you too much already," Andrew repeated, relief softening his face. "But yeah. He's the head of the Freedom Army. He's tied to the gadget. And Peter. Dear God, Mel," he gulped, glancing around furtively. "One last thing. They're getting close to Mom. *Liam's* blacksuits, not the few I still control. They'll let Sarah take Mom, force an upload. Then kill her. At least I'm hoping it's Sarah and not Peter who takes Mom. She'll at least be benevolent. In comparison."

"*No.* You can't let them do that, Andrew! You know what that means!"

"Yeah. I do. And I have no control over it." He looked sick. "It's *his* deal, Mel."

"Liam?"

"No. *Him.*"

Her skin crawled as she realized who he was talking about. Peter.

I can't leave Drew in that snake pit. Even if he is a son-of-a-bitching jerk. He's my brother. I can't let this happen.

"Andrew." She reached over to her hologlobe, began calculating. "Drop everything. Make a break for it." She frowned at the globe, then nodded. "You can do it if you move fast enough. *I can help you.* Together we can stop them."

Andrew swallowed hard, glancing down and dropping his chin to his chest. Then he raised his head. His mouth twisted and his eyes glistened, and for a moment her brother reminded her of a lost and despairing child ready to burst into tears.

"I *can't,*" he whispered. "I just *can't,* Mel. It's too late. For me. For everything. I don't know how long I have before *he* comes back. If *he* finds me before I get to you, it's too late, even if I'm on the run. He won't just kill me. He'll upload me. No. I can't. Do what you can. I know you will."

The screen winked out. She slammed her fists on the desk.

"Damn it!" she said aloud. "Damn it, damn it, *damn it*!" She drew a deep breath. There had to be a way around this.

<Can we get a warning to Mom without catching their attention? Use Ness, perhaps?> she asked Marty.

<Too much electromagnetic flux over the North American continent.>

<I definitely need to go with you. Damn it all, I'm not going to sit here and let them take her!>

<Mel, think about it.>

<Mel, if we go off half-ready, we're screwed.>

<Andrew gave us a chance, Marty!> She chewed on her right thumb, thinking back to Andrew's behavior, Andrew's words. <He took the risk to give us this information. I'm not letting that go to waste. Put together a team. *I'll* talk to the Board and figure out who'll be in charge here while I'm gone. *You,* Angela, and Nik figure out how we're getting over there unobserved, and how quickly we can track Mom down. We leave after Dad's funeral this afternoon.>

She half-expected Marty to argue further, but he winked out of her brain instead. For a moment, she stared at the wall, wondering if she'd made a wise decision.

Then, hoping against hope, she toggled her mother's link to see if there was a text response yet. A blue icon flashed. She blinked on it.

Melanie. This is Kathy. I'm sorry about your father. I'll get the news to Diana when I can. We had to split up. She's running hard, under complete silence, with her Dialogue completely off. Those blacksuits are getting too damned close. As far as I know, she's still free.

"That's it," she said aloud. "I am definitely going now."

Take the fight to Sarah.

And Peter? God. If Sarah was less toxic than Peter, then what the hell was her uncle?

Melanie exhaled. Inhaled. Then she started putting together the visible support team to keep things running while she was gone; a team that might need to replace her should the worst happen.

"YOU'RE SURE YOU STILL WANT TO GO?" MARTY ASKED AS THEY DRESSED for the funeral.

She nodded. "Yes. You heard Andrew. You saw the fate Liam and Peter want Mom to have. If you can't send Ness to stop the shadow, I need to go with you."

"I don't think that Ness and Will together could do anything from here."

"I think a direct attack is the only thing that can stop Sarah."

"I just wish you would stay. You and your mother are the last ones left of your family who are free from Sarah's influence. One of you has to stay safe."

She took his hand and shook her head. "I've already been through this argument with the Board, hon. Contingencies were set in place seven years ago, when I became North American Do It Right head, in part due to Mom's age and the risk I faced staying behind. No one's happy about my doing this, but the Board—reluctantly—supports my reasons."

"I suppose I can't overrule the Board." He scowled.

"There's also the personal element. I *can't* stay behind. Not knowing whether you're alive or dead. I'm not that tough. Not like Mom."

And I'm not yet strong enough to leave you alone with Ness.

"But what do we gain by you coming along?"

"I know links and sources that neither you nor Mom would know. Other help I've cultivated over the years in North America. Personal connections. I don't know that they'd work for anyone but me."

Marty sighed. "So you and the Board set up contingencies? Won't people notice you're gone?"

She nodded. "A governing body will manage things and issue orders in my name. We're not publicizing my absence. Wouldn't be the first time the Board has done something like that. Mom has needed to go dark several times in the past. So has Dad. Routines are in place."

"All right." He kissed her. "I confess, even though I'm worried, I'm glad you're going to be with me."

"Good. So what's going to be happening?"

Marty rubbed her face. "We decided that the best route is through Free Victoria, then gather information in Portland. Go from there."

"I thought she was organizing in the Midwest."

Portland is a good place to start, though.

"She was, but she's gone even more dark. Those cells aren't talking, but we haven't received failure alerts or any sign that they've been betrayed. If she's running hard, she'll go to places where she has old connections. The Northwest is where she'll be," Marty said. "That's what *my* sources say."

"They'll look for her there, especially up on the Mountain."

"I don't think she'll go there. But that's a line you can check once we arrive."

She nodded, and would have said more, but the chime calling them to Will's service tolled.

WILL'S FUNERAL SERVICE WAS SHORT AND SIMPLE, A VARIATION OF THE standard funeral Mass with Shinto and Buddhist overtones. Melanie steeled herself against emotion, against tears, prepared to face the public scrutiny from the presence of local Do It Right staff, the thirty-or-so dignitaries from Japan, China, and the New Federated government-in-exile who had managed to arrive in time, and the limited press.

She *thought* she was steeled against emotion.

All that went to hell the moment Marty walked Melanie down the aisle of the small chapel.

Pictures sat on Will's simple pine coffin. She couldn't sit until she looked at them.

Marty stood next to her, his hand supporting her back. She looked at each one, tears catching her by surprise. Her parents on their wedding day. Will snowboarding. Melanie as a young child on skis, supported by her father. A formal family portrait of all four of them, taken when she and Andrew were in their early teens. Drew and their father kayaking on Waldo Lake. A recent picture of her parents on a boat, both looking relaxed and happy, laughing. A shot of herself and Will from the past few days, the two of them concentrating on a computer screen.

I'm taking that one to Mom.

Tears blurred her eyes. She needed Marty's hand to guide her to the pew. Melanie fumbled for the kneeler and collapsed on it, resting her head on the back of the pew in front of her. Marty rubbed her back soothingly.

Bells finally drew her away from her tears, as the priest processed down the center aisle, swinging the thurible that emitted stinky smoke as he blessed the attendees. The habits of her occasional Catholic upbringing kicked in and Melanie murmured her way automatically through the responses, unable to stop the tears leaking from her eyes, barely aware of Marty's arm around her.

Oh God. Mom should be here. It shouldn't be like this. Not this way.

She was grateful for the bells that replaced the traditional hymns. If she had to hear any of the traditionals, she'd break worse than she already was.

At last the ceremony was over. No open casket. Marty guided

Melanie through the mechanics of reverence and then to the reception hall, while she worked on regaining her composure.

<You all right?> Marty asked.

She nodded. <I was sandbagged by the pictures, Marty. I didn't think they would hit me that way.>

He gently patted her back. <It's the little things that get you.>

<Yeah.> She leaned into him for a moment, then steeled herself to meet the dignitaries. The Do It Right colleagues would be easier to face. She at least knew them.

To Melanie's surprise, Julia was one of the first to come up to her.

"I'm surprised you came," Melanie said.

Julia squeezed her arm and chuckled, more like Will's than anything Melanie had ever heard from Julia before.

"I couldn't *not* come," she said. "Besides, Will *wanted* to attend his own funeral."

Melanie half-choked, half-snorted the water she'd been sipping.

Julia pounded Melanie's back until she stopped coughing.

"So did he like it?" Melanie was finally able to croak.

Julia grinned. "He had a running commentary going through the whole damned thing. Good and bad. He did appreciate your tears throughout. He was impressed that a tough cookie like you reacted like that."

Tough cookie. Yeah. Riiight, Dad.

"The pictures nailed me. Hard. Every damned one of them, of a family that no longer exists. Did he pick that last one of him and me?"

"Yes, he did." Julia paused, then patted Melanie on the arm, a Will move. "Hang tough, girl. Bring it home, help your mom win, and make him proud." Her tone changed from the slightly deeper note and rhythms of Will to her own lighter cadence. "*I* say, good luck and godspeed, Mel."

"Thanks." Melanie stared after Julia. Then she shook herself and went back to work meeting and greeting, spreading the cover story that Janine had created. She and Marty were supposed to be leaving for an exclusive hot springs resort right after the reception. Purportedly this was for an upper-level Do It Right management retreat, intended to consider the impacts of Will's death and Diana's continued absence / possible disappearance on the company.

That bought them a little bit of time, at least. Melanie had recorded statements to cover contingencies. Diana's death. *Her* death. Disability of either her or her mother, both short-term and permanent. Diana's successful takeover of the North American Confederation. Announcing her own death had been the weirdest of all—but she hoped it wasn't needed.

Marty caught her eye, after an hour or so of social interaction. <Time to head out.>

<All right.> Melanie made one last round of the room to ensure she met with everyone important. Instead of heading for their quarters, they went to Marty's lab, where their travel equipment was stashed. Angela waited for them.

"Ready to kick some ass?" Melanie asked Angela.

Angela's dark eyes twinkled. "I'm more than ready. I want to check up on Mama and Sophie, and eat some good tamales. Too much fake raw fish here."

"Save me some of your mama's chicken tamales. I miss her." Melanie hurried into the changing area.

<Hey. It's me,> Marty said.

<Come in.>

Marty slipped in, tubes in one hand. His face looked darker, more swarthy, almost African instead of his typical Native American.

"We need to make you less obvious. This isn't fancy, and won't hold up under a lot of scrutiny, but it's better than nothing. You're already brown-haired, and we'll give you skin to match. Pigment nanos that spread through your system through facial application, within five minutes. We have to apply it nightly. Supposed to last forty-eight hours, but I don't want to risk it."

"How are we getting in?"

"Free Victoria, then a skimmer drop to a Makah fishing boat. They'll truck us to Portland."

She started to nod, then stopped as he grumbled wordlessly, still spreading the nanocream over her face. It tingled.

<Sorry. Okay. Hope the transfer is smoother than our getting over here was,> she subvocaled.

He grunted and used a tissue to wipe the corner by her nose. "It will probably have complications. Free Victoria always does. But it's the quickest thing Angela could arrange. Hold *still,* damn it! Need to get this on straight. Looks weird if it's streaked—wish the application was somewhere else than the face, but that's the best method of transmission. It has to be smooth on the face before it spreads to the rest of your skin. I don't know why because I didn't design it. However, it works. I used this every day in National Security, so I'm comfortable with it. I don't think there are any long-term effects."

"How'd you get the face hair so fast?"

"Stuff I'm a little less comfortable with. Quick-grow. It manipulates hormones. None of this is going to hold up to close scrutiny, so we need to be discreet. On the other hand, I went through years like this at National Security, and no one looked closely at me. But I didn't give them reasons to look. Behavior is as important as disguise."

"Okay."

He sighed, then pulled her close for a kiss.

"Time to go!" Angela yelled through the door.

They split apart and grabbed their packs.

CHAPTER 12

There's something about this place that screws up travel plans.

Melanie stared out into the early morning darkness from a different safe house in Free Victoria, not able to see very far thanks to the wind-whipped rain.

Four fucking days. And now this damned storm.

At least it would hide them from the jumped-up patrols in the Strait.

Good thing it's the Makah fishers doing the boat work.

If anyone could get them across the water safely, it would be the Makah fishers, with their knowledge of the Strait and its moods. For everyone's safety, while Angela knew their names, names never came up around Melanie. All the same, she hoped they would have the same men handling the boats. She *might* not interpret every slap of waves against the bow as a sign they were capsizing.

She jumped as Marty suddenly appeared next to her.

"You okay?" he asked.

"Yeah. You just surprised me. Moving pretty quietly tonight."

"Good. I'm trying to be quiet. Nik said I needed to work on it."

"You're doing a good job."

"It's work. I'm not used to thinking about how I move."

"Maybe you need to take up aikido."

"Maybe," he agreed. "Nik says five minutes before we leave. Full cloaking. It sounds like it's going to be a pretty grim trip. You get seasick?"

"Sometimes." Melanie shivered. Until the last trip across the Strait, most of her boating experience had come from rare trips to the relatives living in Neahcom on the Oregon Coast. She had learned fear of the sea from them, especially after one almost-capsizing incident. Makah fishers did things totally different from her relatives, and for *that* she was thankful.

"Maybe you ought to take a pill," Marty said.

Melanie shook her head. "It won't make any difference. I'll get sick if I'm going to be, pill or no pill."

Besides, I'd much rather be conscious and alert.

She sensed Angela before she saw her. Angela pressed something into her hands.

"Night goggles. Put them on. Once we're outside, no speech. Dialogue only, stealth mode. Stealth everything. Got your stealthsuits on?"

"Yeah," Melanie and Marty said.

"Good. Be tough getting across. The patrols are still out there despite this damned weather. At least the weather covers us. We're the lucky ones. All four of us are going to be under the bow because we're known quantities and we can't risk being seen. The others will be out in the weather."

"Won't we be in trouble if we get water in the boat?" Melanie asked.

Melanie could barely see Angela's shrug. "The fishers don't seem to think it's a problem."

"Okay." Melanie pulled on her night goggles, blinking in a random sequence as she adjusted to them, then calibrated her Dialogue overlays.

Nik glided into the room. <Let's go,> he texted.

They followed their Security to the waiting truck. It was a short ride to an out-of-the-way dock. Then Melanie and Marty were hustled across the dock and into the boat. Melanie cringed at the smallness of the boat. Even though it was bigger than the sixteen-foot craft her kinfolk took over the bar of the Neahcom River into the ocean, it was still an open boat with a closed bow, meant for day fishing. At least she recognized the fishers from their previous trip. *These* people knew what they were doing.

She hoped.

Nik stashed them in the bow. As the smallest person, Melanie was right up at the front, Marty tucked in next to her.

Dear God. If we swamp, we're toast.

Once she and Marty were settled, Nik set up scatter generators around them, then shoved Angela in, and finally himself, tucking his long legs up as far as he could and bracing them against the side of the boat.

Melanie tensed as the motors roared into life. All too soon the bow was slapping hard against big waves that jarred her every joint. She clenched Marty's offered hand and bit her lip to keep from crying out. Marty occasionally stroked her shoulder, but they dared not speak or share Dialogue comments. All they could do was endure.

A couple of times the engines cut out and the boat quickly swung parallel to the waves. Melanie tightened up even more when that happened.

I will not cry out. I will not whimper. I will not think about getting swamped. This is not Neahcom; these aren't the Stephens kin. The Makah people have been crossing the Strait for generations, in smaller boats than this one, without engines.

Each time the engines fired up again and they roared off. Melanie didn't ask. She grimly held on, not wanting to know whether there was a problem.

Finally, the boat slowed to trolling speed. The waves quieted. A few minutes later, Melanie heard voices outside the boat. The boat banged against something.

Dock. At last.

Nik and Angela rolled out.

<Stay,> Angela texted. <Might leave. Don't move.>

Melanie stifled the groan she wanted to make and rolled her head against Marty's chest. He rubbed her back in circles, then stroked her cheek. She lifted her head, feeling woozy and sick. He kissed her forehead gently. She closed her eyes, relaxing into him, trying not to think about her roiling stomach.

Then she felt hands pulling at her legs. <Go,> Angela texted. <Stealth until inside.>

It was hard to uncurl from the position she'd locked herself into, tough to straighten cramped legs. Marty had to help her while she helped him.

At last Melanie worked her way free, climbing over the side of the boat with wobbly legs, grateful for the hands that steadied her even as they whisked her along the dock as fast as she could move with her cramped legs.

To her relief, they guided her directly to a decrepit old trailer.

Fishing camp, I'll bet.

The trailer smelled of mold and looked dingy in the faint light as she stripped off her goggles. But it wasn't moving, even though the world around her swayed. Melanie staggered over to the old sofa and collapsed on it, sneezing as she raised some dust. She shivered and started looking for a blanket.

"You okay?" Marty asked. "That was a rough one."

"Yeah. Hurt all over, but that's to be expected. I'm colder than hell, though. Can't get warm."

"Ready for food?" Angela asked.

Melanie shook her head. "Just want to lie down. Stretch out. I bet I'm bruised all over. Want lots of blankets."

"Come on. I'm ready for some sleep in something that's not moving." Marty guided her to a bedroom. The double bed was big enough for both of them to stretch out. Marty piled blankets on Melanie before joining her under the covers.

She dropped off quickly to a dreamless sleep.

THEY WAITED TWO DAYS BEFORE LEAVING THE FISHING CAMP. MELANIE spent the time reading the musty, disintegrating paperbacks scattered around the cabin and talking quietly with Marty. There wasn't enough open space to practice her katas. But the restlessness that had possessed her in Free Victoria was strangely quiet here.

Finally, they loaded into the truck, hidden behind stacks of dried fish, next to the cooler that held the fresh and frozen fish. Nik and Angela huddled with them during the two-day trip, while the other four members of their Security entourage took turns being visible as assistants to their driver.

They squabbled over Portland information-gathering strategy in loud whispers when it was safe.

"I don't like the idea of you and Marty going off alone," Angela argued during one of those sessions.

"Ange, *I can handle it.* Too many of us in a clump will draw attention. We absolutely need to prioritize information gathering. But more than two people together is asking for trouble. Plus we have a lot of ground to cover. Four groups of two make more sense than one group of eight or two groups of four. We have different connections throughout the city. Let's cover them in one night."

"Then why does it have to be you and Marty? Why not you and Nik, or you and me?"

Melanie sighed. "I'd much rather bed down with Marty, for one. For another, Nik going with me will attract too much attention where I want to go."

"Which is—" Angela glared at Melanie.

"Sellwood. The snowboard crew there."

"She's right. Too many people know my family," Nik inserted. "And not all of them are safe. Ange, you need to be the one talking to your brother."

Angela exhaled, hissing through her teeth. "How the hell are you getting down there, Mel?"

"Drift that direction with homeless folks heading for nighttime shelter. That'll give me cover to get across the bridge. From there it's an easy fade along the river and into Sellwood."

"This is getting worse and worse," Angela growled.

"Mel *does* know how to fade into homeless camps," Nik inserted.

"I *know that!*" Angela snapped. "But that incident was over twelve years ago!"

Luckily Nik sat behind Angela so she couldn't see him roll his eyes. Melanie stifled a grin. She and Nik had done private training sessions in east Portland during the last seven years, when Melanie was staying at Do It Right's downtown condo for business.

Someday you might want to disappear into the shadows, Nik had said when he started training her. *Best you have some practice in fading out of sight fast.*

Why not tell Ange what we're doing? she had asked.

Deniability. If National Security takes her to be interrogated, she doesn't know the extent to which I've trained you. I have—protection she doesn't.

And since Nik was the shadow side of Angela's role of Head of Security, trained directly by Will Landreth—Melanie didn't argue with him further about keeping Ange in the dark about what she did and didn't know about urban survival.

The question of who went with whom was still unresolved when they reached Portland But at least they got there without being discovered.

"I still don't like you and Marty going off on your own, without Security as part of your team," Angela said. Nik stood next to Angela; his arms crossed but not saying anything. Yet. "I understand the reasoning, and that you and Marty want to stay together, but I'm not happy. At least you have your father's weapons. We'll have to hope that's sufficient. Where shall we meet tomorrow?"

"The soup kitchen by Lloyd. That work?"

"Sounds good. Time?"

"Nine-ish."

"Exercise Dialogue discipline," Marty said. "Short-range, short bursts, local communication only, highest shielding you can raise. Otherwise, no contact except for emergencies. Since Andrew's told us National Security knows about Dialogue, they'll be watching for that type of communication activity."

"Let's go," Melanie said. She and Marty shouldered their packs. "Ange, Nik, everyone, take care of yourselves."

"*You* take care of yourself," Angela said.

"I'll make sure she does," Marty said.

They walked away from the others, heading south.

"So now what?" Marty asked her.

She squeezed his hand, then dropped it. "I want to fall in with a group heading for the shelters. Might get more info that way, and it's less likely that we'll attract blacksuit attention. Just follow my lead. Don't talk—be strong and silent. Pretend to be hearing-impaired. I'll probably be doing that as well."

Another role that she had studied under Nik's supervision.

"Okay."

They climbed the staircase to the Hawthorne bridge deck. As Melanie expected, walkers crossed the bridge in assorted bunches. She timed their pace so that they fell in with a small group of three men and two women.

"Luck today?" one of the women asked her.

Melanie grunted in return and shook her head. "The stuck ups wouldn't even give me a chance," she whined.

"Too bad. I've got me a good gig that needs a hand tomorrow."

"Me and the man are going to try our luck on the East Side tomorrow." Melanie slurred her speech slightly.

"You sure you want to try East Side?" the woman asked in a low voice, her eyes darting around quickly, slinking closer.

Melanie pretended not to hear. The woman's behavior bothered her.

Find an excuse to get away from her. Too snoopy. Damn. Did I fall in with a National Security mole?

Or did the woman work for one of the local gangs that preyed upon the poor and homeless?

"Hear me?" the woman repeated.

"Sorry. Don't hear so good any more. Got beat up by the man before this 'un. One blow too many to the head. This man's hearing is worse than mine."

The other woman turned her head so that Melanie could see her lips before speaking again.

"You sure you want to try East Side?" she asked. "Things are purty tight there. Security's running hard and y'all have to go through checks even to do yard work."

"Not a posh place I'm going to. Someone I used to know from way back."

"They got room for others?"

Melanie shrugged. "Don't know if they even have anything for me and my man. We thought we'd hike on over, see if they have a crash for the night, and work in the morning."

"You better be careful if you have to go too far. Security don't like us on the street after dark."

"Thanks for the word. What's up with Security, anyway? Somebody big die?"

Her informant shrugged. "Just heard the big top bitch bought the big one. But nothing's changed, least not for the better. Sure thought it would change. Another big bitch is supposed to be pushing for change, but ain't seen no sign."

"Don't seem to matter whatever changes happen up top, us little folks are the ones who get screwed." Melanie spotted the distant flash of lights from a Security checkpoint, and stopped at the staircase leading down to the old Eastside bicycle path. "Think we'll get off the drag here."

"You watch out there now, you girl. Tough 'uns if you go thataway. Better to chance the Security."

"Got friends with the tough 'uns, or used to, anyway. Thanks for the word."

The woman walked off with her group. Melanie led Marty down the staircase.

"Be ready with every damn weapon you have," she said, once they were out of earshot. "She wasn't kidding about tough ones down here."

"How the hell did you ever get involved with homeless folks?"

"Nik and I have been training. Top secret. Angela doesn't know." Melanie shrugged. "Since we're together, you might as well know."

"Surprising that he keeps secrets from her."

"Part of his role as Angela's shadow side." Melanie swallowed hard. "There are things you don't want to know, Marty."

He nodded curtly. "Understood. So why *not* go through the camps?"

"If Mom's nearby, Kathy will be around. I'm half-hoping to find her. That one camp with the 'tough 'uns' is her favorite underground hideout. Nik and I have met her there before."

Marty raised his brows. "Ah. I see."

Melanie picked up a steady long, rolling stride. She wanted to break into a run through this stretch. No. That would attract unwanted attention. She forced herself to look bigger, more confident than she felt.

They marched past the old OMSI building, underneath the ruins of the old light-rail and pedestrian bridge, and set a course for the Ross Island Bridge.

Before they reached the bridge, she pulled Marty aside.

"Time to get fully armed," she explained. "That camp below the bridge is full of a lot of toughs. If we're obviously armed, they'll leave us alone." She strapped a heavy pistol on her waist.

Marty nodded, and pulled out a folding assault rifle from his pack that he quickly put together. "Good enough?" He grinned at her. "You're not the only one who thinks of these things."

She grinned back at him. "More than good. Let's go."

They proceeded along the path, under the bridge and were just past the camp.

"What's the password?" A lanky, dreadlocked, dark-skinned man dressed in shapeless fatigues stepped out in front of them.

"Don't need no fuckin' password," she growled back.

"I say you do."

She pulled out her pistol. Marty clicked his rifle into firefight mode.

"This and my friend there say I don't." She jerked her head toward Marty.

"Melanie?" An older woman came out from the shadows behind the dreadlocked man. "Stand down, Crispin."

Perfect. Kathy is here.

"Kathy." Melanie lowered her pistol.

Kathy Miller raised her brows. "A surprise to see you here. What's going on?"

"We need to talk."

"I have a place to crash. Follow me."

They followed Kathy around the outskirts of the camp, with Crispin tagging along, ending up at an old warehouse on the edge of the Sellwood district. Kathy led them to a windowless room, and switched on a single light and a small heater.

"Home sweet home, such as it is." Kathy looked over at Crispin. "Extra watch. Get Harry and Annie out to cover. Three people per shift."

"Not going downtown tonight?" Crispin asked.

Kathy shook her head. "This situation just bumped that priority."

Crispin nodded and ducked out.

Kathy sighed. "Things are tighter than ever here, Mel. As you can see."

"What's going down?"

"I'm getting worried. You can't even breathe without Security around. I don't know what tipped them off, but they think she's here."

"*Is* she here?" Melanie asked.

Kathy's eyes darted over to Marty, obviously reluctant to say anything more with him there.

Marty chuckled. "Kathy, you flatter me. I guess my disguise is better than I hoped if *you* don't recognize me."

Kathy peered at him. "Marty Fielding? Jeez. You don't look anything at all like you used to. Hell, though, the only way I recognized Melanie was when she spoke."

"That's good," Marty said. "I was hoping the nanocream worked that well."

"What's the story?" Melanie asked.

"Well, they want me bad, for obvious reasons. But they want *her* even more." Kathy looked over at Marty. "What Melanie said in that text to Diana. You're Ness's host?"

Marty nodded.

"Any way I can consult with her? I have some ideas about what's going on with this Netwalk stuff and the shadow."

"We're willing to listen to anything," Melanie said. "But the shadow is Sarah. She wants Mom. Blacksuits have orders to hunt her down, turn Sarah loose on her to run an upload, then kill her. You know what that means?"

The shocked look on Kathy's face was enough to convey her understanding.

"But how does that work?" Kathy asked.

"The same way that Will was killed," Marty said. "If it hadn't been for me, Melanie, and Ness, plus help from our lab techs, Sarah would have Will, too. We managed to save Will. He uploaded directly without Sarah getting him."

Kathy looked at Melanie. "Mel?"

She shook her head. "Not me. Julia Hawkins."

Kathy nodded. "Good. So, how do I consult with Ness?"

Marty paused, then spoke. "Ness doesn't recommend I bring her out right now. She's monitoring the local security networks. If she appears, that would bring not just the shadow but the blacksuits down on us, hard. But she's listening. I can relay her comments."

"Okay, good." Kathy paused. "Just how the hell are we fighting this shadow?"

"I don't need to consult Ness to give you part of that answer," Marty said. "That's why we're here. Every Dialogue needs to learn the Netwalk transfer process, as either host or Netwalker. We are *not* going to lose any more Dialogues to that shadow."

"How do you propose to do that?"

"How many Dialogues are in your group here?"

"We all are."

"Everybody gets taught the basics. Then we make up a training team. They find other Dialogue cells and train them," Marty said.

"How many of these—Netwalkers, you call them?—do we have?"

"Ness and Will."

Kathy scratched her chin. "And how many do they have?"

"Possibly as many as twenty. Peter and Sarah for certain. We know Sarah's predatory and running wild online. Peter seems to ride pretty close to Andrew. The others—may not be as coherent as those two. Hopefully that means they're easier to beat," Marty said.

"Those are pretty long odds."

"It's not perfect. Will and I were working on measures to control hostile Netwalkers just before he was killed. Something we'll have to figure out. One thing we've learned from Ness is just how damn hard it's going to be to kill them permanently. That forced our hand." Marty shrugged. "Kathy, if you have suggestions that I can stick into our trainings here in the field, I'll gladly incorporate them. I'm hoping you have some input."

"Let me think about it. Do you have any ideas why Security's so tight here?"

Melanie shrugged. "Short of them thinking that Mom's in Portland, or a leakage from our people, no, not really. I've a crew gathering information. Marty and I didn't come here alone. Unless—" she paused delicately. "The—*gadget* seems to be involved, at least with Peter. It may be kicking things up. I was told that you or Mom are the only ones with authority to talk about it. I need to know more."

Kathy scowled. "I'm not feeling its particular little touch in this mess, so far. You say Peter's affected?"

"Yes."

Kathy nodded, chewing her lip thoughtfully. "I'd prefer you talked to your mother about it. If she can't—then I will. But, really, she's the one. Meanwhile." Kathy paused. "Why did you two choose to come back here, when you were safe in Nagano?"

"Andrew told me Peter's plans for Mom. A deliberate tip, during the one time he was free from supervision. We couldn't let that happen. Plus—I need more information about the gadget. Everyone keeps referring me to you or Mom."

Kathy nodded. "Is Andrew's disclosure a trap?"

"Very possible. But there's more to it. I don't know how much of this plan is Andrew's idea and how much if it is Peter's doing. And then there's Liam and his connections."

"Liam?" Kathy scowled. "Just how the hell does he fit into all this?"

"He's Andrew's minder. Andrew claims Liam leads the Freedom Army."

Kathy shook her head. "Melanie, this is sounding worse and worse. Why did you come back to this hellhole?"

"Did I really have a choice? Besides finding out about the gadget, I wanted to make sure that Mom has the help she needs when she faces the final showdown with Sarah. It'll take me and Marty and Ness on her side to give her the edge she'll need with Peter and Andrew. Plus

Liam and the Army. And maybe the gadget." Melanie took a deep breath. "If I have to, I'll host Sarah myself. But doing this requires me being here. Not in Japan. Here."

Kathy shook her head. "You're crazy."

"Maybe so. As I told Marty, I have links around here that he doesn't. The old Mountain ties hold on pretty good."

"The Mountain. Jeez, Melanie, anybody could think of that."

"Kathy, if I hadn't told you, would you have thought about me and the old-time Mountain families? Or, for that matter, the old-time County families from Gramps and Mom? Yeah, my ties to Hoodland and to Skene County are in my bio for anyone to look up, but come on, who really thinks that there's any serious connections between the two places? Not even Liam took those links seriously."

Kathy sighed. "It's an Oregon thing, I guess. But I'm from here, so I'd think of it."

"Maybe. You also know us."

"I also know you and your crew would sneak a ski run in tonight, if you could. That would be predictable. You're a ski bum gone Corporate, and you surround yourself with ski bums who can keep up with you." Kathy tapped her chin thoughtfully.

"I'm hoping that Mom uses the community links right now."

"She probably is. Sounds like you think she's in the Northwest somewhere. Where do you think she is?"

Melanie twisted her lips, thinking. "Any blacksuit action near the old Andrews Ranch?"

"Let me check," Kathy said. She got up and stuck her head into the adjoining room, speaking so quietly that Melanie couldn't hear what she said.

"So were you expecting this?" Marty asked her.

"No. Not at all. I was heading for the snowboarders in Sellwood. The exiles who have day jobs so they can ride on weekends. I was planning to shoot by the apartments where they used to hang out, see if I could rouse anyone. If not them, then I wanted to check out that fourth-generation Sellwood crowd of skaters who also snowboard. Nik's family. That's why I couldn't bring him. Not all the snowboarders like the Morleys."

Kathy returned. "So. What do you know. Blacksuit action heavy around the old Andrews Ranch."

"Damn." Melanie studied her thumbs. "I'm not positive, and I could be wrong, but Mom always was fond of the back of a good horse. More so than skiing, even. I'm betting she might have taken off for the old ranch, seen the excitement there, and headed for the Reserve."

Kathy shook her head. "She couldn't get through. Remember, I had to go through that Reserve to hook up with her."

"So where would she go from the Andrews Ranch?" Melanie mused, leaning back in her chair and staring up at the ceiling. She spotted a faint twinkle of a star through a tiny hole in the roof. "It's winter. Hopefully she's running with good and knowledgeable folks."

"Last I heard, your number two security team had hooked up with her. But they're small in number."

Sergio and Erica, with Jennie, Noel, Keith and Ken. Small in number, but big in heart. Melanie wanted Sergio and Erica to come to Nagano with her instead of Steve and Paul, but both preferred to stay. Their families had grown up with Diana, and while they had Mountain ties, they were also connected to—*aha.* Fishermen and loggers through Erica's family.

"I may want to check in with the boarders before we leave Portland," she said to Kathy and Marty. "But I'm pretty damn sure I know where Diana is now."

"Where?" Marty asked.

She gave him a big, shit-eating grin. "Neahcom."

Marty's eyes widened. "Oh, hell. You mean we came all this way and she's in Neah Bay?"

Kathy shook her head. "Wrong one."

"Sarah's old stomping grounds in Neahcom," Melanie said.

Neahcom, on the northern Oregon coast. Not Diana's favorite place, nor Sarah's. A grim little coastal logging and fishing town where the Stephens family had first made its timber fortune, and left once opportunity allowed.

The perfect place to confront Sarah. The location Sarah had spent her entire life running from, the past she never liked to talk about.

Yeah. It made sense.

"We're going to Neahcom," she decided. "After Marty and I do your Netwalk training, and we meet up with our Security."

"Mel, I promised Sergio I'd keep my mouth shut. But I figured you'd know where to go when you heard she was with Sergio and Erica, and that the Mountain and the County weren't a possibility."

"Not that hard of a thought process, at least not for anyone who knows Sergio and Mom."

"Thank God that rules out most of National Security. Unless Andrew or Liam remember."

Melanie shook her head. "Not unless we had a really good mole in our system who was better than the ones I've been pruning over the years. For all the time we spent together, Liam didn't really pay attention to family and friend dynamics. Steve and Paul are my visible number twos, and we took them to Nagano. Serg and Erica have always been buried pretty deep in my system. I've let Angela and Nik have a free rein in setting up the order based on their own family structures, and kept out of it except for a need-to-know basis. Anyone wanting to poke into my Security systems needs to know a turncoat from the Mountain. I don't think there are any from my close circles. Could be, but unlikely."

"It's not a pattern Sarah would understand?" Kathy asked.

"It's not a pattern *Andrew* would understand, and he grew up with it," Melanie said.

She hoped she was right about that assumption.

CHAPTER 13

"WE WON'T HAVE TIME TO CHECK IN WITH THE BOARDERS," MELANIE SAID to Kathy, over a quick breakfast of Security travel rations. "Which puts me in a spot. I hoped to catch a ride from them over to Lloyd, so we would be at my rendezvous point in time."

"I can help you," said Kathy. She nodded toward the back of the warehouse. "I've a four-seater that needs to be returned to the carshare site near Lloyd. Crispin knows the drill. He and Annie can go with you. They want to go to Neahcom."

"Who the hell goes to Neahcom if they don't have to?"

Kathy laughed. "He's from there, Mel. He has family."

"Oh. I'd better ask about them."

"No need. They're an old Stephens Timber family, the Ruskins."

"Oh yeah. I know the family. Old-timers."

"Thought you would." Kathy paused. "Anyway, I'd like to send them back to Diana. They're from her Security, and she needs them more than I do."

Marty entered the small office. "Done with the training and reprogramming." He scooped up a ration bar and sat in the remaining chair, slumping slightly. "Went better than I thought. Processes do work, after all."

"You weren't sure?" Melanie asked.

"Never sure about any of this stuff until it's field-tested. Kathy, your staff's all Dialogue-upgraded and Netwalk-transfer trained. I did the bare bones programming. No lab work, no major tweaks, just simple reprogramming. It's all I can do in the field. But they can start training other Dialogues linked into your group."

"Thanks, Marty."

Marty nodded. "Mel, I'm worried about our time. It's running late if we're walking."

"No problem. Crispin's driving us."

"Lap of luxury, hmm?"

"If you call a sharecar that," Kathy said wryly.

Crispin stuck his head into the office. "We're ready to leave."

Melanie gulped the last of her tea. "Let's go."

THE ELECTRIC FOUR-SEATER WAS A TIGHT SQUEEZE FOR FOUR ADULTS AND their packs, even with two smaller adults like Melanie and Annie. Crispin let Marty and Melanie off near the soup kitchen.

"We'll take care of the rig, then hook up," he said. "It'll look more natural."

"Right," Melanie said.

They headed into the park next to where a shopping mall had been. Melanie found a good spot to observe people walking in and out of the park, near the soup kitchen. At some point they would fall into line for free food, but lounging around in a small group, waiting for others to join up with them, was normal. Other small groups who had split off to spend the night at various shelters or night jobs were doing the same. Some were recognizable as small family groups; others were friend groups. Melanie kept an eye out for anyone she might recognize. Some of the boarder community used soup kitchens, although the Sellwoodies would patronize their local one unless someone was working over here.

The blacksuits working undercover were easy to identify. They circulated the park in three groups of two, too clean, too well-dressed, with obvious deliberately-aged clothing. They wandered around looking at everyone, instead of picking their spot and hanging out. A few people greeted them and talked, but for the most part the blacksuits were studiously ignored.

At least their brief companions from the night before weren't friendly with the blacksuits. One of the women from that group visibly steered them as far away from the blacksuits as she could. At the far end of the park from Melanie, they met up with a gang. That confirmed Melanie's suspicions that the woman who had been talking to her was the one who lured unsuspecting prey into the clutches of their group.

At last, Angela and Nik wandered into the park. Unlike the blacksuits, they tried to blend with those around them as they drifted in, heads down, moving with an economical shuffle.

Blacksuits could learn a lesson from them.

Angela and Nik made their own meandering circuit of the park before they got to Melanie and Marty.

Angela winked at Melanie, tapping her bag. "Chicken tamales from Mama. Got a whole big batch of them," she murmured. "Not many of our folks in Hoodland right now. Too crazy. Blacksuits spending too much time poking around up there, only folks who like shooting at them or folks too scared of town are left. Neither fits my mama, that's for sure, especially with Sophie in tow."

"They okay?"

"They moved in with big brother. Mama got tired of ducking the blacksuits every time she wanted to go somewhere, and they were *waaay* too interested in Sophie. Mama likes to do what she wants, when she wants, and she's worried about Sophie. Big bro's having a time with it, but that's his problem. He can't admit Mama's pretty tough."

Melanie grinned, thinking about Angela's mama Brenda and just how tough a lady Mama Brenda was. Mama Brenda had been amongst Diana's first Security staff. *She* wouldn't mess with Brenda.

"Hope there's enough tamales to hold us out for a run to Neahcom," she said.

"Neahcom, hmm?" Angela said. "We got info pointing to Neahcom as well. Sergio's been in touch with Mama, figuring it was one way to get news to us."

Melanie told Angela about Kathy Miller.

Angela shrugged. "Glad you found Kathy. Serg's been leaving messages with selected Mountain folk that are hiding out down here, figuring if anyone came to town they'd connect up. Mama was worried last night, 'cause Kathy was supposed to drop by. Then, after we got there, she thought that maybe Kathy ran into you on her way and all was well."

"What's their Dialogue status?"

"Trained everyone last night. Kathy's been tuning up everyone she runs into, so we didn't have to do a lot of maintenance work. Mama says to tell you that she wants to come visit in Nagano after this all gets settled. She doesn't believe me about the raw fish stuff."

"Did you tell her it was mostly fake fish?"

Angela chuckled. "She'd believe that one even less." She glanced around quickly, then whispered. "I got us temp IDs and passes so we can use transit. Not for long, but at least we can get out of town. Working connections for other transport."

"Thanks, girlfriend."

Angela shrugged. "Wasn't hard."

The remaining three pairs of their team drifted in slowly. Melanie urged them toward the food line, eying the National Security group drifting closer. Angela caught her glance, and nodded.

<Covered,> she texted. <Kirsten and Robbie.>

<Thanks.>

They got through the food line without incident, and joined the crowds walking toward downtown. Angela directed Carol and Julio, Crispin and Annie, then Kirsten and Robbie, to break off and meet them out by Hillsboro, using different transits. Halfway through their transit trip, right after they emerged from the tunnel under the West Hills into Beaverton, Angela's mood changed from relaxed but alert to tense and edgy.

Melanie scanned the crowd around them. Nothing to account for Angela's sudden tension.

"Let's get off here," Angela muttered to her at the next stop, clearly avoiding Dialogue use.

Melanie nodded, even though they planned to get off three stops later. *Something* had triggered Angela into high alert.

Nik picked up on Angela's tension. Melanie caught quick, covert hand and eye signals between them. Security shortcodes she wasn't trained to recognize. Then he and Angela talked softly in a tonal language Melanie didn't know, but recognized a few key words from past occasions when Nik and Angela suddenly started using it.

Mixteco.

Oh shit. They don't do that unless something's really wrong. Shit.

Angela marched them briskly down the sidewalk. Melanie found an excuse to drift close to Marty.

"You see it too?" he muttered to her out of the side of his mouth, keeping his lips still as possible.

"Yeah. They aren't texting. You hear them talking? It's Mixteco." She followed his lead and tried not to move her lips, almost like she was subvocaling. Except subvocals were easier.

"I thought something was up when we got off transit early. Then I saw Angela talking to you, not texting. And the shortcode. Don't know any of those signs."

"We need to learn some of that. Could be useful for us." She didn't bring up learning Mixteco. Angela had brushed Melanie off when she suggested that previously.

"Yeah."

Angela stopped them on a busy cross street where other worker groups lingered.

"Wait here." She walked over to a tall man directing teams to different areas. Angela spoke with him. After exchanging a few words with the tall man, and taking a package from him, Angela rejoined them. Without speaking, she handed out ponchos from the package the man had given her, and tucked the remainder into her backpack. Then they merged with a small group standing furthest away from the larger crowd. Within five minutes, an open-bed truck pulled up. They climbed into the bed.

Melanie discreetly eyed their companions as the truck took off. A mixed group, some clearly heading for field work or tech work. Most carried at least a small pack which probably carried food and a change of clothing. These days that was what a wise person did who depended on transit and worker transports.

Marty stayed next to her, glaring at anyone who jostled her.

"Playing your role well," she whispered to him at one point.

"You're a good-looking woman. It's my job to be territorial in this setting."

The truck let them off on the far side of Beaverton. They spent the rest of the day trekking through the squalid remnants of what had once been expensive neighborhoods. Angela kept them close to the greenspace edges, never straying too deeply into the mazes of buckling concrete and multi-family occupied houses. Several times they struck off into the wetlands, avoiding people entirely. Melanie was glad for the shapeless gray ponchos. They looked like just another lost labor crew on their way to a job.

Finally, they arrived at an old, apparently abandoned, barn near the airport. They staked out a space among moldy straw bales.

Eventually, Crispin and Annie, then Carol and Julio, arrived.

"Blacksuits got Kirsten and Robbie before we even left downtown," Carol said.

"Shit!" Melanie tensed.

"Take it easy." Marty whispered to her. "Look at Ange and Nik. They already know."

"But Kristen and Robbie have Dialogues. If they get Netwalked, we're in trouble."

"We'd have known."

"Any idea whether they got away?" Melanie asked Carol.

Carol shook her head. "No idea. We think they were fingered by those blacksuits at the park. They were grabbed the minute they approached transit."

Melanie looked over at Angela. "Is there anything we can do?"

Angela shook her head. "They're gone. For good."

"I don't understand."

"Suicide Red gone," Angela said grimly. "I'm keeping my folks on isolated floating links, including you two. Will set it up for me before he died. Haven't had a chance to tell you about it. Keeps you and Marty separate unless it's absolutely necessary, which means you wouldn't feel them go but I would."

She was almost afraid to ask the next question.

"Did they—" Melanie's voice caught on the words.

"Angela. Quick Link," Marty said, raising his hand to cut Melanie off. "That is, if it's secure now."

"It's secure," Angela said.

Angela and Marty stared at each other, texts flashing in their eyes.

<No,> he told Melanie. <They didn't upload. They exercised their Security fail-safes.>

She closed her eyes tightly. Two gone. "We'll avenge them," she said, a harsh note in her voice. "We'll make sure that their sacrifice counts."

"They'll pay, those who forced them to this." Nik said. Her Security looked at each other with hard eyes.

"They'll pay," they repeated. Without hesitation, Crispin and Annie joined in.

A chill ran up Melanie's back. This had the marks of a Mountain Security bonding ritual.

Kathy didn't tell me Crispin and Annie were sworn Mountain Security. She just said they were Mom's Security.

Only sworn Mountain Security would know the rituals, at least as far as she knew.

Just how many Mountain Security teams did Mom have in Nagano that I don't know about?

One question she failed to ask before they left Nagano.

Angela and Nik would know.

"And the price they'll pay?" Nik asked.

"Death."

"And who will enforce this sentence?"

"The Mountain Security of Do It Right."

Their Security team moved together, intertwining their hands.

"We swear it by our blood."

Melanie and Marty watched, transfixed.

<The National Security blacksuits don't have this,> Marty told her. <They operate on fear, not sworn trust in their companions.>

<Makes for a tighter bond. Is this common with all our Security or is it just Mountain Security?>

<Who knows?> Marty said.

<But Crispin and Annie aren't Mountain Security. Are they?>

<They were originally Mountain Security before they went to Nagano with your mother. They told me that when I trained them in Netwalk procedures.>

She nodded. <I can't track everything.>

Marty gave her a quick hug. <Trust and delegation. That's what makes Do It Right different from the Confederation. Go back to vocal, not Dialogue. Not safe to do it for long.>

Melanie nodded. He picked up her hand and squeezed it, then wrapped one arm around her and pulled her close.

At least I have Marty.

Melanie slept poorly that night. Even curled up with Marty, she was cold and restless. The moldy straw bothered her sinuses, and she kept hearing things. She wished they could be in a tent, but tents would just attract attention.

Worries kept racing through her brain. What if this were a trap? What if her mother wasn't in Neahcom? What if Sarah—*or the gadget*—was lurking out there, ready to pounce upon her once she fell asleep?

Marty stirred and wrapped his arms more tightly around her, kissing her neck gently.

<Sorry to disturb you,> she sent, risking the brief contact.

<I'm not sleeping well either.>

She rested her head on his chest. <I'm cold. That's part of the problem. Even with my hat on and socks, I'm cold.>

<It's not that cold. Are you coming down sick?> He felt her forehead with the back of his hand.

<Don't think so.>

He clucked. <My thermometer suggests you're maybe a degree below normal. If it's working right. Not surprising. You don't have thermal clothing and it's damp.>

<What? You have a thermometer implanted in there or something?
>

He was slow to respond. <I had several diagnostic tools implanted in my hands before we left. One way to get around the problems of non-lab upgrades, and it's stuff that Ness can manage for me.>

<How much am I missing that I should know?>

He sighed softly. <Lots. Some of this is need-to-know, Mel. The less you know, the better. I don't even know it all. Let's just say that there's more tricks out there.>

<When will I know more?>

<When we finally get some time to debrief in a safe location. Which isn't right now. Here. Let me get you more comfortable.> He shifted around onto his back and tucked her between his body and his arm. Then he adjusted their coats on top of the sleeping bag so that most of the weight was over her. He pulled up the edge of the bag so that she was covered all the way up to her mouth.

<Better?>

<Yes.>

She warmed slowly with the heavier weight on her body. Finally, she slept.

NIK ROUSED THEM INSTEAD OF ANGELA. SHE WAS GONE, BUT HE SAID nothing about it, and his grunted responses kept Melanie quiet as well. He handed out rations, which they ate silently, then huddled together until Angela returned.

"Got another transport," she said. "Going to Tillamook. We can make it to Neahcom from there."

"Sounds good," Melanie said.

"Bit of a hike to it, though. Out by the old highway." Angela pulled out her flask. "I also got this. Pretty potent. Just a touch for everyone, a little hit to give us all a bit of heart." She took a quick swig, and handed the flask off to Crispin.

When it was Melanie's turn, she was surprised at the smoothness of the high-quality tequila.

Ange outdid herself this time. Trust her to find booze when we need it.

They shouldered their packs and followed yesterday's pattern. Once at the highway, they joined a small group of workers. An hour later, an open truck arrived, with the front already full. They sat in the back, bunching together for warmth and sharing ponchos to keep dry in the driving rain.

The truck ducked and dodged its way among potholes in the old Wilson River highway, occasionally stopping to drop off packages and passengers and pick up new ones. It was a combined labor and mail transport, with local labor getting the privilege of sitting up front. Melanie leaned on Marty and drowsed when she could.

The truck struggled up the side of the mountain, and finally wheezed over the pass to drop into the Wilson River drainage. Then Angela tensed, half-rising to look ahead, yell something at the driver, who hollered something back to her.

<Blacksuit blockade ahead,> Angela texted. <Need to jump soon.>

When the truck slowed almost to a crawl before rounding a corner, her team leapt off. They raced up the side of a steep, brushy hill, zigging and zagging at a quick trot, hustling to make time.

By the time they'd reached the top of the small ridge, Melanie was breathless.

<Adrenaline can only take you so far,> she subvocaled to Marty.

His subvocal response was wordlessly profane, projecting mood but not words.

Angela called for a break. She passed out water bags, herded Melanie and Marty into the center of the Security team, then set up scatter generators.

"Too bad we had to trade the stealthsuits for the ride in Neah Bay," she said to Melanie. "Hope to hell we can get more from Sergio and your mom."

"There wasn't any way to bring them along?"

Angela shook her head. "I used them as part of the payment for getting us across the Strait. Makah fishers need them bad. Survival issue."

"What's the plan now?"

Angela called up her GPS projection. "We're going to head off this way, and drop into the Neahcom River drainage." She traced the path. "One day hike to get there, if we don't run into trouble. Another day to get into Neahcom. That'll take us in the back way, and we can try to hook up with your mom. Serg's probably moving her around. Any ideas?"

Melanie scratched her chin. "I want to check out Larry's place on the river first. I don't want to go into town right away. If Larry's there, that will save us half a day at least."

"Think about the options, and we'll talk about them at our next stop."

Angela passed the flask around again, and then they were off. The small mouthful of tequila was just enough to create a tiny sensation of warmth and ease Melanie's aches.

By nightfall, they were at the headwaters of the Neahcom River. The team set up camp in a small clearing carpeted with frost-browned bracken ferns. Marty sank down on one of the logs, and Melanie collapsed next to him.

And I thought I was in good shape!

Definitely no match for her team's condition, however. And Marty had been quiet most of the afternoon. Worrisome, given their rigorous pace.

<You holding out okay?> she asked.

<I'm in lousy condition,> he answered. <Too damn much easy living at National Security.>

<Yeah. Riiiight. Like National Security's a pleasure camp. Gonna make it?> She twined one hand in his.

He squeezed it back gently. <Yeah. I'm just tired, Mel. And thinking. Any idea if we're here for the night?>

<I'll check in with Angela.>

Melanie turned toward Angela.

Marty screamed.

<MEL!> Ness screeched.

Melanie whirled. The shadow settled over Marty. He fell off the log and thrashed among the ferns, arms outstretched, the shadow between his hands, a hologlobe forming around him.

How?

She leapt toward Marty, bursting through the hologlobe perimeter as it expanded.

"Link up with me!" she shouted to the others, grabbing Marty's arm and throwing every bit of *herself* against the shadow, automatically cueing the trigger that sent her into Netwalk.

No sign of the sphere this time. *Thank God,* she had time to think.

And then, just like before, gargoyle-faced Sarah with the long fingernails appeared before her. Marty grabbed Sarah by the throat and held her away from him. Ness hovered, shifting back and forth from tiny, Tinkerbelle-esque human to falcon, screeching and tearing at Sarah's head.

The Security team pushed strength into Melanie as she dived for Sarah's shoulders. An electric shock scorched through her as she pulled Sarah away from Marty's grasp.

Ness stooped down hard on Sarah in her falcon form, continuing to tear at Sarah's head. Marty shifted to his bear avatar and bounded toward them with teeth bared, roaring loudly, keeping Sarah from turning on Melanie. She held Sarah's shoulders, energized by her Security support to keep Sarah contained.

Then, suddenly, the shadow shimmered out of existence. Sarah's disappearance slammed Melanie back into the world of dusk and damp ferns, her arms wrapped tightly around Marty while her Security clung to her and each other. The hologlobe shimmered out of sight, back into Marty's forearm. Melanie collapsed, gasping for breath and quivering, her stomach tightening with dry heaves.

Melanie was dimly aware of Angela's hands helping her upright. Angela eased a juice pak tube between Melanie's lips while Julio and Carol steadied her. She drank gratefully, noting out of the corner of her eye that Nik, Crispin and Annie were doing the same for Marty.

Julio offered her a protein cube. Melanie gratefully gobbled several, then shook her head at more. She leaned back, breathing deeply, her hands resting on her thighs. Every ounce of her body cried out for rest and sleep—but Melanie was pretty damn sure that this incident ended any hope of staying in this site.

"Now *this*," Angela said to her team, "is exactly why us Dialogues dare not be alone. With even one support person you have a chance to survive. *This* is what killed Will Landreth. Because Marty's a Netwalk host, and our Head of Research, he had some tricks that saved him. And us. This time."

What if Sarah's using us to track down Diana? Or was this the gadget doing dirty work for Peter?

She checked on Marty. He was pale, but steady.

"You okay?" she asked.

He nodded. "I'll be moving slow for a little bit. That's what I was feeling earlier, that thing in the back of my mind."

"Damn. She's tracking us?"

"It's possible," Marty said.

"Marty," said Angela. "Is she plugging into Ness, or do you think it's a Dialogue link?"

Marty shrugged. "I wish I could tell you, but right now I don't know."

"Is it—you know what?" Melanie asked, keeping her voice low so that only they could hear.

Marty shook his head.

Angela let out her breath slowly. "I don't like this. We need to move on. Sorry, folks. I know you're tired, but we can be tagged too damn easily if we stay here. Sorry. Let's have something to eat, then keep on going. Keep the scatters on until we're ready to go. Cold tamales tonight."

Melanie helped Marty back onto the log, and fetched him some tamales. They ate silently, slowly, conserving their energy. She watched him carefully, even more worried than before by the way he was moving. She knew how she felt, especially after that brief but furious Netwalk battle.

She reached into her pocket and pulled out a box of Burnout tabs. Without saying anything, she held them out to Marty.

He shook his head and gently pushed her hand away. "No."

"But they'll keep you going."

"No. I'll find a way."

"This isn't going to work. You're struggling." She began to go through their packs, moving some of the heavier items to hers.

Angela came over to them. "Melanie. No need for that. We'll take most of your stuff. You just lug a survival bag each."

"You sure?"

Angela nodded. "I'm damn sure Marty would benefit from not carrying a load after that last bit of excitement, and you're not in much better shape. Let us do it."

Marty heaved a deep sigh. "Thank you, Angela." Melanie huddled close to him. At least he was still warm, not turning cool or clammy.

They rested, minds quiet, until it was time to move again.

Crispin came up to them. "Marty?"

"Yeah."

"Your Netwalker. Ness Ryan, right? Fighting for you there?"

Marty sat upright. "You were able to see it all?"

Crispin nodded, then paused, face twisting as he struggled to find words. "Ness Ryan was my aunt's cousin," he said finally. "Thank you. Thank you for saving her."

"Thank Melanie as well," Marty said. "If it hadn't been for her work, and Will's, it wouldn't have happened."

Crispin awkwardly took Melanie's hand and shook it.

"Thank you. Thank you." Then he turned away from them.

"Ness's cousin," Marty mused. "He's from Neahcom, right?"

"Yeah. Crispin's family tends to be pretty tight-knit. Once folks find out about Ness being your Netwalker, you'll likely get more thanks, except for those who might want to try an exorcism. But they tend not to be in the mainstream in that family."

Just in mine, at least the batch left in Neahcom.

Fortunately, she could avoid the crazy Stephenses just by staying away from their gated compound.

Far too soon, Angela gave the signal to move on. She passed the flask for a final mouthful apiece. When the flask came back to her, Angela shook it, then wordlessly handed it to Marty. He took a swig, and handed it to Melanie. One last mouthful. The liquor gave her a quick warm glow, softening her aches once again.

This last slog was worse than the high-speed sprint up the ridge. Melanie walked next to Marty, her hand in his. The warmth from the tequila eased her tension. Let Security deal with problems now. It was easier if she didn't think about anything, just ducking branches and hunching deep into her clothing.

Moving. Moving. Moving. At some point the clouds cleared and she saw stars. Then the moon rose, shimmering light on the path ahead of them. By now, they approached places which were vaguely familiar from her childhood. Given her memories of Neahcom, that was almost worse than the darkness. Especially with the shadows that made Melanie twitch, thinking about Sarah.

Sarah. Neahcom. The place that twisted Sarah and started her rise to power. Where their ancestors had built a worldwide timber empire which was the precursor of both Stephens Reclamation and Do It Right.

Too many shadows here.

Not the place she would have chosen to fight Sarah. There was too damned much about Sarah's Neahcom past that Melanie wished she knew. Diana had kept Melanie separate from the Stephens relatives for the most part. Melanie had spent time with her Andrews grandfather instead of the Stephens family for most holidays, even when policy dictated that she should have gone to Neahcom instead. The few encounters she had with the Stephens relatives centered around fishing and boating mishaps.

Could have stood to miss the boating screwups.

But her father had liked to fish. Had supervised every one of the fishing trips, which was probably why they had been allowed to happen.

Dad.

The memory of Will fishing on the ocean brought tears to Melanie's eyes. She grabbed at Marty's arm to steady herself. He pulled her close to him and they walked together stride for stride.

At last Angela stopped. "We've gone far enough. Let's make camp here."

It seemed like forever before they crawled into their tent and slid into the sleeping bags, curling up as tightly together as they could.

If they dreamed that night, or if a Netwalker tried to poke at Marty, neither of them noticed it.

CHAPTER 14

"Mel. Marty. I'm sorry, but it's time to get up." Angela's voice was tired and hoarse as she scratched on their tent door.

Melanie groaned in response. Barely any light around them. Every muscle ached. She could stand a few more hours sleep, a warm bath, and warm food.

"You're making me feel hungry and cold," Marty grumbled at her.

"Sorry. Not meaning to project."

"S'okay. You project those feelings strongly through your Dialogue, when you're tired or stressed. When we get the chance, you need to learn how to block better."

"Whenever that'll be." Melanie rose slowly, pulling on clothing over her datasuit. Her breath puffed white clouds in the growing light. Marty sat up next to her. She fell against him before she could stand on sore, wobbling legs.

"Sleep better last night?"

"Yeah. Too tired not to."

They sat together for a couple of moments before shaking themselves out of the bag, and climbing out of the tent. Melanie turned to pack up the bag and tent, noticing that they were the last ones moving.

"Let us do that." Angela handed Melanie a plate of tamales to match the one Marty held. "Focus on eating. You two need to keep your strength up for travel."

Angela was right, much as Melanie hated to admit it. Her legs were rubbery and weak. Everything cramped when she tried to sit. The combination of cramps and weakness meant it hurt less to walk than to sit, but she *had* to sit occasionally, or risk falling down.

Compromise.

Melanie walked around camp until her legs quivered, and then she sat. Angela gave her a cup of coffee. As she ate, her legs steadied, so she started walking again, sitting down occasionally.

Angela joined her during a walk period. "You know the area better than we do. How do we find Larry?"

Melanie thought for a moment. "Let's see. If we're where I think we are, then we have forest for another three miles, before we hit a road. Then we better tweak our gear to appear local."

Angela nodded. "After that?"

"We look up Larry."

"He's reliable?"

"He's an old friend of Mom's from way back. Logger turned priest. He and his family were always friends of Mom's rather than Grandmother's."

"How likely is it that the blacksuits know about him?"

Melanie shrugged. "He's no Dialogue, as far as I know, and he and Mom kept contact low-key. At some point the blacksuits have to prioritize. Otherwise, they'd have the entire Northwest paved with their people."

"But after last night—"

"Yeah. That could bring more attention to Neahcom, if they had a GPS lock on Marty. I think it's possible to block it. I'll ask."

"Marty?" she called across the clearing. "Could the blacksuits have gotten a GPS lock on us last night? Or could Sarah give them location info?"

Marty shook his head. "Not likely." He walked stiffly over to them. "The floating links give a false locator to anyone lacking the right codes. Code-matching is not one of National Security's strengths. They would have to triangulate better than they could have. While the Coast Range isn't as weird with wireless as the Cascades are, they're still going to give some false readings." He glanced at Melanie. "From what you've told me, since it's Sarah you're worried about—I don't think we need to think about the other contingency."

"That's a relief."

Angela nodded. "Let's move on. Mel, who do you want to try after Larry?"

"It'll be tougher. Valerie, old friend of Mom's. Zechariah. They're less likely just because Zech is on the waterfront and Val is getting up in years. If Mom isn't at any of those places, then we start working Sergio's connections."

"Let's hope we find someone who knows where she is, fast."

"Yeah. I'm worried after last night."

Angela and the others took their packs again. Melanie was glad of the reprieve. Marty seemed to be moving better as well. The three-mile stop just out of sight of the road was a good break, though, and she used it to eat the last of her rationed tamales. Then she had Marty apply nanocream remover to her face.

"I need to be Melanie Landreth," she said. "It's more dangerous otherwise."

"You're not worried about your relatives here?"

"Hell, no. They're barricaded on the hill above town. If any of 'em are still here. It's winter, and they're probably all down in Cabo or Palm Springs instead of this cold wet place."

Marty grunted.

Melanie rummaged through her duffle as her darkened skin faded, looking for clothes that fit Neahcom better than Portland or the Mountain. She settled on a heavy flannel shirt to go under her poncho, and jeans with a nanodry weave in them.

After changing, they set off, this time with her in the lead instead of Angela. About a half-mile from Larry's place, just before they broke out onto the road, she stopped them.

"Marty and I will walk along the road. Angela, you and Nik follow in the trees by the road for about another quarter mile. There's a curve at that point. Wait until we disappear around the far end of it before you pop into sight. You two only on the road. Crispin, you remember Larry?"

"Yeah. He usually runs a bull with his cows."

"Right. Stay within the tree line. It'll open onto two pastures. That's Larry's property. Follow the tree line along the pastures until you hit a long, rutted road. That goes up to Larry's spring system. Be careful around that area. Larry used to grow pot there, and he might still have a trap or two set up to discourage thieves. Wait on that rutted road until you hear from one of us."

Angela frowned. "I'm not sure I like this much distance between me and my Primaries."

"Without transport, a group of four is pretty damn obvious. If Marty and I are walking along with our packs, we could just be a couple hitchhiking from the Valley. Four would attract attention. Make sure you give us enough space, okay?" She turned to Marty. "Ready to go, love?"

He shrugged on his pack. "As ready as I'll ever be."

They crashed through the brush, down into the deep bar ditch, splashed across the knee-deep water at the bottom, then scrambled up the gravel shoulder to the main road. Melanie took a deep breath and walked down the road, leading while Marty followed.

She sure hoped this notion paid off and fast. Walking along the road in the open made her feel vulnerable. If only someone would come cruising along to give them a ride. No, they'd have to justify not taking it, as anyone along here would give them a ride into town instead of to Larry's. Plus she could just imagine the anxiety their hitching a ride would give Angela.

They rounded the corner, and the fields opened up in front of them. She spotted Larry's house across the field, a ramshackle old farmhouse. Smoke rose from the woodstove chimney. Someone was there. Melanie picked up the pace, feeling even more exposed.

A vehicle coughed into life in Larry's barnyard. She watched it anxiously, worried that whoever it was planned to leave. So close, and yet so far. Would the sight of two hitchhikers startle Sergio into moving Diana if she were there?

Probably not.

She hoped. If she and Marty were blacksuit decoys, leaving would catch more attention than not. Sergio was too savvy to be stampeded.

She watched as the beater truck chugged its way down the long driveway to the main road. It was too far away to see who was in it. The truck hesitated, then turned in their direction.

Shit!

"Could this be a problem?" Marty asked.

"I don't know. I don't know."

"I've got my hidies ready. You?"

Melanie nodded, tensing as the truck coughed toward them. The truck slowed as he drove by. Not Larry, too short for Larry. But Melanie couldn't see the driver's face because his brimmed rain hat was pulled low over his face. Only one person in the vehicle.

That she could see.

"It's turning!" Marty yelled.

They turned to face the truck. Melanie's heart pounded. Had they been found out? Should they run? Where the hell *could* they run in these open fields, even if they could get through the woven wire fences quickly enough to keep from being shot?

The truck roared to a stop next to them. The driver turned his head, hat brim pulled low over his face.

Melanie tensed.

He said something she couldn't hear, then pushed his hat back, grinning big at her.

Sergio!

Perfect.

The passenger door popped open. Her mother sat up from where she'd been lying on the seat, smirking as she slid out of the truck cab and disarmed her ancient shotgun.

"About time you two showed up." She reached out to hug first Melanie, then Marty.

THEY CLIMBED INTO THE CAB AND BACKTRACKED TO PICK UP ANGELA AND Nik, then whistled in the rest of their team. Melanie sagged against the back of the old truck's bench seat, squeezed in between Diana and Marty, more than happy at this moment to hand over the responsibility of gathering up her people to Diana and Sergio. They had made it.

"Is Larry back at the house?" she asked Diana. "I wasn't sure if he was still around, but I wanted to try his place before Val's or Zech's."

"He's there," Diana said. "His sensors caught your folks. You must not have brought stealthsuits."

"Couldn't. Traded them for transportation."

Diana nodded. "How come you came down the hard way instead of the easier passage around town?"

"Blockade on the Wilson River Highway. We lost two of the team in Portland. Somehow, they got fingered by blacksuits. They went Suicide Red. We weren't sure if that blockade on the Wilson was a standard sweep or someone looking for us, so we booted out of the transport and hustled over the hard way."

"That blockade's a standard site for floating checks. I came through it okay, but Sergio and Erica had me stashed in a bag in the back of the worker transport with scatters all around." Diana winced. "I've had to do that more often than I want to think about recently. Sergio and Erica have Larry's basement tweaked to hold at least twenty of us if we need it. No one around here's going to bother Larry, as long as we aren't in their face about our presence."

Melanie nodded. Trust her parents to keep up hidden contacts without sharing with her or with her local Security. "So are those sensors stuff Sergio set up?"

"No. Larry and your dad." Diana winced, pausing for a moment. "Your dad kept Larry's place wired up. Larry's one of our hidden Dialogues. He's up-to-date on all the latest upgrades. Kathy sent me a message that you were on your way. We've been watching for you."

The truck stopped in the barnyard. Melanie noted that the path from the truck to the house suddenly was surrounded by the shimmer of a scatter generator.

"Hurry up and get in," Diana said. "We can't keep this on for long. Too obvious. Larry's got a *real* breakfast going for you guys."

"We've been eating Angela's mama's tamales," Melanie said.

"Anything left?"

"Unfortunately, no."

"Well, we'll have to see Mama Brenda soon, then, won't we?"

Melanie snorted as she climbed up the steps, stomped her feet clean, ducked inside and sat on the handy bench to pull off her boots. As if seeing Mama Brenda was at all feasible right now.

"Hey, Melanie. Long time no see," Larry greeted her, turning from the wood cookstove with spatula in hand. She left one boot on and hobbled across the room to hug him, reveling in the sweet scent of home-raised bacon, fresh-laid eggs, and toast.

"Sorry I brought so many folks."

"De nada. It's a party! Girl, it's good to see you. And who's this?" Larry asked, looking over at Marty. "I hear you have someone special these days. He the one?"

Shyly, she introduced them, then the rest of her team, before Diana shooed them into the farmhouse's spacious basement. A huge wood furnace put off waves of heat that felt exquisitely good after several days in the cold, driving rain.

After eating, showering, disinfecting and redonning their datasuits, and switching into dry and comfortable clothing, they gathered around the furnace on the several couches set around it. Melanie curled up next to Marty, drowsing off.

Her mother shook Melanie awake.

"Mel. I'm sorry. I know you're tired, but we need to talk. My office is on the other side of the wall."

Melanie rose, waking Marty. "C'mon, Marty." Aside, to her mother, "He has stuff to tell you too." She was suddenly wide awake, suspecting just what it was that Diana wanted to discuss in private.

Diana nodded. Silently, they followed her into the next room, where a small fan vent puffed in heat from the woodstove. Melanie fell into one chair while Marty sat in the one next to it. She picked up his hand and held it tight. This was not going to be easy.

Diana sat at her desk, looked down at the top of it, and heaved a heavy sigh. Then she looked back up at them, her face held tight and expressionless.

"Tell me," she said, her voice soft yet deadly, all professional and Corporate, the personality that had kept Do It Right going despite adversity. "What *really* happened to your father?"

Melanie drew a deep breath. She began the story of their work with

Ness, with Marty occasionally adding data but otherwise just holding her hand, giving her wordless support.

She faltered as she began the story of the actual attack itself. She had to close her eyes for a moment and calm herself as tightness choked her throat. She didn't know if she could do this.

<I'm here,> Marty said.

At last, she opened her eyes and looked full into her mother's face, describing what had happened. Her voice choked and faltered again as she recalled seeing the memories skittering away from Will's brain, her efforts to capture them, and stop them from flying off. Then kneeling to hold in what she could.

"Memory cascade," Marty interrupted, tersely. "The first stage of any Netwalk attack. Forced memory upload."

Diana nodded, her eyes focused on Melanie, wetness forming around her eyes. Melanie continued, her eyes blurring with tears as she described the rest of it. Diana winced as Melanie mentioned the fleeting bright vision of the gadget, but didn't say anything.

"The transfer worked?" Diana asked.

"It did," Marty confirmed. "He uploaded successfully, and on his own terms. Sarah has nothing of him, Diana. He fought her every step of the way. Maybe if he hadn't been riding the Burnout dragon as hard as he did, he might have survived."

"You couldn't have stopped him." Diana shook her head. "He was just too determined to pull this off. Mel, as you might have guessed, he and I were texting regularly almost up to the end, when it became too dangerous for me to contact him regularly, even on a floating link. I tried to get him to stop the Burnout." Her voice broke and she dropped her head into her hands, her entire body shaking.

Melanie gulped, her tears breaking free.

At last Diana raised her head from her hands, her cheeks damp. "Thank you for trying." She drew a deep, shuddering breath. "I knew he was dying. He knew he was dying. We weren't sure we would see each other again in this life. It was a hard choice I didn't want to make. He wouldn't let me stay. Not after the Interim appointment. I know that's why he was riding the dragon, hoping to keep his cancer at bay until we got this situation solved." Her voice broke again. "I just wish we could have pulled this off and I could have been there with him."

"Mom."

"But you were there. At least you were there. Someone from the family was there."

Silence fell over the room. They sat silently for a few minutes, calming themselves.

Diana's voice was harsh when she spoke again. "*She* has one hell of a lot to answer for." She let the statement hang. "What happens now?"

"We program and train all of you in Netwalk procedures. That's even more crucial after what happened last night. *She* came after me." Dispassionately, Marty described the attack from the night before. "We must ensure you know what to do," he finished.

"Peter's plan is to capture you, sic her on you, then have you killed," Melanie added. "Andrew told me that, the one chance he was free to talk to me without being watched. He's apparently Peter's host. Not a full-time host, he's one of two hosts." She hurried to continue as her mother opened her mouth. *If I don't ask now we'll get sidetracked.* "Mom, everyone keeps putting me off. I keep asking and no one will tell me anything. The gadget is involved. More on Peter's side than Sarah's. But it's involved."

Diana winced. "First of all, if the gadget is involved, that's not Sarah's plan. Your grandmother takes that device very seriously, more so than Peter ever did. Drew—" she shook her head. "If they play with his mind much more—especially Peter driven by—the gadget—" She sighed. "He's a host now?"

"Drew said he was Peter's host, and Sarah's enslaved other Netwalkers to stay charged. It's not just Sarah and Peter," Melanie said. "Liam is involved as well."

"Liam?" Diana asked. "You're sure of it?"

Melanie nodded. "Andrew confirmed. Liam's his minder, and he leads the Freedom Army. Liam may be Peter's other host."

Diana sighed again. "Peter. *My* brother, damn it. Freedom Army means Peter's the negative influence on Drew. Not so much Sarah. Damn. I can handle your grandmother. Peter, though, that's different, especially if he's tied into the whatchamacallit."

"Mom, just what is the gadget and why won't anyone tell me about it?"

Diana sighed. "It's a longer story than I really have time to tell. There's also oaths and disclosure agreements."

"Damn it, won't *anyone* tell me what the damn thing is?"

"Part of the situation is that we really *don't know* what the damn thing is!" her mother snapped back. Diana brushed a strand of hair out of her eyes. "Sorry. It is a war machine-like device that caused the Disruptions. That's about all we understand. There are certain—requirements—for you to know much more. It's been getting restless. Sarah was researching means to settle it before her death."

"Who would make such a thing?" Melanie whispered.

The rumors were true, then. The Gizmo caused the Disruptions. Chemical-biological attacks on random cities that had happened before she was born. The attacks had stopped as suddenly as they had begun, with no explanation. No wonder her father had been reluctant to say anything.

More than that—

Sarah and Mom were working together on this? Sounds like it.

Which meant this Gizmo was bad stuff. *Really* bad stuff, to bring her mother and grandmother together, in the face of their conflicts over the last seven years.

"We've never been able to find out," Diana answered. "Sarah said she had Ness Ryan working on a project—"

"Just the Netwalk stuff," Marty said.

"Then Netwalk may be an attempt to control Gizmo," Diana said. "Which means we need to control it. *We need to control Sarah as Netwalker and keep Peter and the Freedom Army away from it.*"

"Ness did nail Peter pretty good, before Will died, hopefully enough to keep him down for a while," Marty said. "He tried to affect Melanie through Andrew and failed. Peter isn't tied into Andrew the way that Ness and Will are locked into their hosts. He uses Andrew and another host as a means to keep separate. We're hoping that he remains disabled for a while yet."

"Andrew was free from Peter when I talked to him eight days ago."

Melanie said. "And I don't think Sarah was drawing on Peter or anyone else last night."

"Ness says that it takes some time for a Netwalker to reintegrate," Marty said. "The danger is that every time that a Netwalker goes through disintegration, we run the risk of them turning crazier than ever."

Diana nodded curtly. She spun her chair to stare at a picture of Will. "Okay," she said, turning back to them after a few minutes of thought. "Let's give you and your team a couple of hours to get rested. Do this training. Then, we're going hunting."

"Hunting?" Marty asked.

"Sarah hunting. We had better damn well get moving if we want to disarm Sarah and get her under control as a foil for the *thing* before Peter gets himself together and finds a means to send it after us. Trust me, we really don't want that. Once I get you—*both* of you—sworn to the Courts, you'll know more about the whys and wherefores. Can't tell you more before then for your own protection."

"But you *will* tell us, correct?" Melanie asked.

Diana nodded. "Next. We have to do something about Andrew before this business with Peter pushes him over the edge. He's still my son and your brother, and I want to save him if we can."

"Agreed."

"And then there's Liam and the Freedom Army. Sarah has always been skittish about them but she won't go into details. We have several alliances to be concerned about. Sarah, and whoever's allied with her. What worries me is that Liam and the Freedom Army seem to have some control over her. That wasn't supposed to happen. Then there's Peter. His alliances have always been sketchy. Andrew—who is he really allied with? Sarah? Peter? Liam?" Diana sighed. "So much to figure out. And then there's the leadership of the country."

"A real mess."

"Uh-huh. I *have* to get this situation worked out with Sarah before I can fix things politically. You two plus Ness are going to help me win, with me as Sarah's Netwalk host."

"Mom," Melanie protested. "I need to be Sarah's host, not you!"

"*No,* Melanie. The only way we're going to defang Sarah is to tie her to someone who knows more about her secrets than you do. We'll figure out what to do with Peter and the rest of her crew of Netwalkers after we get Sarah under control." She paused. "Besides, if we take care of *this,* the political arena will suddenly become a lot easier to manage."

Melanie sighed, exasperated. "Mom, I think you're just too close to all this. You haven't seen what Sarah's like now. I've stared her down twice already. Stopped her with Marty. If only I had figured it out before Dad died!"

"No." Diana's voice was flat. "I'll need you to be my backup if something happens to me. Not the other way around." Her voice went even quieter. "I know what soft spots she has. Not something you would know." She shook her head. "I don't want to burden you with this job."

"I don't want to lose you."

"I understand. But I'm still a tough old broad. I've been fighting with her for longer than you've been alive. Plus being her host should make it easier for me in the political arena. Her followers will respect me if I show I can control her."

"How are they going to know?"

Diana raised a brow. "The same way that too damn many of them know that she and Peter survived online. If I have to bring her out to show them, I will."

Melanie spread her hands wide, shaking her head. "I can't change your mind," she said in a low voice. "I'll support you all the way, Mom. But you exploiting her for political power is not something I want to see."

"There's another factor as well," her mother said quietly. "You deserve a right to create your life with Marty without *her* being a part of it. One Netwalker in a relationship is enough. I'd like to spare you that, if I can. You'll have your hands full figuring out the gadget when this is done."

"I guess I understand," Melanie said softly.

"Hon, I—" Her mother blinked hard, shaking her head. "I just wish —" She brushed away tears with the back of one hand, then dropped her head into her hands.

Melanie hugged her mother, rubbing her shoulders gently. Diana reached blindly for Melanie and hung on, bawling.

"Will. Oh God. Will. What a way to go," Diana groaned into Melanie's shoulder, shaking her head violently. "What a *hell* of a way to die. Oh God. I wasn't there. *I wasn't there, damn it!*"

A fresh wave of tears jolted through Melanie's body and she held her mother close. At some point, she was aware that Marty left them.

Finally, her mother pulled away. "Thank you. Thank you for being there. And for coming here. With you by my side, I can do this. Thank you for taking the risk to tell me this in person, to support me. Thank you for being here."

"I'll try my best to support you," Melanie said. "*We'll* try our best."

"Get some rest now. It could get pretty crazy before all this is done."

Melanie went into the other room. The others had thrown down sleeping bags in front of the furnace, taking advantage of the warm, safe place to rest comfortably. Marty had placed theirs in one corner, affording them a small amount of privacy. When she slipped in with him, he pulled her close, wrapping himself around her.

"You going to be okay?" he whispered.

"Yeah. Thanks for giving us the time alone."

He kissed her. "I knew you needed it. I hope you can get some sleep."

"You too."

When the training for Diana's Security started, Melanie was the only one on guard upstairs. She sat in the spacious front room, near the pellet stove, watching the road and the fields through the huge picture window. Sun warmed the room, a rare sunny day for the Coast Range in winter. Binoculars close to hand, she wrapped herself up in an ancient crocheted afghan blanket to sit her vigil.

It was a nice day to sit in the sun and do nothing. In other circumstances, she might have chosen to read. Right now, it was relaxing to not do anything but watch for trouble. For the first time in three weeks, she felt relaxed.

Had Sarah's death only been three weeks ago? It felt like forever. At least she had some downtime that wasn't a function of resting up from a cyberattack or traveling.

It was enough to watch the single hawk circling high above the fields as the cattle grazed. An occasional rig chugged by, but none slowed. No skimmers. Just trucks. Most people out here lacked the cash to support a skimmer. Melanie idly wondered if this much traffic was typical, but decided against distracting the training process to ask. It probably varied.

Besides, the blacksuits wouldn't drive trucks. They would come in skimmers.

When plans started to pop up in her thoughts, Melanie ruthlessly pushed them back down. Now was not the time. It was downtime. The simple duty of standing watch. Rest her mind for the job of supporting her mother when it came time to go Sarah hunting.

She'd worry about Gizmo and other issues later.

Melanie wasn't sure how long it was before evening shadows spread across the fields. A small herd of elk ventured out from the edges of the trees, holding themselves separate from the cattle.

Soft-shod feet scuffed on the polished wood floor behind her. Her mother rested one hand on Melanie's shoulder, briefly, before grabbing another afghan and curling up on the couch next to her. Melanie noticed the new appearance of dark circles under her mother's eyes.

She had a rough one.

"Tough session?" she asked.

Diana nodded, curling her long legs to her chest and resting her chin on her knees.

"It's really weird seeing and talking to Ness like this," her mother said finally. "*Really* weird." Another pause. "She offered to link me with Will and Julia. It wouldn't have been much of a connection. Will's not that strong, too close to his original integration, she says. But I could talk to him." She hid her face for a moment.

Melanie reached over and rested a hand on her mother's shoulder. "Did you?"

Diana shook her head, looking back up. "I'm not ready for that. Not yet."

They sat silently for a few minutes.

"Second thoughts about hunting Sarah?" Melanie asked.

Her mother shook her head again. "No. Talking to Ness confirmed it. We can't let Sarah go on like this. Not just for our sake, but hers."

"Agreed."

"It's one thing thinking about this in theory. Talking to Ness brings home what I have to do. And it's pretty overwhelming."

"I've had it thrown at me so hard that I haven't really stopped to think until now," Melanie said. "I've been trying not to think too much."

"That's good."

"Weeks on the run. Weeks reacting. I'm tired of reacting."

"You and Marty have been through one hell of a tough time."

"Yeah. But we've not had much of a choice."

They fell silent again.

"What's the schedule now?" Melanie broke the silence. "Ready to go hunting?"

Diana grinned ruefully. "Not until I've had some dinner and a chance to rest up. My God, Mel. I'm surprised that you and Marty are still on your feet."

Melanie shrugged. "You do what you have to. Are we waiting until tomorrow?"

"Later on tonight. I don't want to put it off too long. Ness gave us some good strategies to use, and we'll go with that. But I want some food, I want to rest, and Marty needs some rest as well."

Melanie nodded. "He's been pushing it hard. I wish I could get Ness to tell me what his physical state is. I worry about him."

"You can't control the men, kiddo. It just causes you more problems. I know from your dad."

"Dad was pushing hard at the end, too.

Diana sighed. "Normal for him. He was active by nature, even with the cancer. You get your activity level from him." Her mother blinked back tears. "Knowing he was dying ripped me up. It was better for him when he couldn't see how his sickness was tearing at me. I'm sure that was why he was so firm about me leaving."

They fell silent again.

"So. Dinner. Then how do we go about hunting Sarah?" Melanie asked.

"Larry's cooking us a feast. We'll eat, then rest. Then about nine-ish, we'll convene up here. Make sure we have a nice warm fire going, candles, get the ambiance up in a way that *she* absolutely hates. She thrives on that sterile lab setting. We'll have those members of our Security with higher Netwalk aptitude to back us. Then we'll have Angela, Sergio and the rest of the crew patrolling outside in case we attract any blacksuit attention."

"You think that's a risk?"

"The activity online might set them off. We'll call Sarah. I'm hoping she comes without any need to chase her down. We ambush her, and then pare her off from that posse backing her." Diana's lips tightened. "Get her subdued and locked down in my chip's host area."

"Does Ness think that Dad can help?"

"Because of the way the transfer happened, she says he's not that strong."

"Damn. Two Netwalkers against one might be useful."

"I'm just grateful that she thinks Peter might still be out of commission. Otherwise—" Diana stared off in the distance. "If she's wrong, it might come to you to take care of Peter. I hope it doesn't. I really hope it doesn't."

Melanie shuddered. "Me too."

"Okay." Diana got up, other footsteps echoing in the kitchen. "Sounds like it's time to get dinner going. You helping?"

"We have someone else available to be on watch?"

"Now that we're done, yeah. Come on, it's been a while since you cooked with Larry. Let's get ourselves some *real* food. You're way too skinny."

"That's what Marty says."

"He's right." Diana hugged Melanie, then they headed for the kitchen.

CHAPTER 15

MOONLIGHT POURED DOWN ON THE FIELDS BELOW LARRY'S HOUSE. THE elk herd still lurked cautiously near the tree line, dark shadowy forms moving slowly. Larry's herd of Angus beef cattle grazed closer to the house, a mixed herd of cows and older calves with one bull. Melanie shivered, wrapping her arms around herself. It all seemed so peaceful. So quiet.

The quiet before the explosion.

At least no one thinks the gadget will interfere.

Marty came up behind her. Melanie leaned back into him, tingling at his touch, marveling at how quickly he had become a necessary part of her life. His lips brushed the top of her head.

"It's pretty out there," he said.

"It is." Melanie shivered again.

"You okay?" He pulled her closer.

"Yeah. But now I'm scared," she said. "Scared something will happen to Mom. Scared something else goes wrong. Scared something will happen to us."

"You're right to be scared," he said. "But not for us. I won't let you fall. You know that."

"I do. But I don't want to lose this. Us. I look at Mom now, without Dad, and I think, that could be me if something happens to you. Or you if something happens to me."

"Oh, darlin'," he whispered. "It could happen at any time. You know that. Doesn't need to be now. What's eating at you?"

"It's not just losing each other; I worry that things will change between us. That you'll wake up one day and think that this happened too fast and just who the hell is it that you are in bed with?"

Marty chuckled softly into her hair. "Melanie, honey, some things will change. Some won't. What won't change is that I'm here. Now. Will be in the future. Our future." He rested his head against hers.

"Thank you."

"I can't believe the stuff we've done together so far. I'm amazed at what I can do with you at my side. I know I can't do it without you."

She dropped her chin to her chest, smiling. "Then no regrets?" she asked.

"No regrets," he repeated. He turned her to face him. "Melanie Landreth, you are one amazing woman. I've always respected you as a colleague and as my superior in Do It Right. When Ness died, when it was time for me to come home, you were one of the things that I knew would make it right. I looked forward to seeing you. I didn't know why, but I knew that I could come home, that you would be there, and that somehow you'd make it stop hurting."

"Ness's influence?"

He shook his head. "No. Absolutely not."

"I just wonder."

He shook his head again. "No. When we became lovers this time, I found this different side of you. I don't know why I didn't see it when we were dating before."

"You've been there, you've always been someone I've enjoyed being around, but suddenly it was as if I'd never noticed you before."

He kissed her, at first brushing her lips softly, tentatively, delicately. Then his arms tightened around her and his lips pressed down more firmly on hers, and they kissed furiously, deeply.

At last, he lifted his head. "I love you."

"I love you, too."

She rested her forehead against his chest. They stood like that for a few moments, then Marty gently took her face in his hands.

"Once Sarah's under control and your mom is set up as Interim

President, let's consider a contract. You name the type. Civil, covenant, ceremonial, whatever. If something does happen to one of us," he paused. "I want you to know that this is the commitment I want to make. Wanted to make. If you're willing."

"I'm willing," she whispered.

He pulled her close again. They stood together, quietly, for a few more moments. Then Marty sighed and pulled away.

"Time to start getting ready. Do you know what your mother has in mind?"

She nodded. "I'm waiting for her to light the candles."

"Those make me nervous. We could start a fire by accident. We don't know enough about the effect these Netwalkers have on the physical world. If Sarah-as-Netwalker can kill your father, and Ness bring out bruises on you, then what could they do to candles and flame?"

"I'm okay with it. They're pretty safe," she said. "She's placed them in areas where they won't get knocked over."

"But can they be used against us?"

Melanie shrugged. "So far none of the Netwalkers have been throwing stuff at us."

"There is that."

"We also have nastier stuff in the labs. If Sarah had wanted to get ugly when she killed Dad, she had access to dangerous material. Easily. What does Ness say?"

"She's not worried about it. Am I being silly?"

"You're being cautious. A good thing. Thinking about things we take for granted is what I pay you for." She grinned up at him.

"Yes, boss." He chuckled.

Melanie turned serious. "We'll keep fire safety in mind. But Mom's not worried, because she's had Larry bless them. He used to be a priest. I think he still does a secret Mass."

Marty raised a brow. "I didn't think of your mother as religious."

"She's very private about her beliefs."

"Is this something you share? Just curious. Not seen it before."

She waggled her hand. "A little. My involvement with the Church is not the same as hers. I went through Confirmation, occasionally still go to Mass a few times a year. It was something she shared with Dad. I think he converted her."

Marty winced. "Ouch. Netwalk impacts their belief system."

"Maybe. Maybe not. Dad didn't seem to have a problem, but he was always a pretty pragmatic Catholic. Mom's spoken out pretty firmly in the past when research crossed her personal moral line, but she hasn't said word one about Netwalk. I don't know if it's something they researched years ago with Dialogue, or what."

"I hadn't a clue about this."

"I don't have a feel for whether Dad's survival as a Netwalker makes it worse for Mom. Dying like he did without her there, yeah. That was hardest on her."

"And you?"

She took a deep breath. "I'm pragmatic. My own belief tells me that it doesn't really matter what survived in the upload, that his essential self isn't there. Just like Ness's isn't there. Or do you feel that way?"

Marty frowned, then nodded. "A Netwalker is—and isn't—the same as the real person. There's a piece missing. Not as much as with a digital thought clone—there's more of the real person in a Netwalker—but like you said, the essential self isn't there."

"Whether it is or not the real person, I don't want to see that digital persona abused. By Sarah or anyone else."

"Agreed."

"It shouldn't matter, what matters is that he was—" her voice caught. "Dad was a good person." She wiped her eyes with one hand.

Marty kissed her forehead. "I'm sorry. I didn't mean to make you cry."

"It sneaks up on me. What time we did spend around Neahcom was usually here. Sometimes that was just me and Dad and Drew, while Mom dealt with family."

Footsteps sounded in the room beyond. Marty took Melanie's hand as Diana, Larry, Crispin and Annie entered the big living room. Annie carefully set a hologlobe generator down in the middle of the room. Larry wore vestments and carried a small vial of holy water.

"Everyone have the new datasuits?" Annie asked. After their

assents, she keyed up the hologlobe. Melanie quivered as it tingled through her.

The boundaries stabilized at the edge of the room.

"All right," Diana said. "Larry is going to quickly bless each of us, unless someone objects. It's okay to object if you don't want it. This is just for me. If it helps you, great. If it hinders you or makes you uncomfortable, then don't do it."

She looked around, meeting their eyes, waiting for their assent. "After that, I'll light the candles, and start some music. We'll have a moment of silence for you to pray, meditate, or think 'oh shit!' Then we'll begin. Any questions?"

No one spoke. Diana nodded to Larry. After they were blessed, Diana began lighting candles. She shook her head at Melanie's silent offer to help. Melanie stepped back and took Marty's hand.

Then Diana took Larry and Melanie's hands, and nodded at the others to join in a circle. They stood for a few moments, quiet.

Make this work. Please. Just make this work without anyone getting hurt.

Diana took a deep breath, slipping her hands free from Melanie and Larry. She braced herself, feet standing in line with her hips and shoulders, knees slightly flexed, shoulders back and upright, her hands at hip level. She tapped out codes in the air along with the music, subvocaling rapidly.

This isn't spontaneous. How long has she been preparing for this confrontation?

The Netwalk schematic framework sprung up around them, pulsing with the beat as the music segued into a bluegrass/rock jam. Melanie's senses took a couple of seconds to adjust to the virtual world.

<Time to raise Ness,> Marty warned.

<I'm ready,> she told Marty.

Slight prickles raced up Melanie's right arm, followed by a sensation of heat in her right hand. Then Ness appeared in falcon form, apparently from their conjoined hands. She perched on Marty's right shoulder. The falcon dipped her head toward Melanie, acknowledging her. Melanie nodded in acknowledgement.

They waited. Then Ness alerted, head swiveling toward the southeastern corner of the room. Diana stopped subvocaling and tapping code, turning to face that area. Falcon Ness raised her wings slightly, fluttering them.

<No,> Marty sent to Ness. <Not yet.>

<Mel,> he said to Melanie.

<Yes.>

<We'll do this together. Follow my lead!>

<As long as I know what to do!>

<You shouldn't have any problems.>

The shadow formed in the southeastern corner of the room, gingerly avoiding the areas where candles flickered.

Interesting.

Melanie's heart pounded and her breathing sped up while her mouth went dry. Maybe her mother was right about the effect of the blessed candles. Or else Diana's own faith in the candle effect was communicated to the shadow. Sarah wasn't Catholic, had never been Catholic.

Marty raised their entwined hands. He whistled to Ness, who rose off of his shoulder, then landed on their hands. As Ness's talons contacted Melanie's hands, electric shock raced through her body, followed by warmth and a feeling that she was racing fast down a well-packed ski run with a light dusting of powder, accelerating toward a yet-unknown point at the bottom.

The three of them. Together.

The shadow stopped short of Diana. It coalesced into the gargoyle-Sarah shape. Elongated and pale head. Shimmering fangs poking beyond her lips. Red eyes staring out from her skull. White hair sticking out in splinters. Blood dripping from long, narrow, almost-skeletal fingers with claw-like fingernails.

<She's disintegrating,> Ness said. <Losing control. Where's her posse?>

More globules of shadow stuff appeared, also shying from the candles. They formed an arch around Sarah, remaining as indistinct shapes.

That must be her captive Netwalkers.

Marty walked forward. Melanie followed, until they stood two steps from Diana's right hand. Suddenly Melanie remembered when she and Marty stood together at the beginning of this struggle, supporting her mother, *just like now.*

The memory felt forced.

<No memories!> Marty snapped, part him, part Ness. <No reflecting! Memory cascade trigger!>

Melanie shoved the memories away.

Sarah hissed at Diana, her words incoherent. She yelled. Then she lunged at Diana, flicking out her claw-like fingernails at Diana's chest.

Diana sidestepped toward Melanie, whirling into a crouch as Sarah plunged past. Sarah matched Diana's posture, snarling. Her eyes darted back and forth among the living, as if she were seeking new prey.

Sarah lunged toward Crispin, on Marty's other side. He stumbled as he tried to evade Sarah's grasp. Sarah keened triumphantly as she bent over him, tearing at him with her fingernails. Crispin screamed as one fingernail hit home, tearing into his arm.

<NOW!> Marty snapped. They flung Ness into the air while Marty changed into the bear shape. Ness stooped hard on Sarah, striking at her head, sending strands of hair flying. Marty growled and snarled, backing Sarah away from Crispin.

Why aren't I changing?

And then the transformation occurred. One moment Melanie was all human. Next, she moved on cougar paws, thinking cougar thoughts, striding forward to glare into Sarah's eyes.

I don't fear you now.

A globule moved between them as Sarah broke and ran. Melanie dived upon the globule, tearing at it with claws and teeth as white pieces of data scattered with each scratch.

The globule disappeared. Melanie stopped, looking around, tail switching. Larry wrestled with a globule. It faded away as Melanie watched. Crispin curled up in a ball, shaking and moaning.

Where's Marty?

She finally spotted him. Marty shambled to where Sarah and Diana wrestled. Ness struck at Sarah's head. No reaction. Sarah's form grew more distinct. And her globules were gone. Inside her, maybe? No. A few still remained, drifting around Sarah and Diana, heading toward Diana's back.

Diana held Sarah at arm's length while Sarah lunged at her throat. But her arms quivered with the effort. Soon, Sarah would break through.

She keeps on coming at you, and at you, and at you until your strength fails.

NO! Melanie bounded toward them. She used her big cougar paws and strength to pull Sarah away from Diana, like she did during Sarah's attack on Marty.

A sharp electric charge lanced through Melanie, throwing her onto the floor and switching her back to her human shape. Sarah hovered over her, ready to pounce. Melanie rolled away as Sarah dove for her. She leapt to her feet. The cougar form didn't return. Sarah rose, snarling. Melanie's lips pulled back from her teeth, and she stood her ground.

I will not back down. I will not let you bully me.

Sarah swiped at Melanie. One fingernail brushed Melanie's cheek. Marty's shambling mass struck Sarah, knocking her sideways. Sarah turned on him. One fingernail scraped his throat.

No!

But she couldn't move fast enough to help Marty. Shadowy globules clustered around her, slowing her movement. Melanie batted at the globules, trying to break free.

Another of Sarah's fingernails found Marty's throat. Blood sprayed across the room. Marty screamed.

Melanie could no longer touch his Dialogue.

No!

Sarah bent her head to tear at Marty's throat. Too far away, too far away, *too far away.*

"*ENOUGH!*" Diana bellowed. She grabbed Sarah's head and yanked her away from Marty, knocking Sarah to the floor. Ness continued to strike at Sarah's exposed body as Diana tried to pinion Sarah. Melanie hesitated.

Oh God. Marty.

Stopping Sarah came first.

Melanie jumped on Sarah and straddled her chest, seizing Sarah's hands, ignoring the shocks pulsing through her. Sarah kicked at Melanie. Bony virtual knees thumped on Melanie's butt, dispensing tiny zap charges. Ness hovered over them, screeching and stooping on Sarah when an opportunity opened.

"It's time you learned who's in charge here," Diana growled at Sarah through gritted teeth. "You can't run wild like this. You're going to move inside my chip, you're going to learn some boundaries, and maybe once in your life you're going to behave! Now!"

She snapped Sarah's neck with a sharp twist, yanking the head free from the body. Sarah's body faded under Melanie. She collapsed to the floor.

Diana raised Sarah's shrieking head to eye level, pushing on it. Faint black lines streamed between them, terminating at Diana's Netwalk chip. Sarah's head kept screaming as it shrank, until there was nothing left in Diana's hands. Then Diana's hands dropped to her side, and she stood there, shaking her head, as Larry hurried over to her.

Melanie half-ran, half-crawled to Marty's side. With trembling hands, she tore a strip of cloth off of her sleeve and pressed it against the wound on his neck. He breathed fast, shallow breaths that were almost gasps, moaning softly.

"Hang on, Marty. Hang on. I'm here," she crooned to him. His eyes rolled under his lids and his head rocked from side to side. "Damn it, Marty, *stay with me!*"

Ness, now in human form, sparkled into being on Marty's other side, nearly transparent.

"He's not responding to me!" she wailed. *"I can't get back in!"*

Oh God. Oh God.

"Marty, damn it," Melanie groaned. Her mind blanked and the only thing she could think about was *Marty dying.*

Larry knelt next to her, medkit in hand. "Let me take care of the medical stuff. You support him."

"His Dialogue's offline!" Melanie yelled. "I need Dialogue help, now!"

"Easy, girl. Can't you fix it?" Larry asked.

"I can't remember how!"

Diana slid in next to her. "You can reboot him with my help. We can do it."

"How, with *her* in you?"

"You'll do the work. Come on, Melanie! Girl! Snap out of it! We have to get Ness back in! Come on! Get back with me!"

Her mother's tone shocked Melanie into action. She placed both hands on Marty's temples. That was as much as she could remember.

How did I get affected? What blanked my brain?

No time to figure it out right now.

Diana directed her through the external tapping reboot code. As the code progressed, Melanie calmed. Soon, she remembered the sequence without being cued.

Ness faded.

"No!" Melanie cried.

Diana placed a hand on her arm. "It's okay. He's active again. She's recharging. You did it."

"I can't tell!"

"Easy. Deep breath. He's stable. You were so focused on the sequence you couldn't notice."

Melanie made contact with his Dialogue. She sensed the faint hum of a working Dialogue whose owner was unconscious. Ness was in the Netwalk section of Marty's chip. But there was no response otherwise.

She sagged back onto her heels, moaning as she buried her head in her hands.

No. God, no.

Diana shook her. "Mel. Hon. He's *okay*. He's in recovery mode. We'll get him airlifted to better support as soon as—" She hesitated, then continued. "As soon as I get this next situation settled."

Melanie raised her head. "*Next* situation?"

Diana nodded. "I need you. Outside. Now."

"Why?"

"We have blacksuits."

Melanie thought she saw a faint reflection of Sarah in Diana's eyes. Then it winked out. Her mother's face was tightly drawn and haggard.

She's damn near running on empty.

"You won't be able to bring her out yet," she said.

"No time to integrate. But if I have to, I'll bring her out. I'll need your help to make her behave if I do."

Melanie nodded. She kissed Marty's forehead. He stirred and moaned softly, but did not rouse. Then she followed her mother.

Diana thrust a heavy coat at Melanie. "It's cold. Wear this."

"What about you?"

"Don't worry about me." Diana handed her a pistol. "Be ready."

"You have one?"

"I still have your father's hidies. If it gets to that point, I'll bring *her* out. I'll have no time to deal with any more weapons."

They marched outside. The headlamps of both National Security blacksuits and their own Do It Right Security illuminated a standoff. Angela, Nik, Sergio and Erica stood at the bottom of the steps, weapons locked and ready, facing at least twenty blacksuits who uncharacteristically milled about instead of standing in rank. As Diana marched out, they straightened up.

One blacksuit stepped forward.

"Diana Landreth, Melanie Landreth, you are under arrest. Come with us."

"Under what authority?" Diana demanded.

"Under the authority of Andrew Landreth, President of the Confederation of North America."

Diana laughed. "*I* am the Interim President of the New Federalized United States of America. My appointment has been ratified by the Congress-in-Exile. My son has no authority! His position has not been ratified by any recognized entity, either Confederation or Federalized American!"

The blacksuit took another step forward.

"Halt!" Sergio commanded. He snapped his weapon to his shoulder. The red dot marking his target held steady on the blacksuit's chest. Simultaneously, Erica, Nik, and Angela dropped to a one-knee shooting position, their weapons sighted on the chests of the first line of blacksuits.

Melanie shivered. She pulled her weapon and aimed at the one blacksuit remaining in the front row who didn't already have a target dot on him.

A distant light flickered at the bottom of the driveway. A truck turned up the drive.

No. Two. Three. Four trucks. Melanie kept her hands steady as Diana stared down at the blacksuit, maintaining silence. Reinforcements for the blacksuits? Not likely. Trucks, not skimmers. Blacksuits wouldn't use trucks.

Help has arrived.

At last, the blacksuit spoke. "I have orders."

"I'm not coming. Neither is my daughter. We do not recognize Andrew's authority."

"Then it'll have to be by force," the blacksuit said.

"You're outnumbered," Diana told him.

Now it was the blacksuit's turn to laugh. "By what? You and this handful of Security?"

"By *my* Do It Right Security, yes," Diana said calmly. She nodded toward the trucks. "And by *them.*"

People poured out of the cabs and beds of the four trucks. All carried weapons of various vintages.

"Shit!" the blacksuit turned, raising his weapon. "Company, prepare—"

Oh shit, it's going all to hell, just at this very last moment.

Melanie tightened her hands and prepared to shoot.

"HOLD!"

That's not Mom's voice.

Melanie's head snapped toward Diana. A shimmering shape formed next to her. Sarah.

Oh my God, Mom's brought her out to play.

She stepped close. If her mother couldn't control Sarah, they were in trouble.

The blacksuits froze at the familiar voice. Slowly, they turned toward Diana, Sarah, and Melanie. Melanie lowered her handgun and moved close to the Sarah manifestation.

If the bitch even twitches funny, I'll nail her.

Sarah looked strained, but at least she wasn't the gargoyle figure.

Instead of the stealthsuit in tatters, she wore one of her favorite gray and black suit ensembles, black slacks with a gray and black patterned jacket that zipped up to her chin.

"Stand down," Sarah commanded. "You know who I am. She has the power she claims." A sour look flitted across her face. "I *reluctantly* acquiesce to her authority."

<Ness. Can you hear me?> Melanie had never tried talking directly to Ness before, but damn it, if ever she needed backup fast, it was now.

Her shoulder tingled on the side by Sarah. She looked and saw Ness perched there.

<Can't do this for long. Draws too much from him.>

<Thanks. I may need help getting Sarah back in.>

<I'll try. May need to go back without warning.>

She nodded.

The new arrivals swarmed the now-unresisting blacksuits, disarming and cuffing them. Kathy Miller led them.

"I raised the Pacific Northwest for you, Diana!" she called out. "This was the only string left untied! What do you want us to do with these damned blacksuits?"

"Lock them up," Diana said, tersely. "Then come in. I have wounded that need a higher level of assistance. Do you have any skimmers you can send to Uni Hospital in Portland?"

"Waiting just down the way." Kathy pointed behind her shoulder with a thumb as she walked up the steps. "I see you have *her*," she said in a lower voice. "Under control?"

Diana's lips formed the word, "Barely."

Kathy's eyes darted to Melanie. "Where's Marty? I see Ness."

"He's down," Melanie whispered. "She's just barely able to help."

Kathy nodded. "Send her back."

Melanie nodded. <Hear that?>

<Yeah.> Ness's presence was gone.

"Sarah. Back," Diana commanded.

Melanie tensed, holstering her gun. This was the telling moment.

Sarah pulsed brighter. A hint of the gargoyle shape twisted her form.

"Back."

Sarah pulsed stronger. Melanie and Kathy exchanged quick glances, and took one step closer as Diana whirled to face Sarah's form.

"You two move *off*, damn it!" Diana snarled at them through gritted teeth. "Stay out of this! I need to show my control of her publicly, without help!"

Reluctantly, they moved back two steps.

Diana grabbed the Sarah-shape by the neck.

"Do I have to do this to you again?" she demanded. "I *will*, you know! Get back in there!"

Sarah glared at Diana. "One day you'll make a mistake."

"Like hell I will. Not with *you* there. Now *get back in there before I snap your neck again!*"

Sarah faded, streaming toward Diana's temple. When Sarah was gone, Diana visibly relaxed.

Melanie bit her lip.

I'm not comfortable with the way those two are relating to each other. I hope they start cooperating. Damn it. I should have taken control of Sarah myself.

Diana turned back to the crowd of allies and disarmed, cuffed blacksuits.

"Thank you," she said. "Thank you so very much for your help. This is our new beginning. Our means to taking back what is truly ours. The revival of the New American Federation." She smiled at them, more of a weary grimace than a smile. "Many of you are friends I've known from childhood, or from families I've known from childhood. I thank you for your loyalty and your support. Now I ask you to keep the faith. We have the Northwest. Other regions will be joining us. Our big push now is to take over D.C., and I need your help. Some of you have to take care of things here. But I want a group to go with me to D.C."

Diana took a deep, shuddering, breath before continuing. "Decide amongst yourselves. I'll take however many choose to go all the way. For those of you employed by National Security, we will welcome your assistance if you support us. Thank you, and good night." She spread her arms wide, as if in benediction.

The group cheered. Diana turned away. "Keep me on my feet if it looks like I'm gonna fall," she muttered to Kathy and Melanie. "I'm about ready to collapse, and I sure as hell can't do it here."

Melanie pressed close, supporting her mother with a hand on her back while Kathy opened the door for them. Once they were safely inside and the door closed behind them, Diana's legs buckled and she sagged to the floor.

"You okay?" Kathy asked.

"Yeah. I'm just beat. She damn near didn't go back in. I've *got* to get some rest. Food. Fast. Damn, controlling her is going to be a *bitch*! I'm glad we worked out the protocols—" Diana broke off.

"Is this a gadget thing?" Melanie snapped.

Diana and Kathy exchanged quick looks.

"Procedures we've developed with the whatchamacallit, yes," Kathy answered.

"Melanie, we can talk about this once I've rested," Diana said.

"I'll take care of Mom," Melanie told Kathy. "But we have two people down, Crispin, and Marty. Get more help for them, Kathy. *Please.*" Her eyes met Kathy's, pleading.

I'd help him but I can't. I have to help her. She needs me too. Damn it. Help him for me.

Kathy nodded sharply, as if she heard Melanie's silent plea. "I'll take care of them."

"Just let me see Marty before they go," Melanie said.

"Of *course,* Mel!" Kathy turned away, already focused on her two charges.

Melanie knelt beside Diana and draped one of Diana's arms over her own shoulders. "Okay. One-two-three." They heaved up and stood there, Diana's taller form swaying against Melanie. "Let's get you fed. Larry have a place for you to crash upstairs?"

Diana nodded. "Back bedroom."

Right off of his kitchen. Perfect. She coaxed her mother along until they were in the kitchen. Melanie eased her into a chair next to the woodstove. Diana shivered violently, so Melanie hurried back into the living room for an afghan, pausing to notice that two medics worked over Crispin and Marty, getting them ready for transport.

Good.

She wrapped Diana in the afghan, leaving one arm free so Diana could feed herself. Then she peeked in Larry's refrigerator. Their rescue fruit drink had made it into the fridge from the supply packs. Melanie poured a generous amount into a mug, and helped Diana drink it. Then she pulled out protein and chopped it up into small, easily-eaten bits, snacking as she worked with shaky hands. Ham, roast beef and turkey slices. Cheese, both cheddar and mozzarella. No easy high protein stuff here, not like at the labs, but enough to remedy a cybercrash.

She fed the small bits to Diana, interspersing it with sips of the fruit drink, until Diana held up a hand.

"No more. I can't eat more."

Melanie glanced over at the small pile of meat and cheese. "The more you force yourself to eat now, the better you'll feel when you wake up."

"Mel."

"Netwalk eats you up. You need to do this."

Hell, I need to do this.

Melanie reached for the fruit drink and poured herself a glass.

Kathy leaned around the doorframe between the kitchen and the front room. "Mel. It's time."

Melanie chugged her drink and glanced at her mother. "You'll be okay?"

"Go see him off."

"I'll be right back." She pointed at the food. "Get that down your gullet! I don't care how, just do it!" Melanie winced at her snappish tone.

I'm close to crashing.

"*Go,*" Diana said. "I'll be fine until you get back!"

Marty was awake as she knelt beside him. His eyelids fluttered as he watched the medics—they had him on monitors and an intravenous line. Melanie caressed his forehead and leaned her head into his shoulder. His lips lightly brushed her hair. She raised her head.

"Thank God," she breathed.

"You're okay," he whispered. "When she went for you. Worst thing I could imagine. When I couldn't see you here, I was afraid to ask."

"I was taking care of Mom. Sorry. I couldn't be in two places, I wanted to be here, oh God, Marty, it was my worst nightmare when she nailed you."

"Sorry. Just too slow. Damn, she's fast. Your mom?"

"Has Sarah. Brought her out to stand down the blacksuits. Sarah almost didn't go back in."

"Damn. I should have been there."

"I borrowed Ness for a moment. But that took too much out of you."

"You borrowed Ness? We can do that?" He smiled. "Damn, Mel. That's good news. We learn more about this stuff every time we do it."

"Any idea what's up with you?"

He shook his head. "Feel like hell. Feel worse than when I integrated Ness. Some sort of poison inside my system from Sarah's attack."

Melanie picked up the hand that wasn't tied into the intravenous line and held it to her face. "I wish I could stay with you."

He caressed her face. "We're not ordinary people. You're not an ordinary person. Don't have the luxury. I *understand,* hon. No blame. No regrets."

Tears blurred her eyes and she kissed Marty's hand. He stroked her face.

"Call Ness for help to control Sarah as long as distance allows," he ordered. "She can't charge off of you. Can't stay in your chip. But you can direct her. Use her. I'll do what I can remotely, 'kay? Just log what you're doing. Use the info later to figure out what we're doing. You're likely to learn more than I will."

Kathy touched her shoulder. "It's time."

Melanie blinked back more tears. She kissed Marty, then took his hand as the medics activated the floating stretcher. The blacksuits were no longer in sight, and two trucks were gone, but the occupants of the remaining trucks stood on alert.

It took all of her willpower to walk out of that skimmer and stand clear, watching as it lifted into the early morning darkness.

But she did it.

Then she trudged back to the house and into the kitchen.

Her mother snored with an empty plate beside her. Larry cut up more meat and cheese, snacking as he worked. Melanie grabbed a quick handful of ham chunks, washing them down with fruit drink, before shaking Diana awake.

"Let's get you into the bedroom."

Diana grunted agreement. Slowly, carefully, Melanie guided her into the bedroom and got her settled into the bed. It was all she could do to keep from falling into it with her mother and nodding off herself.

Need to eat first, she reminded herself. She turned to the door and started to walk out.

"Mel." Her mother's voice, though drowsy, was still compelling. Melanie went back and sat on the bedside.

"What's up?" she asked.

"You gonna take care of yourself? Spent all that time on me, but you're wiped out too. I saw it."

"Yeah, Mom. Doing it now."

"Good." Diana rolled onto her side, and her eyelids drooped down as she eased back into sleep.

Melanie drifted into the kitchen, picking up one of the plates of meat and cheese Larry had set out. She started eating absentmindedly.

Then everything they had done tonight struck her.

She shivered and dropped into a chair, for a moment resting her head in her hands.

Dear God, I wish Marty were here.

Or that she was with him. She desperately wanted to make certain that he was recovering properly.

But she had greater responsibilities.

CHAPTER 16

"THIS IS IT," DIANA ANNOUNCED TO THE PEOPLE WAITING OUTSIDE THE next morning. "We're leaving. You're coming?"

The crowd cheered and whooped in response.

Melanie stood two steps from her mother's right shoulder, Nik and Angela next to her, Sergio and Erica flanking them. If anything, she thought the crowd was bigger and more enthusiastic than it had been last night.

"Do you believe this?" she muttered to Angela.

"It's the only way we'll be able to pull this off," Angela whispered.

"I sure hope so."

"This has been pretty standard behavior when your mom speaks to an audience," Sergio whispered into Melanie's ear. "She's a pretty good politician."

Diana pointed to the approaching skimmers. "The folks in those skimmers will brief you. Load as quickly as possible. Good luck. We're on our way to take our country back!" She went inside the house, Melanie following.

"You talked to Julia yet?" Diana asked Melanie.

Melanie nodded. "Yes. We have the hologlobe/hologlove protocol worked out for Sarah. Lockdown codes and everything else they think I'll need."

Diana patted Melanie's arm. "Good. We'll be working with her as soon as we're on our way."

MORE PEOPLE KEPT COMING, SOME BRINGING SKIMMERS. DIANA ORDERED more skimmers from—somewhere, while Melanie helped with organization. The skimmers filled Larry's front field. The count was up to several hundred people by the time everyone was loaded into the skimmers, early in the afternoon.

"We'll reach a neutral site sometime in the middle of the night," Diana said as they took off. "Then we'll make our move in early morning. We've a couple of stops to make along the way. Plus we're plotting a random course. All that adds to the time."

"Okay."

"Let's get to work with Sarah."

Melanie took a deep breath. "First. How did you develop the yanking the head off theory about controlling Sarah? I need to know where that came from before we start." She eyed her mother cautiously.

And to what degree are you working off your anger at her for killing Dad by doing that?

"Kathy knew a little bit about Ness's Netwalk research. Not a lot, just enough to formulate some theories. When I let her know that I was planning to host Sarah, she suggested that as a desperation move. We shouldn't depend on it."

"Is there anything else you and Kathy have developed that I should know about? Especially with Gizmo?"

"Don't call it that out loud around me and Kathy!"

Melanie flinched back. "You haven't told me that!"

"Sorry." Diana sighed and spread her hands. "There is—feedback if the word's said around those sworn to it in unprotected settings. Melanie, we don't know what's going to be helpful. I talked it over with Kathy. Adding Netwalk into the mix, plus defusing some of the fail-safes we put in to protect Zoë—"

"How secure is that com channel?"

Her mother raised one eyebrow. "It's Kathy. What do you think? Especially where *the object* is concerned."

"True," Melanie conceded. She swallowed hard.

I'm not going to get any more out of her until I go through that damned swearing process, whatever it is. Have to get through this, first.

Now, more than ever, she wanted Marty by her side.

I can do this.

Melanie activated the hologlobe, keeping it small for fingertip-level operation. Then she called up a link to Ness, holding her in reserve while she tapped the limiting codes into the globe's programming that would help control Sarah. She pulled on her hologlove and handed another to her mother.

"All right. This is remote Netwalk management. Put the gloved hand into the hologlobe."

Diana complied.

"Now tell Sarah to go through your hand into the globe."

"How?" Diana asked.

"She can slide through your arm and fingers." Melanie quickly subvocaled a question to Ness about the process. "Ness says to tell Sarah to think of herself as a blob or a wave of energy. Also, tell her that I'm watching in case she tries something."

<As am I,> Ness added. Ness manifested herself as a red cloud around Melanie's glove. <Can't do this for long,> Ness added. <Range issues.>

The shadow oozed down Diana's shoulder and into her arm. It hesitated at Diana's elbow. Melanie poked at it. A sharp shock vibrated down her finger. The shadow pulsed twice, then moved quickly along Diana's forearm and into the globe.

<Good. She's there. Call me when you put her back.> Ness winked out.

Sarah's shape changed from shadow to a small version of her physical self.

"You didn't *have* to do that!" she complained.

"When you're transferring, I want you to move quickly," Melanie said.

Diana broke in. “We don’t have time for this. I want data from you, Sarah. Let’s start with the level of defenses around Andrew.”

Sarah frowned. “But what if I don’t want—”

Diana sighed. “Sarah. Now that you’re reasonable, we have to cooperate. I have reason to believe we have—um—whatchamacallit issues.”

“Oh, *lovely*.” Sarah grimaced, her expression changing from defiance to worry. “Is Melanie sworn?”

“We won’t have time until after we settle this business with Andrew and Peter.”

Silence. Diana and Sarah stared at each other.

Sarah glanced up at Melanie’s hand, and shook her head. “A mess. A royal, fucking mess. Like everything else with that device. Okay,” she said in a conciliatory tone. “Here’s what you need to know about that first range of defenses.”

BY EARLY EVENING, THEY STOPPED IN NEBRASKA. SARAH’S COOPERATION seemed to be improving with each session, but Melanie was suspicious of Sarah’s sudden compliance. It just didn’t seem right that all animosity between her mother and grandmother stopped when Gizmo came into play. She took advantage of her mother’s rest break of the evening to check with Ness.

<This will have to be our last long talk,> Ness cautioned. <I can’t keep this up. Too stretched. Too thin.>

<Why are Mom and Sarah all kissy-kissy when the device comes up? It’s as if the last seven years haven’t happened. What’s going on?>

<If they’re collaborating because of the widget, it’s for real.>

<It’s *that* bad.> Melanie shook her head. *Why* hadn’t anyone told her about this before?

<Yes. It is just that bad,> Ness said grimly. <But there are other factors for their cooperation that have to do with Netwalk design. Having a host is addicting. Sarah is getting used to having a regular charge instead of constantly looking for a charging bond. She’s becoming dependent upon your mom.>

<But you and I can talk without Marty. Couldn't Sarah do the same with Andrew or someone else?>

<I don't think so,> Ness said slowly. <I can't talk to anyone but you and Marty outside of a hologlobe. Will can't talk to anyone without Julia being present. Maybe you can once he integrates further. The possibilities for independent communication exist but work still needs to be done. That third form of Netwalk in Peter is different from what Will devised—or my National Security Netwalk variant, which is me and Sarah. If we can figure out how they can be independent—>

<Yes.>

<What the three of us have is based on the relationship between you and Marty. But. Your vocal tones give you a real power over Sarah that Diana doesn't possess. I think you could hurt me. Or any other Netwalker.>

<Good to know.>

<Time to go. Marty's waking. Connection's too thin with him awake.>

<How's he doing?>

<Wiped out. The distance makes it worse on him—why we have to stop. Something about that poison which works only on him, not on me. Julia thinks that's part of what killed your father. They're calling it a Netwalker toxin.>

<Ah, crud. This is something new?>

<Yes. Trust yourself. You're shaping up to be a pretty good Enforcer.>

Melanie sighed and settled back into her seat.

Diana blinked awake as she did so. "Getting any rest?"

"Not really."

"I'm surprised at how well you're doing with Sarah. I wonder if you have that effect on other Netwalkers. Maybe the ability that makes it problematic for you to host might have other uses."

"What do you mean?"

Was Sarah somehow monitoring her conversations with Ness and relaying details to Diana? Suspicious that this discussion was happening now.

"Sarah thinks of you as a sort of law enforcement type. An Enforcer. I think we need to develop that image more."

"Funny," Melanie said slowly. *Is this a leak from that damned gadget? Careful, Melanie. Play along, but—be careful.* "Ness just called me an Enforcer. Must be a common imagery among Netwalkers."

"Let's keep it in mind. This is weird. I'm getting used to it, but it's still weird." Her mother tapped her fingers on her armrest. "Change of subject. Our final strategy. We need to use that rabbit hole Sarah told us about to pop up in Andrew's office without warning. I can't believe they have all those vulnerabilities."

"It's a National Security mentality. They don't count on anyone from outside getting inside, but they want to be able to pop in and take control of each other."

"Could be." Diana frowned. "I don't want to use D.C. as a capitol. I don't trust anything there."

"Is there anything that says that the New Federation U.S. capitol has to stay in D.C.?" Melanie asked.

"Tradition."

"To hell with tradition. If we're going to change things, then let's *change things*. The East Coast's a mess. Neahcom or the Mountain might be a little much for anyone to take, but I bet you could make an argument for San Francisco. Or Seattle."

"Seattle," Diana said firmly. "Or—the New Feds want to keep up the Confederation's inclusion of Canada. I'd go for Vancouver to keep them happy. Or Free Victoria, if we could bring them in."

"You think the New Feds would go for it?"

"Shorter distance for them to travel from exile." Diana shrugged. "Maybe we need to have regional capitols, rather than one big one."

"And what role do you want me to play in all this?" Melanie asked.

"*Do* you want a political role?"

"No. I'm here because you need me. Do It Right needs someone in charge. I like monitoring research. Managing research. I could quite happily go back to being Do It Right North America instead of International, except that you need an International head."

"Until I finish this presidential gig. I don't think I'll stay with this political stuff, not after I get things reestablished and settled in."

"You sure?"

"I have no idea if I'll win reelection once we get this situation worked out. But President-for-Life doesn't appeal. The Corporate Courts need reorganization and—well—you'll see what's involved when it's time."

"That's assuming we can pull this off."

"Yeah." Her mother fell silent. Melanie settled back and closed her eyes, resting.

ABSENCE OF MOTION WOKE MELANIE. BESIDE HER, DIANA SUBVOCALED and tapped out commands.

"Are we there?" she asked, during a lull in her mother's communications.

"Yes. Getting set up right now. The distraction's just about ready to go."

Showtime.

Melanie unfastened her shoulder and belt straps, stretched, pulled on her long, quilted formal winter coat she'd rescued from Larry's storage, and snowboots, then crawled out of the skimmer. She was immediately grateful she'd brought them along. Winter was definitely in full display here, with six inches of snow on a cold, clear night.

She noticed that Nik and Angela were following behind her, close but not too close. Tighter Security.

That will probably never go away now.

It had been bad enough when she was just on the Mountain. Now...well, at least Nik and Angela were in charge.

Melanie turned back to their lead skimmer. Her mother climbed out as she reached it.

"The distraction is leaving now," Diana said.

"How are we getting to Andrew?"

All but three of the skimmers lifted as she spoke.

Diana waited until they were gone.

"Skimmers to the rabbit hole. There's ground transport once we hit the tunnels."

GETTING TO ANDREW WAS A BLUR. SECURITY MADE BOTH MELANIE AND Diana tuck out of sight on the skimmer floor. At last, they stopped. Angela's hand pressed on Melanie's back, keeping her down. She and Nik exchanged a few terse phrases of Mixteco. Then Angela's hand lifted off of Melanie's back.

<Move,> Angela texted. <Fast!>

Melanie nodded, unkinking her stiff legs. Nik and Angela hustled Melanie out of the skimmer, then drew their weapons, pressing shoulder-to-shoulder with Melanie, Nik on her left, Angela on her right. Melanie glanced around to get her bearings as they moved away from the skimmer. A grassy area near a leafless forest, bare branches reaching high into the sky—landscape, not natural forest. Earth-bermed building that only revealed a row of four small windows and a single door without handle or visible lock.

Diana, flanked closely by Sergio and Erica, strode over to the door. For a moment, Diana hesitated. Then she snapped up a hologlobe and pulled her hologlove out of her pocket. Melanie started forward to help her mother, but Angela stopped her.

Melanie glanced over at Angela, her mouth opening in protest. Angela pinched Melanie's wrist and shook her head.

"It's covered," she mouthed.

Melanie watched, misgivings rising as Sarah slid into the hologlobe. This time her pantsuit was pastel green instead of black and white. Diana stuck her right hand into the hologlobe. Sarah's shape transformed into a black cloud that fitted around the hologlove.

Melanie caught her breath.

What the hell are they doing, and why aren't they telling me about it?

Diana pulled her hand out of the globe, staring at it for a moment. Then she pressed her hand against the door, where a palm lock would be.

Oh. Now I get it.

By wearing Sarah the Netwalker on her hand, Diana hoped to release a biometric lock tuned to Sarah.

But will it work?

The door clicked open. Diana closed the hologlobe, leaving the black-clouded glove on her right hand. Raising the hand high, she led them inside.

As she ran down the corridors behind her mother, Melanie's stomach tightened as they suddenly became familiar—from the glimpses of the place through Marty's nightmares.

National Security Central Labs.

Located in a rural suburb, not in D.C. proper.

Andrew's retreat.

They burst into an office suite. An assistant half-rose, reaching under her desk with one hand. Steve and Paul pulled her away from the desk, Steve covering her mouth with one hand while Paul held his gun to her head.

Diana stopped and shook her right hand. Sarah formed next to her. Diana twitched at her jacket and slacks, ran her hands through her hair to straighten it, then took a deep breath which seemed to add six inches to her height. She nodded to Sergio and Erica.

"Come on, Sarah, Melanie. Let's get this done."

Sergio was first through the door, followed by Diana with Sarah close behind, then Erica, Nik, Melanie and Angela.

Andrew rose from his chair, spluttering.

"Where's Peter?" Diana demanded.

"You must be joking!" Andrew yelled. "You killed him!"

Melanie elbowed past their mother and slammed her hands on Andrew's desktop, leaning forward to glare at Andrew. "He's a Netwalker. He's been using you to recharge. We know it. *Where is he?*"

"I don't know." Andrew's eyes widened as he stared at Sarah. "God. You've got *her*, too?"

"Yes," Melanie snarled. "Ironic, isn't it? *Mom won.* Now. Where's Peter?"

"I haven't been able to raise him for a couple of days, thank God."

Melanie turned to Sarah.

She shrugged. "I don't know where he is, but he's not tied into Andrew."

"So they're not linked as host and Netwalker," Melanie muttered. "How the hell did that happen? I thought he was Peter's host!"

"Peter must be floating out there," Diana said.

Melanie shook her head rather than say anything more in front of Andrew. "That means we have to chase Peter down."

"That's your job, Melanie," Diana said. "I have a country to put back together." She fixed Andrew with a stern glare. "Under my authority as the Interim President of the New Federated United States, I'm putting you under arrest. The North American Confederation is no more. Tell your forces to stand down."

Andrew's shoulders sagged. "Mom, I can't. They took that authority from me yesterday."

"Who?"

"Liam and the Governing Board."

"Where's Liam?" Melanie moved in again.

Andrew stared at her. "Little sister, I haven't the faintest damned idea where your ex-boyfriend is."

Melanie sighed explosively through her teeth, her muscles tightening as she fought back a desire to grab her brother by the throat and shake the information out of him.

"Just who the hell is Liam in this government?" she demanded.

"I don't know," Andrew said. "Really. He's taking his orders from someone else."

"Who?"

Andrew shrugged.

As Melanie gathered herself for another explosion, Diana gently put a hand on her wrist.

"Don't," was all she said to Melanie. Diana turned to Sarah. "Inside," she ordered. Melanie tensed but Sarah winked out of sight quickly. Diana stared at the wall, subvocaling and tapping code.

"All right," Diana said finally. "I have the Governing Board located and surrounded by our people." Her face turned grim. "My commander issued them an ultimatum. Five minutes to surrender."

Melanie quickly set a countdown clock running on her Dialogue overlay.

"Or what?" Andrew asked bitterly. "You'll talk them to death?"

Fire flashed in Diana's eyes as she glared at her son. "The facility they're in is mined by National Security. Sarah just gave me the detonation codes."

What. The. Hell? Can Sarah be trusted? What kind of agreement does she and Mom have for her to do that?

Melanie swallowed hard. That issue could be dealt with later.

If that's mined, then what about here?

She checked the time she set after Diana's announcement, her gut tightening with fear.

Andrew stared at their mother. "I suggest," he said, in a tight, strained voice, "that if you've gotten detonation codes from *her* for one facility, that we get the *hell* out of this one. *You* may trust her but *I* sure as hell don't."

"For once, that's an excellent idea," Diana said. "I don't trust her not to trigger a chain reaction."

Andrew nodded. "Or Liam."

"So. Are you with us?"

"I can't be," Andrew said tightly. "I'm not safe."

"Sergio. I'm not leaving him here."

Sergio nodded sharply, pulling out an injector. Andrew flinched as Sergio strode across the room.

"Hold," Melanie said quickly. "Drew. Will you resist?"

Andrew shook his head. "But I won't help."

"Damn it, Melanie, you're wasting time!" Diana snapped.

"Mom. Don't. Just—don't." Melanie didn't dare look away from Andrew. The muscles in his jaw softened, though his gaze skittered sideways to keep track of Sergio and the injector. "We have to bind you."

Andrew nodded. "I won't fight."

"Ange. Bind him."

Nik and Angela hurried over to Andrew. Nik hoisted him up while Angela snapped nanocuffs on his wrists.

Sergio put the injector away.

"Let's get the hell out of here!" Diana whirled and led them out the door, flanked by Sergio and Erica, then Nik and Angela pulling Andrew along between them. Melanie and the remaining Security hurried behind them, back to the skimmers.

Then she thought of something.

Where's Liam?

Melanie sprinted to catch up with her mother.

"Liam's with the Governing Board?"

Diana shook her head. "No idea where he is."

"I don't like that. Not with his connections."

"Neither do I," her mother said. "But I'm not waiting around to figure it out. I'm announcing that I'm in charge in five minutes, no matter what happens to the Governing Board." Her face tightened. "Let's pray they decide to surrender. I'm not backing down from this."

As they lifted off, the timer flared in Melanie's left eye. A few moments later, she heard a low rumble, and spotted a distant cloud of smoke. Not the nukes, thank God.

"They didn't surrender," said Diana, her voice flat and dead. "On to the Capitol."

They sat in silence after boarding the skimmer. Andrew leaned back against his seat while Melanie and Diana looked out the narrow side windows. It didn't take long to transition from fields to suburbs, to townhouses and apartments, then to urban structures.

Soon enough, they were in the Capitol area itself. The streets were eerily silent, even for this early in the morning. At the very least there should have been National Security patrols and early morning workers trudging about their business. Almost no one was on the streets, not even homeless people. Twice, they slowed for large packs of grim-faced people standing around fires in the middle of the street, carrying motley assortments of guns and machetes.

They stopped at the third fire. Sergio slipped out of their skimmer. Andrew sat up, peering out of the window.

"That's not official staff at that blockade. We had one here just yesterday."

"Things are changing," Diana said. Her face tightened as she watched Sergio, and her hands closed briefly into fists before she breathed out softly and opened them wide before closing them, repeating the move several times.

Melanie straightened up and blew out the breath she'd been holding, squaring her shoulders. Getting ready—for what?

<What's happening?> she texted Angela.

A pause before Angela responded. <Citizen patrols, Sergio's giving our bona fides. Face recognition required. No electronic clearance. This stop's the last one. Serg getting safe and fastest route updates. Changing by minute. Avoiding fighting.>

<Will we need to fight?>

<We may.>

Melanie left it at that. Sergio jumped back in and they were on their way again. Andrew sank back against the seat, closing his eyes.

"We're cleared for the rest of the way," Sergio said.

"Thanks." Diana's jaw relaxed. Melanie rolled her shoulders.

Too easy. Especially if Drew says they had patrols here yesterday. Or are things that much in flux?

That much in flux, she decided after looking outside again.

They landed near the Capitol steps. Melanie and Diana crawled out, leaving Andrew behind with three Security staff.

"What's the plan?" Melanie asked.

Diana turned a bleak face to her. "God, Mel, I feel sick about what just happened. But it was either blow up the Governing Board or spend days shooting it out with them. Now I'm going to say what I did and why. Announce that I've taken power."

"Sounds like a start."

"And I'm going to do it with *her* speaking. Bringing *her* out will bring about more cooperation and save lives and time."

"No." Melanie grabbed her mother's arm. "You're not going to give her that much influence. Not over you, not over the government."

"Melanie, Sarah's followers will support me if they know she's in me, even in a digitally uploaded version. They'll accept me as being her." Diana pulled free from Melanie.

"No," Melanie repeated. She clenched her fists and took a deep breath. "That's absolutely stupid. Or is *she* saying that through you?"

This qualified as an emergency. A *major* emergency.

<Ness! HELP!> she sent. A long shot, given the distance.

Diana glared at her. "I don't believe you just said that."

A small nudge in her brain. Ness was faintly there, then gone. She was on her own. Damn.

"I said it. What the hell have we been fighting for, just to hand it all back to her again? That's stupid. You might as well hand your brain over to *her*. You aren't her. You can't be her. You *won't* be her!" Melanie snapped the last phrase out hard, sharp, visualizing the crack of a bull-whip as she spoke.

Diana raised her hand as if to slap Melanie. Then she dropped the hand, staring down at it and shaking her head.

"No," she whispered finally. "No. God."

Melanie grabbed her mother by the forearms. "Look at me. LOOK AT ME!"

Shadow formed in Diana's eyes when she finally met Melanie's gaze.

"BACK!" Melanie subvocaled. "Leave. Her. Alone. NOW!" She pushed with every ounce of her being.

The shadow faded. Diana blinked. She frowned, looking around quickly, stared at Melanie for a second, then nodded.

"Dear Lord. I didn't realize—thank you," she said. "She was pushing hard there. But still. Why is it a bad idea for me to wear Sarah when it'll save lives and time? It worked for us last night."

"Mom, we have to do this part straight. You've been given that power, legally, by the Congress in Exile. Sarah's supporters have to make their choice based on what you have to offer. Not a false image of Sarah."

Diana shook her head. Melanie tensed for another confrontation.

Sarah hasn't let go of her completely yet. God. Even with the collaboration she's trying to take over. Is this the deal Mom struck for Sarah's help?

"Lives, Melanie. Lives."

"False pretenses. Lies. *You're going down her path.* She probably felt she had good reasons for doing what she did all those years ago." Melanie dropped her hands to her sides. "I can't support you in a lie, Mother. I just can't."

Silence. Diana turned away from Melanie, hands in her pockets. She started to walk away, then stopped.

"You're right. But damn it, Melanie, it would make things so much simpler."

The world erupted in blast and flame. The blast concussion pushed

Melanie down. She screamed, her hands flying up to protect her head and neck as she fell. When she stopped rolling, she caught her breath. Inhaled. Exhaled. Went through her post-bad-fall mental checklist.

Anything broken? Toes wiggle? Fingers wiggle? Weird shooting pains anywhere? Head pains?

Bruises. She'd be stiff and sore soon. Nothing broken. Her ears rang, and she swallowed, several times, popping one open, but the other remained dull and echo-ish. Possible broken eardrum?

She raised herself up to her knees and looked around for her mother. Diana moved slowly and stiffly, but seemed to be okay.

"Was that *her*?" Melanie asked, recalling Andrew's warning.

Diana shook her head, her face tight and grim.

"That's one *she* didn't know about."

Then Security had them hustling back to the skimmers.

CHAPTER 17

NIGHTFALL FOUND THEM IN AN ANONYMOUS HOTEL SOMEWHERE NEAR Hartford. Diana had announced her Presidency in New Haven. Melanie continued to watch for another attempt by Sarah to dominate Diana. But Sarah appeared to be docile, feeding Diana information as requested, retreating into a quasi-robotic mode when Diana brought her into a hologlobe to report.

Maybe the hologlobe lessened Sarah's influence. Melanie didn't know, and at the moment, she was too tired to care.

Nothing was settled yet. Buildings exploded throughout D.C. and Virginia, with Confederation loyalists, New Federalists, the Freedom Army, and little splinter groups taking responsibility for each action. Liam appeared as the public face of the Freedom Army, claiming to be their leader.

Be a wonder if anything's left when the fighting stops.

Melanie slumped in one of the overstuffed chairs in the living area of the hotel's second-best suite, her entire body aching and sore. Andrew sprawled in another chair, staring at a newscast on the big screen, for the past hour unresponsive to anyone's comments or actions. She wasn't sure if he was sleeping or, like herself, just overloaded.

He had shut down like this when they were kidnapped as teens. While Melanie had to be drugged to stop fighting, Andrew had gone mute. She couldn't do that. She would be pacing right now if she didn't feel so tired that she didn't want to move.

Nik and Angela sat at a table in the far corner, consulting their hologlobes and viewscreens, keeping track of developments and occasionally texting the results to Melanie. Right now the New Feds had the upper hand, but it was clear that on the East Coast, at least, there had been a pack of other underground groups entertaining notions of taking over D.C. and parts of the East.

The West was solidly New Fed. The Confederation and the Freedom Army controlled small chunks throughout the South and Midwest. Enough that Diana couldn't claim either area as being New Fed. The Northeast declared for the New Feds, which was one reason Diana announced in New Haven, then gone on to Hartford for security's sake, in case someone was trying to predict their actions.

This hotel was one of the few willing to take on the responsibility and liability of being viewed as the current New Fed seat of government. Security cleared it out, paying for new space for those they evicted, putting everything on the Do It Right tab.

Might as well. No question where our corporation falls.

Just like there was no question about Stephens Reclamation, although Andrew still claimed he had no power over that entity.

Andrew. She was ticked off at her brother's apparent powerlessness.

No control over anything. Is he really that useless, or is he waiting for Peter to make a move?

She didn't know which possibility it was. A good reason to keep him in sight.

Peter, damn it. Kathy and Julia had relayed more information to Melanie. If he was loading a secret charge off of Andrew, he needed to come back tonight to keep it viable. Otherwise, he would only be able to charge off of Liam. Peter wasn't stupid. He would want to keep his options open.

I thought Sarah would be the tough Netwalker to handle. Not Peter.

Maybe she let too much of Andrew's arrogance as Peter's aide lead her into underestimating her uncle. Andrew was no Peter, much as he tried to be.

But then there was Liam—another subject that Andrew clammed up on.

And just how and when did Liam hook into the Army?

It made too much damn sense that he had been a part of the Freedom Army for a long time. Looking back, Melanie could identify things Liam had said and done that suggested that he was infiltrating Do It Right for the Army years ago, and that their relationship had been his means of gathering information.

If she had the energy, Melanie would be angrier. But there were too many other things to think about right now. Like going to bed. But she was the ranking Dialogue. She had to be on watch. Peter would come back to Andrew, soon. Every time she thought about *sleep,* those thoughts reminded her of her duty.

The suite door opened. Diana swept in, followed by Sergio and Erica. Melanie eased herself slowly out of her chair as her mother moved in front of the big screen Andrew was watching. Andrew jerked, but kept staring at the screen as if their mother wasn't standing there.

"It's improving," Diana said. "We have Virginia, Kentucky and Maryland now. Just the Carolinas, Georgia and Florida to go for the South."

"Nothing new in the Midwest?" Melanie asked.

Diana winced. "The Freedom Army has a tight hold in that area. You and I have been denounced as 'Satanic bitches.' Interesting. But it's the latest from Liam that worries me."

"How's that?"

Something's not right.

Melanie moved between her mother and Andrew, observing him. A brief twitch flitted across his face. A brief shimmer near him, almost like a Netwalker.

What's that?

She blinked, and it was gone.

I'm too damned tired. Seeing things.

"They say we're possessed by electronic implants that direct our every move," Diana said. "We're agents of the New World Order,

World Government, that sort of blather. How much does Liam know about Netwalk?"

Andrew smirked and chuckled softly. Melanie turned on him.

"And what do you know about *that*?" she snapped, fatigue making her voice sharper than she intended.

His chuckle changed to an open laugh.

"Answer me!" Melanie started toward him, but their mother stopped her.

"Melanie. Don't." She moved toward Andrew, stopping short of him. "It's not just Liam," she said. "Peter still has his independent connections with the Freedom Army, doesn't he?" Her voice was soft and deadly. "He never broke them off, despite Sarah's direct order, right?"

Andrew nodded. "It's been right in your face. He was even able to keep *her* fooled, up until *her* death. Oh, that's such a pretty thing to see."

Melanie jerked to full alert.

A Peter phrasing.

She stared at Andrew. Was it happening?

"You know-it-all ladies. And he's been playing games with you under your noses." A deep chuckle, from a voice deeper than Andrew's.

A chill raised the hair on Melanie's arms.

Peter's coming. This is it.

And this wasn't going to be a weakened Peter, but a strengthened Peter with a hidden host.

Andrew's face changed while he kept chuckling, features tightening into a facial structure more like Peter than Andrew.

He's using Andrew's body. Not like other Netwalkers. Possession?

This had to be handled carefully. Correctly. Precisely. She shook a trap door chip—one of Marty's new devices—designed to catch rogue Netwalkers into her palm. Tapped to prepare the capture matrix, setting it up so that it was ready to spring with a quick touch.

A last resort, because there was no way out of a trap door chip. Not acceptable for Sarah, but for Peter—

No time for that. Focus.

Sarah had been black clouds, with a following of black globules. Ness had been red. What would Peter be?

Melanie moved closer to her mother. Diana glared at her, Sarah rising high in her eyes—*she must sense the trap door chip.* Melanie ignored them, single-mindedly focusing on Andrew. The shimmer flared up again, this time around her and Andrew.

"Are you going to take charge of *him*?" she bluntly asked her brother.

Andrew startled at her question. "What the *hell* are you talking about?"

She was certain, now. Peter stared back at her from Andrew's eyes. Shadow. Like Sarah, yet unlike, a smoky gray streak.

He's a sneaky bastard. Oh, but he's sneaky.

How long had Peter been tiptoeing in and out of Andrew while they were sitting here?

If Andrew was even aware of it.

She shivered.

Andrew couldn't be Peter's primary host. Without Peter, Andrew was merely untrustworthy. With Peter, Andrew would be a spy. An agent of both Peter and Liam, unable to exercise his own will.

Plus whatever Peter is to Gizmo.

God, she could just about *feel* that presence, a deep subsonic rumbling that vibrated her bones.

I don't hear anything. My imagination?

Melanie shook her head to dismiss that distraction.

"You don't fool me, Peter," she whispered. "I've got you now, you son-of-a-bitch."

Andrew shot out of his chair. He lunged at her, hands reaching for Melanie's throat, just as the bright red and blue of a secured, impenetrable hologlobe flickered into full strength. The subsonic vibration she'd felt earlier grew in intensity, shaking though all of her body.

"You little smartass, I'll teach you who's boss!" Peter's voice snarled.

Fortunately, Andrew had never been the athlete she was, and even with Peter in him, she still had the advantage. Despite his greater weight, she was able to roll and pin him. Then more strength came into his arms and he flung her off, lunging to grab her throat again, slamming her hard up against the hologlobe's suddenly stronger wall.

This isn't Andrew's strength. This is Peter in him.

The crazed eyes staring back at her weren't Andrew's. She jabbed at them with her fingers, trying to get him to release her throat. One landed home.

"Ow!" Peter's voice again. Deeper rumblings, thrumming through her body. His knee came up and slammed into her belly. Hard, almost electrical in contact. She gasped hard as she fell forward, black spots dancing across her vision, her gut in agony. She snapped at his free hand, the subsonic vibration shaking both of them so much she almost missed. Her incisors missed his hand and pinched his forearm. She bit down hard and gnawed desperately for a stronger grip.

Where the hell's my Security?

Beyond the hologlobe that was secured against them, most likely. But secured hologlobes could be hacked. Marty could get through one.

But Marty isn't here. And there's no one else here besides me who could do it fast.

Andrew's hand slipped from her throat to yank at her hair. His knee struck her hard in the gut again. She managed to twist away from him, gasping as she reached for something, anything, to stop him. Her vision blurred. She couldn't tell which one was Peter and which one was Andrew. Or was there any difference?

She could discern a difference between Sarah and Diana. She couldn't see any separation between Andrew and Peter. The smoky gray and black cloud swirled in and about and *through* Andrew, throbbing with the same deep bass pulsations that shook her body.

Then he was on her again, smashing Melanie hard with his fists.

Melanie fought back, unreasoning, with fists and teeth and nails and leverage, managing a few blows on his jaw and gut. His muscles failed for just a second. She tripped Andrew and landed a hard blow on his jaw.

He rolled, sprang back up, and swung at her again, smacking Melanie against the hologlobe wall. She recovered, ducked low and darted behind him. Yanked on his hair, half-turned him and jabbed at one of his eyes from the side. This time she solidly hit the eye. Andrew hurled her away and she crashed across the table, rolling over it and onto the floor. Sobbing with pain, gasping for breath, she dragged herself back up.

The tapping code. She had to trap him. Now.

She tapped.

Nothing happened. No cage. She flicked the chip out of its hiding place and tried again. Still nothing. She shoved it back into her sleeve pocket.

Shit! What went wrong?

That blurriness of Peter and Andrew. Had to be the key. They were mixed together, not separate like the Netwalker pairs she already knew. She needed to separate them.

He shambled toward her. Were they alone? Why wasn't anyone stopping him? Why wasn't someone breaking into the hologlobe? Even a secured hologlobe could be hacked. What was taking them so long?

She glanced around frantically for something to use.

I have to kill him.

She didn't stop to think about who "he" might be, whether it was Peter or Andrew. This was a fight to the death. Someone's death. Not hers, if she could help it. There had to be a weapon. Somewhere.

Chair. Too big.

Lamp. Too light.

Vase. She picked the clear glass vase up, found it surprisingly heavy. Leaded crystal, most likely, with a good thick bottom. But it was small, and could she reach him with it before he took it from her?

He laughed. Bright, neon-green light flashed around them as the vibration threatened to shake the vase out of her hand. Peter/Andrew pointed a hand toward her as the copper-colored spiky sphere slowly took shape behind him.

Is he attacking me with that?

She didn't wait to find out. Melanie whirled and whacked Peter/Andrew on the side of the head with the heavy bottom of the vase as he reached for her, right on his temple. Astonishingly, the vase didn't shatter.

Vibration stopped, as if a switch had been flicked. The spiky sphere disappeared. Peter/Andrew sank to his knees. Melanie raised her arms high and brought the vase down hard on the side of his head. He shook his head back and forth, falling forward on his hands.

Go down, will you, damn it!

It was agony to do this. She wanted to scream, to cry.

Just give it up!

She couldn't do this.

Had to do it. She brought the vase down on the back of Peter/Andrew's head with the full force of what strength she had left.

Andrew screamed, collapsing to the floor.

Andrew's voice, not Peter's.

As he moaned, the black and gray cloud swirled free of his body. Melanie dropped the vase and crouched, waiting for a shape.

The cloud swirled malignantly, coalescing into a sphere as it headed for her.

"*No. Stop.*" She shook the chip out of her sleeve pocket and tried the tapping code again.

This time the code brought up the cage. The loosely formed sphere dodged it, heading for her.

"*Stop.*"

She pushed at it. Tiny vibrations prickled up and down her body. She ignored them, pushing as hard as she could—*there! That's what I need to do!*

The shape lost its spherical form, fading into a swirl of dust-like motes.

She pointed to the cage. "In there."

It resisted.

She pushed.

"In *there,*" she repeated, more firmly, pushing harder. It moved backward slightly, fighting.

Then it shrieked, a long, wavering electronic shriek that ripped deep into her gut and stirred up all the pain and agony that tightened inside her.

She screamed back, a long, wordless scream of pain, frustration, anger and fear. Her scream overwhelmed the shriek of the gray-black swirl and shrank it, drove it into the cage. She slammed the door shut, then tapped the cage down until it was a small chip once again.

"And may you rot in there forever," she whispered, wrapping her hand tightly around the chip, sinking to her knees, then rolling to the floor and curling up tightly, groaning and sobbing as agony and pain swarmed over her.

The hologlobe flared out of existence.

Noise. People moving around her. Voices.

She screamed and kicked out when someone touched her, a mere brush of their hand sending red-hot waves of pain throughout her body.

"Oh my *God*, what the hell were they doing?"

"Jesus, I knew it was bad when they went to the globe, but *that* bad? They beat the crap out of each other!"

"Melanie. My God. Melanie. MELANIE!"

Someone turned her into a recovery position, gently straightened her out despite her screaming and thrashing every time they touched her.

Breathe. She had to breathe. That was all she had to do now. Breathe. Keep breathing. Sobs broke loose from her throat as agony crashed down hard upon her. So *much* pain. She couldn't pass out because it hurt so bad. She wanted to pass out. Wanted to sleep. But pain drove unconsciousness away.

"Medic, damn it! We need emergency transport NOW! Two people down!"

Hands. Hands moving her, voices asking her to do things. She couldn't respond to any of it except to scream at every touch.

Pain was her world. Pain. Throbbing, knifing, stabbing pain. It wouldn't go away. None of it would go away.

Someone tried to pull the chip from her hand. She shrieked and struck out at them. No. No one should have this. She *needed* to hold onto it. The right person wasn't here to take it from her. She had to keep it for the right person.

"She has a neural implant. Wireless computer interface. Communication and command device."

None of the words she heard made any sense. Her breath sobbed in and out. In and out. It was important to keep breathing. Something fitted over her nose and mouth. Breathing became easier.

Someone was shouting orders while sobbing. That didn't seem right.

Warm fuzziness seeped into her consciousness. She fought against it, desperately struggling to stay conscious.

Mustn't lose it. Mustn't stop thinking. Mustn't stop.

Then the fuzziness covered her pain, and she could hold on no longer.

CHAPTER 18

AWAKENING. VOICES. MORE PAIN. HOSPITAL BED. TUBE UP HER NOSE. PICC line. Staring at unfamiliar masked faces, then one she knew even with a mask. Angela. Must have been one hell of a ski race crash this time.

Wrong. She hadn't been skiing. Faint memories of a fight with Andrew surfaced. Melanie moaned as for one quick moment it all came back to her.

The chip wasn't in her hand any more.

She screamed. Thrashed around trying to find it in her bed. Hands touched her and she shrieked again, still hurting every time someone touched her.

Finally, the hands went away. She blinked, but couldn't see clearly.

Worried voices. Angela leaned over her, talking in soothing tones, in words she couldn't make out.

Warm fuzziness again. This time she didn't fight it. Angela was here. Her Security was here. Safe. Someone she trusted watching her. Someone protecting her.

THIS TIME SLEEP WASN'T SO PLEASANT. PETER, LIAM AND ANDREW; Andrew, Liam and Peter, changed shapes and melded together into one being, then separated, chased her down a long hallway. At the end of the hallway, the copper-colored sphere pulsed and rumbled. She whirled away from it and ran hard, trying to hide, trying to get away.

Melanie snapped into awareness; her throat raw from screaming.

She heard her mother's voice coming from far away, hoarse, edged, almost at the brink of tears.

"They went into a globe and damned near killed each other. She said something about Peter coming, Peter being in Andrew before the globe came up. A *secured* globe. None of us could hack it, not until it was all over."

Damn. It hadn't been just a dream.

Pain crashed down over her, and suddenly she was caught up in the memories again, pain and fear and *ohmygod where's the chip where's Peter ohmygod that's Gizmo!*

Melanie gasped and moaned, panting as she thrashed around.

She heard Diana's voice, but she couldn't make out the words.

Marty's voice. Marty's hand on her brow. For once, touch didn't hurt her. Had to be because it was Marty. Marty. Marty here. Security and Marty. She was safe. She was okay. She blinked hard, trying to focus so she could see him, confirm that *this wasn't a dream.*

"Mel. Mel. It's okay. I'm here. It's okay. *I've got the chip.*"

Her breathing slowed. Marty bent over her. She focused on his thin, wan face, his smile.

"Rest," he said. "I'm here. It's okay. *I've got the chip,*" he repeated.

It was all right. Marty was here. Marty had the chip. It was all right. She could rest. Everything was covered. Melanie leaned her head against his hand, pain easing even before the wave of warm fuzziness swamped her yet again.

THIS WAKING WAS SLOW, FROM A PEACEFUL, RESTFUL, SLEEP, AT A PACE OF awareness almost like surfacing from a deep dive in a warm ocean.

First, sound. Beeps of monitors, distant voices.

Next, touch. The warmth of the hospital bed and the stickiness and sharpness of hospital stuff hooked up to her.

Melanie opened her heavy eyelids, focusing slowly, for the first time able to think instead of react.

She blinked. No Dialogue. Blurry focus as she looked around. More blinking, and she could clearly see her surroundings for the first time.

Yes, definitely a hospital room, by herself. *Serious* life-support stuff hooked up to her. She looked further, just moving her eyes. The slightest motion of her head sent waves of pain down her spine, but someone was sitting next to her bed. Who?

Finally, she found the right combination of minuscule head and eye movement to see the person.

Marty. Thinner and paler than she remembered. His face that pale under creamy brown which she now recognized as Marty being sick, with dark circles under his eyes. He wore reading glasses as he scowled at a hologlobe projection. One of his hands was connected to a medication line, like hers, only his was a mobile unit strapped to his arm.

She made a noise, not quite able to coordinate her mouth just yet. Marty looked up and smiled, then switched off the projection, putting the hologlobe cube on the table next to him.

God, but his face lights up when he smiles like that at me.

She wanted to smile back, and tentatively tried it. Her face didn't hurt as badly as she thought it might.

"Hey." He picked up her hand, the one without tubes or patches on it. "Looks like you're finally surfacing, huh?"

"Yeah," she husked. Her mouth was dry and full of cotton. She tried to cough but nothing cleared. "Drink?"

He reached for a cup, dipped a spoon into it, and deftly eased some ice chips into her mouth. "Try this. I've been feeding them to you before now. You haven't been awake enough to remember."

The ice chips soothed her parched, raw throat. But they melted quickly, too quickly. "No. I haven't been. More, please."

This time he ladled a larger spoonful into her mouth. "Couple more of these, and I'll grab a straw. There's just enough water in here for you to have a decent drink."

Melanie felt better after she sucked down the last chips and drained the cup's water. Marty put it to one side.

"I'll get more in a couple minutes, unless you want some now."

She started to shake her head no, and winced as pain shot through her head and neck.

"Careful," he cautioned. "You've had a pretty rough time of it. Don't move unless you absolutely have to."

"How bad?" she whispered.

Marty looked away from her, his face briefly twisted in a wince, pressing his lips together tightly. He sighed, then looked back at her.

"We thought you were dying. It's been iffy until the last twenty-four hours. I've been here for two days, as soon as I was healthy enough to come." He gestured to his arm. "As you can see, I'm still under treatment. Kathy wasn't happy about me coming here, but I wasn't going to stay put. I had this weird romantic notion that you needed me here to get better. Don't know if it was true, but it sure seems to be working."

"I remember waking one time and you were there, telling me you had the chip."

"Yeah. That was right after I got here. You chose that time to go into one king-hell of a seizure. I don't mind telling you, hon, this has scared me more than you going to the brink of Suicide Red did. At least then I had faith that the bioinoculate would protect you. But this time, there weren't any guarantees." He stroked her cheek gently. "I hope this doesn't hurt. You've been screaming any time anyone's touched you, except me."

"Feels good."

"It's hard to find a spot that doesn't have a bruise or a cut. If I hurt you, please tell me."

"I will. I was seizing? I thought I was looking for the chip and couldn't find it."

"Hon, it was a full-blown, major seizure. Maybe it was connected to the chip, or—the gadget. Both your mother and Sarah saw—it, but they couldn't do anything. Anyway, you stopped having seizures shortly after I told you I had the chip. You'd been having them regularly for several days. Trauma, possibly some Dialogue feedback, maybe—" he grimaced. "Stuff they won't tell us yet that's tied to the damned device. Your mom had the chip until she gave it to me. She took it from you, but she couldn't get it out of your hand until you were so doped up you couldn't keep any muscle tense, much less your hand. She kept it for me."

"Destroy it," Melanie told him, in a flat tone.

"Destroy it?"

"It's Peter. He's more dangerous than Sarah. We don't dare link him with any host, Marty. I couldn't tell him from Andrew, my God, it was nothing like Ness or Dad or Sarah." She broke off, suddenly tensing up and trembling.

"Easy. Easy. Don't think about it now, hon. Don't."

"I can't *not* think about it," she whimpered. "It was awful, Marty. He sprung a secured hologlobe on me. I was fighting for my life. I don't know if he was trying to kill me and force an upload, or if he was trying to subdue me to make me his host, but it was awful." Tears welled up in her eyes. "The—thing—was there. He was going to use it on me at the end."

Marty stroked her cheek. "Hon. It's all right. You've taken no harm. You're clear of any touch of Peter. I checked. Ness checked. Your mom had Sarah check too. She says Sarah's pretty rattled."

"How is Andrew?"

"You worked him over pretty hard, Mel. He's still in a coma. How much of it is what you did in that fight and how much of it is what Peter—and the widget—did to him is still impossible to tell. From what we can figure out, Peter trashed Andrew's implant. Sarah says it wasn't National Security work, and Ness confirms. We think that Liam's connected. Somehow, Liam knows about the implants, and may have one himself. If Andrew wakes up, we can learn more from him. *If* he wakes up. You're in better shape than he is."

"How long has it been?

"Five days. You've lost a lot of blood. Internal injuries. Broken bones. Blunt force trauma to your head. The seizures. Spinal cord bruising, there was some worry about paralysis. Fortunately, that swelling's going down." He looked at her mournfully. "Girl, I love you to death, but do you suppose we're ever going to go a week without one of us landing in the hospital?"

Melanie tried to laugh, but it produced enough pain that she had to stop. "Hon, I'd like nothing better right now than to be tucked into a nice little cabin up on the Mountain with just you and me, walking distance from a good slope. To hell with all this other stuff for a while."

He grinned at her. "I can echo that sentiment. We've done plenty right now for the New Federalized States."

"How's that going?"

"Your mom's buzzing around picking up the pieces. When Peter got caged, that seems to have stopped a lot of the resistance, except for Liam and the Army."

"She'll be President for real now." Melanie hesitated. "Can you hold me?" she asked. "Please. I don't care if it hurts. I just want the touch."

"I don't know what I can do without hurting you, but I'll try. Don't you move!" He sat gingerly on the side of the bed, then carefully leaned over until he lay next to her. He placed one arm across Melanie, easing it over her chest, barely touching her and keeping his arm stiff so that the pressure was not too great.

"Thank you," she whispered. "Thank you."

They lay like that for a few minutes, just being together, their breathing falling slowly and quietly into a matching, soothing rhythm.

"I feel guilty," Marty said, reaching up and gently stroking her brow. "Sorry. My arm's getting tired."

"It's okay. Why do you feel guilty?"

"I told you I wouldn't let you fall. And then this. I wasn't there."

"Hon, you were in no shape to be there. It wasn't your fault," she said.

"I still feel guilty, okay?"

"You have no reason to feel guilty."

"I'll be there next time," he promised.

The door opened. Marty startled in place, then carefully, slowly, sat up.

"Well, she *must* be better, if you two are snuggling." Diana walked to the foot of the bed, eying Melanie carefully. "Girl, you look one *hell* of a lot better than you did." Her voice softened. "Thought we were going to lose you for a while."

"That's what Marty said."

"Recovery must be going around. Andrew's starting to come out of it. But he's in pretty damn bad shape."

"I'm sorry for my part in it," Melanie said. "But it was me or him. And I couldn't get Peter out of him any other way. I couldn't tell them apart. Especially when Peter was about ready to use—*it*—on me."

Diana nodded. "Peter took Sarah by surprise. We couldn't see much through the hologlobe." She shuddered. "I'm surprised that either of you are still alive."

"We have to destroy that chip," Melanie said. "We can't trust Peter loose, even if we had a host strong enough to keep him under control. He's slippery, and he knows how to manipulate the thing."

Diana nodded. "Matches what Sarah's telling me." She looked over at Marty. "And Ness?"

"Ness concurs."

"Will would like to study the technology," Diana said, a dry tone in her voice. "But I'm not inclined to play with Peter and his connections to—things you'll learn about when you get better. I'd much rather find the Freedom Army designer who came up with that choice little Netwalk version that ties into the gadget. Pump them for information, rather than retro-track it from Peter. I'd love it even better if it were Liam we were grilling. I suspect he's been spying on us for a long time."

"I've figured that one out," Melanie said. "He has a mole in DIR. It's a girl, has to be a girl. But he's seduced so many women in Do It Right that I wouldn't know where to start looking. Possibly Anna, but she's so obvious and in-your-face that I wonder if she isn't a cover for someone else."

"I can get that investigation started," Diana said in a tight voice. "It's a high priority."

"One more thing," Melanie said.

"What's that?"

"I want to see that chip destroyed myself. With my own eyes. Then I'll believe *he's* really gone."

Her mother studied Melanie for a moment. "Fair enough," she said. "And then you can tell us what you learned from this encounter."

"I'm sure we can pick enough out of my brain to keep us all occupied for a while. In Research," Melanie hastily added. "Not politics."

Diana gently laid a hand on one of her feet. Melanie winced, and her mother cringed, pulling it back.

"Melanie. You've done enough politics. Your job now is to get well, then figure out Enforcer provisions for Netwalk, understand where and how Netwalk can manage—the thingamabob—and make sure your team understands the Peter variant of Netwalk so we can fight it. It won't go away. I'm sure of that. But your time in the political side is done. Unless you've changed your mind and want to go into politics?"

"No fucking way," Melanie said. "A nice, quiet, Research management position is quite enough for me right now!"

"Then Research it is for you, m'girl." She smiled sadly at her. "Get better, quickly."

"I'll be back on the slopes by March," Melanie said.

"I've heard that line before, that time you got caught in the avalanche."

"And I was, wasn't I? Just took me two months to be back on the slopes by March that time. We're almost at New Year's. Plenty of time."

"I think you do better tangling with avalanches than Netwalkers!" Her mother alerted, blinking at a Dialogue prompt. "Damn. I've got to go. Meeting." She moved to the head of the bed. "Excuse me, Marty. I'm going to say a proper goodbye." She kissed Melanie on the forehead. "Get better, okay?"

"I will. Back on the slopes by March!" Melanie said.

Marty rolled his eyes.

"You're sure about that, Mel?" he asked after Diana left.

Melanie snorted. "It's what my mother expects to hear from me. She's as invested in the image of her ski bum daughter as the media is. Look. Marty. *Something* is going on between Mom and Sarah. I don't know if it's the device or what, but they became best buds on the trip out."

"Ness told me about your concerns." Marty scratched his chin.

"What does she think?"

"She's concerned, but doesn't have the answers. It could just be Netwalker and host bonding."

Melanie frowned up at the ceiling. "Damn it. And then there's Liam."

"I thought you were going to rest and think about skiing," he said.

"I—don't quite trust how this is all playing out," Melanie said. "Mom's up to something. It's connected to the device. And Dad. How Sarah plays into all this, I don't know, but—we don't dare let them shut us out of what's going on."

"I agree," Marty said. "But for now—you need to rest. All right?"

"All right," she conceded.

CHAPTER 19

It took two days to reinstate Melanie's Dialogue. Another day before Marty and her doctors agreed that Melanie was sufficiently healthy to sit up long enough in a floater to witness the destruction of the chip containing Peter the Netwalker.

Even at that, two nurses, one male, one female, eased her into the floater, wrapped her in thermal blankets, and took charge of the floater while Marty fretted. Nik and Angela grimly supervised each step, hands openly resting on their weapons.

Are these nurses reliable? Why are Nik and Ange so tense?

Bad enough that she needed *two* nurses in addition to Marty, Nik and Angela.

Remember that convalescence makes you grumpy.

Perhaps that was why Nik and Angela were so tense. Of course, she had to have the nurses, because of her current fragile state. Of course, Nik and Angela needed to be present for this excursion. Neither she nor Marty were capable of self-defense at the moment, and things were still far from settled in the political arena.

Doesn't mean I have to like it.

At least the Gizmo work was postponed, until she and Marty were physically stronger. *You'll need to be 100% for the swearing,* her mother had said. *It involves—some physical rigors.*

From what she had seen of the gadget so far, Melanie could just imagine what her mother might mean by that. Meanwhile, they still had Peter's final banishment to accomplish.

They traveled down several hospital levels to a skimmer parked at the security entrance. Nik took over the controls of the skimmer while Angela supervised Melanie's loading. It was only after she was settled and strapped in that the nurses gave her enough space to hold Marty's hand.

<I feel like you about all this,> Marty grumped at her. <Not just one nurse, but *two*? Meddlers!>

His annoyed tone made her feel guilty. <I'm sorry. Have I been broadcasting? I didn't mean to.> Her control after this last Dialogue reinstatement was not what it had been.

He rolled his eyes. <Big time, honey. *Big* time. I don't think you can help it, but I feel your pain every time they touch you in a sore spot.>

<I'm sorry. I didn't mean to do that. I guess I'm a bad patient.>

<No worse than I am, really. Two nurses. Wouldn't one be enough?
>

She had discovered by now that shrugging *hurt*, so Melanie kept herself from shrugging, but just barely. <Guess they assume we need one apiece in case we both fall apart. Mom's doing, probably.>

<Probably.>

She gently squeezed his hand, and he stroked the back of her hand softly with his thumb.

No one challenged Nik at the gates of the National Security test facility.

One advantage of being the President's daughter.

The skimmer bypassed the usual parking area and pulled up at a side door. They unloaded, and the nurses firmly took charge of Melanie's floater once again, although she noticed that the man placed himself closer to Marty than to her. Backup, indeed. That told her about his current condition.

Curling up in a cabin on the Mountain, with a nice pellet stove going strong. That's what we really need.

Tension radiated from Marty.

<What's up?> she asked.

<This place makes me nervous. Neither Ness nor I worked here.

I'm not certain it's completely secure. A lab this big will have hidden accesses all over—probably why we have so many Security staff around us.>

Diana and her entourage met them in an observation room.

"We can't go any further," she said. "But we can observe." Her mother waved at the thick glass separating them from the lab. "This facility is designed to incinerate some pretty damn nasty stuff. We had to clear it room by room—this is the wing in best shape—and it's the only surviving trustworthy D.C. location with a reliable incinerator."

An anonymous figure in a hazard suit clumped into their room.

"The chip?" He popped the helmet, revealing his features. Sergio.

Good. Chain of custody, all the way to its destruction.

"You're doing it?" she asked.

"Yeah. I'm the lucky bastard who's been trained to chuck it into the furnace for you."

"Good."

Marty held up the chip, enclosed in a transparent plastic container. "This is it, Mel?"

She studied it. Faint red-brown traces stained the chip.

My blood. She shivered. *No wonder Nik and Ange were so tense. They knew Marty had it.*

"Yes."

Marty handed it over to Sergio. He took it delicately between his gloved thumb and forefinger and turned to leave.

"Wait," Melanie said. She gestured to the female nurse. "We're following him," she ordered. "I'm paranoid. Sergio, wait until we're back in the observation deck before you destroy it. Nik, I want you with me. Stay by the lab door. Make sure no one else goes in. Marty, can you watch from here to make sure that nothing weird happens before it's incinerated?"

Marty shook his head. "I'm going with you. Your mother can supervise this part."

"Mom?"

"I've got it," Diana said.

Marty moved to her floater, reaching the controls before her nurse could, glaring at the nurse.

Sergio replaced his helmet and clumped out of the room, Melanie and Marty followed him to the lab door, watching while he went inside and double-locked the door. Nik caught her eye and nodded sharply. Marty turned her floater back to the observation room. As they did, another person in a hazard suit tramped by, hesitated, then continued on his way.

Melanie signaled Marty to stop. She stared after the anonymous walker. Something familiar about the way that person moved. The way the walker half-lifted, half-dragged the right leg. The movement of an otherwise normal-walking someone who limped from an old injury when fatigued.

I know this person. Who the hell is it?

<Angela,> she texted.

<What's up?>

<Suspicious hazard suit just went by. Hesitated when they saw us. Provide backup for Nik.>

<Gladly. I'll bring Erica.>

"Wait," she told Marty, still watching the walker.

Erica and Angela came out of the observation room. As she passed, Angela dropped a small handgun into Melanie's lap. "One of my extras. Just in case."

"Thanks, Ange."

"Yeah." They took up position next to Nik.

As the hazard suit approached the end of the long hallway, memory clicked in.

Liam.

"STOP!" she yelled. Nik and Angela snapped to attention. She raised the gun Angela had given her, taking aim. "LIAM MICHAEL JEFFREYS, STOP!"

He broke into a run. She shot. Nik and Angela bolted toward him. She shot again. Liam staggered, stumbled, one hand rising to his chest, but kept going.

"Follow them!" she ordered Marty. Instead, the nurse pushed him onto the floater with her and took over the controls, pushing the floater to its highest speed. Marty grabbed her shoulders to keep his balance. It hurt, but she focused on Nik and Angela.

They spun around the corner and the nurse expertly braked the floater so that they had a view of both hallways, then jumped off. She pulled out a weapon, bracing in a defensive position. Her partner raced down the hall, brandishing his weapon. Nik and Angela peered into doorways and alcoves.

Security. DIR Medical Security.

Her mother must have brought them in from—Rio? Nagano? Melanie didn't know either of them. But they moved like they had been trained by her father.

"Nothing," Nik called back. "If he has codes, he could have ducked into any of the labs."

"Let's just get this damned chip killed," Melanie said. "The longer it takes us to do the job, the more time they have to recover it. Get the alarm out!"

Nik nodded curtly.

"Let Sergio know what's happening," Melanie added.

"I've told your mom. She's telling him over the speaker. No Dialogue contact inside the lab. Sergio's Dialogue is temporarily disabled."

"Good." Melanie said.

They processed back in silence. Angela and Nik rejoined Erica at the lab door. The nurses followed them into the observation room. Diana whirled to face them as they entered, weapon in hand, along with Steve and Paul.

"You're sure it was Liam?" she asked Melanie.

Melanie nodded. "It took a couple of moments to recognize his limp. It's him."

"Damn," Diana growled. She turned back to the window. "I'm calling up more reserves. Either there's more of them out there, or he's desperate."

"He's desperate," Melanie said. "Liam wouldn't be here if he could get someone else to do his dirty work."

Sergio walked toward the lab's incineration chamber.

"All okay out there?" he asked.

"Liam's still at large," Melanie said.

Sergio nodded. "I'm ready." He gestured toward an assault rifle lying on a worktable, within easy reach. "I don't trust anyone else in here with me. So, if they enter, I'll shoot."

"We're good to go, then," Melanie said.

Sergio reached over, punched a few buttons, and picked up a pair of tongs, carefully fitting the chip container into them.

<Has to wait for a minute to get the heat up,> Marty said. <We need to flame it for a good five minutes to make sure it's gone. This lab is electronically shielded, along with Sergio's Dialogue being disabled. That means Peter can't jump to him, even if he calls for help from our mechanical friend. Had Ness check too.>

<You think of everything, love.>

<You aren't the only paranoid one in this family.>

Motion caught her eye. Another hazard suit *moving in the lab*, walking toward Sergio, with Liam's characteristic limp.

Sergio carefully put the tongs down and picked up the assault rifle. He fired several shots.

Liam fell. Sergio put the weapon back down and picked up the tongs.

Marty's hand closed tightly on her shoulder. It was painful, but she didn't flinch. Instead, she raised her good hand and tapped his hand until he moved his hand to hers.

"Sorry," he muttered.

Sergio thrust the chip inside the incinerator, then closed the door, setting a timer that displayed a digital countdown. The other suit moved again, rising to hands and knees, shaking his head, then leapt for Sergio, a wire between his hands. Sergio deflected his leap, the assault rifle spinning across the floor. As Liam landed, his helmet went flying.

Both men scrambled for the assault rifle, grabbing it at the same time. Shots rang out. Liam's head jerked. Sergio kicked him away, then backed up, rifle in hands, continuing to fire until Liam dropped to the ground, the middle of his suit red with blood. Sergio fired twice at Liam's head, aiming at the right temple, where an implant would be.

Dead. Did he upload?

Marty's hand tightened hard on Melanie's.

<I'm *okay*,> she told him. <It's *over*. Long over.>

"Can't use mind speech right now," Marty muttered to her through clenched teeth. "Don't *dare*. *Bastard*. Deserves every piece of that. Wish it was me instead of Serg. After what's been spilling from your nightmares the past few days."

"It's okay," she repeated. "Marty, it's *okay*. The son-of-a-bitch won't haunt me anymore." God, she hoped that was true.

Did he upload?

<Sarah? Did he upload?>

<Not that I can tell. No sign of—*it*—either.>

Diana stepped away from the window, subvocaling.

Maybe Peter attacking me was the last I'll see of the thing.

Melanie didn't believe that possibility. At least they'd dealt with this particular manifestation.

I can only hope it will wait to get up to—whatever the hell it's planning—until I'm sworn and know more.

The timer zeroed out. Sergio waited for another minute, then opened the door. He sifted through the ashes, scooping them onto a tray and picking through them for any bits.

Nothing but ash. He poured the ash into another container and left the room, carrying his weapon.

"Okay," Diana said, tensely. "Let's move. They're attacking this facility. We need to go to another exit. Quickly!"

Nik, Angela, Erica and Sergio, still in his hazard suit, joined them as they rushed out the door and down the hallway, not bothering to close any doors behind them. Melanie clutched the weapon with her good hand, tense until they slipped into a tunnel, then popped up in another building and out to their skimmers.

Diana stopped them before they entered the skimmer.

"New orders," she said. "Including you two," she said to the nurses. "I'm sending you home, Mel. To the Mountain. You're safer there, among our own." She looked at the nurses. "This is the contingency clause I told you about yesterday. You'll meet the rest of your team when you get to your destination. Your job is to monitor these two, get them to safely, then prep local staff on what's to be done. Understand?"

They nodded. "We have a complete twenty-four-hour supply of

their medications," the woman said. "Packed, on us, ready to go at all times, as you stipulated."

Diana smiled. "I *love* having good help. Thanks. I knew I could trust you." She kissed Melanie on the cheek, and hugged Marty. "Go home. Get well. I need you two healthy and able to do research for me."

"You keep yourself alive," Melanie said. "I want to be on the slopes with you when I'm back on my feet."

"I will," Diana promised. She strode off toward her fleet of skimmers.

Melanie looked at Marty, then at the skimmers that awaited them.

"I guess we can go home now," she said.

"Yeah," Marty said. "Sounds like a good idea to me." He stroked her cheek, then stepped aside as the nurses took over, guiding her floater to the skimmer.

Home. At last.

She'd never thought that the prospect of a quiet time at home could sound so good.

CHAPTER 20

EARLY AFTERNOON, LATE MARCH SUN POURED THROUGH THE THICK GLASS of the view window overlooking the front steps of the High Reaches Main Lodge. Melanie stood two feet back from the window, looking at the skiers below as her attendants fussed over the simple white sheath dress and veil she wore, consciously conserving her strength. Maybe she'd have enough energy left for them to ski a couple of runs, besides the surprise they'd planned.

Maybe. Her left ankle and knee were questionable, and she still fatigued easily. Her first introduction to Gizmo as a consultant to the Corporate Courts last week had taken more out of her than she liked. Plus her recovery was not yet perfect, thanks to the toxin effect. Odds were good that she would never regain the physical strength and endurance she'd had before.

Netwalker toxin reaction, Reiko and Julia called it. For both her and Marty.

But here she was, three months after being damned near beaten to death, and she was on her own feet. She had survived her first meeting with Gizmo. Small victories were better than no victories, and each one deserved to be celebrated.

Janine twitched Melanie's veil so that it lay smoothly, then guided her toward the huge stone fireplace in the main lobby where the ceremony would take place. The media that was allowed to be present moved in. Big news both locally and internationally. Melanie was, after all, not just the daughter of the President of the New Federalized United States, but the head of a major international corporation. Much as she really wanted this whole ceremony to be private, *that* wasn't going to happen.

She caught Angela's eye. Angela nodded. All was clear. Good.

The crowd parted to allow Marty to enter the circle. She grinned at his gray-green tuxedo and spiked hair, complete with discreet snowboard boots. He hadn't gained back the weight he'd lost during his convalescence, but neither had she. At least they could stand on their own two feet without floaters or canes, and walk around for a reasonable period of time without fatiguing. If it worked out, after the ceremony, they could ski one run. Maybe more.

The cams flashed as they took hands and kissed.

<What a circus,> she said to him.

<Yeah. Got your stuff on underneath?>

<Yeah. Don't know if I can even take on Designer run, though. Might just have to be Bunny slope.>

<Bunny's the better photo op, anyway.> He smirked impishly at her. She grinned back. They'd managed one private ski session already. What would happen after the ceremony was their own idea.

She winked at Angela and Nik, also wearing ski gear under wedding attire. She and Marty, along with Diana, their daughter Sophie, and Mama Brenda, had stood as witnesses to Angela and Nik's formal commitment ceremony yesterday.

The cams fell silent again as DIR and Presidential Security formed a tight aisle, and her mother strode through, followed by Larry, in his vestments. Diana kissed Melanie on both cheeks, then moved to Melanie's side. Security tightened, Nik and Angela at the head of each line, allowing the photographers, both live and remotes, only one angle to shoot as Larry took his place. Melanie caught the faint shimmer as Ness slid out to observe, tucking herself unobtrusively onto Marty's shoulder.

The actual vow-making passed in a blur.

Ness gave her a faint, ghostly caress. <I'm going to lock myself in the chip unless you need me. That's my wedding gift to you two. No Netwalker over your shoulder.>

<Thank you,> Melanie whispered back.

Then Melanie kissed Marty, kissed and hugged a lot of people who gathered around her. Signed the contract with her new name. She had decided that she wasn't going to share a name with Andrew, who was still being a butthead, even without Peter in him.

Besides, what difference did it make what she called herself? She knew who she was, and the world damn well knew who she was. It didn't matter if she called herself Landreth or Fielding.

"*This one's for Liam*!" a female voice shouted. Melanie's first reaction was to spin toward the voice—*Anna*—she realized.

It doesn't look like her!

Angela sent Melanie sprawling as shots rang out, covering her protectively. A babble of voices surrounded Melanie, arguing and screaming, but no more shots occurred. She tried to raise her head.

"Keep *down*!" Angela hissed. "She's not under control yet!"

"Is anyone hurt?"

"Not that I can tell, but right now I'm just worried about you. Keep down! Ahh, now they've got her!" Angela eased off of Melanie, but kept a hand on her back, forcing Melanie to lie flat while Angela sat up, gun in hand. "Okay. All clear."

Melanie sat up slowly. "Who is it?" she asked, even though she knew.

One of our own. Liam's mole, revealed at last. Figures that it would be Anna.

<Ness!> She invoked the emergency code.

<No Netwalkers involved,> Ness told her. <I'm going back now.>

But the person struggling in Steve and Paul's tight grip as Sergio and Erica applied restraints didn't *look* like Anna. Plastic surgery?

Sergio pulled a mask off of her face.

"Anna Johnson," Angela said bitterly.

Melanie caught Marty's eye. He helped her to her feet. "You okay?" he asked. <*Really* okay?> he asked silently.

"Just sad," Melanie said. <Yeah, I'm okay.> "Ange thinks everyone's okay," she said out loud.

Marty nodded. "Anna's a lousy shot. I saw part of it. Steve deflected her gun." He wrapped his arms around her. "More excitement than we needed. Figures. At least we're not on our way to the hospital."

"Yeah. I should have realized she was the mole, not a distraction."

Janine approached them. "Melanie, Marty, I'm so sorry."

Diana broke free from her Security. "You two okay?"

"We're fine," Marty assured her. "Did anyone got hurt?"

Diana's mouth twisted. "We'll have to fix a few windows, but that's it."

Melanie straightened. "I want to talk to her."

Nik and Angela appeared at her shoulders, pressing in close to form a human wedge.

"Don't get too close," Angela said. "While Steve says she's clear of any detonators, she might still be loaded with poison."

Melanie nodded in acknowledgment. She moved through the crowd, heading for Anna, still struggling against her restraints.

Anna stopped resisting as Melanie approached.

<Far enough,> Angela said.

Melanie and Anna surveyed each other.

"Why?" Melanie asked.

"You bitch," Anna snapped. "You cold, cynical, manipulative, exploitative, arrogant evil *bitch!* You and your whole family are a blight on the face of the Earth! You never, ever, understood at all!" She continued to rant while Melanie stood, keeping her face impassive.

This has to be one hell of a photo op.

Melanie concentrated on Anna, waiting for her to stop.

There were many things she could say to Anna. Multiple defenses of her actions.

But there was the faintest kernel of truth in what Anna spewed at her. At times, Melanie *was* as manipulative and exploitative as Sarah had been. Deny it though she might, she was as much a product of Sarah's attitudes as she was of Diana's.

This situation called for a nasty Sarah response, not a measured, political Diana reaction. To hell with caution and measured, thoughtful action. She had to upstage this with every bit of arrogance she had picked up from years of vying with Sarah. Had to show flash, glam, and action, as opposed to Anna's fervent venom.

She caught Angela's eye.

<Say one thing. Then slopes,> she texted.

<Give time for setup. You safe first.>

<Okay.>

<Bunny?>

<No.> For one wild moment Melanie considered the black diamond runs. No. There was action, and then there was stupidity. Neither she or Marty could handle black diamonds in this condition. <Designer,> she answered Angela.

As Anna's vitriol slacked, Melanie forced herself to smile pleasantly at her. "I don't deny any of this," she said sweetly. "Do you have a point?"

Anna's face twisted. "I loved him and you didn't care! You killed him!"

"That, my dear," Melanie allowed her most Sarah-esque, sarcastic, and poisonous tone to creep into her voice. "Is complete, total, and utter bullshit worthy of the man himself. And you'd be wrong. Once upon a time I loved him."

"You killed him!"

"Damned right I did. He damned near killed me."

"That's a lie!"

"Is it? He lied. Constantly. To me. Probably to you as well. Now." Melanie raised her chin firmly. "I have a wedding to celebrate. To a good man I love completely, utterly, and deeply; who's more than three times the man Liam Jeffreys ever was on his best day."

She executed a sharp, precise turn, walking back toward Marty and carrying herself with every ounce of pride and arrogance she could muster. She took Marty's hands, raised them to her lips and kissed them as she looked into his eyes. He smiled and slipped free, giving her another deep, passionate kiss.

<Damn. That was a magnificent performance,> he said.

<I didn't overplay it?>

<No. You got the attention back on us.>

The cameras swarmed around them again. <You up for Designer?> she asked. <We have to make a splash after this.>

<Yeah. I'll be slow, but I can do it.>

<Ready,> Angela texted. <Copying Janine.>

"They're ready," she murmured to Marty. He nodded, and kissed her again. Then he spun her around, took her hand, and they ran, to the surprise of much of their audience.

At the edge of the crowd Janine and Crispin came forward. Melanie threw her veil to Janine, then held up her hair as Marty unzipped her dress. She carefully stepped out of it to reveal the ski suit, and handed her dress to Janine while Marty gave his suit to Crispin. Then they took off again, getting a quick head start on those who hadn't been briefed on this turn of events. Only the remote bug cams followed them down the front steps under the snowshed.

"Don't slip!" Marty shouted as they veered to the right of the Day Lodge.

"I grew up running on this!" she yelled back at him.

Nik and Angela waited for them at the edge of the plowed parking lot. They helped with skis, snowboard and quick entry boots. Melanie pushed off fast, thrilling to the feel of the snow underneath her skis.

It's working. I can do a good solid run.

"Don't kill yourself, Mel!" Nik shouted. "You're not that damn strong yet!"

She flipped him off, then picked up the pace as she hit the main slope, testing her body. No, she wasn't going to make a speed run, and it was only going to be one run, judging from the way her knee was twanging at her.

But damn, it was good to be back out on the slopes, even if it was only for one run, the slopes turning rosy around her as the sun set.

A low cloud skittered overhead and cast a golden light over the snow and their small group. Melanie gloried in the moment, drank in the cold air, thrilled to the soft crunch of the powdery coating over a layer of solid snow underneath, thanks to last night's providential and marvelous dry, flaky flurries. Powder over Cascade concrete. Lots of powder.

Things couldn't get much better than this.

She beat Marty down the slope, and waited, with Nik, until Marty and Angela reached them. The mechanics of kissing while on skis and snowboard were awkward, but they did it, then caught the chair back up, Marty's arm around her shoulders, holding her tight and exchanging little kisses.

"Up for another run?"

She shook her head. "One's plenty for me today."

"Yeah." They kissed again. Then it was time to slide off the chair, hand in hand, to the flash of cameras and another round of kissing, this time for the cameras. Her mother grinned at them.

"You stinker," Diana murmured as she stood next to them for a picture. "You should have told me. I could have joined you!"

"We weren't sure it could happen." Melanie whispered back. "A last minute plan."

"You did good. Going for another run?"

"Not tonight. Maybe tomorrow."

"I'll kick you from here to Nagano if you don't let me know about it. You promised me time on the slopes together, remember?"

"I did. But today was for Marty. And me."

"It's good to see you back on your feet."

"Yeah. But now we're demanding private time."

"I'll set it up." Diana subvocaled orders to her Security. Melanie looked back at the rose and golden glow, then grinned at Marty. They unbuckled their skis and snowboard, handing them off to Nik and Angela. Marty grabbed her hand and pulled her close, looking deeply into her eyes.

"Now. Forever. Always," he said softly. "No matter what, I won't let you fall."

"I'll hold you to that," she whispered back. "Now. Forever. Always."

As he took her in his arms for another kiss, the snow glowing pink and gold around them, Melanie couldn't think of any other place she would rather be but on the Mountain, in Marty's arms.

Now. Forever. Always.

"Let the party begin," Marty whispered.

She squeezed his hand in response. "Yes."

My husband. My mountains. As long as I have them both, all will be well.

THE END

NEWSLETTER

Like what you've read? Want to follow Joyce either through her monthly newsletter or through an email feed of her irregular blog posts?

Sign up for Joyce's newsletter here:

https://tinyletter.com/JoyceReynolds-Ward

Or follow Joyce's irregular blog posts on her Substack, here:

https://joycereynoldsward.substack.com/

BOOKS AND PUBLICATIONS

The Martiniere Legacy

First Meetings: A Martiniere Legacy Short Story
Inheritance: The Martiniere Legacy Book One
Ascendant: The Martiniere Legacy Book Two
Realization: The Martiniere Legacy Book Three
A Belated Christmas Honeymoon: A Martiniere Legacy Short Story
The Enduring Legacy: The Martiniere Legacy Book Four

People of the Martiniere Legacy

The Heritage of Michael Martiniere: A Martiniere Legacy Novel
Broken Angel: The Lost Years of Gabriel Martiniere: A Martiniere Legacy Novel
Justine Fixes Everything: Reflections on Mortality

The Martiniere Multiverse

A Different Life: What If?
A Different Life: Now. Always. Forever.

Goddess's Honor titles currently available (chronological order):

The Goddess's Choice: A Goddess's Honor Short Story
Beyond Honor: A Goddess's Honor Novella
Exile's Honor: A Goddess's Honor Novelette

Birth of Sorrow: A Goddess's Honor Short Story
Pledges of Honor: Goddess's Honor Book One
Return to Wickmasa: A Goddess's Honor Short Story
Crown Anniversary: A Goddess's Honor Short Story
Challenges of Honor: Goddess's Honor Book Two
Cleaning House: A Goddess's Honor Outtake Story
Unexpected Alliances: A Goddess's Honor Rough Draft Outtake Story
Choices of Honor: Goddess's Honor Book Three
Judgment of Honor: Goddess's Honor Book Four

Netwalk Sequence Author Preferred 2022 Editions

Life in the Shadows: Book One
Netwalk: Book Two
Netwalker Uprising: Book Three
Netwalk's Children: Book Four
Learning in Space: Book Five
Netwalking Space: Book Six

Bright Star Fair Witches

Becoming Solo: A Bright Star Fair Witches Novella

Non-Series Titles currently available:

Alien Savvy: A Western SF Novella
Klone's Stronghold
Beating the Apocalypse
Bearing Witness

Vella Titles:

Falcon of the Martinieres (part of *Justine Fixes Everything*)
Bearing Witness
Beating the Apocalypse
A Different Life—What If? An Alternative Martiniere Legacy Novel
Becoming Solo
A Different Life—Linda's Story: An Alternative Martiniere Legacy Novel
Federation Cowboy

Audiobooks Available:

Alien Savvy: A Western SF Novella

Released from other publishers:

"Queen of the Snows," in *Once Upon A Winter: A Folk and Fairy Tale Anthology,* edited by H. L. Macfarlane

"My Man Left Me, My Dog Hates Me, and There Goes My Truck," in *Black-Eyed Peas on New Year's Day: An Anthology of Hope,* edited by Shannon Page

"Lost Loves," in *All Worlds Wayfarer*

"The Wisdom of Robins," in *Whimsical Beasts: A Campcon Anthology,* edited by Joyce Reynolds-Ward

"The Cow at the End of the World," in *Well…It's Your Cow,* edited by Frog Jones

"To Plant or Pull Up Stakes," in *Pulling Up Stakes: A Campcon Anthology,* edited by Joyce Reynolds-Ward

"The Notice," in *Children of a Different Sky,* edited by Alma Alexander

ABOUT THE AUTHOR

Joyce Reynolds-Ward has been called "the best writer I've never heard of" by one reviewer. Her work includes themes of high-stakes family and political conflict, digital sentience, personal agency and control, realistic strong women, and (whenever possible) horses. She is the author of *The Netwalk Sequence* series, the *Goddess's Honor* series, and the recently released *The Martiniere Legacy* series as well as standalones *Klone's Stronghold, Alien Savvy,* and *Beating the Apocalypse.* Samples of her Martiniere short stories/novel in progress and her nonfiction can be found on Substack at either Speculations from the Wide Open Spaces (general, writing) or Martiniere Stories (fiction). Joyce is a Self-Published Fantasy BlogOff Semifinalist, a Writers of the Future SemiFinalist, and an Anthology Builder Finalist. She is the Secretary of the Northwest Independent Writers Association, a member of the Science Fiction and Fantasy Writers Association, and a member of Soroptimists International.

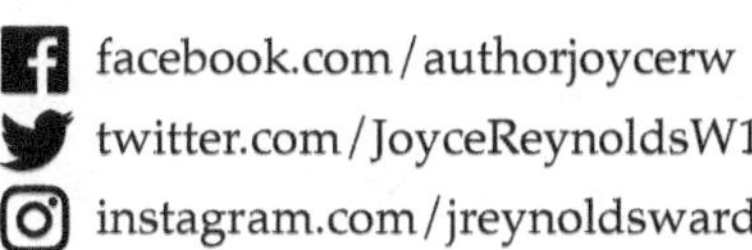

facebook.com/authorjoycerw
twitter.com/JoyceReynoldsW1
instagram.com/jreynoldsward

www.ingramcontent.com/pod-product-compliance
Lightning Source LLC
Chambersburg PA
CBHW030806210726
48290CB00002B/455